BECAUSE OF YOU

Because of You

First published in 2016 by Fridhem Publishing

1 2 3 4 5 6 7 8 9 10

A CIP catalogue record for this book is available from the British Library.

Paperback ISBN 978-0-9954907-0-3

E book ISBN 978-0-9954907-1-0

Typeset by Elipsis Digital Limited, Glasgow
Printed and bound in Great Britain by Clays Limited, Bungay, Suffolk

www.fridhempublishing.com

I dedicate this novel to my beloved parents, who instilled in me a passion for life and literature.

Rest in peace — you're always in my heart.

H.

PROLOGUE

WOKEN BY THE persistent ringing of the phone at 5am on a bitterly cold morning, one glance at his face confirmed the voice at the end of the line delivered the news they had dreaded for so long.

"It's over — no more pain and suffering," he whispered, arms around her, adding, "We're all he has left; today's the start of the rest of our lives without her."

Later that day, while she was busy putting together a eulogy in the house holding such fond memories, a shadow of a man carrying a brown envelope suddenly appeared.

"She made me promise to give it to you after . . ." he mumbled in a broken voice, eyes sad and empty.

"What is it? Please stay!" she cried, clinging to his arm.

"You'll soon find out. Always remember how much she loved you." Feigning a smile, the frail figure squeezed her hand, leaving as quietly as he had entered.

Later still, seated in the semi-darkness of the room, letters scattered around her, her only thought: "He never ceased to love me . . . blaming myself won't change what I did."

Too distraught to focus on anything but the flashbacks in her head, she let herself drift off to a distant, happier time.

CHAPTER ONE

1978

BARRY WHITE'S DEEP tones echoed through the rooms of the Stein bungalow in Limhamn, an affluent suburb of Malmö in the southern part of Sweden. Close to local shops, harbour and beach, with large bay windows and glass doors leading onto a big garden, it was home to Zadie, Walther, Hannah and Peter. In her late thirties, tall with an olive complexion, brown eyes and jet-black hair, Zadie was a strikingly beautiful woman. She smiled fondly at the young girl sunbathing next to her in the heat of July. Recently graduated from college, she was the opposite of her mother: petite frame, red hair and green eyes, yet both shared the same vivacious personality and ability to empathise. Watching her firstborn, Zadie wondered what had happened to the mischievous, freckled tomboy always up to something.

"Your graduation party was the perfect end to college and that chapter of your life, sweetheart,"

Her gentle tone made Hannah smile in return. Reaching over, she kissed her mother's soft cheek. "I couldn't have done it without you and Pappa. You're the best!"

"We love you very much, sweetie." Reminiscing about the party, Zadie remarked on how pretty Hannah had been in the blue satin dress they'd purchased in a boutique in Malmö. "The boys couldn't take their eyes off you!"

"You would say that, seeing as you're my mother," Hannah teased, completely unaware of her own beauty.

"You listen to me, Hannah Stein! There's a *je-ne-sais-quoi* quality to you *and* you're a nice person, indeed a rare combination." Pretending she wasn't listening, Hannah asked if they'd miss her. "Of course! It's only natural. But just imagine all the fun you'll have in London. Your grandmother's dying to see you." Zadie felt certain Peter would miss her too. Fair and blue-eyed like his father, with only a few years between them, he preferred spending time with his sister as opposed to hanging out with his friends.

Soon Hannah would depart for Golders Green, a Jewish suburb in North West London buzzing with activity, shops and restaurants. Despite not being religious, the Steins took pride in their heritage and culture, frequently joined by friends during the Sabbath, Chanukah and Passover. Accompanying her daughter, Zadie would be staying at her mother's flat in nearby Hampstead until Hannah settled and enrolled on an English course.

Momentarily uncertain she'd made the right decision to spend a gap year in London, far away from the people she loved, Hannah felt her mother's eyes searching hers.

"You'll be fine, sweetie! Besides, we're only a couple of hour's flight away. Did I tell you your grandmother called? She's arranged a meeting with Ella Rifkind as soon as we arrive. She wants me to tell you how nice she is."

"Really?" Hannah sighed. "If Granny approves, who are we to question it?"

"That's right – your grandmother and I have great intuition!"

In her mid-seventies, Zipporah Friedman left Stockholm for a new life in London. Having lost most of her friends, an acquaintance suggested she start afresh, leaving her old life behind. Widowed at a young age, Zipporah raised Zadie single-handedly, supporting her by working part time in a shoe shop. Her late husband, Julius, was the love of her life. Born in Russia, Zipporah kept her strong accent, had many – mainly Russian – friends, and a contagious zest for life. The moment Hannah was born, both shared a special bond. "Your grandmother knows you're independent," Zadie continued. "She won't mind that you're not staying with her."

Listening to her mother, Hannah felt much happier. "Are you and Pappa planning on travelling to Lugano?" It was a favourite family destination in the Italian part of Switzerland, close to Milan.

"What with celebrating your birthday and travelling to London, we've simply no time," Zadie replied, shaking her head. She and Walther had booked a trip to Paris in the autumn. The 'City of Love' came second to the house in Limhamn. Each time they travelled there, they'd bring back a suitcase crammed with lesser-known artists' paintings discovered in galleries outside Paris, joking as the years passed that they were sitting on a fortune, seeing as most of the artists became famous and sought-after.

Renowned for their flamboyant parties, Zadie and Walther regularly invited friends to dinner, dancing to the likes of Sinatra and Bacharach, serving delicious food and tiny squares of pizza in the early hours of the morning. Content to be a housewife, Zadie long since formed a book and French conversation group, immensely proud of her husband's law firm in Central Malmö. "I know how much you look forward to studying for a degree and teaching, Hannah," she would frequently tell her daughter. "Just

5

remember this: however satisfying, a career's no substitute for a fulfilling personal life." Apart from a few crushes, Hannah didn't have a boyfriend and continually achieved top grades at school.

One week prior to departing to London, the Steins celebrated Hannah's eighteenth birthday at The Savoy, an elegant hotel and restaurant in Malmö. Eager to fuss over her, Walther announced he'd opened an account in her name.

"We'll send you a monthly allowance – it's our birthday gift to you."

"But what about Peter?" Hannah's eyes were wide. "Will he receive the same amount?"

Glancing at her husband across the table, Zadie replied, "You're very loyal – yes, if your brother wants to spend a year abroad, we'll match the amount."

The last days leading up to leaving everyone behind consisted of packing and saying goodbye to friends and Hannah's tearful attempts to memorise her bedroom: tiny red roses on the wallpaper, lace curtains and vanity table with framed pictures of ABBA. Back in 1973, Hannah, Peter and Zadie had attended an ABBA concert in The People's Park, Malmö, where, from her privileged position in the front row, Hannah watched her idols perform the songs she knew by heart. The following year the group entered the Eurovision Song Contest and the rest was history, making that night a special memory.

Bidding farewell to her father and brother was the hardest thing she ever did. They were at Copenhagen Airport, only a few hours before catching their flight when Walther held her close, whispering, "If for any reason you don't want to stay, all you have to do is call and I'll come for you." His little girl was embarking on a new adventure and he knew he mustn't let her see how upset he was.

"Are you okay, sis? Keep in touch! I'll update you about what's going on in Limhamn." Giving her a bear hug, Peter wondered how he'd feel not having her there to talk to. Promising to call as soon as they arrived, Zadie and Hannah waved; the latter's eyes brimming with tears.

Putting an arm around her, Zadie smiled. "Stop worrying so much. They'll be fine – I'll make sure of it. The moment you've been waiting for is here: London, we're on our way!"

Arriving at Heathrow on a hot Sunday afternoon, collecting their suitcases and walking outside to queue for a black cab, both noticed the sky turning dark. The driver laughed, seeing their expressions as they seated themselves in the back.

"This is London! The city boasting four seasons in a day!"

Talking amongst themselves, they looked out the window, thinking how dirty it was outside in comparison with neat and tidy Malmö. It took almost an hour getting to the address, the driver announcing, "Here we are, luvvies! I've parked outside the number you gave me."

"My daughter's on a gap year – we're not sure if she'll be living in that house," Zadie murmured.

"A pretty girl like you – you'll have a great time! I hope you don't mind me saying, I can see where she gets her looks from."

Laughing, Zadie paid the fare, adding a generous tip. "You're very kind. Take care." The driver helped them carry their suitcases onto the pavement, then drove off. People were milling about everywhere. Zadie and Hannah's eyes fixated on a couple of benches oddly positioned in the middle of the street causing cars to pass by with caution. Looking up, they spotted a sign: Rodborough Road NW11.

"Let's get this out of the way – your grandmother's awaiting us," Zadie said, gesturing towards a building at the top of the road. "Look, there's a cinema and Jewish delicatessen just around the corner. You're in a good location – the station's only a five-minute walk from here."

But Hannah wasn't listening. She felt butterflies at the pit of her stomach looking at the house in front of them; an old Victorian property quite unlike their modern house in Limhamn.

"I bet it's seen a lot of changes," Zadie said in a cheerful voice. "Are you ready, sweetie?" In summer frocks, both were anxious to get inside before there was another downpour. Catching her breath, Hannah pushed the doorbell.

After the distant sound of footsteps on the inside, the door swung open and the pair found themselves staring at the smallest woman they'd ever seen. Shorter even than Hannah, her hair was white as snow, and she had red lips and bright-blue eyes. Supporting herself on a stick, she looked them straight in the eyes.

"You're Miss and Mrs Stein? I'm Ella Rifkind, please call me Ella – everyone else does. I'm sorry I can't greet you properly; arthritis is such a nuisance! A sign of old age. Welcome to my home." Talking in a melodic, soft voice, her accent and manner were impeccable.

Following her inside the room further down the dark passage, Zadie and Hannah noticed she walked with a limp.

"This is the dining room, it's awfully stuffy this time of year but it's my favourite place to relax and watch television," Ella explained. Hannah took in the antique furniture and framed photos on the walls, just as Ella asked, "Can you cook my dear? As you can see, I'm fairly limited."

Hesitating, Hannah looked at her mother. "A bit . . . Granny taught me how to make chicken soup."

"The 'Jewish penicillin' – splendid! By the way, you're very pretty, my dear. The young men around here will take a shining to you!" Blushing, Hannah was at a loss for words. It was the second time that day someone had commented on her appearance. "Would you mind terribly if I requested your help in getting tea ready?" Ella asked Zadie.

"Of course not! Kindly lead the way to the kitchen and we'll do it in no time."

Looking very pleased, Ella steered them into the small room adjacent to the dark dining room, the only furniture a small table and four chairs with hardly any space to move. Showing them where she kept the biscuits, it didn't take long to lay the table. There they sat, sipping their tea and munching on cakes. Watching them, Ella noticed how beautiful Zadie was with those big, brown eyes.

"I've a daughter but no grandchildren, Carmen and Jim, that's her husband, visit on Saturday mornings. At best not religious, I keep kosher. It's not easy changing one's habits at eighty!"

"Ours is a liberal family; proud of our roots," Zadie replied, raising her voice slightly when she realised Ella was also hard of hearing. As she helped clear the table, Ella mentioned her cleaner, Margareth Dudley, was coming in the morning.

"But I was under the impression that's my responsibility," Hannah interrupted, eyes confused.

"Certainly not. All I ask is that you keep me company from time to time, do a bit of cooking and shopping – anything above that's selfish. You're in London, my dear!"

Relieved to hear that, Hannah asked if she could view the room intended for her.

"Of course! Please follow me upstairs. There's hardly much point showing you the rest of the rooms downstairs. My late husband dictated they're finished almost identically." Hannah and Zadie held their breath, climbing the stairs behind Ella, who took one step at the time. "Phew! This is quite a struggle for me," she exclaimed, when standing on the landing, face red and flustered.

Spotting the separate bathroom and toilet, Hannah almost blurted out she'd never seen anything like it, thinking Ella's large room at the end of the corridor quite lovely, with white lace curtains, armchair and light pink covers on the bed. Across the hall was her own room. As they entered, Ella pointed at the furniture. "Please feel free to move it around. I want you to feel at home, my dear."

Pleasantly surprised, Hannah's reaction was short and sweet. "I love it!"

There was a huge bed in the centre, an open fireplace on one side and a couple of cosy old armchairs by the window. The curtains, similar to those in her bedroom in Limhamn, and antique vanity table enticed her the most along with the view of the street outside.

Looking as pleased as her daughter, Zadie smiled at the old lady. "Hannah clearly approves! I too think it's a wonderful room."

"I'm pleased to hear it. Could you live here, my dear?" Ella's voice trembled slightly.

"Yes, please!" came the immediate response.

"I'm so happy! It's my daughter's room . . . She has excellent taste." When Hannah told her she'd enrolled on a course of English, the old lady frowned. "But your English is excellent, my dear. Better than most people's around here."

"She's attending university next year, studying to become a teacher." Zadie was unable to contain the pride in her voice. Ella couldn't believe her luck; the girl wasn't just pretty and mature, but clever too. Turning to Zadie, she asked, "Are you comfortable with the idea of her staying here with me, Mrs . . . Zadie?"

"Without a doubt. My mother's right: you're a lovely lady."

Blushing with joy, Ella asked them to lock up on their way out, handing Hannah a set of keys. "I usually take an afternoon nap – today's an exception."

They arranged to talk a few days later with a view to Hannah moving in at the end of the following week. Bidding farewell, mother and daughter embraced the kind lady who so readily welcomed them into her home.

"I can't tell you how much I look forward to having you living here with me, my dear. Please give Mrs Friedman my fondest regards."

It was early evening by the time they left Rodborough Road, with the sun shining above them and the sound of birds singing. Carrying a suitcase each, they walked towards the station.

"What's it like knowing this is where you'll live for a year?"

Hannah beamed at her mother. "Wonderful! I've a feeling Ella and I will be the best of friends." Catching a passing cab to Lyttelton Road and Zipporah, Hannah gazed out the window at the heavy traffic on the North Circular, cars hooting around them, thinking how she couldn't wait to tell her grandmother about Ella and the house. As the cab driver parked outside the familiar block of flats, she felt like the luckiest girl in the world.

CHAPTER TWO

THE DELICIOUS AROMA of chicken soup, chopped liver and freshly baked Challah filled Zadie and Hannah's nostrils as they waited outside the third floor flat. Opening the front door, Zipporah greeted them with open arms. "Thank God you're here – you must be starving!" Slightly plump with an ample cleavage, Zadie's brown eyes and Hannah's red hair – albeit tinted nowadays – she wore a black jersey dress, matching shoes and pearl necklace, making the effort to apply blue eye shadow and pink lipstick.

"You look wonderful – I don't know where you get the energy from!" Zadie exclaimed, kissing her mother's cheek. Laughing, Zipporah raised her hands in the air.

"My dear friends Katja and Tanya insist it's our duty to look our best, living each day as if it's the last . . . Oh, and staying out of the sun." She looked at least a decade younger than her years. "My face is as soft as a baby's bottom, I drink lots of water and use an inexpensive moisturiser. But don't just stand there – come into the kitchen, we've a lot to catch up on!" Speaking in a mixture of Swedish and English, Zipporah's Russian accent was as strong as ever. Barely pausing for breath, she informed them that Hannah would be sleeping on the couch in the living room and Zadie in the guest room next to her bedroom. Too cramped to fit a table, the kitchen was heaving with delicacies. "You must help me carry everything into the living room!"

"It looks delicious. You went to all this trouble for us," Hannah said, taking the linen cloth, crystal glasses and porcelain to the dining room table adjacent to the couch.

"Only the best for my girls!" Looking extremely pleased with herself, Zipporah took a closer look at them. "You certainly don't take after me in the looks department! Unless my eyes deceive me, you're even more beautiful than I recall. You're his flesh and blood, alright!" she told them, nodding to a framed photo of her late beloved husband on the mantelpiece.

"Don't be ridiculous! Hannah and I have your hair colour and eyes!"

The cosy combined living and dining area was furnished with pieces Zipporah had brought with her from Stockholm, and her friend Tanya's paintings decorated the walls, colours so bright and bold they felt as if they were somewhere exotic. "She's had a lot of interest, even an exhibition in London."

Admiring the abstract splashes of colour, Zadie nodded. "They're certainly not like anything I ever saw before!"

Keen to sample the dishes they rarely ate at home, the minute Zadie and Hannah started eating they realised how hungry they were.

"This is by far the best meal I had in a long time," Hannah announced between mouthfuls. "I can't believe I'll soon be moving into Ella's house."

"Really? That's wonderful news. I'm glad you like her."

"Very much, Granny. You're right, Ella's a darling."

"We're pleased for you, sweetie." Leaning across the table, Zadie pinched Hannah's cheek, turning her attention to her mother. "Walther and I wish you'd come and live with us. Are you okay living by yourself?"

Shrugging her shoulders, Zipporah smiled at them. "I'm blessed with good health and friends, something I thank God for every single day. Can you guess what we're having for dessert?" she asked, eyes full of mischief.

Pretending she didn't have a clue, Hannah replied, "Is it what I think it is?"

"Perhaps . . . It's definitely your favourite!" She disappeared into the kitchen, returning a couple of minutes later with the cake Hannah had loved since she was very young. "It's apple pie – I made it especially for you." Between them, they finished the pie in hardly any time, leaving a tiny piece. "Tanya's quite partial to it . . . She'll be disappointed I didn't bake one especially for her."

"How come I never succeed in getting it right?" Zadie asked. Despite being an excellent cook, this was the only recipe she always failed at.

"The secret's in the blending of sour cream and cinnamon. It takes a lot of practice – my friends keep asking me for the recipe but I tell them my lips are sealed. I once brought it with me to a restaurant in Swiss Cottage. Cosmo offers Eastern European cuisine – the supervisor tried to bribe me, but to no avail." Hannah vividly recalled the food and ambience. "Anyway, are you determined to go to university, my darling?"

"Definitely! You know how much I want to teach. As soon as the year's up, I'm returning to study."

"I'm very proud of you, we all are . . ."

"But?"

"I want to see you married with a family of your own. Your mother feels the same. Perhaps you'll meet a nice Jewish man?"

Shaking her head, Hannah started to giggle. "I'm too young to settle down. At my age all I want is to have some fun, I've plenty of time yet." Wisely neither Zipporah nor Zadie pursued the matter, secretly hoping she'd make friends in Golders Green, conscious of the fact she was fiercely independent and would resent anyone interfering in her life.

After washing up, it was time to go to bed. After unpacking their suitcases, Hannah and Zadie immediately fell asleep, unlike Zipporah, who lay in bed reading until the early hours of the morning – a habit she'd adopted since relocating to London.

Time passed very quickly as the Steins visited nearby Golders Green and Lindy's, serving Zipporah's favourite dish, 'chicken in a basket' with coleslaw and fries, also the Italian bistro, Luigi's, in Lyttelton Road close to the flat. The day Hannah moved into Ella's flat arrived much too soon, yet after leaving her mother and grandmother, it wasn't long before she adapted to her new home. She found her landlady easy to get along with, both falling into a comfortable routine. When Zadie declared she was returning to Malmö, it suddenly dawned on her this was it: her adventure was about to start.

"I'll miss you terribly, sweetie. Between your grandmother and Ella, you'll be fine. If for any reason you don't want to stay, your father and I will book a return flight." Holding her close, Zadie gazed into her eyes. "Be sure to look after your grandmother for me and remember: don't let anyone talk you into doing something you don't comply with. Listen to your head, not your heart."

It was a sound piece of advice – she'd do well to keep it in mind.

Waving goodbye from the kitchen window in Zipporah's flat, Hannah held onto her grandmother's arm until Zadie and the cab were out of sight.

By late September Hannah attended her first English class, soon discovering how much further ahead she was than the rest of the pupils. She decided to join the advanced group, which would eventually enable her to pass with distinction.

Every Friday Hannah made Sabbath dinner of roast chicken with all the trimmings, her culinary skills extending to stews and omelettes. Afterwards, she and Ella would watch the latest dramas on television, feasting on a bag of vanilla fudge. Ella's daughter and son-in-law visited every Saturday morning, but it was clear to Hannah that they weren't in the least interested to get to know her, much less have anything to do with her and Ella's life. Sundays were usually spent having lunch at Zipporah's flat, where the three of them enjoyed Hannah's favourite food, with Ella too polite to ask for the recipe of the apple cake.

One Friday evening in late October, Ella looked at Hannah, asking, "Why don't you explore the neighbourhood? You're too young to keep me company – as much as it pleases me, it's not fair on you."

"But I don't want to leave you! Mrs Dudley told me your legs are getting worse. Her son Tommy saw you trip over something the other day. I'd never forgive myself if you had an accident." Her eyes welled up. Ella was as dear to her as her own family.

Whenever she took a nap, Hannah spent hours in her room watching the 'world pass by' outside the window. Apart from tending to Ella's needs, Hannah didn't have much to help pass the time. Margareth and Tommy were her friends but they had their own lives. After she finished cleaning the house, Margareth took her young son to an activity centre then continued working to provide for them. Ella told Hannah Tommy's father had left when he was born and that they lived in a small flat in Temple Fortune, only a bus ride from Zipporah's.

"They're as fond of you as I am, my dear. Margareth agrees the idea of having a gap year is to make new friends. You're much too pretty and clever to hide from the outside world."

"Are you trying to get rid of me?" Hannah joked.

"Not at all. I just want you to be happy."

It was turning cold outside, late autumn was slowly making way for winter and Hannah couldn't help missing her family and life in Limhamn.

I have to start somewhere, she thought to herself. *Going for a walk is as good a start as any.* During the following weeks Hannah explored the local area and surrounding boroughs, venturing out to Hendon and the recently opened shopping mall at Brent Cross, and catching a bus into London, visiting her favourite stores, Selfridges and Fenwick.

One night, on the way home from one of her excursions, she noticed crowds of young people crossing the road to Ranch House, a local bistro in the high street only a few minutes' walk from Rodborough Road. She debated whether or not to return home, conscious of Ella spending the day with her daughter, eventually deciding to pop into Ranch House to see if it was to her liking.

Strolling down the street in her new green tweed jacket, Hannah's red hair tumbled down around her shoulders. A couple of men wolf whistled, making her feel attractive and sophisticated.

"Are you eating, Miss?" the short, dark haired waitress asked the minute she entered.

17

"Yes please." Following her to a table in the centre of the room, Hannah could tell it was popular with the locals, everyone laughing and talking around her. Furnished in rustic, earthy colours with tables and chairs made of wood and wine bottles decorating the shelves around the walls, the place felt relaxed, oozing with ambience. After ordering a toasted tuna sandwich with crisps, Hannah asked the waitress from where she originated.

"I'm Iranian, although I've been living in this area for many years. My name's Aziza, what's yours?" Hannah informed her she was Swedish, also living in the neighbourhood and studying English. "You're kidding right? Your English is perfect – I wish mine was as well." Aziza was fluent yet spoke with an accent. "You made the right choice; our tuna sandwich is very popular – enjoy your meal."

She was right, the toasted double decker with tuna, sweetcorn and mayonnaise served with crisps and coleslaw was delicious. *I'll put on weight if I continue eating this way*, Hannah thought. Ranch House was much nicer than Lindy's – packed with people of her own age, giving her a sense of belonging.

Back at the house, when Ella enquired if she'd had a good time, Hannah assured her she did.

"You ought to browse *The Jewish Chronicle*," Ella said. "I've a copy upstairs in my bedroom. Take a look at the advertisements. It'll do you good to socialise with people of your background, my dear." Taking her advice, Hannah's eyes fell on a young singles event the following Saturday at Hendon Hall Hotel, not far from where she lived.

"My concern is that it's aimed at those wishing to meet a partner."

"Don't worry – it's an opportunity to make new friends. But

you must book a cab to take you there and back; your mother expects me to keep an eye on you!"

After giving it some consideration, Hannah decided to give it a go. She made a special effort to look her best, choosing a green dress matching the colour of her eyes. *I could bump into my knight in shining armour*, she thought, kissing Ella goodnight.

"You're certain you'll be fine on your own, my dear?"

"Of course."

"You look lovely, enjoy the party!"

As she arranged for the cab driver to collect her at midnight Hannah felt awkward, wishing she were at home, curled up with Jilly Cooper's latest novel. There was a crowd of people waiting to get in, further emphasising the feeling of intrusion. As she stood by herself in a dark corner of the large foyer, a waiter passed, asking, "What's your preference, red wine or Pimm's, Miss?"

"Pimm's, please" she replied in a shaky voice. Sipping the fruity drink, Hannah couldn't help but feel embarrassed that she didn't have the slightest clue who anyone was.

"Hello, my name's Melanie Gordon, I'm the organiser of tonight's event," said a slim woman with dark hair. Shaking Melanie's hand, Hannah admitted she'd never attended a Jewish do before.

"I come from Sweden," she said nervously. "I'm over on a gap year. As soon as it's over, I'm going to take a degree in teaching."

Melanie studied her appearance, seeming to take in every detail. "I'm into Economics," she replied, "which is just as well seeing as I've no patience with kids! You're eighteen, right? I'm nearly twenty-five, celebrating it with a party in a few months. Why don't you come along?"

"But we're strangers!"

19

Shrugging her shoulders, Melanie burst into laughter. "Not anymore! I never knew there's a Jewish community in Sweden, I guess one learns something new every day." She proceeded to introduce Hannah to her friends. With Melanie by her side, Hannah found herself relaxing sufficiently to open up to them about herself and life back home.

"See those guys over there?" Melanie whispered. "They've been staring at you since you arrived." She couldn't help thinking this girl was different from the others. It wasn't so much the unusual colour of hair and eyes as the way she came across; seemingly more mature than most girls her age.

Blushing, Hannah replied, "But you're the attractive one – they're probably looking at you." Indeed, Melanie looked very feminine and smart in a blue trouser suit, matching her big blue eyes and olive complexion. If it hadn't been for her hospitality, Hannah would have felt like a fish out of water.

Seating herself at a table at the centre of the large dining hall, she watched the guests piling delicacies onto their plates from the lavish buffet and toasting one another in wine and champagne. She admitted to herself that although the evening had been pleasant, not a single person apart from Melanie had made a lasting impression. *Prince Charming's not turned up tonight*, she thought to herself, almost forgetting the cab awaiting her outside.

"Thank you for being so nice to me," she said on the way out, giving the hostess a big hug.

"This is my number – let's stay in touch." Melanie handed her a card with her details. Scribbling Ella's number on a paper napkin, Hannah nodded her agreement. "As soon as my final exams are out of the way, we'll get together," the older girl added. "Tonight's not really your thing; you're much too young to settle down!"

"How about you?"

"No way! I'm focused on my career – not match-making."

"It's been great meeting you, Melanie, good luck with your exams."

Accompanying her outside to ensure the driver was genuine, Melanie called out, "See you in a while, kiddo!"

Hannah smiled. Melanie Gordon was different from anyone she ever met. A short cab ride later, she let herself into the warm, lit up entrance. Climbing the stairs to her bedroom, she was touched to find a note on the pillow:

I hope tonight was special. We'll talk in the morning. Sleep tight. Ella.

Although they called one another several times a week, Hannah and Melanie kept postponing meeting up due to the latter's exams.

"Will you be okay on your own?"

"Stop fussing! I'm fine – We'll get together eventually," Hannah assured her, secretly disappointed her friend couldn't fit her into her busy schedule. But she had tests of her own to study for, and the time soon passed.

After Hannah received her English diploma, Ella and Zipporah invited her for a meal at a bistro in Belsize Park, treating her to *ABBA: The Movie* at the ABC Cinema in Golders Green, reminding her of the time she, Zadie and Peter watched them perform in The People's Park.

One cold morning, Hannah ventured out for a morning walk, followed by a croissant and coffee at Bar Linda next to the station. She stopped off to buy a daily paper on her way back home when the man at the newsstand enquired if she had been to Great Expectations.

"I've probably passed it," she said, warily. "The name sounds familiar."

"It's a disco, next to The Refectory and an Italian restaurant called L'Artista. I work there most nights, tending to the coats. It's a fun and friendly place – you ought to try it out."

"But I've no one to take me!"

"You know me, don't you? I'm Ollie. I'll be happy to show you around. It's the perfect venue to drink, dance and make new friends." In his fifties, balding and with thick glasses, Ollie didn't really fit Hannah's vision of Prince Charming.

"Thanks . . . I'll bear it in mind." Truthfully, she didn't think it was for her. What on earth would she be doing in a place like that?

Prior to Christmas, Ella fell ill with flu. With no appetite to speak of, all she wanted was to stay in bed.

"There's not much point in just cooking for yourself, my dear," she told Hannah. "Why don't you visit that place you like so much? Just make sure you return before the streets are empty." She was referring to Ranch House, a few minutes' walk away.

"I think you're right. Will you be okay without me?"

Smiling, Ella nodded and closed her eyes.

Less than ten minutes later, a smiling Aziza led Hannah to a table by the window. "Let me guess: you're having the tuna sandwich, right?"

"You bet! This place is rather empty tonight."

"It's the weather. One inch of snow and everything stops."

"Really? This time of year Sweden's covered in it!" Tucking into her food, Hannah noticed a tall blonde girl in blue jeans, floppy belted t-shirt and knitted jacket walking by outside the window. She'd noticed her in the area before because she looked Scandinavian, but hadn't approached her. Suddenly curious to find out if she was Swedish, Hannah put some money on the table, picked up her bag and signalled to Aziza that she was leaving.

Just as the girl was about to disappear around the corner of the street, Hannah shouted, "Please wait! I want to talk to you." Stopping in her tracks, the girl turned to look at her.

"I don't know you – what do you want? My bus is due any minute." Her accent was unmistakeably Swedish.

"My name's Hannah – I live a few minutes away from here. I'm Swedish too," she said, swapping to their language.

Laughing, the girl introduced herself. "I'm Sanna. I come from Stockholm but I've been here since July, working as au pair for a family at Henlys Corner, not far from Temple Fortune."

"That's close to where my grandmother lives. She's in Lyttelton Road, next to Market Place."

"I've seen you around – often sitting by yourself at Lindy's or Ranch House."

"Let's go there!" Hannah exclaimed, wanting to get to know the girl. "Don't you just love their Banana Split?"

"But you just came out of there! You're tiny – where do you put all that food? I gain weight just looking at it . . ." The girl burst into laughter, displaying a set of even white teeth.

Debating whether to stay or leave, Sanna said she might as well catch a later bus. It was Sunday, after all, and her day off.

Aziza looked up as the two of them entered.

"Did you come back for dessert?" she teased Hannah, then turned her attention to Sanna.

"I recognise you . . . you and your Scottish friend come here ever so often. I keep forgetting her name."

"Rosie? Oh, she's at home nursing a cold. I told her she'd better get well or risk not coming with me to Great Expectations on Friday!"

Shaking her head, Aziza replied, "The two of you sure love that place."

"Well, it is the only disco charging a pound to enter and handing out free sandwiches at midnight."

Giggling, Aziza left them, returning a couple of minutes later with two enormous portions of banana split, ice-cream and whipped cream. "Enjoy!"

Over their desserts, Hannah asked her new friend if she liked being an au pair. Sanna grimaced.

"It's okay . . . They're kind of nice, yet expect me to do everything. Their kids are three and five, very spoilt. Despite the mother being a housewife, she'd not dream of coping on her own. Can you envisage a Swedish woman agreeing with that? My mother raised me by herself after Dad left us when I was two." Hannah told her about Ella and how fortunate she was to live with someone so nice. "I envy you – my salary's £12 a week – it's not exactly cheap around here, is it?" Hannah omitted telling her about her parents' monthly allowance; the girl clearly struggled to cope. Feeling extremely privileged, she made a mental note to pay the bill.

Suddenly Sanna glanced at her watch and shot to her feet.

"I'd better leave – my bus is due in fifteen minutes!"

"Can't you catch a cab? It'll be my treat – we only just met."

"No way!" Sanna shook her long hair. "Give me your number so we can arrange to meet in the near future."

"Aziza mentioned you and your friend are regulars at Great Expectations – what's it like?"

"Fabulous! Lots of fun, music and guys to die for." Hanna smiled, thinking how different they looked physically. Sanna was the epitome of a blonde, blue-eyed Scandinavian woman with a curvaceous figure bound to make men drool over her. "I can't resist anything in this place!" Sanna continued, licking a last bit of cream off her spoon. "You'd better finish that plate. Bread and candy taste better at home; it's the burgers and fries I can't resist!" She handed Hannah a piece of paper with her number.

"There. Now we've swapped numbers, you must join Rosie and me at Great Expectations. She'll go mad when we speak Swedish in her presence!"

"Are you close?"

"Very – Rosie's my best friend. Just like us, she's on a gap year. We're returning home in the summer. I'd better warn you, Rosie's blunt – what you see is what you get." Hannah couldn't believe her luck; she'd already made two new friends in Melanie and Sanna. Perhaps Rosie would be the third? "Hey, I never told you my surname," Sanna added. "It's Göransson. What's yours?"

"Stein."

"That doesn't sound Swedish?"

"It isn't. We're Jewish. My parents were born in Sweden, but both my grandmothers originate from Russia – my maternal grandmother moved here in the early seventies."

"Wow – what an interesting background. Now I know why you're so pretty – I love your red hair!"

When Aziza gave them the bill, Hannah refused to let Sanna pay.

"You refused my offer to take a cab but this is my treat. Once you get to know me better, you'll realise I'm very stubborn . . ."

On the way to the bus stop they talked about their plans for the future. At nineteen, Sanna was determined to become a social worker. In turn, Hannah revealed her ambition was to teach.

"That doesn't surprise me," Sanna replied, "you're very articulate. Oh look, here's the bus, it's actually on time for once! Hey, why don't you join me and Rosie at Great Expectations next Friday?"

"It's the Sabbath – Ella and I always have dinner together."

"Tell you what, the disco doesn't get going until late, you'll have plenty of time to eat and join us later. We'll call each other during the week." After a quick hug, Sanna jumped on board, calling over her shoulder, "I can't wait to introduce you to my friends – just imagine all the fun we'll have!"

CHAPTER THREE

1979

TRUE TO HER word, Sanna called a couple of days later, suggesting they meet up at The Refectory next to L'Artista the following Friday night.

"You can't miss it! That place reeks of garlic. I can't tell you how much I look forward to introducing you to my friends and Great Expectations."

"I'll get back to you," Hannah wasn't sure if she should go. "Ella's recovering from two bouts of flu."

"I'm sorry to hear it." Sanna told her she'd call later that week.

As the days passed, Ella didn't get better, but the older lady insisted Hannah should go and meet her new friend.

"You're sure you'll be okay?" It was nearly time to go, but Hannah still felt uncertain. "I hate leaving you on the Sabbath." She assisted Ella upstairs and into bed. Lying against the pillow, it was obvious how frail she was.

"Nonsense! Dinner was lovely, I'll be fine after a good night's sleep." Hannah gazed down on what had now become a very dear face. They'd spent Chanukah and Christmas with Zipporah and her Russian friends. Zadie, Walther and Peter had called, wishing them a Happy New Year and updating Hannah about life at home. Telling her how beautiful the snow was that year, Hannah wished she were there with them. She contemplated booking a flight, opting to stay and find out what lay ahead in 1979.

"You must promise to be careful walking back in the dark," Ella commented in a weak voice.

"You've nothing to worry about – Sanna's watching over me." Bending to kiss her cheek, Hannah noticed the uncharacteristically frightened look in her eyes.

"You're looking very pretty my dear – I'd give anything to be young again, dancing the night away. I hope you have a wonderful time."

Switching off the light on the bedside table, Hannah went downstairs to pick up her bag. It was much too cold to wear a dress, so she opted for a pair of black flared jeans, a purple top, heavy coat and boots, red hair falling loosely down her shoulders, eyes heavily made up. It didn't take long to walk to the pub. Sanna was right. The overwhelming smell coming from L'Artista was making her nauseous.

"There you are! I was about to send out a search party."

Elbowing her way through the crowd of people standing at the bar, Hannah embraced her friend and joined her up on a high stool. "Wow! This place's certainly popular." Sanna asked if she wanted a drink. "Bacardi and Coke with a slice of lemon please."

Sipping their cocktails, the girls began to catch up on each other's news, but the young man serving them enquired if they planned on visiting the disco.

"Yeah . . . later. What's it got to do with you?" Sanna snapped, conscious of the way he was looking at them.

"Sorry I asked! As soon as my shift's ended, I'll go there myself." He gave them a dirty look, laughing.

Ignoring the comment, Sanna declared, "Let's find another place to sit." Embarrassed, Hannah followed suit, squeezing in at a table close by. "Don't take any notice – he's just a kid."

It was time to change the topic.

"I like your shoes," Hannah said. "I'm amazed you can walk in them." In a short black skirt, diamante-studded blouse and spiky heels, Sanna looked very sexy. Leaning her ample cleavage over the table (and drawing the stares of some nearby men in the process), she whispered in Hannah's ear.

"Me neither! It's the reason I brought these with me." She gestured at a pair of boots in a plastic bag. "You look gorgeous – the guys will fancy you rotten!"

Blushing, Hannah asked, "What's it like? Expectations, I mean?"

"It's a cross between a disco and pick-up place."

"Meaning what exactly?" She almost regretted coming out.

"The name's misleading, everyone's really nice yet also dubious . . . just don't believe everything you're told, okay?" Glancing at her watch, Sanna told her they'd better make a move. They grabbed their bags and coats, heading for the exit.

Outside, a queue of people waiting to get in stretched well onto the pavement. It took the girls almost half an hour to climb the narrow staircase down to the basement, dim lighting streaming from the dark dance floor and bar.

After they'd paid the one pound entrance fee entitling them to free sandwiches at midnight, two men greeted them, one of a stocky build in a grey suit, the tall guy next to him sporting a baseball cap. "Aren't you going to introduce us to your pretty friend, Blondie?" the former asked in a deep voice.

"Hannah's my new Swedish friend."

"Pleased to make your acquaintance, love. My name's Bob, the

29

geezer next to me is Ronnie. We're employed to ensure you ladies are well looked after." Turning to his friend, they heard him add, "They're a sight for sore eyes. What'll we call Blondie's mate?"

"That's a no-brainer! We'll refer to her as 'Ginger' – you don't mind do you, love?" Ronnie bent to kiss her cheek.

"Of course not," she mumbled, feeling out of place.

"Go say hello to Ollie, and ladies, have a good night!" Blowing them a kiss, Bob turned his attention to the crowd waiting to get in. Sanna took Hannah's arm.

"Those two wouldn't hurt a fly," she whispered. They're old enough to be our dads – I've lost track of all the times they came to Rosie's and my rescue, helping us get rid of unwanted attention. Beneath that bolshy exterior, Bob and Ronnie are a couple of rough diamonds."

As they made their way towards the cloakroom at the back of the room, Hannah instantly recognised the guy from the newsstand at the station.

"You decided to give it a go then?" Ollie commented, taking their coats. "Well, don't you worry. Between them, Sanna and Rosie will ensure you're having a good time! See you in a while . . ."

After touching up their make-up in the small Ladies behind the cloakroom, the girls made their way to the dance floor, where ABBA's 'Take A Chance On Me' followed by Bee Gees hits from *Saturday Night Fever* belted from the stereo.

"I can't believe I've not come here until now!" Hannah was mesmerised by the size of the place. She looked around her, watching the floor filling up with people their age, seated on plain black chairs and couches along the wall, round tables scattered all over, laughter and music filling the room. Struggling to hold a conversation over the din, Hannah noticed a tall slim man accompanied by a short woman with dark hair enter.

"That's John and Rosie – he's a Londoner, she's Scottish." As Sanna introduced her friends, both spontaneously gave Hannah a hug. It was almost 10pm and the place was heaving.

"We'll find somewhere to sit and talk," Rosie shouted. Grabbing some chairs, the four of them sat down at a table close to the toilets.

John insisted on buying a round of drinks while Rosie and Hannah got to know each other. Returning with their drinks on a tray, he commented, "You probably guessed I'm older than most – people refer to me as 'residential artist'. I draw visitors too drunk to notice!"

"Are you famous?" Hannah asked, surprised by his admission.

"I wish. There's a lot of talent out there – I'm not too bad."

"He's much too modest!" Rosie protested proudly. "You ought to take a look at his paintings – they're the best!" She and Sanna were clearly his biggest fans.

"I paint on the back of paper plates meant for ham and cheese sandwiches." John's accent was immaculate.

"You'd be mistaken for a Swede with those blue eyes and fair hair," Hannah remarked, thinking he was very smart.

"Sanna tells me I must travel to Sweden. Although geographically close, it has somehow escaped me so far."

Taking a sip of her Bacardi and Coke, Hannah's gaze drifted to Rosie, noticing her eyes were the same colour as sapphires. In a pair of fitted blue jeans, starched shirt and bangles, Sanna's best friend looked very cute. As if sensing her thoughts, Rosie turned to look at her.

"I'm so pleased we finally get to meet, Hannah. Sanna tells me you're from Malmö, quite a distance from Stockholm where she was born. I work as au pair in Hendon. Don't you just love this place? Sanna and I met here." Touching John's arm, she added, "In case you've not figured it out, John's actually gay. The good ones usually are . . ." Blushing, Hannah looked the other way.

"You mustn't worry about me!" John laughed. "Subtlety's never been Rosie's strong point – she's always brutally honest. It's part of who I am – the guy who prefers men to women." He wasn't in the least offended, looking directly into her eyes without flinching.

"Good for you. Where I come from, it's not a big deal."

"I'm pleased to hear it. Will you let me paint you? I love the colour of your eyes and hair."

"I'm flattered." Hannah felt her face turning red. The foursome spent the rest of the night dancing to their favourite tracks, until Hannah glanced at her watch, exclaiming, "It's almost midnight! I'd better leave or my landlady will wonder where I am . . . I really enjoyed tonight, thank you everyone."

"Won't you stay until you've eaten your sandwiches?" Rosie asked, determined to not leave before getting what she paid for.

"It's late . . . you can have them."

"Let's talk in a couple of days," Sanna intervened, voice drowning in the noise from everyone queuing up at the bar to collect their sandwiches.

"Are you sure you'll be okay walking back on your own?" John enquired. Too embarrassed to admit she'd rather not, Hannah bowed her head. "Well, I'm coming with you," he insisted, sensing her apprehension. "You two can wait for me to return and give you a lift back."

"We're okay with that," Rosie and Sanna said simultaneously.

"But that's not fair. You were looking forward to those sandwiches."

"What's unfair is letting a pretty girl wander the streets alone. Please say you agree – it will ease my mind."

"You're sure you don't mind?" Hannah asked the others.

"Of course not. You're in safe hands; John's not just gay, he's a gentleman too!" Rosie teased. Giving Hannah a hug, Sanna added, "I promised I'd make sure you're alright, didn't I?"

Handing them their coats, Ollie asked if Hannah had a good time.

"It's been ages since I enjoyed myself this much!" she replied, just as Bob and Ronnie left their position at the entrance.

"That's what we want to hear, see you again soon, Ginger!"

Hannah and John strolled arm in arm through the dark, empty streets of Golders Green, ten minutes later turning into Rodborough Road and Ella's house.

"I'm very grateful you offered to come with me," Hannah said, kissing John's cheek.

"The pleasure's all mine, I really enjoyed getting to know you. You're serious about letting me paint you, aren't you?"

"I can't wait!" Watching her enter and lock up, John waved and walked off.

Taking off her jacket and boots in the dimly lit hall, Hannah tiptoed upstairs and was startled to hear a voice ask, "Was tonight as nice as you expected, my dear?" Ella stood waiting for her on the landing, wearing a robe over her nightgown and slippers on her feet.

"You should be fast asleep, not worrying about me! Let's get you back to bed." Taking her arm, Hannah felt tears sting her eyes.

"Will you be seeing them again?"

33

"I might . . . They're almost as nice as you are." Ella viewed her as family, hence the reason she awaited her return.

Ten minutes later, tucked up in bed, Hannah felt happy to be alive.

CHAPTER FOUR

S ANNA GÖRANSSON, ROSIE Andrews and John Munro were the reasons Hannah spent Friday nights at Great Expectations. While the girls danced the night away, John retired to a spot further back, drawing them on the back of paper plates. Seeing her likeness for the first time, Hannah was quite overcome. "You succeeded in catching my spirit, not just appearance; I must pay you!"

"No way! I never charge my mates," John replied, standing his ground.

"I didn't mean to cause offence . . . won't you at least permit me to buy you a drink?"

"Alright – you twisted my arm. Did I mention I'm having an exhibition at a friend's gallery in Hampstead? What with preparing for that, guiding tourists through the streets of London and seeing you lot, I've got my hands full . . ."

"Hey John," said Rosie, pushing through the crowd. "Did it slip your mind we're entering a dance competition? It's the reason we regularly practice – my feet are living proof of it!" She moaned, pretending she was in agony.

"It's a breeze compared to ungrateful moaning tourists," John replied, giving her a hug.

"How come we weren't informed about this competition?" Sanna raised an eyebrow.

"She's right," Hannah intervened. "Why are we the last to know?"

"It's not until spring," Rosie said. "The disc jockey's announcing it after deciding which couples he thinks are good enough to take part. He approached us a while back."

"I reckon we're just as good as Newton-John and Travolta in *Grease*," John said, smiling broadly.

"I bet my bottom dollar the two of you will win it!" Hannah told them, thinking they had natural chemistry. Indeed, the following week John and Rosie found out the disc jockey had included them among the other contestants taking part.

"You're amazing! Hannah and I are so very proud," Sanna told them warmly, wishing she was as talented.

"It's Seventies night . . . How about we wear sequins and platforms?"

"You're mad!" John looked genuinely shocked, scratching his head. "We'll look ridiculous in platforms – I quite approve of the sequins though," he added, pinching Rosie's cheek.

Too busy to be part of the weekly get-together at Ranch House, John didn't object to the three of them meeting for lunch and gossip every Sunday afternoon. One day it rained so much that they gave up on the idea of venturing out into the neighbourhood, instead opting to stay put, ordering their usual tuna and club sandwiches, fries and milkshakes. Seated near the door, they watched people passing by outside, carrying umbrellas.

"I do wish spring would arrive early," Rosie said. "Hey – you'd better stop pinching my fries or risk not fitting into your new Miss Selfridge jeans."

Sighing, Sanna complained she only had to look at food to gain weight. "Why can't I be as slim as you two?" She pushed away her plate. "I was looking forward to dessert but you're right . . . I'd better not." Sympathising with her, Hannah and Rosie skipped ordering chocolate fudge cake with marshmallows and vanilla ice-cream, the latter's mind elsewhere.

"Look at those guys in the centre of the room. I bet they never saw a blonde, brunette and redhead together until now . . . What a pity neither of them is remotely attractive!" Her voice could be heard all over.

Joining them, Aziza roared with laughter. "Rosie Andrews! You're very bad for business – they'll never set foot here again."

Agreeing with her, Rosie pulled out a chair. "Stay and join us discussing our future, Aziza. I bet you've got a plan."

"Perhaps . . . No, I'm taking a rain check, my boss doesn't approve of staff mingling with customers. You're on your own!" Taken aback about the fact they were expected to have an in-depth conversation, Hannah and Sanna frowned.

"Well, what else is there to talk about?" Rosie persisted. "The weather's awful; we may as well come clean about our future plans. I'll begin shall I?" Taking a deep breath, her blue eyes lit up. "Flowers! It's hardly a secret I'm crazy about them. Imagine the intoxicating smell of a room packed with all kinds of arrangements? I'll start with a small shop, expanding to a chain of florists catering to weddings, birthdays and bar mitzvahs. What's your ambition, Hannah?"

"It's hardly a secret. For as long back as I can remember, my heart's been set on becoming a teacher."

"Really? Personally I can't think of anything worse, just imagine having a kid . . . Who'd want them?" Rosie replied, feeling nauseous.

"Don't you want a family of your own?" Hannah asked.

"Maybe when I'm in my thirties with a successful career. It's not possible to have both."

Listening to her, Sanna's eyes flared up. "What a ridiculous thing to say! My dad abandoned us when I was two. Mum brought me up single-handedly, insisting anything's achievable if you put your mind to it. I'm considering becoming a social worker."

"You can't be serious! You'd willingly get involved with drug addicts?" Rosie began to view her friend in an entirely different light.

"What's wrong with that? Someone has to. Why not me? I enjoy participating in all kinds of situations. John recently told me life rarely turns out the way we plan it. Here's to us and our future!" Toasting each other, the three of them downed their milkshakes.

Hannah suddenly recalled her mother's advice: "Success means nothing without that special someone to share it with." Instead of sharing it with the others, she decided to keep it to herself.

Whenever Sanna visited Hannah, she'd acknowledge her presence by throwing small stones from the pavement onto the bedroom window. Enjoying her cosy bedroom and fireplace, she and Rosie thought Ella was the kindest person they'd ever met. Occasionally Hannah and Ella invited the girls round to Sabbath dinner, introducing them to their culture and cuisine.

"Is your family religious? My brother and I were brought up Catholics yet became atheists."

Rosie loved the atmospheric Friday dinners and scrumptious food Hannah spent hours preparing, adding to her initial small repertoire.

"My parents keep kosher and we're proud of our roots. Granny's traditional yet very modern. Did I mention her moving to London in her seventies? She lives in Market Place."

"Can we meet her?" Sanna asked, longing to get acquainted with the woman Hannah constantly raved about.

One Friday afternoon sitting in Ella's cramped kitchen, Hannah suggested they meet up at Cosmo, a cosmopolitan restaurant in Swiss Cottage. "It's very popular among Jewish people – the food's great!"

"The Purple Pussycat is off Finchley Road," Rosie added. "It's a nightclub run by two brothers. Ricky's the oldest, with a larger-than-life personality. Sanna and I can't wait to introduce you."

"Is it as nice as Expectations?" Hannah asked.

"Sort of, only smaller." Sanna suddenly thought of something. "It's John's thirtieth birthday on Saturday. He's invited us round for a drink."

"We'll get him a bottle of wine and truffles, seeing as he's got such a sweet tooth," Rosie said. "His flat isn't exactly what you'd expect," she added, warning Hannah it was a typical bachelor pad.

It turned out she was right: with paintings scattered everywhere, it wasn't particularly tidy or clean.

"I wish I could afford somewhere bigger, Hampstead's getting increasingly expensive," John told them, sipping his wine.

"Do you have someone helping you to clean? Ella's cleaner, Margareth, is brilliant. Would you like me to enquire if she's available?" It was meant as a joke; Margareth Dudley detested travelling further than Golders Green.

"You'd better not! Mum drove me crazy constantly nagging me about the state of my room – it's the reason I moved out!"

Although John's own appearance was immaculate, the girls politely declined his offer of sandwiches and cakes, thinking it was probably safest to toast him with wine. They were on their way back to Golders Green when Rosie piped up, "I dread to imagine what might have happened had we said yes to his offer of food – we'd probably have ended up being poisoned!"

Shortly before Easter, Zadie called, sounding distraught.

"What's wrong?" Hannah asked.

"Your father wants me to tell you your grandmother hasn't got long to live."

An only child, Walther adored his mother, Esther, being all he had left when losing his father many years ago. As a Russian immigrant, she had refused to accept her adopted country, not even wishing to learn the language and customs. She and Zadie respected each other yet weren't close. Still, feeling eternally indebted to her, Walther never forgot how much she sacrificed to give him the life he craved, thinking that without her support and unselfishness, he wouldn't be where he was today.

The complete opposite to Zipporah, Esther came across as hard and unforgiving, questioning everyone and anything, including Hannah, Peter and Zadie; partly the reason they kept a healthy distance. "She's too set in her ways to change," Walther told them. "My father's untimely passing turned her into a shadow of her old self."

Now, taking in her mother's words, Hannah expected the worst.

"I'm sorry, sweetie, I'm having to postpone my visit – your father needs me. We'll see one another in the near future. Give your grandmother and Ella my fondest wishes."

When Walther called a week later informing her that Esther had died in her sleep, Hannah asked if he wanted her to attend the funeral.

"What's the point? I'd much rather you remember her like she used to be – she loved you very much, darling."

Hannah and Ella sent a card expressing their condolences, and Zipporah showed respect by lighting a candle in Esther Stein's memory.

As soon as Easter and Passover were over, Hannah organised a meeting between her grandmother and friends. "I booked a table at Cosmo," she told the girls. "Ella and Granny's old friends Katja and Tanya will be joining us." May was approaching and with it, sunny hot weather. The ladies made the effort to look their best. Opting to wear a light-blue dress, her hair in a soft shade of red perfectly matching her lips, Zipporah admired Tanya and Katja's bright kaftans, the latter wearing a turban to conceal her loss of hair due to old age. Meanwhile, Hannah assisted dressing Ella, choosing a lavender dress with matching jacket. Rosie and Sanna also made the effort to dress up.

Seated at the large table in the buzzing restaurant overlooking the crowd around them, Rosie kept thinking everyone looked wonderful. "You look years younger than your actual age!" she blurted out, referring to each by surname.

"Please don't! Unless you refer to us by first name, we'll feel ancient," Zipporah whispered in her ear.

It was difficult choosing from the extensive menu. "I'm postponing my diet," said Sanna. This place's worth it."

Nodding her agreement, Katja replied, "You're a girl close to my own heart. Women are wrong assuming being thin as a stick's attractive – men prefer a fuller, feminine figure!" Her Russian accent matched that of her friends'. Beaming, Sanna wholeheartedly agreed.

"I'd never contemplate cutting down on my food, neither would Tanya," Katja added, winking at the larger woman seated next to her.

"Hence the kaftans!" The latter's laughter echoed in the room, attracting a lot of attention from the other guests. "You must attend one of my exhibitions," Tanya continued. "Did Zipporah mention I only started to paint in my eighties?"

Watching her old friend, Zipporah replied, "Hannah's seen your bold splashes of colour – all of which enhance an at times dull world!"

Roaring with laughter, Tanya addressed them all. "I want you and your young friends to join me in one of my 'London By Night' outings. It's an excellent opportunity to familiarise yourselves with the capital! My combined chef and driver knows the city like the palm of his hand."

"Do you recall the first time you came along, darling?" Zipporah asked her granddaughter.

"I most certainly do. I felt as though London belonged to me – nobody else."

"Then that's settled! Life is for living, darlings. Will you be gracing us with your company, dear?" Tanya raised her glass in a toast to Ella, who was shaking her head.

"I'd better not, seeing as I usually get queasy in a car."

The meal turned out to be a great success, Rosie for once keeping her thoughts to herself and listening to the ladies reminiscing about the past.

The following Saturday evening Tanya's chauffeur collected everyone outside the entrance of Zipporah's building, wearing a formal uniform and cap.

"My name's Leo, Mrs Levy's driver and chef. I wish you a pleasant night." He was clearly in his sixties, judging by the glasses and grey hair. As he assisted them into the large, black limousine, the girls felt as if they'd been transported to another planet – one inhabited by the very rich.

Rosie felt exhilarated. From the comfort of Tanya's limousine, she stared out at the impressive properties in Park Lane. "I never saw anything like it!" she marvelled, sipping champagne out of a crystal glass.

"What's the verdict, darlings? It's not every day you get the chance to be in the company of such distinguished old broads!" Leaning closer towards them, Zipporah kissed their cheeks.

Uncorking another bottle of Dom Pérignon, Tanya had a wistful expression in her eyes. "All of us lost people we love in the Holocaust. It's our duty to make the most of whatever remains of our lives, for them as much as for ourselves." Filling up their glasses, she added, "You've such a lot to be grateful for, never forget it."

Watching her closely, Rosie was close to tears. "How can you be so positive after everything you endured?" she asked in a low voice.

"Because you only get as much out of life as you put into it, darling." Stroking her hand, Tanya smiled through her own tears.

It was almost midnight when Leo dropped them off outside Ella's house, where they'd spend the night in Hannah's room. Embracing the older ladies, the girls vowed to keep in touch.

"Thank you for the most magical night of my life – we'll never forget it," Sanna told them, following her friends up the path.

Chapter Five

THE SPOTLIGHT FELL on the dance floor as the DJ announced the competition was due to begin. At 9pm on a Friday night in late May, the disco was packed with people forming a circle around the contestants, everyone wearing their best seventies outfits, shoulder pads, flared trousers and platform shoes. In their psychedelic halter-neck dresses, heavy make-up and sprayed hair, Hannah and Sanna were barely able to move, watching the ten couples competing for the title of 'Mr and Mrs Saturday Night Fever'.

With the crowd cheering them on, each couple performed as if their lives depended on it. Yet John and Rosie were a cut above the rest. Having practised around the clock, they were everyone's favourite to win. Looking extremely dashing in a matching white suit and dress covered in sequins, John and Rosie danced as if they owned the floor.

"Look at them – Rosie looks exquisite!" Hannah whispered in Sanna's ear.

"I love her asymmetrical haircut and glamorous make-up." Sanna couldn't take her eyes off her friends as they danced to the Bee Gees' 'Staying Alive', 'How Deep Is Your Love' and many more. Oblivious to everyone around them clapping and shouting their names, the contestants moved to the music until the DJ shouted:

"Time's up!"

Collecting the cards with everyone's favourite name, Ronnie and the DJ retired to the back of the room. After all the agonising, practising and tension, the contestants prayed their efforts had paid off as they joined the crowd for a well-deserved short break.

Close to midnight a beaming DJ with Ronnie following closely behind returned, declaring they were about to announce the winners. Positioning themselves in a line on the floor, ten couples shut their eyes, praying their names would be read out. Surrounded by happy, excited faces, Hannah felt certain she'd never forget that night. Great Expectations attracted people from all backgrounds; some of them making lasting friendships just like her, Sanna, Rosie and John.

Stepping up to the microphone, the DJ addressed the crowd.

"Ladies and gentlemen! I'm about to crown the winning couple – perhaps you already guessed who they might be?" he teased.

"Yes!" everyone shouted simultaneously, stamping their feet and clapping their hands.

"In third place . . . I give you Karen and Lenny!" The spotlight zoomed in on the young couple holding hands, faces red with excitement at the prospect of receiving a certificate and a bottle of red wine. "In second place and runners up . . . we have Lisa and Sam!" Everyone applauded as they too collected their certificate and bottle of wine.

After a brief silence, the DJ continued. "The moment we anticipated for so long has finally arrived! I'm thrilled to announce the winners of tonight's competition are . . ." The spotlight fell on the remaining couples, zooming in on Rosie and John. "The contestants receiving two thirds of the votes are our very own Rosie Andrews and John Munro! Please be so kind as to collect your diploma and bottle of champagne." Shell-shocked yet extremely pleased to have won, Rosie and John walked arm in arm through the cheering crowd, smiling from ear to ear.

That night Great Expectations stayed open longer than usual, with everyone congratulating the winning couple and dancing until the early hours of the morning. Seated at the back of the room, Rosie rubbed her feet, declaring, "Tonight was great fun but I for one won't participate in another competition. How about you John?"

"Who knows?" He shrugged, smiling. "Perhaps if I've someone as formidable as you to team up with . . ."

Blushing with pride, Rosie looked at her friends. "I'll never forget tonight. Winning's great yet it's nothing in comparison to our friendship." She gave each of them a big hug.

Later that night as Hannah headed towards the exit, her eyes fell on a couple standing at the bar.

"In case you're wondering, that's Mark and his latest conquest, Denise," John remarked in a flat voice. In her early twenties, sporting a black t-shirt and jeans, the tall black girl looked very sexy. She was leaning against a slightly shorter, muscular man holding a black leather jacket, hair short and mousy, prominent nose and fleshy lips. His stare caught her off-guard, gazing through the crowd as if nothing and no one escaped him. Conscious she was being watched, Hannah noticed the cleft in his chin and muscle twitching in one cheek. As he turned to say something to the pretty girl beside him, his voice was drowned out by the noise around them. Averting her eyes, Hannah accompanied her friends out into the street.

Chatting to some passers-by outside, she suddenly heard someone ask, "I never noticed you until tonight . . . What's your name?" Turning to see who it was, Hannah's face turned red.

"I'm Hannah – Hannah Stein – I never clapped eyes on you either . . ."

Holding onto her boyfriend's jacket sleeve, eyes narrowing, the tall girl cooed, "Mark, honey, let's go back to my flat. We've got the place to ourselves."

But Mark cut loose from her grip. "You'd better make the most of it. I made other plans."

"But I was under the impression . . ." Her voice faltered.

"We're not joined at the hip!" The muscle in Mark's cheek twitched furiously as he abruptly left the girl too upset to respond, and stalked off in the opposite direction. Oblivious to the destruction left in his wake, Mark approached Hannah.

"What's someone as beautiful as you doing in a dump like that?" he asked, his eyes flicking momentarily back to the disco.

"My friends and I meet up every Friday. If it's not to your liking, I suggest you don't return." She'd had enough of his rude behaviour. Who did he think he was and how dare he chat her up in front of his girlfriend? Ignoring his stare, Hannah joined her friends further down the pavement.

"What did he say to you?" Sanna asked in a contemptuous voice, the others following suit. "You're looking upset!"

"I've never met anyone as arrogant. I bet he thinks he's God's gift to women!" Livid that he'd treated Denise in such a demeaning way, Hannah couldn't care less if he overheard her.

But Mark was much too busy watching the girl with her green eyes blazing at him, equally fiery-red hair and curvaceous figure. *I can't wait to see her again!* Mark Copeck was used to getting what he wanted and Hannah Stein was just that.

Catching a passing cab, John, Sanna and Rosie dropped Hannah off outside Ella's house. It was almost 3am. Opening the door to let her out, John stifled a yawn. "Listen to Uncle John's advice: Copeck's in a league of his own. He takes great pleasure in hurting anyone who gets too close to him. You're the only woman putting him in his place."

"Good! It serves him right. How come you're so concerned?"

"Call it sixth sense. Most women are duped by his charm, but as soon as he gets what he wants, he dumps them – Denise is a prime example. I don't want you to get hurt," he said, kissing her cheek.

"Give her some credit," said Rosie, eavesdropping on their conversation. "Hannah's much too clever to fall for that jerk!"

Meeting her gaze, John shook his head. "It's her heart, not brain, I worry about."

Ignoring their comments, Hannah bid them goodnight, waving until the cab was out of sight. Half an hour later, curled up in bed and looking back on the night's events, all she could think was she never encountered anyone like Mark. Was it possible to harbour feelings towards a complete stranger? Albeit a very arrogant one . . .

Against her better judgement, Mark stirred something inside of her. However hard she tried, she couldn't stop recalling how it felt when his eyes looked into hers.

Melanie called out of the blue that Sunday, asking if Hannah wanted to meet up for lunch at Ranch House. "Bring your friends along – I'd love to meet them," she said. But when Hannah requested their company, Rosie told her they were busy getting ready to see their boyfriends, Mohammed and Andy, whom they'd met at Great Expectations two nights previously.

"We're invited to some friend's party later – why don't you join us?"

"You're certain Mohammed and Andy aren't stringing you along? What'll happen if you fall in love with them?"

"Love? Who mentioned love!" Rosie burst out laughing. "None of us want commitment – they're just a casual fling." Hannah sighed. It was great her friends were having so much fun. Now all she needed to do was meet a man of her own.

An hour later, Melanie greeted her with a big hug. "It's great we finally got together." Packed with families having lunch, the Ranch House menu was as tempting as ever. Sitting at a window table overlooking the buzzing high street, the girls filled each other in on recent events.

"I passed my exams and am in the process of starting an accountancy firm," Melanie said. "I'm hoping a fellow student's interested in coming on board – his name's Matthew." Although she looked very smart in a bob framing her big blue eyes, black dress emphasising her slim figure and chunky jewellery, Hannah had the distinct impression she had something to hide.

"Is there something I should know?"

"Such as?" Melanie feigned ignorance.

"Are you and Matthew more than friends?"

"How did you guess?" Her eyes lit up at the mentioning of his name.

"It's written all over your face!"

"I'll be twenty-five soon . . . Matthew's a terrific guy! He's kind, caring and handsome – I can easily imagine him being the father of my children."

"I'm pleased to hear it! When's the wedding?"

"One step at a time. I've got to get my birthday out of the way first. The invitations are in the mail, yours included!" They proceeded to talk about family and friends. "Did I ever tell you about Ben? He's my best friend – we've known each other since nursery. Our parents are very close."

"Is he Jewish too?"

"Have a guess! His name's Benjamin Isaacs and he's the kindest man you'd ever wish to meet; there's not a bad bone in that body of his." She reminisced about all the times he'd let her win whenever they played some game.

"Are you the same age?"

"Ben's slightly older – he's a solicitor, working at his father's law firm."

"I envy you getting your degree. I can't wait to become a teacher but won't qualify until I'm your age."

"You'll be a great teacher! You're extremely pretty and clever – tell you what, why don't I introduce you to Ben? You're similar in many ways: kind, caring and genuine. Did I mention he's very handsome? Tall, dark and the sexiest big brown eyes . . ."

"Sounds great!" Hannah had to smile. Seeing as you're friends, he's bound to be very nice."

After finishing off a bowl of vanilla ice-cream, both paid and left, Melanie reminding Hannah about her party. "I've a premonition you'll not regret it!" she said, with a glint in her eye. For some reason her comment stuck in Hannah's mind.

In early June, Zadie visited for a week, staying at Zipporah's flat and bringing with her greetings from Walther and Peter. They were planning to visit prior to Hannah returning to Sweden. Delighted she had 'her girls' to herself, Zipporah made the effort to cook their favourite dishes and when Ella joined them, she brought with her Jewish delicacies from the delicatessen at the corner of Rodborough Road.

"I'll miss Hannah so much when she pursues her dream of becoming a teacher," Ella said, her sad eyes betraying her upbeat tone. It was obvious how much she detested the thought of Hannah not being around in the foreseeable future, they were both so very close.

The week passed much too quickly, and on her last day in London Zadie invited Sanna and Rosie to a quaint restaurant in Hampstead. John had recently met some man at an exhibition and Melanie was preoccupied with her new job. After they finished eating, Zadie looked around at the three girls, smiling. "I'm so very pleased I got to know you! Hannah tells me you're very close. If you ever plan on visiting Malmö, I insist you stay at our house in Limhamn." With those large brown eyes and lovely features, Sanna and Rosie thought she was the most glamorous woman they ever saw.

When Zadie departed the next day, Hannah and Zipporah waved from the kitchen window, both unhappy to see her leave.

"Oh – you're young with all of your life ahead of you, whereas I'm having to accept I may never see her again!" Zipporah wailed. "Old age – it's a nuisance." Staying the night in the guest room, Hannah hated that she too would soon have to leave her grandmother and Ella behind. What if neither of them coped without her?

After doing some light shopping one Friday afternoon in mid-June, Hannah was walking towards Rodborough Road when she heard someone calling her name. Turning to see who it was, she immediately recognised the man sitting behind the wheel of a black Ford. Pulling up beside her, Mark Copeck looked dashing in a dark suit.

"Hello, sexy! That bag's looking heavy to me – let me give you a lift." He thought how pretty Hannah looked in leggings and t-shirt, her hair in a ponytail and no make-up. Somehow this was even more enticing to him than the first time they met. Rolling down the window, his arm casually dangling, Mark awaited her response. Their eyes locked for a split second.

"Thanks for the offer but I've not got far to walk – this is my road." Hannah gritted her teeth, pretending she didn't give a damn,

"Well you can't blame a guy for trying, can you? I want to see you again. How about tomorrow?" It was obvious how much he wanted her to say yes.

"I'm busy!" she snapped.

"How come? Are you cooking? I love Jewish food. My parents are Polish – our delicacies are similar to yours, especially chopped liver and dumplings." Was it possible someone as ignorant and rude actually had good taste? Perhaps she'd been too hasty judging him. Arm aching from carrying her shopping, Hannah put the bag down on the pavement. It was getting late. She and Ella looked forward to the Sabbath: chicken soup and roast chicken on the menu.

"Please let me drop you outside your house," Mark repeated, already halfway out of the car. Adamant that he shouldn't find out where she lived, Hannah shook her head.

"I'm fine. Thanks for asking."

Disappointed by her rejection, Mark persisted, asking if she'd meet him at the disco next Friday.

"You're sure your girlfriend won't object?" Hannah's words were laced with sarcasm.

"How many times do I have to tell you, there's nothing between us? Denise is just a friend." The muscle in his cheek started to twitch.

"It didn't look that way to me."

"How come you don't believe me? I'm not a liar!" His eyes searched hers.

"You and that girl are of no interest to me."

"Are you seeing someone?"

"That's none of your business!" Hannah was shouting now, her eyes glaring at his.

"Sorry I asked."

Hannah turned on her heels to walk away, but something made her stop. "What brings you to Golders Green? Are you stalking me?"

Seeing how upset she was, Mark put a hand on her shoulder. "Look, I'm sorry I startled you, I happened to see you and your friends leave Expectations the other night . . ." Removing his hand from her shoulder, Hannah felt like slapping his face. All she wanted was to get back and start preparing her and Ella's dinner. "You've nothing to fear from me."

Looking him up and down, Hannah muttered, "I resent being watched."

"You left me no option – how else would I get to know you? I was on my way home from John Lewis. I'm a salesman at the Brent Cross branch. I live in Stanmore."

"Please don't let me keep you – I'm certain we've both got better things to do than chatting in the middle of the street."

"I see . . . you're playing hard to get!" Enraged he immediately assumed she fancied him, Hannah started to walk away. "Alright – I can't stop thinking about you! You're the prettiest girl I ever saw; I want to see you . . . It's not exactly criminal is it?" Mark put his hands up.

"I already made it abundantly clear I'm not interested." Refusing to have anything to do with him, she walked as fast as she could towards Ella's house, thinking, *My head's spinning – I wish he'd have the sense to leave!*

To her dismay, Mark shouted: "I'll be waiting for you at the disco – please don't let me down!" He got back into his car. Hearing the wheels screech, she watched him disappear around the corner of the street.

Who does he think he is?

Despite being upset, Hannah had to admit no one had ever pursued her like that before. It made her feel very special.

CHAPTER SIX

Situated between Golders Green and Hampstead Village, overlooking Golders Hill Park, The Bull and Bush was sought after by the locals. Seated at the entrance, nursing their usual Bacardi with Coke and gin and tonic, Hannah and Sanna were chatting happily when they heard a familiar voice.

"Fancy bumping into you! My local, the Hare and Hound, is just up the road – this must be my lucky day."

It was a sunny afternoon in late July. Both girls wore dresses that revealed their figures, emphasising their legs and sun-kissed skin. Mark enjoyed the startled expression in their eyes as he strolled up to them; evidence of how much they resented his presence. "You, young lady, stood me up the other night. Did you forget we had a date?" Mark's eyes fixated on Hannah.

"I never consented to anything," she replied in an angry voice, eyes avoiding his. She couldn't help thinking he looked nice in tight-fitting blue jeans, t-shirt and sandals.

Sipping his beer, Mark shrugged his shoulders. "Whatever. We'll meet up next Friday at the disco – you and Sanna can come with me to The Purple Pussycat off Finchley Road." Ignoring his proposition, Hannah stood her ground, angry he still expected her to take an interest in someone so arrogant. Mark was a complication she could easily do without.

"Okay . . . Treat me as you wish. We needn't decide here and now. You've been to The Purple Pussycat haven't you, Sanna?"

"That's right. John and Rosie introduced me to it."

"Isn't it great? Bring your friend next Friday – I'll be there waiting for you." His eyes lingered on Hannah.

"We'll decide later . . ." Sanna muttered.

"Can I get you something to drink?" Mark asked, heading in the direction of the bar.

"No, we're off now." Hannah eyed her friend, silently begging her to say something – anything – all she wanted was to get away from him.

"I almost forgot . . . we're meeting up with a Swedish friend," Sanna blurted out.

"Didn't you just arrive? A Swede? Where are you heading?" It was evident by the tone of his voice that he didn't believe them. For the second time since meeting him, Hannah wanted to slap his face.

"What's it got to do with you? And another thing: I never turned up because I want nothing to do with you."

Upset by her comment, Mark's eyes narrowed. "Let me tell you something lady. I wish you'd stop listening to gossip and give me a break – why, you hardly know me!"

"I listen to my gut instinct; it's never let me down so far."

"Is that right? Your intuition's telling you I'm a bad boy? Denise is no victim – she knew the score from the start."

Fed up with listening to their bickering, Sanna interrupted. "I bet she thought you'd change your mind."

On the brink of saying something he shouldn't, Mark had second thoughts. "Denise is an attractive girl. We had a brief fling

– an exchange of bodily fluids if you like." His crude remark made Sanna explode with anger.

"Is that right? You view women as a piece of meat? Something to amuse yourself with then get rid of when you're bored?" She'd unwittingly raised her voice, painfully conscious of people staring at them.

"What's eating you? I answer to no one! Besides, I'm too young to settle down."

"Don't make me laugh. Guys like you don't know the meaning of love and commitment."

"That's enough! You started it, lady. What about you and Andy? You seriously imagine he gives a damn about you? Take it from me – the guy couldn't care less. I wonder who's kidding themselves now. It sure as hell isn't me!" He took great pleasure in watching her squirm.

Grabbing her friend's arm, Hannah hissed, "We're leaving. I'd not meet up with you if you were the only man on the planet." Picking up their jackets and bags, both stormed out. Neither was in the mood to walk back to Golders Green just yet. What started as a relaxing afternoon turned into a nightmare. Just as they were on the verge of crossing the street, Mark suddenly passed them in his Ford. Parking next to the pavement, he got out of the car and reached for Hannah's hand.

"What I told you earlier was unforgiveable. I ought to have kept my thoughts to myself." He looked as if he meant what he said. "I was gutted when you blew me out the other night . . . I can't get you out of my mind, baby." She looked so damned pretty in that blue dress. All he wanted was to touch her red hair and watching those green eyes melt when he kissed her.

Putting a hand on his chest, Hannah felt his heart beat, reluctantly admitting there was a chemistry between them. Pulling away, she went back to her friend, saying, "Sanna's right. You're not a nice person."

"I'm sorry you feel that way. Unlike Andy, I'm not a liar. I say it as it is." His eyes clouded over.

"You needn't worry on our account. We're returning home shortly."

Mark felt as if she'd dealt him a blow. He'd just met the woman he wanted to be with forever and she was leaving. "Please say you'll meet me at The Purple Pussycat. I promise to be on my best behaviour."

Ignoring his plea to give him another chance, Hannah put her arm around Sanna, both continuing to walk back to Golders Green.

"Are you okay?" Sanna sensed Mark's comment had upset her.

"Don't worry so much about me – how about you?"

"Mark knows nothing about me and Andy. We've an under-standing. My boyfriend's not a liar!"

"You mustn't let him get to you. Anyway, you and Andy aren't serious about each other, right?"

But Sanna's eyes told a different story. Andy clearly meant more than she wanted to admit.

"Just ensure you don't get pregnant or catch some disease."

"I wasn't born yesterday." They'd reached the station and San-na's bus was approaching.

"You're falling for him aren't you?" It was Sanna's turn to be concerned.

"Perhaps . . . I'm so confused. There's something about him I can't put my finger on. He fluctuates between being arrogant and sensitive – it's the latter I'm attracted to."

"If it was up to me, I'd have nothing to do with him. Mark has a nasty side to him – that guy's big trouble!" Jumping on the bus,

Sanna waved at Hannah walking towards Rodborough Road, neither of them aware of Mark watching them from behind the wheel of his car.

When Rosie found out about the incident with Mark, she tried to persuade Hannah to not let him get to her.

"The chance of you two bumping into one another at The Purple Pussycat is virtually non-existent," she promised. Anxious to see the place everyone raved about, Hannah agreed to join her friends the following week.

Wearing jeans, t-shirts and stilettos, the three of them met up for a drink at The Refectory, after which they took a cab to the nightclub. It was 9pm on a Wednesday night and a queue was forming outside in the small cul-de-sac adjacent to Finchley Road. Unlike Expectations, The Purple Pussycat comprised of small, dark rooms, combined dance floor and bar, and toilets signed 'Guys' and 'Dolls'. Owned by two brothers, it was the eldest everyone warmed to. The opposite of his timid sibling, Ricky was bold and extrovert. Tending to guests and serving Piña Coladas, Bloody Marys and Tequila Sunrises, he wore black trousers and t-shirt with the slogan, *At Your Disposal*.

"Let's dance!" Sanna dragged her friends to the cramped dance floor. A little while later, Rosie suggested they returned to the bar to order drinks. Time passed quickly and before they knew it, it was nearly 11pm and time to leave or risk missing the last bus to Golders Green.

Saying goodbye to Ricky, Rosie noticed a familiar tall, dark guy dancing with a blonde. Walking up to them, she shouted: "I wish you'd let me know you're seeing someone else!" Horrified she'd found out he was two-timing her, Mohammed struggled to come up with a plausible excuse. "It's not as if we're joined at the hip – it's just that I expected better from you," Rosie retorted, pretending she wasn't bothered.

Looking in their direction, Sanna saw Andy dancing cheek-to-cheek with another blonde. Locking eyes with her friend, she announced, "Are you thinking what I'm thinking?"

"You bet!" Rosie replied.

A united front, both went up to the dance floor. "Consider yourselves dumped!" Angry they'd been caught out, both men kept their mouths shut.

"Mark had a point," Sanna admitted moments later. "I guess it takes one cheat to recognise another." Her voice shook.

Coming up to them, Mohammed turned on Rosie, shouting: "Who the hell do you think you are, treating me this way?" He was fed up with her trying to control him, dictating whom he could and couldn't see. But Andy's face told a different story. He pleaded with Sanna to give him a second chance.

"I'm crazy about you!" She was about to respond when Mohammed interrupted.

"You're out of your mind! Her face is pretty but her arse is too big. You'll do a lot better than her." He succeeded in persuading his friend to join him and the two blondes.

"So much for him being 'crazy' about you." Rosie put a comforting arm around the Swedish au pair.

"We learnt a valuable lesson tonight." Sanna sighed. "There's no such thing as having your cake and eating it. A fling? Bah! Someone's bound to get hurt – I just wish that someone wasn't me." She had tears of humiliation in her eyes.

Rosie was pretty unhappy as well – they'd been taken for a ride. She vowed there and then to never put her faith in anyone. From now on, she'd be in charge.

On their way out, praying they'd catch a cab in the street, Ricky came after them. There was a big grin on his face.

"Ladies! You're looking as if you're in need of cheering up. Please join me at the Greek taverna across the street. It serves the most amazing food – I ought to know seeing as I'm the co-owner. Come on, make your minds up – I'm starving!" Conscious of the fact he was happily married with three kids, the girls readily agreed.

It was after midnight by the time they finished the delicious meal. Ricky was right: The Metropolis oozed with ambience – just the antidote they needed after what happened earlier. Listening to their host entertaining them with tales of his travelling all over the world, the girls agreed: that night was definitely on par with 'London By Night' in Tanya's chauffeur-driven limousine.

Later still, in the back seat of Ricky's old station wagon and close to being dropped off outside Ella's house where they'd spend the night in Hannah's room, Rosie couldn't stop giggling.

"What's up?" Ricky asked.

"We just got rid of our boyfriends yet couldn't care less!"

"Good for you. Those jerks aren't worthy of licking your boots – 'Mr Right' will turn up when you least expect it."

By the end of the summer Hannah was looking forward to returning home when out of the blue, Sanna and Rosie informed her they'd met a couple of guys who had persuaded them to stay a while longer.

"It'll not ruin our future plans – we're simply postponing things until next year." It was a Sunday afternoon and the friends had met for lunch at Ranch House. Sanna asked Hannah when she was leaving and was somewhat surprised by the answer.

"I'm not sure . . . I arranged to go on a date with Mark. He keeps pestering me every time we meet at the disco."

"It's obviously preferably to attending university!" Sanna teased.

"Don't be silly – the main reason I want to stay is that poor Ella's much worse. If it weren't for Mrs Dudley and me, I honestly believe she'd have to go into care. Granny's always telling me her days are numbered. All of it's very depressing." Her voice faltered just thinking about it.

"You'll be here for them and for us." Rosie's eyes lit up. "Just imagine all the fun we'll have!"

"We'll celebrate by having dessert – anyone for chocolate fudge cake with ice-cream?" Sanna asked.

"Aren't you on one of your diets?" Rosie replied with a pertinent question.

"Screw that – there's always another day!" Laughing, Hannah waved to Aziza to take their order.

The following Saturday, Hannah got ready to meet Mark at Villa Bianca in Hampstead Village, adamant he didn't pick her up after work thus imagining they were an item.

"I'll catch a bus at Golders Green Station," she told him, deciding to wear a bright purple dress, a few pieces of jewellery and subtle make-up. She said goodbye to Ella, who was propped up against the pillows reading a book.

The old lady commented on how pretty she looked, saying, "I hope he appreciates you – enjoy tonight, my dear."

At precisely 8pm Hannah entered the cosy Italian eatery situated in a cobbled mews off the high street. Scanning the candlelit tables and dim lighting, she spotted Mark seated by himself at the back.

"You look gorgeous!" He jumped to his feet. She was, by far, the prettiest girl in the room. He couldn't take his eyes off her, certain the other male guests shared his sentiment, judging by the way they gawped at her.

"You don't look so bad either," she replied, thinking he looked handsome in a grey suit, white shirt and tie. Fighting the urge to kiss her, Mark pulled out a chair, signalling for a waiter. After ordering pasta and a bottle of red wine, he leaned across the table, murmuring, "You look good enough to eat." Embarrassed by the way he stared at her, Hannah thanked him for asking her to dinner. "I hope you're enjoying it as much as I am," he said, their eyes locking for a few seconds.

Returning to pour the wine, the waiter wished them a pleasant evening.

"Here's to us!" Mark drained his wine in less than a minute.

"Mmm. It's nice." Hannah sipped hers, savouring the full flavour.

"Only the best for you, baby!" His husky voice, the wine and the romantic ambience of the restaurant relaxed Hannah so much that she started to open up about her future plans. Between mouthfuls of linguine with tomato and mozzarella, she noticed he'd almost finished his plate whereas she had barely touched hers. "I prefer to eat when it's hot – you don't object, right?" Mark told her, moving to top up their glasses. Indicating she had enough, Hannah put a hand on hers. "You'll not mind I finish it off then?"

"As a matter of fact I do – you mustn't drink and drive."

"I'm an excellent driver! A few more glasses won't hurt."

"I rather you don't." It was evident how much he liked alcohol, in particular the pub and beer.

"I'm not an alcoholic."

"I never said you are." Hannah smiled at him, but her eyes were serious.

So as to avoid an argument, Mark changed the subject. "When are you returning home?"

"In January. I so look forward to enrolling at university . . ." Elaborating on life in Limhamn, Hannah could tell he wasn't really interested.

"I wish you'd change your mind and stay. Our universities are just as good, in fact, better."

"That's not the point! Sweden's where my family live."

"I've heard it's beautiful yet hardly comparable to London – wouldn't you agree?"

"I don't as a matter of fact! Life back home is extremely fulfilling. Our standard of living is much better."

Sensing he'd gone too far, Mark once again changed the subject. "I plan to start my own business selling office equipment. Everyone'll soon learn how to use a computer – we'll be swamped by technology."

"How come you're so sure?" She detested the idea of machines ruling people's lives.

"I just am." He went on to tell her he'd recently been promoted to senior salesman.

"Your parents must be very proud of you." But Mark's eyes clouded over.

"As if! My mother's never satisfied. No matter how hard I try to please her, she's always finding fault with me. Had I stayed away for a year, she'd have a nervous breakdown."

"Isn't your father supportive of her?"

"The man's a joke! They've not had sex for decades!" Mark grimaced at the idea of his parents engaging in anything of a sexual nature. Shocked he would disclose something so personal to a virtual stranger, Hannah was at a loss for words. Raising his glass, Mark blurted out, "Don't look so concerned – I've no problems in that department!" Seeing her face turn red, he told her she mustn't take offence. "I'm sorry I embarrassed you . . . It's the last thing I want to do." Reaching for her hand, he touched her fingers, adding, "I've fallen in love with you, Hannah, and can't wait for us to be together – properly."

"Meaning what exactly?" Hannah whispered, holding her breath.

"You're not that naive surely? I want to make love to you."

"You're very direct."

"Perhaps the word you're seeking is blunt?"

"But we hardly know each other!"

"If you're holding out for some 'schmuck' to seduce you with his charm and fancy job, I'm not your type of guy! What you see is what you get. I want you." His fingers caressed hers.

"You're expecting me to respond to what you just told me?"

"I am."

"We're oceans apart – I'm just not the kind of woman who willingly jumps into bed with a stranger!"

"Point taken. I'll be straight with you. You and I can continue as we are but I guarantee we'll end up in the sack! It's only a matter of time. You know it as well as I." Fiddling nervously with her napkin, Hannah averted her eyes. "Look at me! I fancied you the minute I first clapped eyes on you. I know you feel the same." Shocked he saw through her, Hannah admitted to herself he was right.

When the waiter asked if they wanted dessert, Mark smiled. "We're having ours later, mate." Blushing, the shy waiter pretended he didn't hear. Bending to kiss her hand, Mark asked, "What's it going to be, baby?"

Withdrawing from his touch, Hannah hissed, "I'm not going to sleep with you, Mark!" She was furious he assumed she was such an easy catch.

"What a pity! I'm convinced we'd enjoy it very much."

"And after? Will you dump me the way you did Denise?"

"You're not her! You're the woman I love." But Hannah was much too upset to listen to him.

"You asked me out to dinner, expecting me to return the favour by having sex with you. You disgust me!" She rose to her feet and reached for her jacket. Mark tried to appease her but it was too late.

"Please refrain from making a scene – you'll only embarrass yourself and everyone else. I'll make my own way back. Do not follow me!" She ran out of the restaurant without a backward glance, causing everyone to wonder what he said to upset her.

Sighing, Mark signalled for the waiter, ordering another bottle of wine.

As he parked outside Ella's house at past midnight, the middle-aged cabbie asked if Hannah was alright. "I'll be fine," she replied in a low voice, adding a tip.

Too distraught to go inside just yet, she decided to walk around the block. The darkness and drizzle of rain changing her mind, instead she decided to sit for a while on one of the benches oddly positioned in the middle of the street. *Why did he have to ruin everything?* she asked herself, incapable of making sense of it.

Eventually giving up and going back to the house, she was fishing for the keys in her bag when from behind a voice asked, "I gather you're still angry with me?" It was Mark, looking very sheepish. Looking around, Hannah noticed his car was parked further down the street.

"I told you to leave me be."

"I can't let you disappear from my life! I regret everything I told you earlier – please say you'll forgive me?" Waiting for her to respond, Mark added, "Don't you think it's odd we only just met yet feel this instant attraction?"

"You're just randy."

"If that were the case, I'd have settled for anyone. But you're all I want, Hannah. I for one don't want to waste time arguing. Let's make the most of the time we have left before you leave."

"I'll grant you this, you're good with words – it's hardly surprising you're a salesman!"

"Don't mock me for being honest; I'm in love with you, baby." Moving closer, Mark gently cupped her face in his hands, kissing her beneath the light of a streetlamp. A mixture of wine and aftershave lingered in the air and she responded, conscious of the fact she felt the same. Kissing the nape of her neck, Mark mumbled, "Please don't make me wait too long . . ."

Putting a finger on his lips, Hannah whispered, "Shh . . . you talk too much. Start treating me with respect and who knows? Are you capable of that, Mr Copeck?"

"Anything's possible if I have you . . ." Watching her let herself in, Mark walked reluctantly back to his car.

Entering the dark, quiet house, Hannah couldn't stop smiling. It wasn't until she was tucked up in bed that her eyes fell on the card on the vanity table. It was the invitation to Melanie's twenty-fifth birthday party in September. But there and then, the only thing preoccupying her mind was how it felt when Mark kissed her.

CHAPTER SEVEN

FOLLOWING THAT NIGHT, Mark called every day requesting they meet up locally for a drink or meal. Reluctantly accepting they were an item, Rosie and Sanna admitted begrudgingly that he was besotted with her. They were having a drink in The Bull and Bush when Hannah told them he had invited her to his house in Stanmore that weekend.

"What's the catch? It's obvious he wants to sleep with you." Rosie's words echoed Sanna's grim expression.

"Are you willing to take things further between you? If the answer's yes, you must ask your GP to put you on the Pill."

"I'm turning nineteen in a few weeks . . . Sex is the last thing on my mind!" Hannah looked horrified at the very thought.

"Tell him you're not ready. Guys always assume you're up for it," Rosie replied in a firm voice.

Meeting up later that week at The Hare And Hound, Mark repeated his request.

"Are you expecting me to sleep with you? It's too soon," Hannah protested, hoping he'd understand.

"I'd love to but respect you too much to force the issue." She detected an undertone of disappointment in his voice – no one had rejected him until now.

"Alright, then, I'd love to see your house. You can pick me up after work on Saturday," she told him, uncertain as to whether or not she'd made the right decision.

His face lighting up, Mark took her in his arms, exclaiming: "That's great! I can't wait for us to live together, baby!"

Putting her finger to his lips, Hannah repeated what she'd told him earlier. "One step at a time, remember?"

On the verge of saying something, Mark kept his mouth shut.

Mark's house was a two-storey red-brick property on the out-skirts of Stanmore. It had a small front garden with flowerbeds on either side of the front door.

"Dad and I are in the process of redecorating," he said, as he welcomed her into the narrow dark entrance smelling of fresh paint. "I'll show you my bedroom first." Blushing, Hannah fol-lowed him upstairs, past a landing and into a large room with a built-in closet, four poster bed and desk. She kept a healthy dis-tance by the door. "You're looking as if I'm about to jump on you – it's not my style!" Mark commented, laughing.

Mortified that he'd read her mind, Hannah complimented him awkwardly on his bed cover. "You've a nice view of the street . . ."

"I disagree, this place needs a woman's touch . . . preferably yours." He proceeded to show her the other bedroom and box room across the landing, then the bathroom with big tub.

"Are you installing a shower cabin?" Hannah asked. "They're popular at home."

"We're not as advanced in this country." Pulling her close, she felt his lips on her neck, whispering, "Let's return to my bedroom . . ." As his hands wandered down her blouse, Hannah pushed him away.

"Don't! I didn't come here for 'that'."

"Sorry, you're too sexy for your own good." Indeed, she looked irresistible in a short denim skirt, blouse and espadrilles, with her hair cascading down her shoulders. Mark was desperate to make love to her. "We'd better leave or I'll do something I shouldn't," he said, dragging her downstairs.

Too small to fit a table and chairs, the kitchen was adjacent to the large combined living and dining room. There was a plain white couch on one side and a table at the other, by the window with a direct view of the back garden.

"What's your verdict?" Mark asked, eager for her opinion.

"You and your Dad did a great job – a few cushions and photos are all that's missing."

"It's the reason I want you to move in with me, baby."

"You know that's not possible. I promised Ella I'd stay with her until I return home."

"What about us? You're leaving soon – surely that's the reason to put us first?"

"It's not up for discussion – Ella means as much to me as my own family!"

Turning his back on her, Mark replied, "Alright, I hear you. Won't you at least meet me halfway? I want you to come over at the weekend."

"I'll consider it . . ."

"Can I offer you something to eat or drink? There's this quaint café not far from here. They make a mean omelette."

"I'm not hungry. Perhaps some other time – please take me home." She had had enough of his demands.

"Give me a break! How come you're in such a hurry all of a

sudden? I'm sorry I upset you but I'll not apologise for wanting to be with you! Did I mention my mother has a spare key?" Mark's tone was casual, making it sound as if it was the most natural thing in the world.

Too upset to register his words, Hannah paced the room. "Did you just tell me your mother's free to come and go as she pleases? I thought you were desperate to have your own place?"

"She thrives on looking after me. I'm doing her a favour. This way you and I don't have to clean and shop . . . We'll have more time to ourselves." There was no mistaking as to what he meant.

"Your mother deserves your respect. Instead you're willing to exploit her?" The idea of someone turning up unexpectedly made her see red. "Unless you ask her to return her key, you and I are off!"

"Calm down, Hannah. I'll tell her to call first – there's not much else I can do seeing as she and my father own this house." He may as well have dropped a bomb.

"Liar! You told me it belongs to you and him!"

"So what? We're not as rich as you and your family. Besides, I'll soon inherit the lot." His attitude infuriated her – how dare he presume she came from an affluent background? Watching her, Mark suddenly thought of something. "Are you using my mother as an excuse to not sleep with me? Hang on, you're a virgin, right?"

Blushing, Hannah whispered, "How did you guess?"

"It's written all over your face. You freak out whenever I come near you."

"You must think I'm pathetic. A virgin at my age – it's virtually unheard of!"

"Don't worry about it. Now I know, I love you even more." Telling her how proud he was to be her boyfriend, Mark kissed the tip of her nose. Suddenly everything else ceased to matter; her little secret was out in the open.

Dropping her off outside the house in Golders Green later that night, Mark pulled her close. "You know I'm here for you, don't you? You can rely on me."

"What's that supposed to mean?" She wasn't sure if it implied what she thought.

"I'll be careful to not . . . you know . . . get you pregnant. This is the start of something special."

"You're still expecting me to sleep with you?" she asked in a tense voice, the mere brush of his lips against hers making her tremble.

"Is that so shocking? We're in love, baby."

"You're forgetting something . . ." Head spinning, her voice faltered.

"Contraception? I assumed . . ." He'd automatically presumed she'd take care of it. Getting out of the car, Hannah turned to look at him.

"I'm not putting my future in your hands! You'd better see to it as well."

"Okay, I will. You win, again!" Mark shouted, driving off before she had the opportunity to respond.

Later, as she lay in bed, thinking about what she and Mark were entering into, Hannah's thoughts turned to Zadie.

I wish you didn't live so far away, Mamma . . .

That week Hannah took matters into her own hands and visited her doctor. Agreeing to give her a prescription for the Pill, the GP assured there'd be no side effects. "Just call if there's a problem," was her parting comment.

One week later, on a Saturday evening, Mark picked her up outside the station, looking smart in a brown suit and tie. His face lit up when she told him she'd started taking the Pill.

"That's great news! Something less to worry about." As she reached to place her overnight bag in the boot of Mark's car, he spun her round and kissed her. "I bet you've been looking forward to tonight – I sure have!" Uncertain as to what to say, Hannah didn't engage in small talk throughout the journey to Stanmore. Parking in the garage, Mark turned to look at her. "There's no pressure. One step at a time, baby."

Relieved he sensed her apprehension, Hannah allowed him to carry her bag inside and upstairs to his bedroom. He returned a few minutes later and poured them a glass of chilled white wine. "Welcome to 'Casa Mark'! I hope you're as hungry as I am. I got us something to eat from Marks & Spencer."

Helping to lay the table in the living room, Hannah noticed he'd taken her advice, putting up a few pictures on the wall. Returning from the kitchen carrying a tray with smoked salmon, new potatoes and asparagus on a bed of lettuce and cucumber, Mark put it on the table, filling up their glasses.

"Here's to us," he toasted the occasion, draining his wine.

"It looks delicious – you remembered my love of fish." Her eyes were moist with tears.

They finished their meal, idly chatting about his job at John Lewis. Mark started clearing the table, announcing that the dishes could wait until the morning. Putting on ABBA's 'Thank You For The Music', Mark loosened his tie and kicked off his shoes, slowly coming towards her.

"Care to join me for a dance, Miss Stein?" His arms were around her, hands caressing her body beneath the clothes. "Mmm, you smell so damn good . . ." Slowly they moved to the music,

Mark taking her hand and moving it down to his crotch. "Feel how much I desire you, baby!" To Hannah's astonishment, his words and gesture turned her on, even more when hearing him mumble, "Tell me you want me too . . ."

"I do . . ." The words stumbled out of her mouth before she had time to think. Scooping her up into his arms, Mark carried her upstairs to his bedroom.

The next few hours passed in a haze. Undressing in front of him, Hannah averted his eyes.

"You're beautiful. Perfect in every way." Mark couldn't take his eyes off her small waist, generous curves and long legs. With his eyes drifting all over her, Hannah felt the urge to look at him too, admiring his broad shoulders, toned arms and legs. "You're everything a man could wish for . . ."

Their clothes in a heap on the carpet, Mark pulled off the bed-cover to reveal black satin sheets, and laid her down on the bed, the sensation of his body so close to hers filling her with joy. Exploring every part of her with his hands, fingers and mouth, he repeated how much he loved her. Hannah felt his breath on her skin; a mixture of Polo mints and wine. Mark nuzzled between her breasts, asking, "Are you okay?"

"I think so," she whispered, trembling.

"Good . . . just relax and abandon yourself to me." Feeling his lips and tongue gently probe her, she soon started to unwind, a surge of pleasure stirring up inside. "Show me how much you want me, baby!"

Spreading her legs, Mark kissed the inside of her thighs and then raised himself on one elbow, reaching for the small packet on the bedside table. "Would you prefer I do it?" His voice was hoarse.

"Yes, please . . ." As he released the condom and pulled it on, Hannah's eyes were closed.

"Now, where were we?" He positioned himself above her, slowly pushing inside. Soon both were moving to the same rhythm, the initial discomfort turning into pleasure, intensifying with every thrust.

Throwing caution to the wind, Hannah let herself go, stroking his neck, back and shoulders as he too climaxed, kissed her lips and lay back onto the pillow, asking if she was alright.

"It's as if a weight's been lifted off my shoulders," she admitted. "Being a man you wouldn't understand . . ."

Stifling a yawn, Mark declared, "I'm starving! Let's go downstairs and grab a sandwich."

"But it's not so long ago we had a meal."

"You've no idea how long we've been here, have you?" Looking at her watch, Hannah jumped out of bed.

"We've been here for hours!"

"Time sure flies when one's having fun . . ." Patting her behind, Mark had a naughty expression in his eyes. "I love being with you, Hannah. We've yet to discover what turns you on – practice makes perfect!"

"I've no complaints." Knowing how much he cared about her was enough.

Chasing her into the bathroom, Mark pinned her against the wall. "You're all I want, baby . . . We'll eat later." Suddenly he was aching to pick up from where they left off.

"You can't – not so soon! It's impossible . . ."

Mark placed her hand on his crotch. "Still not convinced?" Giggling, Hannah let him drag her back into the bedroom where they proceeded to make love again. Their passion soared and she found herself moaning with pleasure, both climaxing one after the other.

Sanna's right, it's just as pleasurable for a woman, she thought, exclaiming, "Wow, that was incredible!"

"I'm pleased you enjoyed it." Touching her face, Mark looked deep into her eyes. "Please stay the night."

But Hannah shook her head. "You know that's not possible. Ella's expecting me."

"Won't you at least prolong your stay, perhaps until next summer?"

"That's out of the question. I promised my parents I'd return at Christmas. You must visit me in Malmö – it's only a couple of hours by flight."

It was Mark's turn to shake his head. "Nah – travelling's not my style. I'll only end up getting homesick."

"Don't be ridiculous! I'll introduce you to my family and friends."

"We don't need anyone else. Just you and me, that's all I want." They had just finished making love and all he could think about was himself.

"You're expecting too much of me!" The heat rose in Hannah's cheeks. "I'm attending university and that's an end to it."

Angry at her rejection, Mark turned his back on her. Fuming, Hannah took a leaf out of his book, slowly starting to put on her clothes.

"We shared something special and all you can think of is some old woman!" he snarled at her.

All of a sudden everything they meant to each other evaporated; the discarded condoms in the bin by the bed making her feel cheap and exploited. "I appreciate everything you did for me but I'll not abandon my friend."

"You're my priority," Mark said. "How come I'm not yours?"

"I'm too young to settle down. I want to spread my wings; you can just as easily relocate to Malmö."

"Don't be such an idiot. For a start, I can't speak the language and my parents live here."

"Yet you're expecting I leave everything behind?" Her voice broke.

Realising he had said too much, Mark tried to appease her. "You'll return to me, right? Your grandmother lives here . . . London's where you belong!" Putting his arms around her, he added, "I'm sorry I shouted at you. The thought of not seeing you again petrifies me. Come now, let's get something to eat."

"I lost my appetite. Please take me home." She loathed the way he presumed everything revolved around him.

"You're letting a petty argument come between us! We're still meeting up next weekend, right?" He'd had enough of her sulking.

"Perhaps . . ." Hannah was desperate to get away from him.

Pulling on a pair of jeans, shirt and jacket, Mark grabbed his car keys and carried her bag downstairs. They drove in silence back to Ella's house. Lost in thought, Hannah let herself out of the car and into the dark hall, hearing him shout, "Everything will sort itself out – I'll call in the morning, sleep tight!"

A big part of her wished they'd never met.

"Spill the beans: is Mark as good as his reputation?" Rosie asked after ordering at Ranch House that Sunday afternoon.

"Don't take any notice of her." Sanna could tell something had happened, judging by their friend's unhappy expression.

"Everything was fine until Mark insisted I stay a little longer . . . He asked me to move in with him."

"You put him straight, right?" Rosie looked as if she were about to explode.

"Sure . . . He's kidding himself thinking I'll give up on my dream. I never met anyone so self-obsessed! The house isn't even his. It's his parents, the mother has a spare key." Sanna and Rosie exchanged a glance.

"You'll disapprove of what I'm about to say but I'm doing it anyway – it's what friends are for," Rosie said. "Drop him before you get too involved."

"Guys like Mark don't deserve you! Go find someone who does," Sanna added.

Biting her lip, Hannah looked at her friends. "But I'm in love with him. We're lovers . . . I can't just switch off my feelings."

"Mark's nothing but a chauvinistic pig. You're better off without him," Rosie replied, thinking a leopard rarely changed its spots.

"You're attending Melanie's birthday party, right?" Sanna asked.

"I'd not miss it for the world. But how will I tell Mark he's not invited?" Hannah looked as if she was about to cry.

"You're crazy! It's none of his business – you and Melanie are close friends."

"You're right. I'll say an old friend's throwing a party. Will you cover for me in case he starts asking questions?"

"Don't worry about it. Your secret's safe with us."

Suppressing the urge to yawn, Hannah changed the subject and told them she and Ella didn't see much of each other lately. "I'm desperate to have an early night!"

"I wonder why . . . You never told us what Mark's like in bed," Rosie teased.

"Didn't I? Well, just so you know, I've no complaints whatsoever in that department!" Giggling, the three of them placed some money on the table and left.

Parting outside the station, Rosie suggested they celebrate Hannah's birthday at Cosmo.

"That's a terrific idea! We'll ask Zipporah and Ella to join us. What'll I do about Mark?"

"He's superfluous to requirements." Sanna shrugged.

"I'm not sure that's fair . . . Oh, to hell with it! It's my birthday and I'll damn well do as I please!"

Cosmo was the perfect venue for a celebration. Seated in the centre of the restaurant, Hannah wished she were able to freeze the moment.

The previous night Mark had taken her out to dinner in a small bistro close to where he lived, calling to congratulate her in the morning. "You're better off celebrating with your grandmother and friends," he told her, conscious of how much the latter disapproved of him. She and Ella were getting ready to leave when the doorbell rang, a delivery man handing Hannah a large bouquet of flowers with a card attached:

Wishing you a wonderful day
Love Mark XXX

Touched by the gesture, Hannah put his flowers in a vase next to her parents' card, books and confectionery, and Melanie's greeting. Ella complimented Hannah on her floaty summer dress, high heels and hair in a ponytail. "You're very pretty, my dear."

"Look who's talking! I've never seen you as elegant as you are now." They'd spent hours together choosing an outfit, settling for a lilac dress, matching hat and jacket. The result was astounding.

"You're too kind, my dear. Who knows, this may prove to be my last outing."

"Nonsense – you've got plenty of life in you yet!" The sad truth was that, despite her intellect, Ella was deteriorating and she was extremely conscious of it.

Later at the restaurant, choosing from the extensive menu proved much too difficult. In the end everyone chose exactly the same dishes as the previous time. Dessert was an enormous chocolate gateau with nineteen candles. When they'd finished eating, Zipporah and Ella gave Hannah a flat package. Unwrapping it, Hannah pulled out a photograph of herself and her two 'grannies' on either side.

"It's a little something to remember us by, my dear."

"It's lovely! I'll put it on the wall in my room – I'm so very grateful to you both." Walking around the table to embrace them, Hannah raised her glass in a toast. "Today's been the best of times! I couldn't have done it without you – it's all down to you."

Sanna and Rosie chose that moment to give her a large bottle of L'Air Du Temps and some drop earrings they had spent ages saving up for. "I almost forgot." Sanna too raised her glass. "John sends his love and best wishes. Somehow your number got lost while packing – he and his boyfriend are off to the Bahamas." Getting to her feet, Zipporah sang 'Happy Birthday', everyone cheering the birthday girl. It wasn't until later Hannah realised that Mark's absence had never crossed her mind.

"My folks invited us to lunch next Sunday," her boyfriend declared a few days later. She'd agreed to spend Saturday night at his place, convincing herself his mother wasn't as scary as Mark let on. Mark had been going out of his way to accommodate her, talking her into giving him another chance to put things right between them. Yet, waking up in his arms on Sunday morning, Hannah felt a foreboding sense of disaster. She told herself his mother probably wasn't as scary as Mark led her to believe.

They were on their way to his parents' house when Mark suddenly asked, "Would you prefer I give them a call saying we can't make it?"

Demure in a plain black dress and no make-up, Hannah shook her head. "You'll do no such thing! They've been looking forward to meeting me."

It was early September and the sun was shining as, arms around one another, both walked up the small path adorned by flowerbeds on either side of the front door, giving a welcoming impression.

"Let's get this over and done with." A grim expression on his face, Mark banged on the door. The sound of footsteps approached on the inside and the door opened wide. Standing in front of them was a woman in her fifties, with short permed hair, black skirt, starched white blouse and slippers on her feet.

"I'm Mrs Annuschka Copeck – Mark's mother. Please step inside." Her voice as cold as her eyes; her accent stronger than Zipporah's.

"These are for you, Mrs Copeck," Hannah handed her the bouquet she and Mark had purchased earlier.

"Lunch isn't ready yet. I'll see to them while my son entertains you." She barely acknowledged the flowers.

"Is there something I can help you with, Mrs Copeck?"

Looking at the guest up and down, Annuschka replied, "Hardly!"

Eyes pleading with her to stay calm, Mark led her into the living room. It was furnished with chairs and table facing the garden, another small table, couch and shelf with an enormous photograph of the Pope at the other end overlooking the street. Like its owner and mistress, the room lacked warmth.

As Hannah and Mark sat awkwardly on the couch holding hands, a tall, muscular man in his late fifties entered, looking like an older version of his son. "I'm Marcus Copeck. It's such a pleasure to meet you, Miss Stein, you're even prettier than Mark described." Bending to kiss her hand, Hannah saw how much he and Mark resembled one another, in particular the cleft in the chin. Pouring them a glass of port, Marcus exclaimed, "Here's to a nice afternoon!" before gulping his drink.

From the corner of her eye, Hannah saw the look of contempt on Mark's face. Fluent in English and with no accent, Hannah couldn't help wondering why Marcus had chosen to marry someone as plain and cold as Annuschka. She'd never encountered two people being as mismatched as them. Sipping her glass, she heard the hostess call out: "Lunch is ready – you'd better sit down before it gets cold!"

Seated next to Mark, looking down on the lukewarm soup and stale bread in front of her, Hannah watched Marcus help himself to more wine.

"Didn't you get enough to drink at the pub?" Annuschka asked, eyes narrowing.

"Sundays are my day off, dear," Ignoring his wife, Marcus turned to Hannah, adding, "I feel certain you don't mind."

She was about to reply when Annuschka asked, "You're eating like a bird – is it not to your satisfaction, Miss Stein?"

Unable to look into the other woman's eyes, Hannah whispered, "I've not much of an appetite, Mrs Copeck."

"Girls nowadays have no appreciation of food! It's the reason you look like stick insects."

"That's unfair – Hannah's got a lovely figure!" Mark defended her, the muscle twitching in his cheek.

Attempting to change the subject, Hannah told them how great a cook her mother and grandmother were. "They taught me everything I know."

"Such as?" Annuschka enquired, tight-lipped.

"Mostly Scandinavian and Jewish cuisine, Mrs Copeck."

"I'm impressed! Looks like you got yourself the perfect girl-friend, son."

Turning red in the face, Mark was about to say something when Marcus asked if anyone wanted more wine. Putting a hand over her glass, Annuschka hissed, "Unlike you, I'm well aware of my limits." Pouring himself another glass of red wine, Marcus gulped it down in no time.

Turning her attention to Hannah, Annuschka asked, "Are you religious, Miss Stein?"

"Not exactly, but I'm extremely proud of my roots."

"We're Catholic except for Mark. He's an atheist."

"How come you're interested in my cultural background, Mrs Copeck?"

"It's probably escaped you that this area's predominantly Jewish, yet there's no connection between ourselves and the community."

Biting her lower lip, Hannah ventured, "What's that supposed to mean?"

"Aren't you aware of how much Polish people and Jews loathe one another?"

"Mother!" Mark shouted. "How dare you speak to Hannah this way?"

"Tell our guest I'm not an anti-Semite, Marcus – only stating a fact."

Grimacing, Marcus turned apologetically to Hannah. "You must forgive my wife's unfortunate comments."

Pitying him for sharing his life with a racist, Hannah looked him in the eyes. "I do, but only because you're so nice to me."

Ignoring them, Annuschka proceeded to clear the table, minutes later returning with a plate of meat.

"I believe this is what Jews refer to as 'The Unmentionable'. It's the dish my grandmother taught me to make: pork with all the trimmings!"

Too revolted to speak, Hannah felt the room spinning around her as she attempted to stand up. "Please get me away from here!" she cried. No one had ever treated her like that before, and unless Mark complied with her wish, she'd not be responsible for her actions. Throwing his napkin on the table, Mark helped her to sit down on the couch.

"How dare you do what you just did?" he screamed at his mother.

"Please take me home," Hannah sobbed, holding onto his arm.

"Not until my mother's apologised."

"I'm sorry I offended you, Miss Stein." Continuing her meal, Annuschka looked as if she didn't give a damn.

Dabbing at her eyes with her handkerchief, Hannah replied, "I came here in good faith, please be so good as to explain why you feel the need to insult me."

"Are you refusing to accept my apology, Miss Stein?"

"I demand you tell me what I've done to make you hate me so much!"

"You're much too sensitive, Miss Stein. You people weren't the only ones suffering under the Nazis."

"That's true, but my grandmother and her friends lost their entire family to the Holocaust."

"Such is life! I made fruit salad for dessert. Care to join me?" Ignoring Hannah's pain, her voice was ice cold.

"We're leaving," Mark announced, helping Hannah to her feet.

Oblivious to the harm she had caused, Annuschka replied, "Do as you please – young people have no manners these days."

Following them into the entrance, Marcus apologised once more. "You must find it in your heart to forgive her, Miss Stein. Being rude comes naturally to her."

Smiling through her tears, Hannah kissed his cheek. "It's not your fault your wife's ill, Mr Copeck."

"I warned you she's unpredictable," Mark said, as they walked back to his place.

"Please take me home. I want to be on my own."

"Don't let her get to you, baby! We'll be seeing each other soon, right?"

Shrugging her shoulders, Hannah didn't bother to reply. Between them, Mark and his mother had a talent for ruining everything.

"What kind of person does something like that? That woman's a nasty piece of work. Good riddance to her and everything she stands for!" Ella was shocked to hear what Mark's mother had done to her.

"Please don't tell my parents!"

"Of course not. Everything we talk about is confidential." Seeing the sad expression in her eyes, Ella added, "Don't worry about my feelings – people like her don't get to me. Just make sure Mark knows how you feel."

When he called the next day, "Did you talk to your mother?" was the first thing on her mind.

"Don't be silly! She's too old to change. You're not religious — just let it go."

It took Hannah a couple of seconds to register his words. "Are you saying you're letting her get away with it?"

"Forget about her. We're in this relationship, not her."

"You're quite sure about that?" She'd had enough of listening to him, refusing to take his calls for the remainder of the week.

A few days later, she confided in her friends.

"Get rid of him now!" they replied. They were appalled Mark permitted his mother to treat her like that. But Hannah was in love with him, still hoping he'd put her needs first.

CHAPTER EIGHT

A RRIVING AT THE Primrose Hill venue at 8pm on the last Saturday in September, Hannah arranged with the cab driver to pick her up at midnight. Wearing a blue sequinned dress accentuating her figure and small waist, she stepped out of the car, carrying a bouquet of flowers and Belgian truffles. As she entered the foyer of the large premises to be surrounded by strangers, she heard someone call her name.

"You must be Hannah, Mel's friend?"

Turning to see who it was, she found herself gazing into the friendliest pair of blue eyes.

"My name's Matthew Jacobs – Mel's fiancé and associate – I'm pleased we finally get to meet." With his tall, athletic build, short brown hair and big smile, it was easy to understand why Melanie had fallen in love with him.

"Mel's instructed I take extra good care of you! She's busy with all the guests." Taking her arm, he proceeded to introduce her to groups of people, all curious to know what it was like to live in Sweden. A passing waiter offering sparkling champagne. Discreetly watching her take a sip, Matthew agreed with his fiancée. She was completely oblivious of her own beauty and of everyone staring at her, the red hair reminiscent of a rich burgundy wine.

Engaging in small talk, Hannah asked if he minded Melanie having a career.

"Not at all. I want her to be happy, she's the woman I love." Just then, they were interrupted.

"Hannah! Just look at you. That dress is simply divine." Embracing one another, Melanie exclaimed, "I'm so happy you're here!"

"Your fiancé's been very nice to me. Congratulations on turning twenty-five and getting engaged!" Hannah handed her the flowers and chocolates.

"How wonderfully decadent! Sweets aren't good for the figure . . . What the heck, it's not every day one gets the opportunity to celebrate!"

"You've nothing to worry about – I've never seen you as gorgeous as you look tonight." Radiant in a red gown, with matching lips and nails, Melanie wore her hair in a sleek pageboy cut, emphasising her dark-blue eyes. Steering Hannah towards the back, she put an arm around her.

"What do you think?"

"Wow! I never saw anything like it!" Hannah gasped at the sight of pink tablecloths on the buffet, candles and roses.

"There's someone I want you to meet . . ." Walking arm in arm in the direction of a small group of people talking amongst themselves, Melanie made a formal introduction. "This is the girl I've been telling you about. Hannah Stein – Benjamin Isaacs. Ben's my oldest friend, Hannah's over on a gap year, staying with an adorable lady in Golders Green."

His eyes glued on the pretty woman in front of him, Ben replied, "Mel's been singing your praises, Miss Stein. Now I know the reason."

Eyes locking, both felt an instant chemistry, quite unlike anything they'd experienced before. Tall, dark and handsome, Ben bore an uncanny resemblance to Sean Connery, each muscular with dimples in their cheeks. What attracted her most was his impeccable accent, deep voice and big brown eyes, seemingly looking behind the exterior into her soul.

From a distance Hannah heard Melanie say, "I'll leave you to it, you're bound to have plenty to talk about . . ."

"I'm honoured to sit next to you, Miss Stein." Flattered that he'd pulled out a chair for her to sit, Hannah felt his eyes on her. Overwhelmed by her presence, beauty and charm, Ben was acutely conscious of the fact he'd never met anyone like her; the fiery-red hair, delicate features and emerald-green eyes.

Dinner consisted of melon with port, rack of lamb and sorbet with almond biscuits; everything tasting delicious. Ben entertained Hannah with stories of the time he and Melanie were enrolled at nursery, while Hannah told him about her country, silently comparing his interest in everything she told him to Mark, who rarely listened to anything she had to say.

After dinner there were birthday speeches, including one from Ben, who told everyone how fortunate he was to have such a caring, loyal friend in Melanie.

"She's a lousy loser, though. I lost track of all the times I let her beat me at a game," he teased, raising his glass in a toast to her and Matthew, before returning to his seat.

Touched by his words, Melanie blew him a kiss across the table. They'd celebrated her and Matthew's engagement at her parents' house the previous weekend. At twenty-seven, Ben was the brother she had never had.

Turning his attention to Hannah, Ben asked, "Are you planning on leaving in the near future?"

"Not until after Christmas. Then I'm enrolling at university." Relieved she'd be staying a while longer, Ben enquired about her career subjects. "I always wanted to teach."

"Good for you!"

It felt wonderful opening up to him about her future plans. Unlike Mark, Ben seemed genuinely interested and non-judgemental.

"I miss home and my family – it'll be great to go back."

"I bet they can't wait to see you. Mine missed me a lot when I travelled to France and America. Tell me to mind my own business but I have to ask, how old are you?"

"I just turned nineteen."

"I gathered as much. You're extremely mature for your age." Blushing, Hannah asked what he did for a living. "I'm a solicitor, working at my father's law firm – hoping to start my own one day." He proceeded to tell her about his younger sister and brother, who were both still at college. "Mum's preoccupied with her secretarial temping agency. She and Dad are the perfect couple."

"What a strange coincidence both our fathers are solicitors," said Hannah. "My mother's a housewife and extremely proud of it. She speaks several languages. My younger brother, Peter, and I are very close. My maternal grandmother moved to London when she was in her seventies." It struck her how effortlessly they communicated with one another, again, totally unlike Mark who wasn't interested in anyone but himself.

Listening to her, Ben felt much the same, thinking she was special in every way. "I own a flat not far from here," he said. "It's a typical bachelor's pad. I only use it to sleep in." He deliberately wanted her to know he was single, praying she was as well.

Time passed quickly, and while they were engaged in conversation, the other guests drifted into an adjacent room, to drink tea and dance.

"Would you care to join me for a dance, Hannah?" Ben asked shyly, as John Paul Young's 'Love Is In The Air' began to play. She was on the verge of accepting when Melanie approached them.

"Please forgive me for being such a lousy hostess – I'm like a headless chicken," she told them, looking flustered. "Tonight's great!" She went up to Hannah, kissing her cheeks. "May I borrow her for a couple of minutes? I promise to bring her back to you." Sensing Ben's disappointment, Hannah followed her into a corner of the room.

"Ben's completely smitten with you," Melanie enthused. "I never saw him this happy. You're a striking couple. Didn't I tell you you'd be perfect for each other?" She was so excited; she couldn't stand still.

"Before you continue, there's something you should know. I'm in a relationship . . . I'm sorry I never let on." Hannah felt awful she had kept it from her.

"But I was under the impression . . . my mistake. I'm really gutted."

"It's early days but we're committed to each other," Hannah whispered.

"Is it someone I know?" Mel looked as if she was about to burst into tears.

"I don't think so. His name's Mark, we only just met."

"Are you sleeping with him?"

Blushing at her friend's blunt question, Hannah bowed her head in response.

"I see. What a pity. Men like Ben don't come along often. If I were you, I'd not rule anything out just yet. I sure hope that guy appreciates you . . ."

"How about that dance you promised me earlier?" Standing behind her, Ben refused to take no for an answer.

"She's all yours – talk to you later!" Melanie told him, leaving.

"Are you alright?" Ben's eyes probed Hannah's.

At that moment Hannah wished things weren't so complicated. "I'm alright . . . I'd love to dance with you." Taking her hand in his, Ben led her to the dance floor, Burt Bacharach's 'Raindrops Keep Fallin' On My Head' echoing in the room.

Keeping a respectful distance between them, Ben commented, "That song goes straight to my heart." What he meant to say was that she had already captured his. Feeling him so close to her, breathing in the masculine scent of his aftershave, Hannah felt a sense of belonging.

Twenty minutes later she looked at her watch, exclaiming, "I'm sorry but I have to leave, a cab's awaiting me outside." Ben was visibly disappointed.

"Can't you call and cancel it? I'd be pleased to bring you home."

"That's impossible, seeing as it's booked . . ."

"Tonight's special. Will you let me take you out to dinner?" He'd been telling himself she was a lot younger and the last thing he wanted was to scare her off, but he just couldn't help himself.

Not sure how to respond, Hannah started to panic. "Listen, I really enjoyed spending time with you Ben, but I'm leaving soon – take good care of yourself – you're the perfect gentleman."

"Please wait!" His eyes pleaded with her to stay. "Are you telling me you don't wish to see me again? The least you can do is explain." He looked every bit as upset as she was feeling.

"It's nothing to do with you – I'm seeing someone."

Ben's face dropped, the same devastation in his eyes as in Melanie's. "I see . . . That explains everything."

"I'm sorry I gave you the wrong impression."

"Me too." His voice faltered. "I guess it wasn't meant to be. I hope whoever it is realises how lucky he is. Thanks for being straight with me."

Their eyes locked for a split second and Hannah knew without a shadow of a doubt the only thing coming between them was that they'd met at the wrong time.

"You're definitely an item?" he asked, eyes sad.

"We are – yes."

Taking a deep breath, Ben replied, "I wish you every happiness. You're an outstanding young lady, inside and out." He gave her a card with his number, adding, "I'd love to keep in touch . . ."

Listening to him made Hannah feel less upset; the idea of not seeing him again, too difficult to comprehend. "I'll keep it in mind but you mustn't expect it . . ."

As he bent to kiss her cheek, both felt the same chemistry as when they'd first laid eyes on each other. She was on the verge of changing her mind and agreeing to meet up with him, when Mark's face appeared in her head.

"Goodbye, Ben. I'll see myself out."

Waving at Melanie, who was busy talking to a guest, Hannah walked out of the venue and towards the cab waiting for her outside. Exchanging a few polite words, Hannah's thoughts turned to Ben. He'd made such a lasting impression. She could only ask herself if it was possible to be in love with one man yet feel attracted to another.

★

Watching the last guests leave, Melanie and Ben retired to the back of the foyer. Looking into his eyes, she whispered, "I'm so sorry things didn't turn out the way you'd hoped."

"That makes two of us. I'm in love with a woman I just met and lost."

"Listen to 'Auntie Mel': I've a feeling you've not seen the last of her. If I were you, I'd not give up just yet."

"You're seriously thinking I stand a chance?" There was a glimmer of hope in Ben's eyes.

"I do. Trust me on this one, okay?"

That night Ben vowed to not give up on the woman he loved. Mel's intuition had never failed her before. Despite wishing Hannah and that guy she was involved with every happiness, Ben couldn't stand the thought of her belonging to anyone but him.

CHAPTER NINE

THE FOLLOWING WEEK Hannah received a call from Melanie, demanding to be introduced to Mark.

"Let's meet for lunch at Maxwell's in Hampstead Village, say 2pm on Sunday?"

"But we're spending the weekend at his place."

"No buts! Tell lover boy I'm not taking no for an answer."

Mark was furious she'd accepted without consulting him. They'd met up for a drink at The Hare and Hound and he was about to drop her off at Ella's.

"Didn't you tell her we're seeing each other?"

"She refused to be fobbed off. Do it for me, please."

"She's bound to hate me, just like Sanna and Rosie!"

"No one hates you, they're just being protective of me," Hannah lied, snuggling up to him.

"If you say so . . . Oh, alright. As long as it doesn't intrude on our time together."

"You won't regret it. Melanie's a terrific girl."

They spent the rest of Saturday making pasta with cheese and mushrooms, and after finishing a bottle of red wine, Mark asked if she wanted dessert.

"I've got some tiramisu in the refrigerator, if you'd like."

Shaking her head Hannah went up to him and whispered in his ear. "It's not the kind of dessert I was hoping for. Are you sure that's all you have on offer?"

"You little minx! I know what you want – can't say I object." Incapable of restraining himself, Mark carried her up to his bedroom, where they made love for hours on end. It was midnight by the time Hannah fell asleep in his arms, satisfied everything was great between them and looking forward to the future.

She was woken up by the sun streaming through the curtains and the sound of someone unlocking the front door. Terrified it was a thief carrying a weapon, she shook Mark's arm.

"Someone's trying to break in – you have to do something!"

Mark rubbed his eyes and jumped out of bed. Stumbling over their clothes, he put on a pair of jeans and was about to go downstairs when the door opened. Standing there in front of them was his mother, carrying a large bag.

"I've come to deliver your laundry, son. I thought you'd be pleased to have it ready for work on Monday." Her eyes fell on Hannah, hiding under the duvet.

"Pleased? Are you insane? It's 6am on a Sunday morning!" He wanted to strangle her.

"Let me remind you this house is mine and your father's! I have every right to come and go as I wish."

"I'll change the lock."

"Be my guest. I'll make sure your father throws you out in the street."

"You wouldn't dare – we won't let you!"

"Your father does everything I ask of him."

"No, he doesn't! To him you're nothing but an unpaid skivvy."

Mark clearly didn't give a damn about her, especially not now she'd embarrassed him in front of his girlfriend.

Ignoring him, Annuschka turned to look at Hannah. "You must be freezing under that duvet, Miss Stein. Don't let me interrupt you. I am leaving." On her way out, she paused. "By the way, son, Petra called last night. She wants to know why you're not getting back to her."

"Stop interfering Mum! Get the hell out of here or I'll throw you out!"

Shaking her head, Annuschka went downstairs, slamming the door behind her.

Numb with shock, Hannah jumped out of bed and started to get dressed. "I refuse to spend another minute in this house," she shouted, tears of humiliation streaming down her face. When Mark attempted to hold her, she pushed him away.

"Please don't let that woman come between us, baby. I'll make sure today's a one-off."

"I seem to recall you promising that before!"

"Calm down and let's get back to sleep."

"You're letting your mother interfere with every aspect of your life. Can't you see how much she thrives on it?"

"That's unfair! Her life's empty – instead of hating her, you ought to feel sorry for her. No matter how badly she behaves, you're always defending her!" Hannah shook her head in disbelief.

"Stop it. You're beginning to sound just like her. It's getting on my nerves."

"That's rich coming from you! You're such a hypocrite. Guess what? I'm not letting you mess with my life anymore." She wanted to slap his face.

Realising he'd gone too far, Mark apologised. "Let's not argue anymore. I'm sorry I upset you."

"That makes two of us. By the way, who the hell is Petra?"

"Some Polish girl I went to school with years ago. My mother's got it into her head I'm better off with someone of my own background."

"Do you agree with her?"

"Of course not! I feel nothing for the woman. I wish she'd stop pestering me." He went up to her and kissed her. "I'm sorry my mother barged in like that, baby. Let's get a few hours' kip before it's time to meet your friend." Reluctantly Hannah let him make love to her but her heart wasn't in it. At the back of her mind she kept thinking he had something to hide – why else would his mother take such pleasure in mentioning that girl's name?

He woke her up at 11am, carrying a tray with steaming mugs of tea, toast and jam.

"I've got a great idea. Let's go for a drive – we have plenty of time before meeting your friend. Unless, of course, you'd rather I come back to bed?" Putting the tray down, he started to kiss her.

"Please don't take this the wrong way. I really want some time to myself. We'll meet later at the restaurant."

"As you wish. I gather we're not having breakfast together either?" His eyes were dark with anger.

"I'm not hungry, besides we're having lunch in a few hours."

"Suit yourself – I obviously can't do right for doing wrong!" Snapping at her, he picked up the tray and left. Fed up with his temper tantrums, Hannah couldn't be bothered to go after him. Instead she went to the bathroom to splash some water on her face.

Her reflection in the bathroom mirror depressed her – the deathly pale face and swollen eyes reminded her of what happened earlier. After applying make-up, she brushed her hair, and put on a pair of jeans, blouse and boots. Feeling slightly better, she went downstairs to join Mark in the kitchen.

"Don't be late. Melanie's looking forward to meeting you."

"Is she really? What's the point? You clearly don't want me anywhere near you!" His voice was full of contempt.

"You're being unfair. I only want to clear my head, or have you conveniently forgotten what your mother put us through?"

"That's water under the bridge! I wish you wouldn't analyse everything. Let me take you wherever it is you're going. You'd be lucky to catch a bus on a Sunday."

"I don't mind – see you later." She ran out the door, acutely aware of the hostility between them.

"I hope you come to terms with whatever it is that's troubling you," Mark shouted, watching her disappear down the road.

Hannah vowed to not let him ruin the rest of the day. Catching a cab, she asked the driver to drop her at the station in Hampstead Village. The weather was mild for the season and everywhere she looked young couples were kissing and holding hands. Watching them made her wish Mark wasn't such a 'mummy's boy'. After browsing through a couple of shops, she crossed the cobbled street and went into The Coffee Cup, where she ordered a mug of hot chocolate and a croissant. Sitting by the window watching the world pass by, she couldn't help wishing she was as carefree as the people in the street. It was almost 2pm when she slowly made her way to the restaurant.

Melanie was waiting by the entrance, looking very pretty in a red cashmere top and black trousers. She immediately came up to her and gave her a hug.

"Where's that boyfriend of yours? I bet he's busy trying to find a parking space. This place is always packed at the weekend."

"He'll be here any minute." Hannah forced herself to smile.

"Trouble in paradise?" It was meant as a harmless joke, but watching her friend's face crumple, Melanie instantly regretted it.

"What's wrong, sweetie?"

"We've been arguing. I'll tell you later, he's just walked in the door."

Noticeably nervous, Mark walked up to them and turned on the charm.

"You must be Melanie Gordon. I'm very pleased to meet you." Wearing a grey suit, shirt and tie, he looked every inch the up-and-coming salesman.

"Ditto – Hannah's told me about you – we're very close, she's like a sister to me."

Taking in her nice features and short bob, Mark was convinced they'd get along. "Have you ordered yet? I'm starving!" He asked a passing waiter to bring them a couple of menus. "I've not been here for ages – this is one of my favourite restaurants."

After they'd ordered burgers, fries and milkshakes, Melanie decided to come straight to the point. "What's your aim for the future, Mark?"

Taken aback by her blunt approach, he told her he'd recently been promoted to senior salesman.

"I'm impressed. And you've just moved into your own house?"

"That's right. It's around the corner from my parents."

Melanie sensed the tension between him and her friend. "Aren't you too young to settle down?"

"It depends on your outlook on life. I personally believe sharing a house and career is more than enough. Hannah's assured me she'll return to me after she's finished her degree." He reached for her hand across the table.

"But that's not for another three years! Surely you're planning to visit her? Sweden's apparently a beautiful country."

Shrugging his shoulders, Mark smiled at them. "What with everything that's going on in my life, I doubt I'll get the opportunity – perhaps once or twice."

You bastard, Melanie thought inwardly. "But surely if you truly cared about her, you'd make the effort? If there's a will there's always a way, Mr Copeck!" She smiled but her eyes were cold.

He was about to reply when their food arrived. Focusing on the meal in front of them, neither of them said a word. They'd finished eating when Melanie announced she was leaving. "Matt, my fiancé, is awaiting me. He's an angel, always having my best interests at heart. Men like him are hard to come by. I'm certain you agree with me, Hannah?"

They'd spent only an hour in each other's company and she couldn't wait to get out of there. "It's been nice meeting you, Mark," she lied.

"Likewise, Miss Gordon." Standing up, he offered to help her with her coat.

"There's no need. Please let me pay for my share of the bill."

"Don't be absurd. This is my treat." Both women watched as he went up to the till.

"You can't stand him! I can tell by the way you look at him." Hannah had tears in her eyes. The day had gone from bad to worse.

"You're right. That guy is a selfish, manipulative idiot."

"There must be something you approve of?"

"Sadly – no. I can see the attraction. He's not exactly ugly. And boy, does he know it! Don't kid yourself, sweetie. Mark is always going to put himself first. He'll never conform to your expectations. It'll only end in tears. As your friend, I only want what's best for you. Ben's worth a million compared to him. I wish you'd give him a chance to prove it."

"That's not fair on Mark!"

"If it was the other way round, do you honestly think he'd give a damn?"

"If Ben's as perfect as you say, how come he's single?" Hannah was fed up with her friend's disparaging comments about her boyfriend.

"Because we know who he wants – you. Ben's head over heels in love with you, Hannah."

"We barely know each other! One night is hardly a basis for having a relationship."

"You're wrong. Sometimes it's all it takes to fall in love. Ben's mature, kind and caring. He'd always put you first."

From the corner of her eye, Hannah noticed Mark approaching them.

"I'm sorry it took so long. Everyone wanted to pay at the same time."

"Please let me know how much I owe you." Melanie handed him a few notes.

"I thought I made it clear this one's on me, Miss Gordon."

"But I don't want to be indebted to you, Mr Copeck!"

"You're Hannah's friend. Please let that be the end of it."

Debating his words, Melanie sighed and nodded. "Alright. I see your point. I'll let it go for now." Turning to embrace her friend, she murmured, "Don't forget what I said. Bye, sweetie," then, louder, "Good-bye, Mr Copeck. I'll see myself out." Waving at Hannah, she quickly walked out.

"I told you this would happen. All your friends hate me!" The muscle in Mark's cheek was twitching so much, she thought he was having a fit.

"Do you honestly care?"

"Of course I do. She's your friend. I know how much you value her opinion. She despises me. Her sort usually does!"

"What's that supposed to mean?"

"Most Jews consider themselves superior to the rest of us."

"How dare you? First your mother – now you! Anti-Semitism obviously runs in your family."

"Don't be so bloody melodramatic. I'm with you, aren't I? You're not like them, you're Swedish."

Hannah's eyes narrowed. "Meaning?"

"You're not as money-orientated."

"Let me tell you something, Mark – you and I don't work out. Let's call it off."

"Are you dumping me? You asked my opinion and I gave it to you." He was mortified – the prospect of losing her had never crossed his mind.

"No I didn't! You made an ugly assumption about a dear friend of mine. By the way, you're right – she hates you! Must be because of her Jewish roots, right?" Suddenly she couldn't stand the sight of him.

"Hannah, baby, please! All I want is to make you happy. Last night was great until . . . You know, I'm sorry I spoke out of turn, but you pushed me into a corner." Just like before, Mark put the blame on her.

"Don't ever insult me, my family or friends again. If you do, we're finished – is that understood?"

"I won't. I promise I'll never upset you again." He offered her a lift back but she rejected him. Shaking his head, Mark said,

"This is not how it's supposed to be." Turning away from her, he walked in the direction of Jack Straw's Castle, where he'd parked his car.

On her way back to Golders Green, Hannah wished she still had someone to confide in. Rosie and Sanna had recently returned home to pursue their goals, insisting she followed their example. Both had continued to reject Mark's bullish behaviour, particularly the way he'd let his mother walk all over them.

Celebrating their last night together at Ricky's taverna, each of the girls had been touched to receive a silver bracelet bearing the inscription 'Friends for life' from their enthusiastic host. Hugging them one by one, Ricky reminded them to always be there for one another. Saying goodbye at the airport had brought tears to everyone's eyes, especially Hannah's since she was the one left behind. Now that chapter of their lives had come to an end. Sunday afternoons at Ranch House, Great Expectations and The Purple Pussycat were a thing of the past.

As Hannah trudged through the door, Ella asked if she wanted to join her for tea.

"I hope you had a nice weekend, my dear. You've not been yourself lately, is it something to do with Mark?"

"Melanie can't stand him," Hannah sounded as miserable as she felt. "And his mother delivered his laundry at 6am!"

"That's hardly surprising. Between them, Mark and his mother are quite a handful." She leaned forward and kissed Hannah's cheek.

"Oh, Ella – how on earth will I cope without you?" Bursting into tears, Hannah envisaged leaving the woman of whom she'd grown so fond. Rosie and Sanna were young but Ella was old and frail. What if something happened to her and she wasn't there?

"Please don't upset yourself, my dear. You've got your whole life ahead of you!"

"Can you recall the man I met at Melanie's party?"

"Are you referring to Mr Benjamin Isaacs? Your eyes light up every time you mention his name."

"I've decided to go on a date with him."

"That's excellent news! You owe it to yourself to find out if it's merely a fleeting attraction or something much deeper."

Taking her at her word, Hannah called Melanie.

"Ben will be thrilled! What made you change your mind?" Melanie couldn't wait to play Cupid.

"You were right about Mark. He's always putting his own needs first. We argue all the time. I wish we'd never met!"

"Don't upset yourself, sweetie; you and Ben are made for each other."

When Ben called that night asking if she would like to have dinner with him the following Saturday, Hannah immediately accepted.

"That's wonderful. I can't tell you how much I'm looking forward to seeing you again!" His voice was just as warm and kind as she remembered.

"Thanks for the compliment. The feeling's mutual."

"Is it alright to pick you up at 7pm? Mel's given me your address."

"Absolutely."

"Take very good care of yourself – I'll be counting the days until we meet."

Hannah was on her way to Ella's bedroom when the phone rang. This time it was Mark, accusing her of not returning his calls.

"Are you ignoring me, baby? Let's see each other at the week-end. I miss being with you."

"I'm sorry, but I've made other plans." Listening to him gave her an instant headache.

"Are you seeing someone else behind my back?" he asked in a suspicious voice, angry she rejected him.

"That's none of your business! Leave me alone. You're always upsetting me."

"I can't. I love you and want to be with you."

"Tough – because I don't want to be with you!"

"But you're leaving after Christmas. Tell me what's wrong and I'll do my best to put it right."

"We're oceans apart – you have an awful lot of growing up to do!"

After a few minutes silence, Mark asked, "Have you fallen out of love with me, baby? Is that what all of this is about?"

"My problem is I just don't like you very much." She wasn't willing to succumb to him. Every time she did, it ended in tears.

"I'm sorry you feel that way. Just remember this: you'll never find anyone who will love you as much as I do."

She was about to say something but the line went dead.

Just like Ben, Hannah counted the days till Saturday night. When it finally arrived, she made an extra effort to look her best. Ella thought she looked radiant in a purple lace dress, perfectly complementing the colour of her eyes and hair.

"If he's not already smitten with you, my dear, he most certainly will be now!"

Arriving on the dot of 7pm, looking very handsome in a midnight-blue suit, white shirt and tie, Ben couldn't take his eyes off her.

"You look stunning. These are for you."

Their eyes met as he handed her a bouquet of red roses, leaning forward to kiss her cheek. Both felt the same chemistry as on the night they danced together at Melanie's party.

"They're beautiful. I'll see to them as soon as I've introduced you to my landlady." Acutely aware of his gaze, Hannah led him into the living room where Ella was seated by the fireplace, looking very elegant in a knitted blue dress. As Ella raised herself to greet him, Ben immediately offered her his arm.

"I'm very pleased to meet you, Mrs Rifkind, Hannah's been telling me how wonderful you are."

"I'd be lost without her, Mr Isaacs. Perhaps you'd like to join me for a glass of sherry?"

"I'd love to. I grew up not far from here, attending The King Alfred School. Have you lived here for many years?"

"Since my daughter was six. This place, as indeed the neighbourhood, has seen a lot of changes. When my husband passed away, I decided to take lodgers. It was the best decision I ever made." She leaned forward and touched Hannah's arm.

After engaging in some light conversation, Ben glanced at his watch exclaiming, "We'd better leave or they'll give our table to someone else. It's been such a pleasure talking to you, Mrs Rifkind."

"Likewise, Mr Isaacs. Let's dispense with formality and call each other by our first names."

Turning to Hannah, Ben asked if she was ready.

"Where are you taking me?"

"To an Italian restaurant in Highgate. I hope you'll like it as much as I do."

"Will you be alright without me?" She went up to Ella and gave her a gentle hug.

"Stop worrying about me! I'll still be here when you get back, my dear. Have a pleasant evening." She winked at Hannah, indicating she wholeheartedly approved of their guest.

Helping to put her coat on, Ben informed her he'd parked his car across the road.

"It's a blue Bentley. My father gave it to me when I went to university. Over the years, I've become quite attached to it." There was a slight chill in the air, reminding them winter was on its way. Taking her hand, Ben asked if she was cold. Feeling his warm, firm grip, Hannah smiled and shook her head.

"This is mild compared to Sweden."

"I always dreamed of going to Scandinavia," Ben replied. "Unfortunately I never got round to actually doing it." At that, Hannah wanted to invite him to her parents' house but it wasn't appropriate. He wasn't her boyfriend – Mark was. Waiting for her to get into the front seat of his car, Ben said, "You may disapprove of what I'm about to tell you but I'm going to anyway. You take my breath away."

Too embarrassed to look at him, she thanked him for the compliment, adding no one had ever said that to her before.

"Not even your boyfriend? He ought to."

"Mark doesn't know about tonight. We're having a few problems but deep down I know he loves me." Feeling Ben sitting so close to her, Hannah wished she'd kept her mouth shut.

During the drive to Highgate, Ben decided it was best he kept a low profile – the last thing he wanted was to scare her away and risk losing their friendship. He remembered Melanie telling him Mark was a selfish bastard but despite everything he'd put her through, Hannah was in love with him. *She's young*, he thought to himself. *He's her first boyfriend. It won't last. Be patient and let her know you're always there for her.*

Breathing in the distinct lemongrass scent of his aftershave, Hannah watched his hands on the steering wheel: strong, muscular and slightly tanned. She ached to be close to him. Every time she and Mark touched, he always assumed she wanted him to make love to her when all she really craved was his affection.

Lost in thought, she started as Ben announced they'd arrived. After parking behind the restaurant, he went round to let her out. She looked so damn beautiful in that dress, he wished she were his, not someone else's girlfriend. Then he noticed the expression on her face. Putting an arm around her shoulders, Ben asked if she was okay. She was about to answer him when he spotted something glinting under the light of the lamppost and bent down to pick it up.

"Is this yours?" In the palm of his hand lay a small pearl earring.

Checking she hadn't lost its twin, Hannah told him they were a gift from her grandmother.

"The one who lives in Market Place?"

"That's right. She'd like to meet you and Melanie." For the second time that night Hannah wished she'd kept her mouth shut. Why on earth would Ben be interested in meeting her grandmother? Mark was her boyfriend and he couldn't care less. But Ben's response astonished her.

"I'd love to meet her. She's bound to be very special if Ella's anything to go by! Why don't you arrange it and let me know?"

The minute they entered the large candlelit premises with its pretty décor and flower arrangements, a tall, dark man in his fifties came up to greet them.

"Mr Isaacs – how nice to see you! Who's your pretty companion?" He bowed and kissed Hannah's hand.

"Miss Stein's a close friend of mine, Renato. She knows how much this place means to me and my family."

"Welcome to San Carlo, Miss Stein. Over the years my father and I have helped to organise everything from Bar Mitzvahs to anniversaries here." Turning to Ben, he asked if his mother was still as keen on their Piccata Milanese.

"She swears by it. Claims it's the best she's ever had."

"You're very kind. Please let me take you to your table." Ben and Hannah followed the maître d' to a quiet corner of the room, where he waited until they were seated, signalled for a waiter to bring the wine list and wished them a pleasant evening.

Impressed by the ambience and attention to detail, Hannah told Ben she'd developed quite an appetite.

"I'm pleased to hear it! I can't tell you how much being here with you means to me."

When yet another waiter put a basket of bread and butter in front of them, requesting they let him know whether they were ready to order, Hannah couldn't help comparing the evening with her first date with Mark. Unlike the man sitting opposite her, he had never opened a door or pulled out a chair for her. Ben was a gentleman and in his presence she felt very special.

Choosing from the extensive menu, both opted to have Minestrone Soup followed by salmon for Hannah and lamb cutlets for Ben.

"Let's have white wine – it goes well with fish."

"I really don't mind. If you'd rather have red wine, that's fine with me."

"White it is." He signalled for the waiter to take their order.

Feeling guilty for comparing one man with the other, Hannah had to admit that, even in the looks department, Ben won hands down over Mark. She particularly approved of how he treated

Ella – the old lady obviously thought the world of him. Most significantly, both of them shared the same cultural background and strong family ties.

When their food arrived Ben raised his glass, repeating how pleased he was to be with her. "I can honestly say tonight's the happiest I've ever been."

Touched by his words, she reached for his hand across the table. "That's the sweetest thing anybody's ever told me. It is I who should be grateful to you for being so kind to me and my landlady."

"Let me assure you the pleasure is all mine." Smiling at her, he reluctantly let go of her hand and poured her another glass of wine. "It feels as if we've known each other for a long time. I gather Ella and your grandmother want you to stay?"

"At their time of life, every day's a gift; I'll visit as often as I can."

"Your boyfriend must be very proud of you?"

"Mark's idea of having a relationship is me being there for him; since work takes up most of his time, I'll be the one coming over during term breaks." Her eyes clouded over, thinking about it.

Mel was right, thought Ben. *That boyfriend of hers is a complete shit.* In an overly bright voice, he said, "He's lucky to have you. I hope he appreciates it."

"Somehow I doubt he sees it that way." Hannah instantly regretted she'd said too much, smiled and thanked him for a wonderful evening.

Ben assured her the feeling was mutual. What he really wanted was to tell her he would always be there for her.

"Please don't take offence, but I really want to see you again." His brown eyes searched hers.

"You will. I'm introducing you to my grandmother, remember?"

"I know. It's not what I meant. What I truly want is for you to be part of my life."

His direct approach made her blush. She struggled to find the right words. "You're pushing me into a corner. Tonight's as far as it goes. Mark's not perfect but I love him. I'm sorry if I gave you the wrong impression." She looked as miserable as he felt.

"Just my luck. I wish I'd met you first. This connection between us is the kind of thing that only happens once in a lifetime." He looked so disappointed; she wished she could have put her arms around him.

"You're right. One of these days you'll meet someone special. It's a pity that someone can't be me."

"What if you're wrong? What if that special someone's sitting right in front of me? He looked directly at her.

Averting her eyes, Hannah glanced at her watch. "It's time to leave. Ella's waiting for me."

"You've not had dessert yet. At least have some coffee or tea?" He was desperate to extend what little time they had left before she disappeared from his life.

"Thank you for asking but I'm fine." He helped put her coat on and signalled for the bill.

On their way out, Renato asked if they'd enjoyed themselves.

"The food and wine were superb. Our compliments to the chef."

"Bring your parents next time. It's been a pleasure meeting you, Miss Stein. Please come again." He escorted them to the door and disappeared off to greet a guest.

Walking to his car, Ben put an arm around her shoulders. "I've had a wonderful evening. I'm sorry if I came on too strong."

"You didn't. It's like you said; we met at the wrong time."

Turning to look at her, Ben replied, "I hope you get everything you wish for. Just promise me one thing; if things don't work out between you and that guy, will you please let me know?

"Yes . . . I will," she whispered.

Neither said a word on the drive back. Parking outside her house, Ben immediately got out of the car to help her out. "Will you let me know when I can meet your grandmother?"

"Are you sure it's what you want?" Her voice trembled so much that she could hardly speak.

"Absolutely, I'd do anything to be close to you, anything at all." As he waited for her to let herself in, he called impetuously, "I'm in love with you, Hannah Stein, and I always will be."

CHAPTER TEN

O N SUNDAY, BEN was ensconced at his father's office, preparing the following week's case load when his old friend and associate Collin Henderson turned up, reminding him they had an early start in the morning. Fair with deep-set grey eyes and of a stocky build, the two men were complete opposites yet shared the same outlook on life.

"Did I mention we're expecting an addition to the family?" Collin's face shone with excitement and pride.

"That's great news! I guess congratulations are in order." Walking up to him, Ben shook his hand.

"Can you believe it? In less than a year, Karen and I have tied the knot, moved into our own house and now this – a baby! It will be your turn next, mate."

"Chance would be a fine thing. Until then, work's my saviour." Ben's eyes clouded over, thinking about the woman he loved.

"How about Vanessa Westbrook? That girl fancies you rotten."

"Don't be ridiculous! She and I are just friends."

"Really? Then how come she refers to you as her 'Prince Charming'?"

"You've got the wrong end of the stick. Americans and Brits don't have the same sense of humour." Stifling a yawn, Ben cleared his desk and declared he was off. Joining him, Collin stood his ground.

"I disagree. She meant it, alright – perhaps you've given her mixed messages?"

"Give me one reason! Vanessa's not my type. Stop giving me a hard time!" Ben exploded, angry his friend assumed they were an item.

"Okay! I get it – you needn't bite my head off . . . Anyway, who is your type?"

"That's personal. Let's get the hell out of here."

"Hey, what's up? I'm your friend. Tell me, what's wrong?"

"You're not going to take no for an answer, are you? Here goes. I've met the perfect woman. Unfortunately for me, she's with someone else." His voice was hoarse with emotion.

"Me and my big mouth. What happened?"

"I've told you. She's in a relationship. We met at Mel's bash, went out on a date and that was it. She'll be leaving soon."

Listening to him, Collin knew he was gutted. "Can't you at least stay in touch? Who knows what the future holds."

Shrugging his shoulders, Ben quickly changed the subject. "When is Vanessa's father coming over?"

"Ronald? Sometime next year. She thinks we should enter into partnership with him, claiming our skills and his connections are a lethal weapon."

"Does she now? That guy's got a lot of clout – whatever we decide to do, Dad's backing us all the way. I bet you're just as keen as I am to expand our horizons?"

Weighing his words carefully, Collin took his time to respond. "I'm concerned we're signing up for a lot more than we've bargained for. You'd better watch out – that woman is crazy about you." He knew they'd been acquainted at Cambridge, but instead of finishing her law degree, Vanessa had dropped out, boasting about getting a job in one of her father's businesses. Tall, blonde and with legs that went on forever, she struck him as being both shallow and vulgar. "Her kind don't know the meaning of having to work for a living," he said to Ben. "Rumour has it her old man's purchased a mansion in your area."

"I can't say that surprises me. Ronald's worth billions. If I were you, I wouldn't worry so much – she won't risk losing our respect."

"Well, don't forget I warned you. It scares me shitless imagining what she's capable of."

"Vanessa's not as bad as you imagine, try giving her some credit."

Shaking his head, Collin helped lock up, looked his friend in the eye and said, "She's your friend – your responsibility. See you in the morning." Walking in the opposite direction to where they'd parked their cars, both men were desperate to get a few hours' sleep.

The minute he walked in the door, Ben heard the phone ring. Irritated someone had the nerve to call at such a late hour, he grabbed the receiver, snapping, "Who is it?"

"It's me – Hannah. I hope I didn't wake you up? My grandmother's asked me to invite you and Melanie to her flat for tea. How does Saturday at 3pm sound to you?"

Hearing her voice instantly brought butterflies to the pit of his stomach. While a part of him debated if it was best to say no, another much bigger part couldn't bear the thought of not seeing her again.

"It's great to talk to you. Thanks for inviting us. Mel will be as thrilled as I am! Are you okay?"

"Sort of, I suppose. I'm leaving after Chanukah." The very thought of having to leave her 'two grandmothers' brought tears to Hannah's eyes.

"But it's for a good reason, right? You're going home to study." It was just like him to pep her up.

"Let me give you my grandmother's address." Soon after, Hannah ended the conversation, wishing him a good night's sleep.

"You too, little one – sweet dreams" Ben whispered, putting the phone down.

As she lay in bed, the light from the street lamps streaming through the net curtains, Hannah couldn't stop thinking about him. The sound of his voice had stirred up emotions deep inside of her. Unlike Mark, Ben read her like an open book – tonight was no exception.

The scrumptious display of chopped liver, bagels with cream cheese and salmon, pirogues and fish balls took her breath away.

"Oh, Granny, you've outdone yourself! There's enough food to feed an army."

Blushing with pride, Zipporah clapped her hands. "Only the best for my darling granddaughter."

Seated at the dining table, Ella readily agreed with Hannah. "She's been cooking since dawn. I don't know how she does it!" Both women looked very elegant in their best outfits, matching red lips and pearl necklaces.

Nibbling absentmindedly on a fish ball, Hannah reminded her grandmother to not embarrass her in front of her friends.

"As if! I'll be on my best behaviour – aren't I always?" There was a look of mischief in her eyes.

"Let's hope you're right. They've arrived, the intercom's buzzing in the hall."

Looking demure in a black dress with her hair scraped off from her face, a glimpse in the mirror confirmed to Hannah how tense she felt at the prospect of seeing him again. Unlocking the front door, she heard muffled voices in the elevator, the sound of footsteps in the corridor and *voilà*! There they were, arm in arm and carrying a large bouquet of flowers.

"These are for you and your grandmother," Melanie said, handing her the bouquet.

"Welcome to our little tea party. Please let me take your coats." From the corner of her eye, she noticed Ben was watching her, wishing he and Hannah were on their own.

After introducing themselves, Ben kissed the hostess and Ella's hand, the latter addressing him as though they were old friends. Feeling weak at the knees, Hannah couldn't help but notice how handsome he was in that suit, shirt and tie. For a split second she wished she could run her hands through that thick hair of his. The speckles of grey at the temples made him look even more dashing than he already was.

Without warning, Ben looked at her. His dark brown eyes caressed her face. Conscious of the chemistry between them, Melanie lightened the atmosphere by complimenting the two ladies on how wonderful they looked. "You're gorgeous! I'm so glad we finally get to meet!" Indeed, Hannah thought her friend looked effortlessly elegant in a bright-red cashmere dress.

Incapable of taking her eyes off her guests, Zipporah asked if Melanie and Ben were an item. "You make an awfully nice couple!"

"Good Lord, no. Ben and I are not at all each other's type.

We've been friends since nursery – I'm actually about to get married!"

"Please forgive me for making the wrong assumption. Now you know the reason my granddaughter wants me to keep my thoughts to myself."

Blushing, Hannah heard Ben compliment Zipporah on the buffet laid out in front of them. "My late beloved 'Bubbla' loved to cook," he said. "Her favourite was chicken soup with kneidlach."

"I like you, Ben. You're a nice Jewish boy."

"That's exactly what she used to say!"

The ice was broken – Ben and Melanie were just as much a part of 'the family' as Hannah and Ella. Watching them brought back just how frail Hannah and Mark's relationship was. Although he repeatedly expressed a wish to be a part of her life, she was convinced his heart wasn't in it.

They'd polished off their plates when Zipporah turned to Ben, asking, "Since your friend here isn't your type, may I ask who is?"

Before he had the chance to reply, Melanie leaned across the table and touched Hannah's arm. "This one's right up his street!"

Mortified, Ben immediately came to her rescue. "Please excuse my friend's comment. She too finds it hard to keep her thoughts to herself!"

Laughing out loud, Zipporah blinked at him. "My granddaughter's going home to study at university. Ella and I will miss her terribly." Ben wished he could have told her he shared the sentiment. Instead he thanked her for a lovely meal. "But we're not finished yet! Just you wait and see . . ." She went into the kitchen, returning with the *pièce de résistance*: her famous apple cake. Putting a plate and spoon in front of him, she urged him to try it and give his verdict.

Putting a small amount into his mouth, Ben closed his eyes, exclaiming, "It's simply delicious. The best I've ever tasted." Delighted by his comment, Zipporah offered everyone a piece while Hannah silently thanked him with her eyes.

It was almost 6pm when Melanie announced they were leaving. "It's getting late, the roads will be very busy." She and Ben took turns kissing the hostess and Ella on the cheek, thanking them for a wonderful afternoon.

"You're an inspiration to us all!" Melanie said, impulsively giving them another hug.

Looking as if she was about to cry, Zipporah suddenly grabbed Ben's arm. "Soon our lives will be very empty. Do come again."

"It will be our pleasure. As long as Hannah doesn't mind?"

Confused by his response and worried she'd expressed more than she was prepared to give, Hannah replied, "Of course not. Just make sure it's for the right reason. I've already got a boyfriend."

"There's no need for concern." Ben looked extremely hurt. "I get the message, loud and clear."

Too ashamed to look at him, Hannah started to clear the table, acutely aware of everyone staring at her.

"I would like to apologise on my granddaughter's behalf, she's obviously forgotten her manners!" Zipporah couldn't help but interject. "That awful boyfriend of hers will never measure up to you." Shocked her grandmother had such a low opinion of Mark, Hannah turned to look at her. "Please don't refer to him like that!"

"I'm only speaking my mind – he's nothing but a rotten egg!"

Embarrassed at being part of such a personal situation, Melanie reminded Ben they had to leave. Following her into the hall, Hannah helped her with her coat. "Please don't pay attention to what she just said – they've not even met."

"Well I for one happen to think she's very perceptive. After all, I've met the guy, remember?" She kissed Hannah's cheek, urging Ben to get a move on.

"It's been great seeing you again," he said. "I hope everything works out for the best." Bending to kiss her forehead, his lips lingered for a few seconds.

"I'm sorry I was rude to you," Hannah said. "Please accept my apology."

"There's no need. Always remember how much you mean to me. Take very good care of yourself, little one." His eyes didn't let go of hers.

Waving goodbye from the kitchen window, a million thoughts went through her mind. What if this was the last time they met? The idea of not having him in her life felt like a knife in her heart. She sighed and went to join her 'grandmothers' in the living room.

"They're wonderful people," Zipporah smiled at her. "Ben's perfect for you, my darling!"

"But he's not my boyfriend – Mark is! Please say you'll meet him."

"Never. That man's not good enough for you."

"How can you say such a thing? You don't even know him."

"I know how badly he lets his mother treat you."

"Who told you?" Hannah whispered, her face as white as a sheet. Cringing, Ella avoided looking at them.

"It wasn't her, if that's what you're thinking. Melanie told me when we were on our own."

"She had no right to interfere."

"She had every right. We're on your side."

"And you're adamant you don't want to meet him?"

"Absolutely! Don't lose touch with Ben Isaacs. The two of you belong together. One of these days you'll marry and start a family. I pray I'm around to witness it. And, Hannah? Please don't mention Mark's name again in my presence."

Melanie was getting out of the car when Ben pulled her back, asking, "Do you think she and that guy will last?" He looked so miserable; her heart went out to him.

"Only time will tell. But this I know for sure: he's not 'the one'. You are."

"That's absurd, even by your standards."

"I'll one day remind you of that, shall I?"

"Hannah's not a fool. She won't settle for someone as vile as Mark Copeck. I've seen the way she looks at you. Take it from me. It won't take long before he's out of her life!"

When a middle-aged Spanish lady called Letitia applied to take-over Hannah's room, Ella instantly approved, insisting she'd be in good hands.

"There's no need for concern. I'll be absolutely fine, my dear. Nobody's going to replace you but I'm certain Mrs Dudley will make sure everything works out."

But Hannah wasn't fooled. She knew only too well how much Ella wanted her to pursue her goal. "I've made a list of your favourite food, medication and anything that may be useful."

"You're an angel. Between Margareth, Letitia and me, we'll be just fine." Her face crumpled and there were tears in her eyes.

"Oh Ella, you're too good. I've told Granny, now it's your turn. Should either of you need me, I'll be back like a shot! All you have to do is call." She went up to her old friend and embraced her.

"You're what's kept her going, love. That daughter of hers is useless."

A couple of hours later, Hannah and Margareth were in the kitchen tending to Ella's needs. Unable to keep her feelings to herself, Margareth burst into tears.

"Please don't cry!" said Hannah. "You and your little boy mean such a lot to her. Just make sure she's alright – for me?"

Blowing her nose, Margareth looked at her. "Listen to me, love: you mustn't put your life on hold. Apart from keeping you informed, there's not much else I can do."

Chanukah came and went, bringing with it fond memories of her first winter in London and all the fun she'd had with Sanna and Rosie. Somehow the prospect of seeing her family again didn't quite make up for having to say goodbye to her 'two grandmothers'.

During Hannah's last week, she and Mark spent every day in each other's company. He'd even taken time off work, insisting they do all the things both of them enjoyed, such as going for a drive in the country, walking and talking. They were having a meal at Pizza Express in Hampstead Village when he suddenly announced, "I keep imagining you'll end up with some intellectual and forget about me." The muscles in his cheek twitched.

"Don't be silly – you're the one I love! I'll try to visit as often as I can."

"That's all I want to hear. Melanie's wrong: I'll get out of my way to be with you too."

Kissing the palm of her hand, he added, "Are you going to miss me as much as I'll miss you?"

"What do you think?"

"Never forget how much I love you, baby."

"That makes two of us."

It was her last night and they walked hand in hand to his car, neither of them able to keep their hands off each other. As soon as they entered his house, Mark carried her to his bedroom where they made mad, passionate love until they were so exhausted, they fell into each other's arms. Watching him sleep, Hannah was reminded of how much she loved and wanted to be with him. Their intimacy was the main reason she hadn't left him, despite everything he had put her through.

Mark stirred and opened his eyes. "The thought of not being able to touch, kiss and make love to you scares the hell out of me, baby!" He held her so tight she was convinced he'd never let her go. "Please let me take you to the airport."

"We've decided it's for the best I leave on my own accord. Please don't make it more difficult than it already is."

Too upset to respond, Mark kept his mouth shut.

The next morning, watching her getting dressed filled him with so much dread, he almost begged her to stay, but instead he simply enquired if she wanted breakfast. Too distraught to eat, Hannah shook her head, looking as miserable as he felt inside.

"Let's get it over and done with" she whispered.

On the drive back to Golders Green, neither of them said a word. Parking outside the old, familiar house, Mark took her in his arms and kissed her.

"Have a safe journey – don't be a stranger."

Gazing into his eyes one final time, she somehow managed to get out of the car. Her hands were shaking so much that she dropped the keys to the front door.

"Always remember how much I love you, baby," was the last thing he said before driving off, the wheels of his car screeching as he disappeared around the corner of the street.

Holding onto his words, she suddenly remembered Petra's name. She wondered if by leaving him she'd made it possible for someone else to enter his heart. *I've no choice but to trust him.* The thought echoed in her head as she slowly let herself in, desperately trying to get rid of the image of Mark and some faceless woman getting together behind her back.

Her suitcases awaited her in the hall at the bottom of the stairs. The cab taking her to the airport was already booked and all that was left was to say goodbye. Steeling herself, Hannah entered the kitchen where Ella and Mrs Dudley were having breakfast. Dabbing her eyes with an embroidered handkerchief, Ella asked her to join them.

"Why don't you have a piece of toast and tea, my dear?" She looked so upset and frail, Hannah wished she could have stayed – university could after all be postponed for another year or two. But just as she was about to say something, her parents' faces appeared before her eyes, begging her to return to them.

"Thank you, but I've no appetite. I've been looking forward to this day for longer than I care to remember. Funny that now it's here, I feel so empty." She swallowed so as to avoid bursting into tears.

"That's only natural, you're bound to experience a mixture of feelings. Once you're back where you belong, everything will be alright. Try not to worry about your grandmother and me. I'll keep an eye on her." Poor Hannah had already spent hours saying goodbye to Zipporah; now she had to do it all over again.

"She's very fond of you."

"The feeling's mutual, my dear. Won't you at least have a cup of tea? You've got quite a journey ahead of you."

Seated next to her, Hannah kissed her cheek, wishing she could freeze this moment in time. She'd been trying to memorise her

125

bedroom with its old furniture, fireplace and high ceiling. What if Letitia couldn't cope and poor Ella had to be taken into care? If that happened, Hannah knew she'd never be able to forgive herself. As if reading her thoughts, Ella reached for her hand.

"Don't upset yourself – everything's going to be fine."

"Please remember I'm only a phone call away. You must promise to let me know if you need me."

"On one condition: you must give me your word you will never let anybody dictate how to best live your life. Mark's your boyfriend but he's too consumed with himself. Please don't succumb to him. Ben, on the other hand, is kind and caring, always having your best interests at heart. Religion's irrelevant. What truly matters is being with the right person. Never settle for anything less than you deserve, my dear." She squeezed Hannah's hand and hoped she didn't come across as too judgemental. "Have a safe trip. Give my best wishes to your dear parents. They must be almost as proud of you as I am." Clinging to one another, neither of them bothered to conceal the tears in their eyes.

Suddenly the doorbell rang. It was the driver announcing he was parked outside. Disentangling herself, Hannah whispered, "Thank you for everything you've done for me. I love you very much." Her voice was trembling.

"You're most welcome. Since you arrived, my life's been blessed." Ella's eyes were burning with tears. Pretending to wipe something off the table, Margareth Dudley gave each of them a big hug.

"You're a good girl. May God always be with you, love."

"Please look after her for me – I'll miss you all so much." Blinded by tears, Hannah smiled at her 'second granny' and blew her a kiss. Following her into the hall, she and Margareth watched the driver carry the suitcases to the car and as she put the keys on the mantelpiece, Hannah reminded them once more that she would be only a phone call away.

Too distraught to speak, Ella watched her get into the back seat of the cab, where she waved at them until they were out of sight but not mind. While she cried her heart out, the driver didn't say a word until they arrived at Heathrow. Parking outside Terminal 3, Hannah dried her eyes. Yet another part of her life was over and a new part was just about to begin.

CHAPTER ELEVEN

1980

Peter had changed such a lot during her absence. Had it not been for his blue eyes and broad smile, she'd have mistaken him for a model.

"The brother I left behind was a boy – are you sure you're not an imposter?" she teased.

"Quite," he replied. "What you see is the real article. Your hair's grown – it suits you. But you're much too slim!" Her green eyes looked huge in that heart-shaped face of hers.

"Kastrup's not changed a bit! It's positively sterile compared to Heathrow."

"I've missed having you around. Come here!" Scooping her up into his arms, Peter informed her he'd promised their parents to bring her straight home.

"We'd better hurry or we'll miss catching the last hydrofoil to Malmö."

Going through Customs and Passport Control, she asked if their parents were alright.

"Now Granny's gone, Pappa's not as driven as he used to be. I'd say the two of them are even closer."

"Granny told me you and Lena are an item."

"We're mad for each other; she's the best thing that's happened to me." His eyes lit up at the mention of his girlfriend.

"Can I assume Mamma and Pappa don't mind she's not Jewish?"

"Lena's offered to convert to Judaism but we all dissuaded her since we're not religious. All of us love her just as she is."

"Good for you." It felt wonderful talking to him. She'd been missing their closeness. While boarding the hydrofoil to Malmö, she told him about Mark.

"Sounds like quite a guy – are you as madly in love as me and Lena?"

"Definitely. I'm missing him already. By the way, Mark's not Jewish either."

"I guess we can't choose who we fall in love with, sis. He must be dying to meet the folks?"

"Sort of. Mark's busy focusing on his career. I'll book a flight back in the next few months," Hannah replied, slightly defensively.

"You'll what? But you've only just arrived. Shouldn't it be the other way around? If he cares about you, he'll find a way."

"Please don't turn it into such a big deal – he's my boyfriend, warts and all."

"Alright, but if he steps out of line, he'll have me to deal with!" Based on what she'd told him, Peter didn't think much of her boyfriend so far.

Putting her suitcases in the boot of their father's old Volvo, Peter proudly announced he'd passed his driving test. Everything looked the same as when she'd left for London. In less than half an hour, the snow-covered streets of Limhamn reminded her of a picture postcard. As they parked outside the bungalow-style villa, she saw their parents come out to greet them. It was pitch black and bitterly cold, and she was barely out of the car when she felt her parents' arms around her. It was the moment she'd been waiting for.

Pulling away, she saw her brother was right: as distinguished as ever, their father looked slightly older with tiny speckles of grey at the temples. With her trademark 1950s glasses, black slacks and a cashmere top, Zadie looked every bit as glamorous as when they last met.

"Golders Green is nice but it feels great breathing fresh air again!" Hannah took a deep breath, demonstrating how she felt.

"We're thrilled to have you back home, sweetie. I bet you're starving. Airlines aren't exactly renowned for their food."

"Mmm. What's for dinner?" It felt wonderful being surrounded by the people she loved. "Please tell me we're having potato salad with no skin – and salmon with dill and mayonnaise sauce?" Just imagining it made her salivate.

"Perhaps. I'll tell you this much: we're having chocolate pudding with whipped cream for dessert." Hannah ran into her mother's arms, squealing with delight.

It was surprisingly easy adjusting to life at home. The scenery, open landscape and tranquillity were a far cry from the constant buzz of London. The best bit was being able to walk for miles without bumping into a stranger. She'd been missing the house, in particular the small library behind the living room where she and Peter often sat talking through the dark winter nights. The bedroom was such a contrast to the one at Ella's: modern and light. Hannah couldn't help thinking of the fireplace where she, Rosie and Sanna sat gossiping before going to Ranch House, Great Expectations and The Purple Pussycat. Since coming home, the three friends regularly updated each other on what they were up to. Sanna loved working at a shelter for homeless people with drug addictions, while Rosie was so busy learning how to become a florist, she barely had time to date.

By January 1980 Hannah enrolled at Lund University. Similar to Oxford, Lund was an hour's drive from Malmö and was packed with students, restaurants and bars. Planning to study Economics, Lena and Peter casually suggested they rent a flat together but Zadie insisted they wait until they were older. Confident her and Mark's relationship was strong enough to endure being apart for almost three years, Hannah called to ask him if he'd come over for Easter.

"I wish you would come here instead, baby. We'd have the house to ourselves," he enticed her.

"Don't you want to see where I live and meet my family? They're dying to meet you. Besides, I'm exhausted from all my studying."

"Sorry babe – but I'm committed too." He told her he'd been promoted to Manager.

"Think about the difference it will make to our future! Please come . . . for me?" he pleaded.

"I've already told you, no. Spring's on its way. It's such a far cry from the British weather and all that rain."

"Things are pretty mental this time of year, please don't make me do something that's going to jeopardise our future, baby."

"Perish the thought! We'll meet in the summer; that's when Sweden's in full bloom." She was too tired to argue with him.

"But that's months away," he wailed. "Why can't you get your priorities right?"

"That's rich, coming from you!" Hannah snapped, adding, "Let's hope we can see each other before the year's up."

"Okay. You're pissed off with me. We'll talk nearer the time. I love and miss you, Hannah."

But she couldn't care less. Where Mark was concerned, there was always something or someone taking precedence over her.

Later, she confided in Sanna, and her friend asked if she suspected him of having an affair.

"Nah – Mark's pissed off I'm not willing to succumb to him. I have to trust him when he tells me he loves me."

"Take my advice: don't call. If you've not heard from him by spring, you've got your answer."

"That's easier said and done but you're right. I'm not chasing him. He knows where I am."

Taking classes and sitting exams occupied every minute of the day and when, by April, Hannah still hadn't heard from Mark, she felt certain he was seeing someone else and didn't have the guts to tell her. Swallowing her pride, she decided to find out for herself. Dialling his number, he immediately picked up.

"Why are you ignoring me?" she asked, incapable of holding back her anger towards him.

"I'm not. I was about to call but you beat me to it." Vague and distant, Mark didn't ask how she was or if she'd passed her exams.

"Is there something you're not telling me?"

"Such as?" he snapped in a dismissive tone.

"Aren't you at least a bit interested in my progress? It'll please you to know I've passed with Distinction."

"Why does everything always revolve around you? Your bloody family, your bloody exams! I'm sick and tired of listening to you!" He shouted so loudly she almost put down the phone. She was too shocked to say anything other than ask him to calm down. "Does it occur to you what this is doing to me?" he continued. "To us? I've sat here all alone day in day out wondering if we have a future" His voice was hoarse and Hannah knew it was time to give him a piece of her mind.

"How dare you attack me?" she exploded. "If you gave a damn about us, you'd have cancelled everything to be with me."

"I'm sorry I shouted at you, baby. This isn't your fault. I'm just so bloody lost without you. Please forgive my outburst." Before she had time to reply, he hung up on her.

Over the next few hours she sat staring into space, trying to figure out what was wrong. Why had he asked her to forgive him? Had something terrible happened to his parents? Or at work? Eventually she made the decision to travel to London – it was time she visited her grandmother and made sure Ella was alright. But her parents were outraged she was going.

"He ought to visit you, not the other way round!" Walther exclaimed. Every time he and Zadie enquired about her and Mark, she kept making excuses for him, avoiding looking them in the eyes. Privately, Zadie knew Zipporah and Ella didn't think much of him; even going so far as to suggest that his mother was an anti-Semite.

The evening prior to Hannah's departure, Zadie confessed to Walther how much she worried about their daughter. Lying in bed, arms around each other, she cried, "Something awful's about to happen. I can sense it in here," she gestured to her stomach, "and there's not a thing either of us can do to prevent it; except being here for her when she returns."

Holding her tight, Walther couldn't bear the thought of some-one hurting their little girl.

It felt odd being back. The black cab pulled up in front of the familiar block of flats on a rainy Sunday afternoon in late April. Hannah kept telling herself everything was going to be alright. In another few days she and Mark would be back in each other's arms, making plans for the future.

Excited to see her again, Zipporah let it slip that Melanie and Ben regularly called, enquiring about her health. For fear of starting another argument about Mark, Hannah said nothing, instead asking why her grandmother refused to come and stay with them.

"It's too exhausting to travel these days. I'm simply not as fit as I used to be, my darling." Her eyes seemed to have lost their natural spark.

"You'd let me know if something's wrong, right?"

"I'm getting old, Hannah, that's what's wrong. My time is running out. Poor Katja recently passed away, Tanya's going in the same direction."

"Why didn't you call and let us know? Mamma and I should have been here for you."

"It's as it should be, my darling. I'll be joining them soon. I just wish I have enough time to see you happy and settled first."

"But that will take years – I've a career to pursue!" Hannah said in a cheerful voice, trying to light up the atmosphere.

"You'd better get on with it, then!"

Embracing each other, both had a lot of catching up to do and after a light supper, Hannah decided she was ready for bed. Tossing and turning, all she could think of was what it would feel like to see Mark again. Had she been wrong to not tell him she was coming? What if he got angry with her? Their recent phone conversation echoed in her head – especially his last words.

The next morning Hannah announced it was Ella's turn to spend time with her.

"It'll do her the world of good to have you around," Zipporah said. "Letitia tells me she's quite frail. We keep in touch mainly over the telephone nowadays."

But nothing could prepare Hannah for seeing her dear friend looking so unwell. When Letitia informed her she'd come down with flu over the winter, Ella immediately played it down.

"You mustn't worry about me, my dear. At my time of life it's only normal to feel under the weather. You're very pretty. University clearly agrees with you."

"Oh Ella, I've been worried sick about you. You ought to see a specialist about that cough. Please let me arrange it for you?"

"Absolutely not. You're having a well-deserved break. I'm still alive aren't I? Someone up there must be watching over me." Propped up in bed with her head against the pillows, she added, "Please join me for lunch, my dear. It's so boring eating by myself."

Half an hour later Letitia returned with a tray with cucumber sandwiches, tea and coffee. It almost broke Hannah's heart watching the old lady trying to digest her food between coughing and catching her breath.

"If I'd known you were so ill, I'd have come over a lot sooner."

"That's the reason I forbade Letitia and Margareth to call you. You have to focus on the future – your grandmother agrees with me."

"I wish you were able to travel to Sweden. Granny claims she's not got the energy anymore."

Ella reached for Hannah's hand. "I'm afraid she's right. My travelling days are over too. At our age it's best to stay put. Are you and Mark still an item, my dear?"

"I hope we are. He doesn't know I'm here. It's meant to be a surprise."

"He's lucky to have you, my dear," Ella's voice was decidedly flat.

Apart from Letitia's personal belongings, the old room looked exactly the same.

"I feel terrible forcing you to sleep in the box room," Hannah told Letitia. "Please don't feel obliged to on my account."

"No, this was your room – Ella insists you have it while you are here. It's only for a couple of nights. I'll be fine." The Spanish lady started to clear away some of her dresses and shoes.

It felt strange lying in her old bed listening to the birds on the other side of the window. Suddenly a feeling of despair overwhelmed her. *What if he doesn't want to see me? I'd better make sure I'm not late or he'll be on his way to work.*

Hannah was woken by the aroma of fresh coffee and after a quick shower, she made her bed and got dressed. On her way downstairs, she heard Ella coughing and was determined to persuade her to see a specialist.

"Good morning. Did you have a good night's sleep, my dear?"

"I would have, had I not worried so much about you," Hannah replied, kissing her cheek.

"The doctor said it's the aftermath of the flu." Margareth Dudley looked just as worried. Nibbling on a piece of toast, Ella continued, "Old age, it's such a nuisance, my dears." Hannah's eyes met Margareth's and Letitia's. No matter how hard they tried, Ella simply wasn't having it. She'd had enough of being prodded and poked. All she wanted was peace and quiet in her own home. "Oh, I nearly forgot. Zipporah just called asking me to tell you Ben wants you to get in touch before you leave."

Startled that he continued to pursue her despite being aware of her and Mark's relationship, Hannah's face turned red with embarrassment. Why did he insist they meet up when knowing the score and why did her grandmother encourage him?

As if reading her thoughts, Ella whispered in her ear, "Listen to me, my dear. Your grandmother wants what is best for you. Ben's a nice man; you could do a lot worse."

"Like Mark you mean? Both of you hate him. You've never given him a chance!" Hannah immediately regretted her words.

"You know me better than that, my dear. I never interfere or make a judgement; I merely point out what I feel is true. It's ultimately down to you to make a decision."

"Please forgive me. It's become a habit to defend him – I never meant to upset you."

"You've nothing to apologise for. I've already put it out of my mind." She put her hand on Hannah's, squeezing it as if to say she understood perfectly.

That day and the next, Ella tried her best to stay awake but to no avail. Despite reminiscing about the past, in particular the day Hannah and her mother first came to visit, it was evident how much her health had deteriorated. Before Hannah left, the old lady looked deep into her eyes.

"Promise me you'll not let anyone dictate what's right for you, especially not Mark?"

"I promise. Try not to worry so much about me. I'm a big girl now."

"What if seeing him again doesn't live up to your expectations?"

"We love each other. Everything's going to be alright."

With a worried frown between her eyes, Ella reminded herself of how young Hannah still was – those green eyes lighting up whenever his name was mentioned. "Please call to say goodbye. It's such a treat having you here with me. You and I will always stay in each other's hearts."

Touched by her sentiment, Hannah was too upset to speak. Sensing how she was feeling, Letitia came to her rescue, assisting Ella upstairs to her bedroom.

"Please get on with whatever it is you're doing. She'll be in safe hands. Margareth and I will make sure of it." Letitia held onto the old lady while Hannah embraced and kissed her, promising she would return before the week was up.

By the time she'd put her coat on, brushed her hair and spritzed L'Air Du Temps behind her ears and wrists, it was almost 9am. Getting into the cab waiting outside, Ben's face suddenly appeared before her eyes. Dismissing it in favour of Mark's, she quickly told the driver where they were heading, closed her eyes and started to envisage what it would be like to see and make love to him again. When, half an hour later, they pulled up outside his house, she almost asked the cabbie to turn around. Fiddling with the contents in her bag, she applied another coat of lip-gloss and told the driver he needn't wait for her since she'd seen Mark's car in the open garage.

"I'll wait until you're safely inside, Miss. It won't cost you." He'd witnessed too many girls chucked out onto the street by their boyfriends.

"As you wish, but I really don't think it's necessary."

Getting out of the cab, she walked slowly up the path to the front door, wondering why the curtains were still drawn in the bedroom upstairs at almost 9:30am. Was it his day off? She rang the doorbell. Hearing muffled voices coming from inside, she wondered if he had visitors. The sound of footsteps sent butterflies to the pit of her stomach, and she took a deep breath to relax. She heard the rustling of keys, the door opened wide and there he was: the man she loved – dishevelled, unshaven and pale as a sheet.

"What are you doing here?" Mark hissed, attempting to close the door.

"You look as if you've seen a ghost. I thought you'd be pleased to see me—" She gasped as he shut the door in her face. Hannah banged on it with her fists until he had no other option but to open and leave it slightly ajar, or she'd wake up the entire street.

"What the hell's wrong with you? You should have told me you were planning on visiting." He looked angry and scared – as if he had something to hide.

"One of us had to make the effort."

Standing there frozen to the spot, he didn't even attempt to let her in. Her instincts were screaming "leave" but her heart was unwilling.

"What's the matter? Please let me in. I'm freezing," she pleaded, the steady drizzle of rain and dampness making her tremble. Catching a glimpse of the stairs, she tried to get in but he immediately blocked her.

"Why aren't you dressed?" she stammered. This wasn't like him. He'd never been this cruel and horrible. What the hell was wrong with him? Except for an old pair of pyjama bottoms, Mark was naked, his frightened expression convincing her something terrible had happened. What if someone had died? That would explain his strange behaviour.

"I can't let you in. I'll call you – you're staying with your grandmother, right? Please leave immediately."

"Don't be ridiculous. It's not as if I've never seen you naked before, is it?" Why was he so hell-bent on getting rid of her? The two of them should be in his bedroom, making mad passionate love. Instead he just stood there, rooted to the spot and refusing to let her in.

"Why are you treating me this way? Answer me!" Trying to push the door open, she somehow succeeded in getting a full view.

There it was: the answer she'd been dreading. Standing at the top of the stairs watching them was a tall blonde wearing a transparent top barely covering her upper body – it didn't take long to figure out she was at least six months pregnant. Sick to her stomach, Hannah heard her yell, "Who's that? Tell them to get lost. It's your day off for Christ's sake. I miss your body next to mine, babe."

Putting his hand up, Mark sheepishly replied, "Go back to sleep. I won't be long." He turned to look at Hannah and shrugged. "I'm sorry you had a wasted trip. It wasn't supposed to end like this."

Feeling a wave of nausea overwhelming her, Hannah forced herself to not lash out at him. "At least now I know the reason you stopped calling . . ." Then, as the full impact of what he'd done started to register, she cried, "Why? I thought you loved me. I trusted you!"

"I do. I always will. You must believe me." He reached for her hands but she pulled away from him.

"Please say something – anything!" His voice was full of remorse.

"It's her, isn't it? Petra?" She sobbed, tears blurring her vision. Nodding, Mark avoided looking into her eyes. "Your mother was right all along. Who'd have believed it?"

"You abandoned me. I was lonely. One thing led to another."

Consumed with pain, Hannah felt as if she was drowning. It was over. He may as well have put a knife in her heart.

"I never want to see you again," she cried, wishing she had a tissue to wipe the snot running from her nose.

"It was an accident – she tricked me – I'm trapped!" He sounded like an adolescent.

"My heart bleeds for you. I bet your mother's pleased. You've played straight into her hands!" As she turned to walk back to the waiting cab, she heard him say the words she dreaded the most.

"A few weeks ago Petra and I tied the knot."

"You idiot! I hope the two of you rot in hell!" She slapped his face so hard he winced in pain. "That's for betraying my trust in you!"

Touching his cheek, Mark whispered, "My mother demanded I did what's right because of the baby. Why did you have to leave me?"

"You bastard. Don't you dare pin this on me." Her green eyes blazed at him.

"Say you'll forgive me – please!"

"Never. Hell will freeze over first."

Terrified she'd disappear from his life, Mark started to plead with her. "Petra knows I don't love her. I've made such a mess of my life. Please say you'll give me another chance. You're all I want. I'll divorce her as soon as the baby is born."

"You disgust me. I can't imagine ever having loved someone as pathetic as you!" She walked away without so much as a backward glance. If only she didn't hurt so much on the inside.

Defeated, Mark watched as Hannah get inside the cab and out of his life. Dragging his feet upstairs to his pregnant wife, he kept envisaging the empty years ahead of him. Through his own stupidity, he'd entered a prison sentence without parole – most of all he'd lost the woman he loved.

Pretending he hadn't eavesdropped on them, the cabbie thought she'd had a lucky escape. His kid sister was around the same age – if anything like that ever happened to her, he'd kill the guy. Clenching his fingers around the steering wheel, he thought it was best to keep a low profile.

"Thanks for waiting for me. I'd have been lost without you." Hannah started getting out. Paying him, she added a big tip.

"I couldn't possibly, Miss, not after everything you've been through. Don't forget, there's plenty more fish in the sea. Take good care of yourself. That guy's not worth crying over!"

It was lunchtime. Only another five days before her departure. He'd broken her heart, now all she had to look forward to was her career. Wiping her eyes with the back of her sleeve, she stepped into the lift, thanking God she had the flat to herself. Zipporah was spending the day at Tanya's a few blocks away. Entering the silent apartment, Hannah immediately went into the bathroom to remove her smudged make-up. As she glimpsed her reflection in the mirror above the sink, she started to cry; a deep guttural noise making her shake all over.

Get a grip on yourself! Your parents mustn't find out about this.

Blotchy from crying so much, she accidentally bit her lip until it bled. Too distraught to give a damn, she went into the bedroom, undressed and threw herself on the bed. Just as she was beginning to drift off to sleep, she heard a familiar voice whisper, "Just as well I decided to trust my intuition and come home. It's Mark, isn't it? He's finally shown his true colours." Her grandmother was standing there, watching her. Incapable of keeping it to herself, Hannah told her everything.

"They're having a baby!" she cried.

"The swine!" Zipporah's hand shot up to cover her mouth. "No wonder Ella and I never trusted him." Placing her arms around her beloved granddaughter, she started to rock her. "Shh. It's better you found out before – God forbid – you married him. I hope he rots in hell." She bent to kiss Hannah's forehead. "You'll get over him. I'll do whatever it takes to comfort you." She helped tuck Hannah into bed, then left, leaving the door slightly ajar.

The next few days passed in a haze. Zipporah tried to entice her granddaughter out of her bedroom with her favourite dishes. Then a couple of nights before Hannah was due to leave, the phone rang. Answering it, she heard Ben's voice and quickly told him she was on her way out. Too anxious to talk to him, she hung up and ran into the bedroom, barely having touched the bowl of soup in the kitchen. Ten minutes later her grandmother knocked on the door, urging her to finish her supper.

"Ben's such a nice man. I told him you're feeling under the weather, why don't you give him a call later? He's got your best interests at heart."

"Does he know about me and Mark?"

"Of course not. I've only confided in Ella. She agrees with me. That man's a monster. She asked me to send you her love."

"Please don't say a word to Mamma and Pappa. I can't bear the thought of everyone pitying me."

"It'll be our little secret. How about you making that call to Ben?"

"There's not much point. Who's to say history won't repeat itself? He's better off without me." Hannah cut a pathetic figure, wearing no make-up, her eyes swollen from all the crying. Zipporah noticed she'd lost weight.

"Ben's nothing like Mark. That man cares deeply about you." But Hannah wasn't paying attention to what she said – as far as she was concerned, men were off the agenda. "Listen to me, young lady!" Zipporah persisted. "We've all been where you are right now. Life's not a bowl of cherries. Take your mother and me: I lost my husband, she her father. We somehow found the strength to move on. You will too! Life's too damn short to waste on the likes of Mark Copeck. The world's your oyster, my darling."

Listening to her grandmother's well-worn clichés, Hannah started to smile. "I hear you. Deep down I always knew Mark wasn't right for me."

Kissing her cheek, Zipporah replied, "It's easy for me to say but time really does heal everything."

"After the amount of 'Jewish penicillin' you've been feeding me, I'll be resistant to antibiotics for the rest of my life!" Hannah joked.

"Mark is going to regret what he did to you, whereas you, my darling, will find happiness with someone who truly loves you."

"Oh Granny, what would I do without you?"

"I've never heard such nonsense. You, me and your mother don't 'cope' – we're born to survive!"

Debating her words, Hannah came to a decision. "I'll do it. I'll call him. Ben's always there for me. He has a gift for making me feel special."

"Good girl! Do it now. There's no time like the present." Zipporah felt extremely pleased with herself.

The sound of her voice made his heart soar. Biting the bullet, Hannah decided to tell him about Mark. "We're finished. He's married with a baby on the way." It felt such a relief to get it off her chest.

"That's a hell of a blow – how are you feeling?" His voice was warm and compassionate. Mark was a shit; Ben wanted to wring his neck.

"Bruised but not broken." Her voice trembled as she tried to hold it together and not weep.

"It's probably best we take a rain check. Next time you're in London." There was no mistaking the disappointment in his voice.

"Absolutely not! Why don't you and Melanie pop round tomorrow night at 6pm? Granny's visiting Tanya."

"Mel's in Brighton. I'm afraid you're stuck with me."

"That's alright. Please do me a favour? Tell Melanie what's happened. I'd hate for her to say, 'I told you so'."

"Consider it done. I'm sorry he didn't live up to your expectations, little one."

"Thanks for being so understanding. See you tomorrow."

Ben wished he could have told her how much he cared. Instead he started to count the hours, minutes and seconds until the following night.

Ignoring their worried faces, Ella immediately expressed how much she loathed Mark.

"He's lucky neither I nor your grandmother were present or we'd have given him a piece of our mind!" Her kind eyes were dark with anger.

"Ben's coming over tomorrow night. That's something to look forward to," Zipporah replied, blinking at her friend.

"That's wonderful, my dear! He's just the tonic you need."

Blushing, Hannah quickly changed the subject. Watching the two women she loved, she couldn't help wondering how she'd cope when her 'two grannies' were gone. Reminiscing about the past over tea and biscuits, all too soon it was time to leave. Reminding Letitia and Margareth to take special care of her friend, Hannah gazed at the elderly lady sitting at the small kitchen table where they'd confided in each other, Ella's words of wisdom imprinted in her heart.

"Promise you'll remember me like I was when we first met. Always live in the present. Only look back when you need reminding of special moments, my dear." Margareth helped Ella walk to the front door so she could say a final goodbye to Hannah. This was it. The moment she'd been dreading. Bending to kiss her friend's cheek, Hannah felt tears sting her eyes.

"I love you very much. Thank you for everything you've done for me. I'll never forget it." Raising a hand to her mouth, Ella blew her a farewell kiss.

"May all you wish for come true. God bless you, my dear." She watched the girl she viewed as her own flesh and blood walk out the door and into the cab waiting outside.

"Are we set to go, ladies?" the cabbie asked, before driving off. For fear of crying, both bowed their heads. Grabbing her grandmother's hand, Hannah began to sob.

"I'll never see her again. Promise you won't leave me as well!"

Putting her arms around her, Zipporah replied, "I'm not going anywhere until you've met the man of your dreams, my darling."

"It's wonderful seeing you, little one," were Ben's first words as he walked in the door, kissed her cheek and handed her a bouquet of red roses. The scent of his aftershave, his big brown eyes and his smile immediately put her at ease. Watching her, Ben wanted to kill Mark for causing her such pain. She'd lost at least a stone, her clothes hung on her like a sack and her eyes were the saddest he'd ever seen them.

"You're looking very smart in that suit. I'm sorry I've not made an effort to look my best." Truthfully, Hannah felt slightly intimidated by his appearance.

"You're always beautiful to me, Hannah — these things take time to heal." His voice was full of compassion, almost to the point of making her burst into tears. As he followed her into the living room, she told him she'd make them tea.

"You must be starving after a day's work – how about a slice of Granny's cake?"

"Sounds great to me." She looked so miserable, he wished he could tell her how much he loved her but decided against it and instead looked out the window leading onto the park below. Suddenly, unable to contain himself, he turned around.

"You've no idea how much I've missed you."

"The feeling's mutual. The past week's been hellish. First that incident with Mark, then having to part from Ella . . ." Her eyes were brimming with tears.

"Is she really that ill? People like her and Zipporah are few and far between." Ben looked as upset as Hannah felt.

"She'll be gone soon." She tried to blink away the tears.

"And you're so close . . . Come here." He walked up to her, gently touching the contours of her face. "You're special through and through. Don't waste tears on someone like Mark Copeck." He gazed into her eyes.

Hannah wished she could have told him how much his presence meant to her but the words somehow stuck in her throat as images of Mark and Petra flooded her thoughts.

Later, seated next to one another at the dining room table, Ben asked if she planned to stay in Sweden.

"Maybe . . . apart from Ella and Granny, London's not as appealing as it used to be." She sounded so miserable, he tried to cheer her up.

"When one door shuts, another opens wide."

"That's true. After graduating I'll have a brand new career to look forward to." But as much as she loved the prospect of it, she didn't sound too convinced.

"Well, I'd better leave. I have an early call in the morning. Thanks for having me. Give Zipporah my love and tell her I'll be checking up on her." Ben stood up and helped her clear the table.

"There's no need. I'll see to it later. Thanks for the roses, they're my favourite flowers." Standing on her toes, she coyly kissed his cheek.

"Mmm – you smell good! Correct me if I'm mistaken, but isn't that L'air Du Temps?"

"Spot on. And your's Pour Homme, right? It suits you."

Their faces brushed making it almost impossible for him to not kiss her.

"Some things never change," Ben whispered in a husky voice, quickly disentangling himself before doing something he'd regret.

"Promise you'll stay in touch. I'm always here for you."

"You're too kind. Say hello to Mel for me."

"Don't forget how much you mean to me, little one." His brown eyes lingered on her as he picked up his briefcase and let himself out.

Closing the door behind him, Hannah ran into the kitchen, hoping to catch a glimpse of him from the window. As if by magic, Ben turned to look at her, blew her a kiss and vanished into the darkness of the night.

Cleaning the table in the living room, Hannah's eyes fell on a small parcel on the mantelpiece with her name on it. Unable to contain her excitement, she quickly unwrapped it and gasped. Inside was a tiny black box containing the most exquisite heart-shaped crystal pendant she'd ever seen. Turning it around, the inscription read:

My heart's yours – all my love, Ben

He must have left it there when she was in the kitchen getting tea ready. Eager to thank him, she decided it was best to drop him a line. Staring at the beautiful piece of jewellery in the palm of her hand made her tingle all over.

Lost in thought and oblivious to everything else, Hannah didn't stir when her grandmother entered the room and peered over her shoulder.

"My God, the man worships the ground you walk on," Zipporah said. "I'm thrilled for you both." Smiling through her tears, Hannah embraced her grandmother.

"It's the sweetest, prettiest gift anybody's bestowed me. What I don't understand is why he didn't just give it to me. Why all the secrecy?"

"Can't you tell? Ben's not the type of man who likes making a grand gesture. He wants you to know how he feels about you without the added pressure of your having to commit to him."

"That's true. Ben knows what I've been through."

"Compared to Mark, he'll never cause you pain; that's something worth remembering, my darling."

The next morning as she prepared to leave, Hannah almost wished she could have stayed longer. "Do come downstairs and wave me off," she pleaded.

Shaking her head, trying to hide the tears in her eyes, Zipporah insisted they get it over and done with.

"There have been too many goodbyes lately. I want you to do something for me, Hannah. Promise you'll let that remarkable man into your life – and heart." Their eyes met as Hannah slowly bowed her head.

When the pre-booked cab pulled out of the parking lot, she turned to wave at her grandmother, who was watching her from the kitchen window. Ben was right. Some things never changed. Touching the crystal on the chain around her neck, she suddenly looked forward to the future.

CHAPTER TWELVE

ACCEPTING SHE AND Mark were a figment of the past was difficult enough without her brother announcing he and Lena had become engaged.

"It'll be your turn next, sis. Mamma and Pappa want you to join them in Lugano come July. Why don't you change your mind and say yes?" Peter put his arm around her. He could tell she still cared about that jerk. "You're letting him get to you, sis. Lugano's at its most stunning in the summer. Think of all the fun we used to have when we were kids . . ."

"It's useless trying to persuade me to forget him; he's the first thing I think of when I wake up and the last before I go to sleep."

"Hey, do you remember when we beat those Germans at their own game?" Peter was determined not to let his sister wallow in her misery. "They were so desperate to get the best spot in the sun, they'd put towels on the deck chairs at 6am in the morning! I'll never forget the look on their faces." He laughed, shaking his head.

"I know you're trying to cheer me up and it's working, really it is. It's high time I stopped dwelling in self-pity." She kissed his cheek, forcing a smile.

"Good girl! Just wait until I tell our parents – they'll be over the moon. I'll take you to the airport myself."

Catching a flight to Zurich and connection to Lugano in the Italian part of Switzerland bordering on Milan, Hannah, Zadie and Walther arrived on a hot day at the family owned Hotel du Lac. The owner greeted them personally, treating them like old friends as he showed them to their adjacent rooms on the first floor. Setting down baskets of fruit on both balconies, he told them it was a pleasure seeing them again. There were truffles and champagne in the fridge and the view from the window was spectacular; the sea the bluest shade imaginable, matching the sky above them.

"I strongly recommend you unpack, spend a few hours by the pool prior to a siesta. Once you are thoroughly refreshed, I look forward to welcoming you for drinks in the restaurant." The owner put their suitcases by the bed, wished them a pleasant stay, bowed and left.

"That man's hardly changed, just as charming as ever. Where's my Ambre Solaire? It's at least 30°C in here!" Zadie kicked her shoes off and poured them each a glass of champagne.

Sunbathing, relaxing in the piazza and visiting the daily market took up most of their time. Some nights were spent at the restaurant of the hotel where the owner and his elegant wife sometimes joined them, reminding them of previous holidays and serving up one delicious dish after another. Zadie and Walther would persuade Hannah to join them for a nightcap in the piano bar where, seated by herself clutching the crystal heart around her neck, she'd idly watch her parents dancing to evergreens by the likes of Frank Sinatra and Charles Aznavour, totally oblivious of the male guests' admiring glances.

Making an effort to be on her best behaviour, she couldn't help thinking about Mark, wondering how his life had mapped out with Petra and their baby, and if he had any regrets. Her parents looked so relaxed and happy in each other's arms, with her mother effortlessly stunning in a halter-neck Pucci dress and her father in a smart suit. "I wish I could meet someone as loyal as him," Hannah was thinking, just as her mother went up to her and placed her hand on her cheek.

"We're concerned about you, sweetheart. You're much too pretty and young to waste your life crying over that man."

"You know how you keep telling me that time's a great healer?" Hannah asked, feeling miserable. "I must be the exception to the rule."

"I wish there was something your mother and I could do to cheer you up," Walther said, joining them at the table. "Mark's an idiot for betraying you like that." Her father wished the sorry excuse for a man had never entered his little girl's life.

The holiday passed all too quickly and soon it was time to leave. Everyone agreed they'd had a wonderful time and vowed to repeat it in the not too distant future.

Focusing on her degree, Hannah finally managed to push Mark out of her mind. When her tutor suggested she start practising in a school for children with learning difficulties, she jumped at the chance.

"That's the main reason I want to teach!" she exclaimed.

"I've never met anyone as intuitive as you," her tutor replied. "The way you connect with individual pupils is remarkable. I'm certain the owner will agree with me."

As the years passed, Rosie opened two successful florist's shops in Glasgow and was planning to open a third in the centre of

Edinburgh. The three friends had managed to snatch a rare weekend together in Copenhagen, which was easily accessible from Malmö, Stockholm and Edinburgh, and were catching up on all their news.

Sanna and Rosie were upset that Hannah had kept Mark's betrayal from them. They had found out from Zipporah, with whom they kept in regular contact.

"We should have been there for you," Sanna accused her. "It's what friends are for."

Hannah shrugged. "I spend most of my working time supporting people with all kinds of problems."

"Why is it you always have to bottle things up? This is the perfect opportunity to get in contact with Ben so you can finish what you started," Rosie reminded her.

"Stop interfering in my life! I never do that to you." She knew they had her best interests at heart but wished they'd back off.

The last time she and Ben had been in contact was when she dropped him a line thanking him for the crystal heart, so she was astonished to receive a letter revealing his plans to visit Sweden. Mentioning it to her friends, both agreed he was visiting because of her.

"The guy's madly in love with you," Rosie said. "Just think how pleased your grandmother will be to see you ending up getting married!"

"Are you mad? I just came out of one disastrous relationship and you're seriously expecting me to embark on another?"

"That's not fair! Ben's the opposite of Mark. He'd never hurt you." She wanted to kill Mark for turning her friend into such a cynic.

Rosie was currently involved with a sexy Frenchman, slightly older than herself. Marcel was everything she wanted and she wished her friend could be just as happy. "It's only a physical thing. Marriage is not on the cards for us," she informed her friends in a casual way.

"Bullshit! He's lasted longer than all of them put together." Sanna wasn't fooled by Rosie's attitude; certain Marcel was 'the one'. She was simply too scared to admit someone meant anything more than a casual fling.

"Not everyone has the urge to procreate!"

"You're wrong. Most women I know love the thought of settling down. Roger and I are both only children with single mothers," Sanna said of her latest boyfriend. "It won't deter us in the least. We're planning to get a place of our own in a suburb of Stockholm – the Archipelago is much too expensive, as soon as we get our qualifications." Even Sanna's own stubborn, independent mother reluctantly admitted they were perfectly suited.

"Whatever rocks your boat. Can't we at least plan a trip to London?" Rosie asked. "I miss the old haunts. What about in the spring?"

"Sounds great, but not until we pass our exams." Hannah and Sanna envied Rosie her freedom to do as she pleased and now it looked as if it would be quite some time before the three would meet again.

Shortly before graduating, Hannah's worst fears materialised when one night at the end of November, Letitia called from England. It fell to Walther to tell his daughter that Ella had passed away. Fully aware it had only been a matter of time, Hannah felt the room spin around her regardless.

"Was she in pain? Oh, why did I leave her? Perhaps I could have prevented it!" she cried, incapable of accepting the terrible news her dear friend was gone. "I'd better start packing and book a flight." She leapt from her bed, frantically rummaging through the wardrobe for a suitcase. Reaching out to her gently, Walther told her Letitia assured him Ella went peacefully in her sleep. "That daughter of hers doesn't care! Someone has to ensure she gets a decent funeral."

"Which is exactly what Letitia and Margareth are there for, Hannah. Between them they have everything under control." He pleaded with her, insisting she and her friends visit her grave when they went to London. Refusing to take any notice of him, Hannah was about to respond when her mother entered the room, her eyes the saddest either of them ever saw. Seating herself on the edge of the bed, she let out a sigh.

"Poor Mother. All her friends are gone now," she said, referring to Tanya's passing, which had occurred soon after Katja's. I wish she'd reconsider and come and live with us. We'll organise condolences to poor Ella's family. It's the least we can do after everything she did for you. Everyone knows how close you were – try to get some sleep sweetie. Tomorrow's another day."

They took turns to kiss her goodnight, turned the light off and left. But the minute the door closed behind them, Hannah pulled out Ella's last letter from the chest of drawers by the window. Taking in the neat, familiar handwriting, her eyes welled up as she started to read her old friend's words to her.

My dear precious girl,

We will never see one another again. I've had a good life filled with love and happy memories. Please try to remember me as I was, in particular when we first met in the summer of 1978. You've turned into such a remarkable young lady. My biggest wish is that you find someone who makes your heart sing with joy. Always stay true to yourself.

I am watching over you. With all my love now and forever.
Ella.

She must have read it a dozen times. By the time she drifted off to sleep, a new day had begun – the first of numerous without her friend.

Just before Christmas in 1983, Hannah celebrated her graduation at The Savoy in Malmö. The only people absent were Zipporah, Sanna and Rosie. The former had insisted she was too old and frail to travel but sent her best wishes along with a cheque to do with as Hannah wished. Her friends were sorry they couldn't attend since both had pre-arranged commitments. Rosie organised a huge bouquet of flowers to be delivered to the house in Limhamn. But the thing that touched Hannah the most was the beautiful card she received from Ben, expressing how proud he was of her achievement. Since she had never mentioned it to him, Hannah knew Zipporah must have told him the date. It endeared her to think they were still in touch. Putting his card next to Ella's letter, her heart fluttered every time she read it.

"All I have to do now is get myself a job," she declared, raising her glass in a toast to her family.

"You deserve a break first, sis! Aren't you and the girls going to London?" Peter asked, his arm around Lena's shoulders.

"We're planning to stay at The Marriott in Swiss Cottage. In the late 1970s Sanna and I bumped into the tennis player Björn Borg right there. I'll have you know he was charming. We'll figure out a suitable time for all of us. We've all got such busy schedules."

"What about the interview at the school you practised at?" Lena enquired.

"Oh yes, the headmistress, Mary Ohlsson, is quite a character. Extremely protective of the pupils and very demanding."

"Just up your street then – the two of you will get on like a house on fire!" Peter joked, making a toast to her future success.

On leaving their elegant surroundings, Hannah and Peter walked behind the others to the car.

"Who's Ben Isaacs? Granny can't stop talking about him."

"Oh, he's just an old friend someone introduced me to years ago," she replied, blushing.

"I see. A friend with an expensive taste in jewellery no doubt? You love wearing that crystal don't you, sis? Care to enlighten me?" Truthfully, Peter was pleased she'd met someone, especially after everything Mark put her through. But to his dismay she gave him a dark look.

"That's my private business; nothing to do with you!" She stomped off, making him even more determined to find out why she had reacted like she did.

"I'm sorry I asked. You'd think there's something to hide," he muttered to himself. "I'll keep a low profile then pounce on her when the time's right."

Hannah's interview with Mary Ohlsson was nearly cancelled due to severe weather conditions affecting Malmö and Limhamn that week. Arriving at the small office on the ground floor twenty minutes late, Hannah immediately apologised to the tall, formidable woman with short grey hair, piercing blue eyes and a tweed suit, correctly assuming her prospective employer was in her late fifties.

"All buses were cancelled due to the snow and sleet," she apologised. "I was lucky my father offered to drive me or I'd not have made it at all." Conscious of her somewhat scruffy appearance and wet hair, she prayed Mary didn't notice how nervous she was.

"I'm surprised you made it at all. It must be pretty treacherous out there. Mankind can solve most things but the weather is one of the few things we cannot control." Her eyes scrutinised the young girl as she reached for her cigarettes. As she lit one, Hannah began to cough and sensing her discomfort, Mary pushed aside a pile of papers on her desk. "Please excuse my lack of manners – old habits die hard." Opening a window behind her, Mary immediately shut it, so as to avoid the draught entering the room. "You seemed to enjoy studying here," she continued. "Let me get straight to the point Miss Stein: you're the best candidate this school's ever had. I'd go so far as to say you remind me of myself at the same age; same determination and self-discipline."

Flattered by the comment, Hannah felt embarrassed.

"This place requires someone as skilled as you are. I've devoted my life to its existence, the aim being exactly as it always was: to help in the development of each pupil irrelevant of circumstances and background. We are currently in receipt of grants and private donations, the rest is down to me." Mary's tone was modest, but she was acutely conscious of the sacrifices and responsibilities she endured to keep her school afloat. Forgetting her visitor's aversion to smoke, she lit another cigarette.

"I'm offering you the job of Head Teacher/Supervisor of the three–six-year group. Please feel free to reacquaint yourself with the premises before you leave. I expect you here at 8am next Monday. By the way, I can't be bothered with formality; everyone's referred to by their first name. Welcome on board Budding Stars!"

Uncertain as to whether she'd heard correctly, Hannah said, "You are offering me a position I have no experience of. What'll happen if I can't live up to your expectations?"

Smiling at her, Mary removed her glasses. "Why don't you let me be the judge of that?"

"I don't know what to say except how grateful I am to you," Hannah stammered. Overwhelmed by the other woman's faith in her, she slowly raised herself from the chair.

"I do believe you and I will have a very special working relationship. I'll see you again soon." Mary returned to the task at hand, answering the phone, her deep voice echoing down the corridor. Hannah took her cue to leave and strolled through the two-storey purpose built school with its high ceilings and creaky floorboards, exiting via the back entrance.

I always dreamed of working in a school designed to suit every child and that's exactly what I'll do! she thought, barely able to contain her glee.

Quite contrary to her fear of not measuring up, Hannah realised she was born to teach and the staff, pupils and parents seemed to agree, instantly warming to her kind, caring personality.

By March, Mary declared she was appointing her as Supervisor for the entire school. With her trademark cigarette dangling from her lip, she awaited Hannah's response impatiently.

"What will it be? A yes or no is all I need!" she barked.

"And you're quite sure I don't need more time to prove myself?" Hannah asked in a worried voice. "What happens if my colleagues start resenting me?"

"Nonsense! Just like me they're fully aware of how special you are — a cut above the rest."

"What makes you so sure? You've not seen me in action."

"I really shouldn't be telling you this but you're bound to find out. Every time a new pupil or teacher enters the premises, I have cameras surveying them from the ceiling." She laughed at Hannah's shocked reaction.

"That explains why I felt as if I was being watched! At least now I know I wasn't being paranoid."

"For someone as talented as you are, you sure as hell lack in the confidence department. So what'll it be? A yes or no, you're not going anywhere until I know."

"Of course it's a yes! How can I possibly refuse?"

"Good. Didn't I tell you we'd make a great team?" Hannah detected emotion in Mary's voice, something she usually saved for the children. "From now on I demand you start taking pride in all that you achieve, is that clear? And Hannah, just so you know, those cameras were removed after your first day. Usually they're up for at least a couple of weeks."

That evening over dinner, Zadie enquired why she looked so pleased.

"Mary's promoted me to Supervisor for the entire school! Isn't it great?"

Nodding, Zadie and Walther exchanged a worried glance, the latter weighing his words when replying, "We're extremely proud of you, darling."

"How come I detect a 'but'?"

"Your father and I are concerned you'll devote yourself entirely to that school, sweetie. Do you recall what I told you?"

"But I've plenty of time for *that*!" Hannah shouted, anger bubbling up inside her.

"Of course you have. As long as you don't leave it too late." Seeing the look in her daughter's eyes, Zadie wished she'd kept her thoughts to herself.

"You're seriously expecting me to give up on everything I've worked so hard for? For what? To be someone's unpaid wife?" The words tumbled out of her mouth before she had time to think. Seeing her mother's face turn pale, Hannah got up from her chair, asking her forgiveness.

"You know how much we love and respect you," she whispered, utterly ashamed.

"There's nothing to forgive," Zadie sighed. "Your father and I are aware of how much Budding Stars means to you, sweetheart."

The next few years went by so quickly that it wasn't until autumn 1988 when the three friends finally found time to plan a trip to London. Booking a large room at The Marriott, they arranged to meet at Ranch House on a late Saturday afternoon in October, each one arriving from a different city. Hannah was the last to walk in the room.

"You look great, I love your long hair! And those boots are to die for," Sanna gushed as the three of them embraced. Watching them, Hannah thought Sanna was like a rock chick in a tight skirt and heels. But it was Rosie who had changed the most; looking very smart in a blue jacket with shoulder pads, black jeans and fringe framing her sapphire blue eyes.

"I'm dying to revisit our old haunts!" she said. She'd recently branched out with her third florist's shop in Edinburgh and was cohabiting with her French lover, Marcel. "Don't you dare nag me about why we're not married," she warned them. But her friends' expressions spoke volumes.

"It's so rewarding to work in rehab, it's my favourite part of the job," Sanna told them.

"Rather you than me, honey. I can't think of anything more depressing!"

"My life's just as wonderful as I'd hoped what with landing myself a great guy and the job I always dreamed of."

"Good for you. Roger and I have our little house close to Stockholm and . . . we're trying for a baby! I'm sorry you couldn't be part of our wedding. We simply couldn't afford a proper do. Are you still upset with me?" Sanna asked nervously.

"You bet! We're your best friends and you excluded us from the most important day of your life!" Rosie's mouth twitched, belying her feigned anger. "Seriously though, Hannah and I couldn't be happier for you. You always wanted a low-key affair." She had arranged for a beautiful flower arrangement to be delivered from herself and Hannah.

"Speaking of which, how come you and Ben never got it together?"

"Don't be silly!" Hannah said. "I've plenty to keep me busy, I'm sure he has too." But she didn't sound convincing. It was blatantly obvious Mark's betrayal still prayed on her mind, preventing her from moving on.

Sanna was about to respond when a familiar voice interrupted her.

"Hello strangers! It's been ages since you graced this place with your presence." Aziza had hardly changed at all; except for a slightly fuller figure, she looked exactly the same. "I've missed you guys so much! This place is not the same without you." She hugged them so tight they had to catch their breath. "We count ourselves lucky if the odd customer walks in the door these days." Running a manicured hand through her dark hair, she let out a deep sigh.

"This place was always packed at the weekend," Rosie said, noticing for the first time the empty tables around them.

"I keep telling the owner he has to sell up before he's forced out by some trendy coffee place. Time spent lingering over a club sandwich is a thing of the past."

"But the food's great!" Sanna stole a couple of fries from Hannah's plate. They'd ordered their usual tuna and club sandwiches with coleslaw and milkshakes.

"I take it you're not on one of those diets then? I'm pleased some things stayed the same." Aziza's eyes were moist with tears.

"Who cares? Roger loves me just as I am!"

"Then neither of you will mind your eating for two when you're up the duff?" Rosie teased but no one laughed. This was 'their place' and it would soon be gone.

"I've accepted my partner's proposal of marriage," Aziza announced. "Take my advice, girls. It was great while it lasted but it's time to move on. I'm so happy I got to see you again!" She gave each of them a hug.

"But we're not off yet! Let's at least have the bill," Hannah cried, convinced they'd never meet again.

"It's my treat!" Aziza blinked, hoping they'd not notice the tears in her eyes. She blew them a kiss and left.

"I guess that's her gone forever – let's take a look at the neighbourhood, it used to be our 'home from home'. We'll ask to leave the cases behind the till," Rosie suggested, looking as upset as they all felt.

Strolling through the busy streets, it was evident most of the places they used to frequent were gone, turned into either a wine bar or part of a chain of coffee shops.

"I don't know about you but I've had enough of this," Rosie said. "Except for Lindy's, Bar Linda and Water Margin, I kind of feel out of place." The others nodded their agreement as they passed by the restaurant to pick up their bags and headed back to their hotel.

They were in the process of unpacking when Rosie announced she wanted to go to The Purple Pussycat.

"I hope it's not facing the same fate as Ranch House," she muttered.

"Well, there's only one way to find out," Hannah replied, all of them changing into their favourite Saturday night outfits, with big hair, glamorous make-up and jackets with shoulder pads. Catching a bus outside the hotel, it wasn't long before they entered the small cul-de-sac where their hopes of reliving the late 1970s were dashed. Instead of the usual crowd queuing to enter, there were just a few people lingering outside.

"Have we missed something? Perhaps it's a Bank Holiday?" Rosie in particular was so upset, she wanted to return to their hotel, but the others suggested they should stay for a drink. Inside it was even worse than expected, with the walls and floor badly in need of restoration.

But standing behind the bar wearing his trademark black jeans and his trademark *At Your Disposal* t-shirt, was their old friend Ricky.

"You're a sight for sore eyes! Where did you spring from?" he asked, giving each of them a bear hug. "What'll it be? Let me guess. Bacardi and coke, splash of lemon, no ice for Hannah; gin and tonic for Sanna; and vodka on the rocks for Rosie, right?" Before they had a chance to respond, he had returned with their drinks and a bottle of champagne. "This is cause for celebrating! Please join me later for dinner at The Metropolis."

Struggling to find the right words Rosie asked what was on all their minds. "What's going on, Ricky? First Ranch House, now you."

Pouring them all a glass of champagne, he gulped his in no time.

"It's no use pulling the wool over your eyes is it? Not so long ago we had to turn the punters away. Well, those days are gone. If things don't start to improve, I'll have to declare myself bankrupt."

"Are things as bad as that?" Hannah dared to ask, feeling sad.

"Yup. And a lot worse. Wine bars are all the rave these days. Can you seriously imagine this place turned into something 'middle of the road' like that? I thank God I had the sense to invest in The Metropolis. We're thinking of expanding."

Relieved he had something to fall back on, Rosie asked the other question they dreaded the answer to. "What's happened to Great Expectations?" Seeing his reaction, she regretted asking.

"I'd give it a miss if I were you. Someone turned it into some members club." His voice was flat.

"Is it really as depressing as that?" Sanna dabbed at her eyes.

"Much worse. Let's face it, the good old days are well and truly gone!"

"But we used to have such fun at that place! I'll never forget the night Rosie and John won that dance competition . . ."

In less than one day they'd discovered their favourite haunts were either gone or about to vanish. It was after midnight and nobody had entered since they arrived.

"Have you decided to join me across the street later?" Ricky repeated his offer. But there was no shaking their gloom.

"Please don't get upset but I think I speak for all of us when I say we're pretty tired. Perhaps next time." Rosie saw the thinly disguised disappointment in his eyes.

"I'm sorry you've had one disappointment after another. Next time you're over, let me know in advance and I'll pick you up from the airport. Remember you'll always be my favourite pussy-cats!" He gave each of them another bear hug and abruptly walked away before they saw the look of despair in his eyes. The club was his life's work. It broke their hearts that it too was yet another casualty of the recession.

The following morning, assuming it would cheer her grand-mother up, Hannah decided to book a table at Cosmo. As soon as they saw her, however, it was painfully obvious Zipporah wasn't up to it. Her plain grey dress hung on her, feet stuck in ugly san-dals instead of her usual elegant shoes. Her hair was limp and she wasn't wearing any make-up. Worst of all, the sparkle was gone from her eyes.

"I'm so pleased to see you!" Despite her appearance, Zipporah always issued a warm welcome. "Seat yourselves in the living room while I get the cake. I may have changed for the worse but my appetite remains the same."

Tasting the cake, the girls smiled.

"How do you manage to cook and bake at your time of life?" Sanna asked, helping herself to another piece.

"I don't. My carer's responsible for this," Zipporah admitted.

"You've entrusted her with your secret recipe?" Hannah was too stunned to comprehend the meaning of this revelation.

"She's given me her solemn word she won't pass it on without my consent." Changing the subject, Zipporah offered Hannah's friends to stay the night.

"You're very kind but Sanna and I think you need time to yourselves." Rosie felt a lump in her throat looking at the woman all of them now referred to as their 'granny'. Following them into the hall, Hannah promised she'd join them later that week.

A few days later, Hannah asked Zipporah if she wanted her to stay longer. "Sanna and Rosie will understand. I'm concerned you've lost so much weight."

"Nonsense! Just you wait until you get to my age. My carer's arriving any minute. Go! Return to your friends. Make the most of your time together."

"Won't you at least wave at me from the kitchen window?" There was something so endearing watching the same figure wave and blow kisses at her. It wasn't until she was seated in the back seat of the cab on the way back to her hotel that it suddenly dawned on her: The reason her grandmother had rejected having a meal at Cosmo was down to the deaths of her friends. Returning to their favourite restaurant would have been too painful.

Deciding to have a quiet night at the hotel, the girls ordered room service consisting of spare ribs, burgers and milkshakes.

"It's alright for you," Sanna moaned, "you've figures to die for. I must have gained at least another stone!" She pulled at her skirt.

"Didn't you claim Roger loves you just as you are?" Rosie teased.

"He does! I'm the one who doesn't."

"You'd better reconsider starting a family – just imagine gaining all that weight!" Hannah joked.

"Honestly! If I didn't love you so much, I'd wring your necks." Sanna laughed, tucking into her food.

The following afternoon was spent meeting Letitia to visit Ella's grave in the small Jewish cemetery in Golders Green. Arms around each other, each of them thought of all the times they'd had tea together. Hannah was especially affected.

"Thanks for the wonderful memories, no one understood me as well as you," she cried, tears streaming down her face. Before she left, Letitia warned her that Rodborough Road had changed for the worse.

"I'd stay away if I were you. It's hardly recognisable anymore. Most of the properties have been demolished, replaced by ugly blocks of flats; Ella's included."

So instead the friends agreed they should end their visit in style by having their last dinner at Villa Bianca in Hampstead Village. Seated at the window overlooking the pretty mews, they toasted one another fondly.

"To all that we achieved!" Rosie exclaimed, tucking into her Lasagne Al Forno.

"Life's transient but our friendship's forever," Sanna added, between mouthfuls of tortellini.

"May all of us stay as happy as we are now." Hannah poured them another glass of red wine, polishing off her pasta with Gorgonzola and spinach. After sharing a big portion of tiramisu, they requested the bill and Rosie declared she was so full, she wouldn't be able to walk anywhere.

"Don't be such a spoilsport, Sanna and I will help you stand up. I used to love coming to this area at the weekend."

Passing the Coffee Cup, Hannah happened to gaze into the window of Pizza Express. Her face drained of colour.

"It's him! We've got to get away from here before he sees me!" But it was too late: Mark had already seen and heard her voice. As he turned his attention to the woman sitting opposite him, Hannah watched him make his excuses and leave. Rosie and Sanna swiftly disappeared around the corner, reassuring Hannah they'd wait for her across the street.

"Don't let him get to you," Rosie warned over her shoulder.

Mark suddenly appeared in front of Hannah, blocking her way.

"You're even more beautiful than I remember," he marvelled, admiring her curvaceous figure, red hair and those emerald-green eyes. She'd often imagined what she'd feel like seeing him again. But all she felt was a deep sense of emptiness.

"I've nothing to say to you. You'd better get back to your wife."

"Please don't leave. I've such a lot to tell you." Aching to touch her, Mark moved closer.

"You've five minutes: after that, time's up!"

Perhaps it was the light from the streetlamps but it was painfully evident how much he'd aged. His hair was thinning on top, his eyes swollen and red, probably from drinking too much.

"Did you get your degree?"

"Yes."

"Good. It's what you always wanted."

From the corner of her eye, Hannah noticed Petra was staring at them from the restaurant window, her hair just as bleached, her eyes as cold and calculating as the morning Hannah discovered their secret, blowing her world to pieces.

"I dialled your parents' number so many times but lost my nerve in the end," Mark mumbled, his face crumpling. "Not a day goes by when I don't regret what I did to you – to us."

"You're referring to when you were found out?" Hannah turned to face the woman on the other side of the window.

"I wish I could turn back time – you'll never know how much I've missed you, baby."

"Liar!" she spat at him. "Or have you forgotten you're some-one's husband and father?" Just looking at him made her stomach turn.

"Say you'll forgive me. You're the only woman I've ever loved.

Please let me prove it to you." He reached for her hand, but she pulled away from his touch.

"Listen carefully because I'll only say this once: as far as I'm concerned you're dead, is that clear?" Without realising it, she was shouting at him.

"You're lying! You want to hurt me the same way I hurt you. Petra and I are over. We only met up to finalise our divorce. You're all I want, baby. Please don't let one stupid mistake ruin everything for us."

"I stopped loving you a long time ago, Mark. Now get out of my way!" Her eyes were full of contempt as she stormed off to join her friends. Had she cared enough to turn around and look at him, she'd have seen the shock and disbelief in his eyes as he watched her disappear from his life.

"I've just laid another ghost to rest," she told her friends, looking as if a heavy weight had finally been lifted.

"Great! Now all you have to do is let Ben Isaacs into your heart!" Rosie blurted out.

"Don't be ridiculous. Apart from anything else, he's probably married by now."

"I wouldn't be so sure about that if I were you; Ben's the kind of man who only falls in love once."

Refusing to respond, Hannah stopped a cab and gave the driver the address of their hotel.

As they packed and made small talk, the subject of Ben Isaacs wasn't mentioned further. They were having an early breakfast prior to checking out when Sanna decided to bite the bullet.

"You're not fooling us, you know, Hannah. We know you're not as happy as you make out."

"How would you know? Just because you're a social worker, you think you're an expert on how I feel? Well, I've got news for the pair of you: you don't!" It was the first time Hannah had ever shouted at them. They'd had some minor disagreements but never fallen out.

"Stop lying! We've known each other too long for that. All we ask is you meet us halfway and give that guy a break." Rosie was right. It was time she stopped pretending everything was alright.

"I'm sorry I shouted at you. I'll consider it. Just stop going on about it, okay?" Hannah bowed her head.

"As long as you don't take too long and talk yourself out of it. Sanna and I only want what's best for you."

Saying goodbye at the airport was harder than any of them ever imagined. Watching her friends walk in different directions, Hannah slowly made her way to the gate and the flight to Copenhagen. As she sat by herself at the window, she thought of Ben. Was it possible he was waiting for her to make the first move?

Over the next few weeks her thoughts continued to turn to him and she'd almost summoned the courage to call him when Mary announced she was looking to employ a male teacher.

"I need your assistance in finding the right person," she said. "Some of the pupils don't have a father figure."

Advertising for the right candidate proved a lot more difficult than they anticipated. They interviewed one after another, but all were either too qualified or simply not interested in working as a team. In addition to interviewing, Hannah had a lot of responsibilities, what with her role as Supervisor and running her own class. Contacting Ben eventually turned into just another task she didn't have the time or the inclination for. When her friends reminded her of her promise to call him, she told them he was better off without her.

"We're too far apart. I'm certain he's moved on with his life," she said, a feeling of sadness washing over her.

"Has it not occurred to you he's scared of intimidating you after everything you went through with Mark?" Sanna asked. "Ben's not the sort of man who'd willingly force himself on anyone."

"Hasn't it dawned on you he may simply not care? I'm sure if he really gave a damn, he'd pick up the phone; he's not a child!" Why did they always have a go at her, not him?

"Have it your own way," Rosie snapped. You're obviously hell-bent on following in the footsteps of your employer, leaving you lonely and a spinster with nothing to show for all your hard work!" She was conscious of the fact Zadie and Walther also worried about her friend. "Why do you always think you know what's best for you? Sanna and I are concerned you're still blaming yourself for what went wrong with Mark. But that was his doing, not yours. Stop comparing that with what might happen with Ben. He'll never hurt you – the guy's crazy about you."

"Perhaps you're right, but I've made my decision. Ben and I are a thing of the past. Please don't mention it again."

All the same, however hard she tried to forget him, his brown eyes kept haunting her in her dreams.

CHAPTER THIRTEEN

1988

IN THE AUTUMN of 1988 Mary informed Hannah that someone of interest had applied for the position of male teacher.

"I could be mistaken but something tells me we ought to hear him out. After all, we've nothing to lose."

It was close to Christmas and pupils, parents and staff were looking forward to the party hosted each year at the school. Seated in a corner of the stuffy smoke-infested office, a stocky man in his thirties with short, thick blond hair and light-blue eyes jumped up to greet them.

"My name's Linus Johnsson. I always dreamed of working with you, Miss Ohlsson." His voice was a mixture of child and adult, slightly pitched. Sensing how tense he was, Hannah introduced herself.

"I'm the Supervisor," she said, taking his outstretched hand, which was bulky and dripping with perspiration.

"Nonsense!" Mary's tone was brusque, as ever. "Don't be fooled by her modesty – Hannah's the best thing that ever happened to this school. Should we decide you're right for the job, it's her you'll be directly reporting to."

They proceeded to ask about his past jobs and offered to show him the premises. Following them from one part of the building to the other, it wasn't until they took him into the garden that his eyes lit up. Linus approached a group of children on their lunch break, asking if he could join in their games. Watching him interact with them, both felt as if he was already a part of the school.

"They've taken to him like a fish to water!" Mary said.

"The guy's a natural," Hannah nodded.

"Did you get a chance to check him out?"

"Just a bit. Everyone I spoke to agreed he's a hands-on kind of guy, except some headmaster who added he's not keen to do the 'boring' stuff, i.e. the planning and execution of activities linked to development."

"But that's what we're all about!" Mary's face fell. "I guess I was jumping ahead of myself."

"Let's make our own decision – you could of course cover your back by keeping those cameras on . . ." Hannah joked.

"Perhaps you're right. Let's give him the benefit of the doubt."

"There's something else you should know. That same headmaster informed me Linus took some time off a few years ago for personal reasons. He wasn't prepared to reveal any more."

"I see . . . if it seems too good to be true, it usually is. I hope we're not getting ourselves into a situation beyond our control." Mary shook her head, sighing.

They agreed to offer Linus a trial period of six months and when they approached him with the news, he looked as if all his Christmases had come at once.

"I don't know how to thank you. You'll never know how much this means to me." He had to refrain himself from giving them a hug.

In the next few weeks Linus became everyone's favourite. The pupils competed for his attention, while the staff and parents were drawn to him like a magnet. But that headmaster had been right: whenever Hannah asked him to prepare an activity related to an individual pupil, he made one excuse after another.

"I'm dyslexic. Had it not been for my tutors at university, I'd never have passed."

"That's not a valid reason. This school is designed for children with learning difficulties. It's essential you're capable of implementing our curriculum!"

"You're right. Please be patient with me and don't give up just yet." He was desperate to prove himself to her. Mary had been right in saying Hannah was a brilliant teacher. Not a day passed when he wasn't in awe of her – she was also the prettiest woman he'd ever seen.

"Do you want me to offer him a permanent position?" Mary asked when Hannah informed her Linus was dyslexic.

"That's no reason to let you do all the hard work. He's a good role model, I'll grant him that but he has no right to demand you cover up for him. He'll either pull his own weight or he's out the door."

The next time Linus tried to wriggle out of a task, Hannah hissed, "You've no option but to work harder, I'm not covering up for you anymore!"

"You're absolutely within your rights to be upset with me. From now on I'll do my best to learn."

As he bent to pick up something from the floor, she noticed how much weight he'd put on. It was probably the reason he wore baggy clothes barely covering his bulging belly. Perhaps there was an underlying reason for his obsession with food? When Mary asked her if they should give him a permanent job,

Hannah told her if they didn't, the pupils and parents would probably mob them. "Let's give him an actual contract to begin with," she advised, optimistic Linus would prove them wrong.

"He may be everyone's 'flavour of the month' but you're my priority! Have you looked at yourself in the mirror lately? There's not much left of you. He'll get one final opportunity to shape up – if he fails, I'll personally have him thrown out, together with his P45." Hannah had never seen Mary look so angry before. The mere mention of his name caused her eyes to flare.

"You're kidding! She actually gave me the job?" Linus was so excited, he was actually jumping up and down. They were assembling the class after the morning break.

"Only on the condition you live up to her expectations. Don't let either of us down." Her voice was firm.

"I won't – tell Mary how grateful I am. I'll never be able to repay you for fighting my corner. Let me buy you a drink after work." He looked down at his shoes, too embarrassed to look her in the eyes.

Taken aback by his offer, Hannah cleared her throat. "I'm afraid that's out of the question. Mary prefers her staff don't socialise."

"But that's unfair!" he raised his voice.

"So be it – if you don't approve you can always leave and get another job."

"But I thought we were friends! Why else would you stick up for me? Everyone says I'm a better person for admitting to being dyslexic. I'm sorry I made a fool of myself – it won't happen again." His face turned red.

"Just stay true to yourself. Mary's fair – do right by her and you won't regret it."

"Lucky for me you're nothing like her – always accepting me for who I am." He dared to look into her eyes. Did he sense a spark of interest?

"My loyalty, as you know, is with Mary. Speaking of whom, I'd better make a move or risk being late for our meeting." Running out the door, the nagging suspicion he had a crush on her haunted Hannah throughout the remainder of the day. If she was right, Mary had to be informed, which would spell the end of their working relationship and cost him his job. Regardless of which, it was evident he was incapable of differentiating between what was and wasn't acceptable behaviour.

Driving home to his parents' farm in the country, Linus couldn't stop smiling. There was no denying it: Hannah Stein fancied him! Why else did she blush when he asked her out? The only reason she resisted him was Mary and the knowledge she'd object to the two of them seeing one another. Just visualising what it would feel like to make love to her aroused him; the thought of her sexy body beneath his, those green eyes gazing at him when he entered her . . .

It's only a matter of time before she succumbs to my every wish. All I have to do is stay patient until the perfect moment presents itself.

Back in the spring of 1988, Walther's closest friend had been diagnosed with Alzheimer's disease, a devastating condition for which there was no cure. A respected neurologist in his sixties, Dennis was acutely aware of its ramifications and made the decision to take early retirement or run the risk of misdiagnosing his patients. When his condition rapidly deteriorated, his wife Ellen had no option but to have him admitted into a nursing home where he was cared for around the clock, except weekends spent at home with his family. There he stayed, slumped in an armchair in the living room, with friends visiting, listening to him repeating some nursery rhyme, oblivious to who they were. Seated beside him, Zadie tried to comprehend what he told her, and was livid when his friends began to treat him like an outcast.

"I want nothing more to do with them – they're such hypocrites!" she had cried.

Less than a year later, the Steins were woken up by the telephone in the early morning hours.

"Oh my God, maybe something's happened to my mother!" Zadie whispered. Placing his hand over the receiver, Walther replied, "It's not Zipporah. It's Dennis's wife calling to tell us he died."

"I found him on the floor next to our bed with an empty bottle of sleeping pills in his hand," Ellen sobbed. He must have planned it in the early stages of the disease, just after he was diagnosed. My brave, talented husband knew what was in store for him . . . He and I lost everything to that wretched disease. Had it not been for our children, I'd gladly join him!" She was too hysterical with grief to speak any longer. Zadie immediately packed a bag and informed Hannah they'd be staying at their friend's house for the foreseeable future.

"Ellen and the children are in need of our support," she said, as they hastily got dressed and walked out the door.

The following week at his funeral, Zadie was disgusted by the absence of his supposed friends.

"The poor man needed them and they let him and his family down by turning their backs on them." They were at the small church and cemetery in Limhamn.

"I couldn't agree more, my love. Alzheimer's is such a taboo subject; they're probably too scared to talk about it just in case it happens to them." Walther squeezed her hand. Grieving for his friend, he decided to retire from all duties and devote himself to his wife and children.

Shortly after Hannah celebrated her thirty-first birthday, Lena and Peter became husband and wife at the local registry office, after which their closest family were invited for lunch at an Italian restaurant in Malmö. That night Zadie and Walther hosted a reception at their house for family and friends. There, dancing to Whitney Houston and Linda Ronstadt, Hannah couldn't help thinking it should have been her, not her little brother, marrying first.

"It's a damn shame Granny can't be here, she so loves a party!" Peter missed her presence but she'd compensated by sending them a cheque and a letter informing all of them Dr Anderson simply refused to let her travel at her age.

Wearing an off-the-shoulder organza dress with flowers in her long blonde hair, Hannah thought Lena was beautiful as she and Peter danced the night away.

"Hey sis, since you managed to catch the bride's bouquet, I'm certain you'll soon be walking down the aisle!" He winked at her in front of their parents.

"I'm not so sure about that. My career's going from strength to strength."

Peter was about to disagree but seeing the look of disapproval in her eyes, he kept his mouth shut. Pretending she was okay, Hannah smiled at her brother and decided it was time to go to bed. *I wonder what Ben's up to right now, I sure blew my chances with him*, she thought, feeling miserable. Just as she entered her bed-room, the phone rang. Without thinking she ran to answer it, fully aware something must have happened to her grandmother. It was past midnight and everyone was singing and eating pizza downstairs. She needn't have worried – it was Melanie informing her she and Matthew had set a date for their wedding.

"Sorry I woke you up, I always forget you're one hour ahead of us."

"Actually we've been celebrating my brother's wedding. You wouldn't believe how supportive Lena's parents are that she married into a Jewish family. Peter's arranged a trip to Spain for the honeymoon."

"Give him my best wishes. Matt and I can't wait to start a family – preferably before I hit the menopause!" Melanie laughed. "You'd better come to our wedding, Ben's the best man," she added casually.

"Is he still single?" Hannah asked, holding her breath.

"What do you think? Of course he is! And just as madly in love with you. He told me he's been keeping a low profile for fear of interfering in your life, especially after Mark." The girls continued to catch up, with Melanie telling Hannah she had landed a new job marketing companies in the retail industry. "I guess that's all for now – the invitation's in the mail, all you have to do is turn up!"

So Sanna and Rosie were right: Ben was waiting for her to make the first move. Hannah wondered how she'd feel, seeing him again. Then she remembered that they'd met at Melanie's birthday party. Could it be destiny reuniting them at her wedding?

"You deserve a break. London's the perfect place for it. Does Linus know you're leaving him in charge?" Mary asked, puffing on a cigarette.

"He told me he's looking forward to being in charge."

"Is that right? Perhaps your absence will make him realise how much he's been taking for granted. Please don't misconstrue what I'm about to say: he's been bragging about the two of you being an item."

"He actually said we're a couple? Well, I can assure you it's nothing but a vicious lie! I'll be damned if he's going to get away with it." Hannah was angry, but she'd also never seen Mary this upset before – her eyes were blazing. "I was wrong to not confide in you sooner. He asked me to join him for a drink after you offered him a permanent position, claiming it was the least he could do after everything I did for him. Naturally I rejected him on the pretext that it's not appropriate for colleagues to mix socially."

"And he didn't get the message?"

"Apparently not, although I made it very clear I'm not interested." Her face was red with fury.

"Seems we've taken on more than we bargained for. Do you remember that headmaster who told you he'd taken a leave of absence?" Hannah nodded. "Well, guess what? The same guy contacted me the other day, telling me Linus was suspended due to harassing a female colleague."

"But that's exactly what he's doing to me!" Hannah paused to think. "I'd hate to be the one responsible for him losing his job, though. Those kids adore him and when he puts his mind to it, he's good. Let's see how things work out while I'm away."

"Well, this is his last chance," Mary said. "If I hear he's been misbehaving once more . . ." Her words hung in the air.

"And you're sure you can spare me?" Hannah asked, feeling terrible for recommending him in the first place.

"Don't worry about me – focus on that friend of yours instead!"

★

"We need to talk – it won't take long." Hannah led Linus into the furthest corner of the classroom where they'd have a direct view of the children.

"Have I done something to upset you?" Linus looked tense.

"What makes you say that – a guilty conscience?" She regarded the teacher. He'd gained a substantial amount of weight; so much so, his clothes couldn't hide the fact he'd been gorging himself on all his favourite foods; burgers and fries. "Our colleagues are of the distinct impression you and I are an item. What have you been telling them?" she hissed, looking into his puffy eyes.

"They must have got the wrong end of the stick! All I did was tell them how nice you are. Anyway, you're not exactly squeaky clean yourself. Abandoning me so you can go to London to be with your boyfriend," he snapped, tiny beads of perspiration appearing on his forehead.

"I'll pretend I never heard that, shall I? My personal life's nothing to do with you." She didn't wait for his response, not trusting herself to not slap his face if he said something derogative. Reeling with anger, she instead left him there and returned to the class, determined to not let him get to her.

Mary was right: Linus was a liability she was best rid off. During the few weeks leading up to her trip, both kept out of each other's way.

Arriving at her grandmother's the night before the wedding, Hannah immediately noticed how frail Zipporah was. The dress she was wearing hung loosely on her and she'd not bothered at all with her hair or make-up.

"Melanie's a sweetheart, inviting me to come along, but I'm certain your and Ben's presence more than compensates for my absence." Her eyes shone, mentioning his name. Careful not to upstage the bride, Hannah had opted for an emerald-green dress matching the colour of her eyes. It enhanced her curvaceous figure by clinging in all the right places and a split on either side of the skirt revealed toned calves. High heels and glamorous make-up completed the elegant look.

"Ben won't be able to take his eyes off you!" Zipporah beamed and held her granddaughter close, praying tomorrow turned out to be a blessing in more ways than one.

Despite it being late autumn, the temperature was mild with a light wind. Seated in the back of the pre-booked cab taking her to the synagogue in Hendon, Hannah asked the driver to drop her at the corner of the street. Walking towards the impressive old building, she noticed lots of people laughing and talking, waiting to get inside. Melanie's parents came up to her and thanked her for coming, just as the guard ushered them inside.

Facing the 'Chuppah', Hannah's eyes were glued on the bride. Melanie wore an exquisite satin gown in white with a thin veil covering her face. Next to her the groom looked slightly apprehensive in a grey suit and skullcap, whispering something in the bride's ear. Together they turned to look at their guests and Hannah caught her friend's eye. She mouthed the words, *Mazel tov*. The surroundings and ceremony were so touching, that later, when following the other guests into the small courtyard, her vision was blurred with tears. Standing by herself, she suddenly felt a hand on her shoulder.

"Long time no see. I've been missing you, little one."

Turning to look at the man behind her, Hannah found herself staring into the big brown eyes chasing her dreams. In a midnight blue tuxedo, crisp white shirt and bow tie, Ben looked even more attractive than she remembered.

"Your beauty takes my breath away," he whispered, barely able to disguise his feelings. "Will you allow me to be your date for tonight?" He refused to let go of her eyes.

"That would be lovely," she replied, tingling inside. Arms around each other, Ben led the way towards his Bentley, parked further down the street. Opening the door of the passenger seat, Ben decided to throw caution to the wind.

"Let's get tonight over and done with – I have so much I need to tell you." Leaning closer, she felt his lips brush her own, a gesture so tender and loving, she wished it could last indefinitely.

Driving through the empty streets towards the venue holding the reception, neither said a word, both lost in their own thoughts. She turned several times to look at his handsome profile and strong hands on the steering wheel, and felt the same irresistible chemistry they shared the moment they first laid eyes on each other. *So some things do last forever*, she thought, as he pulled outside the restaurant in Central Hendon. Helping to let her out, he asked if she was okay.

"I know you don't know anyone except me, the happy couple and Mel's parents – don't worry, I'll be glued to your side." Lost for words, Hannah simply smiled as he escorted her to the beautifully laid table in a huge room overlooking the gardens outside. They'd been seated next to one another and she felt his eyes on her throughout the meal, consisting of smoked salmon, rack of lamb and peach melba – served with the finest of wines. The speeches seemed to go on forever and when it was the best man's turn to say something, Ben explained Melanie was his life-long best friend and all the guests laughed when he told them about some funny moments at Nursery. Melanie stood up, thanking all of them for coming, especially Hannah whose gift, a silver bracelet, was dangling from her wrist.

While they were mingling with the other guests, Ben pulled her aside, suggesting they find a quiet corner to talk. She was about to agree when Melanie ran up to them. The bride had changed into a Chanel suit and her dark hair was perfectly styled.

"Hannah and I have a lot to catch up on. Don't worry, it won't take long." Seeing the disappointment in his eyes, Melanie added, "I promise to bring her back to you."

"You'd better. We've only just met again and I'll be damned if I'm going to let her disappear!" He'd made that mistake too many times over the years.

Pulling her away from the crowd, Melanie gave Hannah a big hug.

"I've never seen him this happy before! He's mad about you – the question is what are you going to do about it? And don't tell me you're not as mad about him – I can tell just by looking into your eyes!"

"I'm not denying it. But what's the point? We live in different cities."

"Who cares? If there's a will there's always a way! I want you to be just as happy as me and Matt." From the corner of her eye she saw Ben approaching them.

"What are you two ladies gossiping about?" He sensed it was something to do with him.

"It's been great having you – Matt's somewhere in the crowd waiting for me, I must dash!" Melanie kissed both their cheeks, once more reminding Hannah what she'd told her.

"What's that supposed to mean?" Ben asked.

"It's getting late – I promised Granny I'd be back in time to kiss her goodnight." She avoided looking into his eyes, heading towards the cloakroom in the foyer.

"And there's me hoping we'd have some time to ourselves. I'm sure another few minutes won't make much of a difference? I promise to bring you back in no time." His eyes locked with hers as the other guests prepared to leave.

"Alright, but I really have to leave very soon."

They found a quiet spot and as she stood there so very close to him, Hannah felt the electricity between them.

"You must know how I feel about you? Not being able to touch and be near you drives me insane! I refuse to waste more time. Please say you feel the same." His eyes searched hers for an answer.

Aching to tell him she did, a small part of her held back, petrified of giving up on everything she'd achieved.

"I've said too much too soon. Take all the time you need – I'm not planning on going anywhere. We'd better get you back or your grandmother will send out a search party for you!" Ben joked but his eyes were serious. But as he helped to put her coat on, Hannah suddenly had a change of heart. Turning to look at him, she touched the contours of his face.

"You're right – we've wasted too many years. I'm scared my organised existence is about to change and there's nothing I can do to stop it."

Pulling her towards him, Ben kissed her tenderly on the mouth.

"I know one thing for sure: this kind of thing happens but once in a lifetime – Hannah Stein, you're the love of my life." He put her hand on his chest, adding, "You're in my heart, part of everything I do."

"But what are we going to do? We can't just abandon everyone and everything we hold dear!" She looked so upset. Gently, Ben put a finger on her lips.

"Says who? Loving you is all I care about – everything else fades in comparison."

"But Mary wants me to stay a few more years, I can't let her down after everything she's done for me!"

"Who says you have to?"

"It's easier that way – your father and business partner depend on you."

"You're forgetting you are my priority now. Besides, I've always fancied the idea of living in Sweden – so much so I'm planning a trip for Christmas."

"You'd do that for me?" His words touched her so much that she almost started to cry.

"In a heartbeat. Let's get you back or I'll do something both of us may regret." He bent to kiss her so passionately she started to tingle all over.

"Primrose Hill's only a few minutes away – Granny won't mind," she whispered, aching for his touch.

"Don't remind me. I never wanted anyone the way I want you. I want our first time to be as special as you are." Lucky for them Christmas was only a few months away.

Standing close to one another in the elevator to her grandmother's flat, both nearly succumbed to their desire. As he kissed her, Ben caught the scent of her perfume.

"It's L'Air Du Temps, right?"

"Correct. And yours is Pour Homme?"

"I guess some things stay the same."

The moment they appeared on her doorstep, Zipporah knew something had changed between them.

"What took you so long?" she asked, embracing them and thanking God for making her dream come true. "I wish poor Ella could be here to see this! We always knew you were perfect for one another."

As Hannah disentangled herself from his touch, Ben told her he'd call in the morning.

"I bet you have a lot to discuss. Take as long as you need." As he walked out into the corridor, Hannah repeated her offer to come with him. Cupping her face in his hands, he told her his mother had brought him up to be a gentleman.

"I wish you weren't," she whispered, yet was secretly pleased he was.

They agreed to see each other in a few days, then Hannah watched him step into the lift and disappear.

In the following days, Zipporah was so delighted they had finally got it together, that she regained some of her appetite. As they used some of her recipes to make chicken soup and roast chicken, Hannah told her it was early days yet.

"We're living too far apart!"

"If there's a will there's always a way!" Zipporah echoed Melanie's words. "I can't wait to attend the wedding!"

Hannah didn't have the heart to dampen her enthusiasm.

In the end she stayed longer than anticipated and when Ben finally picked her up on her last day before flying back to Sweden, she insisted he show her his flat.

"Are you sure we'll be able to behave ourselves?" he asked, his voice heavy with desire for her.

"I thought you told me your mother brought you up to be a gentleman?" she teased.

"That was before I met you."

Sitting next to her in his car, he had to use all the strength he could muster to not make love to her there and then. In a pair of jeans and frilly top, her hair falling down her shoulders, she looked stunning – so much so he wished he'd never told her about his mother. *Thank God Christmas is just around the corner*, he thought to himself.

Situated in the heart of Primrose Hill, Ben's flat was a typical bachelor's pad mainly used to sleep in and was sparsely furnished with furniture he'd inherited from his maternal grandparents.

"Are you sure you want to see the bedroom?" he asked, uncertain as to whether he was capable of restraining himself. Nodding, she followed him into the large room with a four-poster bed and matching closet in mahogany.

"Hey, let's get out of here or I'll do something I shouldn't."

"On one condition, that you join me visiting Ella's grave." They quickly left the bedroom before either of them had the chance to change their mind and in less than an hour arrived at the small cemetery in Golders Green. With Ben's arm around her and an umbrella shielding them from the gusty winds and rain, both quietly mourned their dear old friend.

"You were right all along, Ella, I've met the man who makes my heart sing with joy. Ben's the only man for me," Hannah whispered, touching the stone carrying Ella's name.

That night Ben took her to his favourite restaurant in Highgate, an Italian bistro serving the best *linguini* she had ever tasted. Reminiscing about their friend, Hannah told him about some of the things they shared.

"She'd have loved seeing us like this."

"I guess she got her wish," Ben replied, squeezing her hand across the table.

The next day, on the drive to the airport, both were too upset to talk.

"How will I manage without you?" she asked, her voice raw with emotion.

"I'm missing you already, my darling."

Standing next to her at the check-in he took her in his arms. "The future's ours, little one."

"I'll find us a nice place to stay over Christmas," she replied.

Ben held her close, kissing her one last time. Hannah reluctantly freed herself from his embrace, picked up her bag, smiled and left.

Watching her disappear into the crowd of passengers heading for passport control, Ben slowly turned around and walked out of Terminal Three.

On the virtually empty flight to Copenhagen, Hannah suddenly remembered telling her grandmother she wouldn't mind moving back to London.

"Promise you won't tell a soul."

"It'll be our little secret, my lips are sealed." But her eyes lit up at the prospect of her granddaughter living in the same city.

What was I thinking? Granny's incapable of keeping things to herself!

Her suspicions were confirmed when helping to carry her suitcase, Peter asked, "You're returning to be with him, aren't you, sis?"

CHAPTER FOURTEEN

1992

CONTINUING HER WORKING relationship with Linus proved much harder than Hannah had imagined. They were busy preparing for the annual Christmas party when she casually commented how impressed Mary had been with him while Hannah had been in London.

"Really?" Linus asked, glaring at her. "I had the impression she couldn't wait for me to slip up! Are you seeing someone?"

"I've told you: my personal affairs have nothing to do with you! Please clear up this mess before you leave." Furious that he dared to interfere with her personal life, on the way out she nearly slipped on a jumble of toys and crackers strewn all over the floor.

"There you are – I've been meaning to talk to you. Let's do it in my office." Putting an arm around Hannah's shoulder, Mary steered her in the direction of her smoky, dishevelled room. Sitting opposite each other at her desk, Mary removed her glasses.

"Judging by the look in your eyes, I gather Linus is up to his old tricks. I knew things were too good to last."

"It's nothing to do with him. I've had a lot on my mind lately." Despite the fact she loathed him, Hannah wasn't willing to cost him his job.

"I see. How was your friend's wedding?"

"Wonderful! Melanie and Matthew are perfect for each other. I bumped into an old friend I'd not seen for years. He's planning on visiting over the holidays . . ." Hannah was careful to keep her tone casual, so as to not create suspicion. Puffing on a cigarette Mary inhaled and exhaled a couple of times.

"Are the two of you more than friends?" It was a direct question deserving an honest answer.

"We've only just met again," Hannah replied, avoiding the other woman's gaze.

"That's not what I asked. Are you in love with him?" Mary persisted, a worried expression in her eyes.

"Ben's a nice man . . . we like each other very much." She wasn't prepared to discuss details belonging only to them.

"He obviously means a lot to you. Are you thinking of handing in your notice in the foreseeable future?" Lighting another cigarette, Mary studied Hannah's red-faced reaction.

"We're . . . um . . . very attracted to each other . . ."

"I'm sorry. You mustn't take any notice of me. I've no right interfering in your life. If I'd taken a leaf out of your book, perhaps my life wouldn't be so empty. Now all I have to show for it is this place; rather pathetic, wouldn't you agree?" she declared, surveying their surroundings.

"I'm sorry I didn't confide in you but nothing's been decided yet. There's still so much to consider . . ." Hannah was distraught that Mary had worked things out for herself.

"You don't owe me anything! Just answer me this: is Ben 'the one'?"

"It's about the only thing I know for sure right now."

"That's all I need to know. Let's talk later. Neither of us is in the mood to discuss next term's curriculum." Putting up a facade,

Mary ushered her out the door. As she walked down the long corridor, Hannah couldn't help thinking how unnecessarily complicated life was.

Several months later, Hannah watching Linus dressed as Santa Claus, handing out crackers to the squealing pupils. A beautifully decorated Christmas tree stood next to the scrumptious buffet laid out in the main entrance. Everyone was busy, talking and laughing. Hannah's thoughts turned to Ben, as she asked herself for the hundredth time if it was right to leave all this behind. But she was certain this was their time to be together.

Last night Mary had invited all of her staff to dinner at a local restaurant to thank them for everything they did for the school. Mary had given each of them a box of Belgian truffles and a bottle of champagne, her eyes catching Hannah's halfway through the meal, mouthing the words, "God alone knows how I'll manage when you're gone."

Returning to the present, Hannah noticed her friend and mentor approach her, saying, "You don't know how much I'll miss you! Had I been blessed with a daughter, I'd have wanted her to turn out just like you."

"How come you're so sure I'm leaving?" Hannah asked, touched by the sentiment.

"I can read you like an open book."

"Am I really that transparent?"

"You are to me." Wishing each other a nice break, both women embraced before leaving the premises.

Eager to get home, Hannah couldn't shake off the feeling she was being watched when she arrived at the car park. Turning around, she saw Linus staring at her from the front seat of his old van. Deciding to swallow her anger and wish him a merry Christmas, she went up to him, just as he pulled his window down.

"You're a fool choosing that bastard over me!" he shouted. Before she had time to respond, he drove off, the wheels screeching on the tarmac.

"It certainly won't be difficult leaving on his account!" Hannah muttered to herself, her heart racing at the shock.

As he pulled up outside his parents' derelict farm, Linus recalled their reaction when he'd first told them he wanted to teach.

"You, a teacher? Don't be stupid! Why, you can't spell your own name – much less string together a sentence, son," his mother mocked him, roaring with laughter.

Well, he'd made them eat their words and he'd do exactly the same where Hannah was concerned. Telling himself he deserved a drink, Linus turned the van around, heading for his local pub. There he ordered double portions of burgers and fries, washed down with several pints of beer. He put some money on the bar, taking great delight in watching the other punters' expressions sour in disgust when he belched loudly on his way out. Parking outside the shambolic wreck of a home he shared with his parents and siblings, Linus's thoughts returned to Hannah.

As soon as that jerk's safely tucked away in London, it'll be me she turns to for support. All I have to do is stay patient and bide my time, he told himself, instantly feeling much better and mentally preparing himself for his mother's vicious tongue.

Her suitcase already packed for the guesthouse, Hannah glanced at her pale reflection in the bathroom mirror. She'd had hardly a wink of sleep, as she'd kept imagining how she'd feel seeing Ben again. The severe weather conditions prevented her from turning up in a nice dress so she joined her parents for breakfast wearing leggings, jumpers and heavy boots. Politely she refused her mother's offer of porridge, toast with jam and an egg.

"I'm so pleased your father had the sense to fit winter tyres on the car," Zadie said. "There's a lot more snow and sleet on the way."

Gulping down a mug of steaming hot coffee, Hannah told her she'd better make a move or risk turning up late at the airport. A quick glance at her watch informed her Ben's plane was landing in less than a couple of hours. Taking twice as long as usual to get there, she parked outside the entrance and rushing into the main lounge, wondering if she should check if his flight was delayed.

Feeling an arm snake around her waist, she heard a voice say, "We ought to stop meeting at weddings and airports. You're even more beautiful than I recall, little one." Wearing a thick black coat and smart suit, Ben looked every inch the successful attorney; his kiss and embrace sending an electric sensation through her body and mind. Oblivious to everyone looking at them, thinking what a stylish couple they made, they held each other close and ventured out into the snow. "I can't believe I'm here at last, my darling!" Ben exclaimed, looking at her.

"I found us a cosy place to stay. It's quite close to my parents' house. They're expecting us for lunch at 2pm," she replied, dreading his reaction when discovering she'd booked them one room each.

"Sounds great. All I care about is seeing you." Bending to touch the thick snow on the ground, Ben proceeded to inform her he'd not seen as much snow since holidaying in Switzerland with his parents when he was ten. Seeing his happy expression and his dark hair covered in snowflakes, Hannah regretted not booking one room. "I can't wait to meet your parents. They must be very special people having you for a daughter." Putting his suitcase in the boot of the car Hannah almost owned up to her mistake when he interrupted her, telling her it was fortunate she was the driver or they'd have ended up on the wrong side of the street.

"It's a pity I can't show you my favourite places due to harsh weather conditions."

"That's alright, seeing as we have the rest of our lives to do it, little one." Despite the steady downpour of snow and sleet, his comment made her feel warm inside.

When they arrived at the picturesque inn, Ben immediately spotted the giant snowman at the gate and beautifully decorated Christmas trees on either side of the entrance.

"How come Swedish people are so much better at decorating than the British?" he asked, confirming she'd found them the perfect place to stay. Happy he appreciated her choice, Hannah watched his eyes light up on seeing the windows decorated with glitter, crackers, stars and gingerbread.

"I told you I'd find us somewhere special over the holidays."

"It's the cutest place I ever saw," Ben said, tightening his coat and assisting her out of the car. As they entered the dimly lit reception, a young girl with blonde hair and blue eyes greeted them.

"My name's Lisa — I'll be checking you in and taking you upstairs to your rooms."

"Did she say *rooms*?" Ben asked, a puzzled expression on his face.

"I'm not sure I heard her," Hannah mumbled, dry in the mouth. Standing closely together in the lift to the first floor, neither had time to clarify things before stepping out into the small, light passage. Lisa unlocked the door to the first room, informing

Hannah she could put her suitcase in the closet by the four-poster bed. "The décor's very Scandinavian and the Swedish flags inspired the colour scheme," she explained as they took in the high ceiling, chandelier and landscape paintings on the walls. The décor was a pleasing mixture of formal and modern. Both approved of the blue bed cover and rug on the floor.

"There are some towels in the bathroom," Lisa said to Hannah. "Will you be needing another room?"

Watching some children playing outside on the snowy ground below, Ben turned from the window, a mixture of hurt and confusion in his eyes.

"I wasn't aware you booked us separate rooms?" he asked in a low voice.

"I can explain!" Hannah replied, turning to the young receptionist. "Can I get back to you about that later?"

"Of course, let me know if there's anything you need." Leaving them, the receptionist couldn't help wondering how any woman would want to reject someone as nice, sexy and good-looking as that man.

As the door closed behind her, Hannah went up to him, asking for his forgiveness.

"I've no clue why I did it – please tell me I didn't ruin everything between us." Taking her hand, Ben shook his head.

"You can only do what feels right," he said, sounding subdued.

"You came all this way to be with me and this is how I repay you!"

"I'm alright. You'd better stay at your parents' house." She detected an undertone of sadness in his voice.

"That's out of the question! I can't believe I behaved so stupidly and badly!" Hannah cried, wishing she could turn back the clock.

"You're neither of those things – just scared – and I'll be damned if I'm going to intimidate you into doing something you're not ready for." Ben began to unpack his suitcase.

"My friends warned me this would happen . . . you're nothing like Mark but if I could hurt so much over his betrayal, just imagine my devastation if you and I don't last?" she asked, tears streaming down her face. Putting aside his own feelings of rejection, Ben took her in his arms, the love he felt for her shining in his eyes.

"Aren't you forgetting the most important thing? I'm the one who loves and adores you, little one. I'd rather die than cause you pain." Slowly registering his words, Hannah reached for the phone, dialling the number to reception. "You're sure this is what you truly want?" Ben asked.

"One hundred per cent – everything I need is right here in this room." She suddenly ached for his touch, body and soul.

"You don't know how much hearing you say that means to me."

"Let me get this straight: this room's on me – it's how the Isaac men operate – you'd better get used to it."

"But you're my guest!" Hannah objected but seeing the determined look in his eyes changed her mind. "The Stein women can be just as obstinate! Just you wait and see."

"Judging by you and your grandmother, I'm not the least surprised."

They were busy helping each other unpack when he suggested they take turns to change in the bathroom.

"Let's take things slowly," Ben told her. Twenty minutes later, his jaw dropped when she returned in a short black dress and high heels. "You're stunning! Those shoes . . . I'd better carry you to and from the car."

"Don't be silly, I'm changing into these when we get there – you obviously have a lot to learn about women!" Hannah joked, relieved they'd recaptured their special bond.

"Won't your parents object to us sharing a room? I don't wish to offend them."

"Stop worrying – Granny's been singing your praises for years!"

"How about you? What have you told them?"

"That I only knew the meaning of love when I met you," she whispered.

"You've no idea how long I've waited to hear you say that, Hannah." Touched by the sentiment, Ben pulled out a blue velvet box from his trouser pocket, placing it in the palm of her hand.

"What is it?" she asked, eyes searching his.

"Just a small token of how much I love you."

"But I didn't get you anything!" she replied, feeling terrible about what happened earlier.

"You're all I want, please read the inscription." Ben watched her open the lid of the box and then gasp at the sight of what was inside.

"It's the most beautiful bracelet I ever saw!" she cried as he helped put it on her wrist, the emeralds perfectly matching the colour of her eyes.

"Why don't you read the inscription?"

"'For my darling Hannah, forever yours, Ben'. She read the words slowly, then threw her arms around his neck. "Thank you from the bottom of my heart. I love you so much!" She wept, feeling his lips against hers.

"I'm pleased you like it. We'd better leave or I'll do something I shouldn't." His voice was full of desire. He broke off, pulling something out of his suitcase she correctly assumed was for her parents.

"You're not looking so bad either, that blue shirt suits you," she said, adding it would take longer to get there in such weather conditions.

She was right: it took them almost an hour to make their way through the snow to her parents' home. By the time they parked outside the bungalow-style villa, with its impressive black-oak door, front garden and garage, Ben couldn't wait to see what it was like on the inside. They were barely out of the car when a tall, strikingly elegant woman in her fifties with gold-framed spectacles and black hair came out to greet them.

"I'm Zadie. We're so pleased to meet you, Ben," she said, her voice soft and melodic as she kissed his cheek, the scent of Revlon's Charlie filling the cold, fresh air.

"Likewise – here's a small gift for you and your husband," he said, handing her a square packet. Zadie removed her glasses, revealing big brown eyes only a shade darker than his own.

"You're much too kind. Please make yourselves comfortable while I get lunch ready. My husband's joining you shortly." She placed his gift on the large antique table in the light foyer, then changed her mind, taking it with her into the kitchen.

Ben looked around at the white-brick walls, low ceiling, crystal chandeliers and parquet floors. The spacious open plan living area was almost entirely decorated in Art Deco with glass doors leading out into the huge back garden, covered in snow. Pouring him a glass of dry sherry, Hannah saw his eyes fixate on the paintings of Chagall and Picasso on the walls when a distinguished looking man in his late fifties with salt and pepper hair entered the room.

"I'm Walther, we're so very pleased to finally meet you." Raising himself from the plush green sofa, Ben shook the older man's hand.

"Swedes aren't as formal as the British," Walther commented, the handshake firm and sincere.

"I agree with you, Mr . . . Walther," Ben replied, instantly at ease with his host's deep voice and presence.

"Will you excuse me while I ensure everything's alright in the kitchen? I hope you're hungry – my wife's been cooking since early this morning," Walther said, leaving them.

"We'd better drink up. I've a feeling Mamma's about to declare 'Lunch is served'!" Hannah said, emptying her glass.

"Isn't he wonderful – and so handsome!" Zadie said quietly the minute her husband joined her in the modern kitchen adjacent to the living and dining area.

"He certainly is. And utterly besotted with our daughter! Did you see the bracelet on her wrist? It must have cost a fortune." Walther was secretly pleased Ben was as generous as himself.

"Take a look at the book he gave us – the girls in my French and book clubs will be green with envy when I show it to them!"

"Hannah must have informed him of how much we admire Picasso's paintings – it was nice of him to remember it."

That late afternoon turned out to be one of the most memorable of all their lives. Seated in the elegant dining room overlooking the back garden, living room and library with shelves covered in books from ceiling to floor, Ben felt as if he had been transported to a Mediterranean country except for the lack of sunshine and flowers.

"Your home is truly extraordinary – I've never seen anything as unique and beautiful," he complimented the Steins.

"I guess we're fortunate it doesn't look like much on the outside yet hides an Aladdin's cave inside," Zadie replied. She had outdone herself, serving a starter of blinis with herring and cream, followed by poached salmon with new potatoes, and almond cake covered in brandy for dessert. Polishing off his plate, Ben raised his glass, thanking them for "the best meal he ever had", adding, "Please don't tell my mother!"

"I'm so glad you enjoyed it. Would you like me to wrap some up for you to eat later?" Zadie asked Ben and Hannah.

"You mustn't, we're full to bursting as it is," Hannah replied, her eyes thanking her parents for making him feel like one of them.

Later, while tidying up in the kitchen, Zadie remarked on how well mannered Ben was.

"Your grandmother's right: he's the perfect gentleman. Your father and I couldn't be more pleased for you, sweetie."

They were in the living room having coffee with cinnamon buns when Lena and Peter unexpectedly turned up, curious to meet the man Hannah had kept a secret for so long. Soon enough, everyone felt as if they'd known each other for years, rather than just a few hours. Catching his sister's eye, Peter put his thumbs up, indicating how much he approved of her choice of boyfriend.

"He's a great guy and very handsome too!" Lena whispered in his ear.

"We'd better leave or risk not being let back in to our guesthouse. Reception closes in half an hour," Hannah reminded Ben.

"It's been so nice getting to know you, Ben, you're one of us now," Lena said, shaking his hand.

"I can't recall the last time I enjoyed myself this much and can't wait to introduce you to my family," Ben replied, following Hannah into the foyer.

"It's been wonderful getting to meet you, Ben. Please come again before you leave," Zadie told him, kissing his cheek.

"The pleasure's all mine! I hope you know how much your daughter means to me?" he said, returning the kiss.

"It's obvious from the way you look at each other how much in love you are," Zadie replied, touched by how much he cared about their daughter.

"I suppose I needn't remind you to drive carefully?" Walther intervened, shaking Ben's hand.

"Hannah's always safe with me – you have my word." Ben looked into the other man's eyes.

Driving back to the guesthouse, Hannah asked if he had enjoyed meeting her family.

"More than anything. It's as if we've always been a part of each other's lives! I'm especially pleased Peter approves of me, seeing as the two of you are so close." As he helped her out of the car, Ben gently brushed away a strand of hair falling into her eye.

"You must be exhausted after today's events?" she asked. Her voice was tense as she anticipated what lay ahead.

"Not at all. Whenever you're near me, everything else ceases to exist," he whispered, fingers tracing the nape of her neck and sending electric ripples of excitement through her body.

"I hope you get a good night's sleep," Lisa the receptionist handed them their key, her eyes saying, "Aren't you a lucky girl?"

Standing close together in the lift, Ben looked deep into Hannah's eyes.

"Would you rather I sleep on the floor? I honestly don't mind."

"There's no need. I'm just a bit tense. It's been a long day."

She felt like a teenager about to have sex for the first time. Walking through the passage to their room, Hannah's hands shook so much she handed him the key, watching it slowly turn in the lock. Switching on the bedside lamp, Ben held her close. Someone had removed the bed cover, revealing blue sheets, duvet and pillows. Feeling self-conscious, Hannah recalled Ben's reaction to her bedroom at the house, its blue tulle curtains, wallpaper with red roses, collection of ABBA pictures and small desk by the window where she kept his and Ella's correspondence.

"It's the cutest room! How come you kept all my cards?" Ben had asked, kissing the tip of her nose. "They remind me of you," she'd replied. Now it was her turn to question him:

"What happens now?" she asked, voice trembling, the only noise coming from the wind blowing outside the window.

"Whatever you wish – all I want is to make you happy, darling."

"That makes two of us," Hannah put a finger to his lips. "Stop talking and make love to me." Feeling his eyes on her, she slowly started to undress, until the only thing shielding her from him was her underwear.

Burying his face in the cleft between her breasts, Ben whispered, "You're everything to me," then in one swift movement he unfastened her bra, letting it fall to the floor. With his lips kissing her breasts, Hannah asked him to remove his clothes, her hand lingering between his legs.

"Only if you assist me – please . . ." Ben watched her hands travelling down his body, helping to unbutton his shirt then coming to rest once more between his legs. Putting his hand over hers, Ben quickly undressed, his clothes joining hers in a heap on the floor by the bed. Touching the triangle of dark hair on his broad chest, Hannah suddenly wished he could have been her first and only lover. The expression in his eyes told her he understood.

"You and me – it's all I ever dreamed of, Hannah." Unable to take his eyes off her tiny waist, shapely legs and honey-coloured complexion, Ben couldn't help comparing it to his own muscular frame and olive skin. Seeing her so abandoned, her red hair spilling out on the pillow and green eyes gazing lovingly into his stirred up a mixture of feelings deep inside of him.

"Don't you know how much I adore you, little one?" he asked, his voice raw with emotion.

Stroking his face, Hannah replied, "You're the only man I ever loved," before burying her face in his thick dark hair. The scent of Pour Homme brought back memories from all the times they spent together.

"Do you trust me?" Ben said, raising himself up on one elbow. "I'd never do anything to hurt you."

"With my life." She traced his lips with her finger. Feeling his mouth, tongue and fingers gently probe parts of her body no one else touched, she started to twist and turn beneath him, moaning softly.

"What are you doing to me?"

"I can't get enough of you, Hannah. Everything about you turns me on." He traced the outline of her nipples with his tongue. Unable to bear any more, Hannah pulled his head up to hers.

"I want you now, it's safe. I've been on the Pill since . . . you know." She instantly regretted saying too much.

"It's alright, the past's over and done with," he replied, gently pushing her legs apart, eyes never letting go of hers as he slowly pushed inside her, their naked bodies moving to the same rhythm, his thrusts deeper and deeper until neither of them could hold back any longer and climaxed, one after the other. Collapsing in each other's arms, their faces on the pillow, tiny beads of perspiration on his forehead, Ben turned to look at her.

"I've never known anyone as passionate as you. It feels like coming home." Hannah blinked in confusion.

"I never knew there were that many," she said, her voice flat. Regretting coming across as being crude and insensitive, Ben held her close.

"There weren't – you're the love of my life, Hannah."

Visibly relieved and relaxed, she stretched her limbs looking like the cat that got the cream. "That was great," she said, tongue brushing her lips.

"I'm passionate about you, my love, please forgive me for keeping you up all night. I promise to make it up to you later . . ."

"Who's complaining?" she teased, turning to look down at the children playing outside. "Merry Christmas, darling – looks like we're having ourselves yet another white one this year."

"The first of many more," Ben whispered, wishing they could stay just as they were. Despite it now being 10am in the morning, his hunger for her was much bigger than for an early breakfast.

"Why don't I order us room service?" Hannah asked, reaching for the phone. "How about scrambled eggs, croissants and hot chocolate with whipped cream?"

"Sounds delicious. But can't we eat later? I'd love to go outside and play in the snow. We'll come back, shower and dry ourselves in front of the fireplace by the bed." Watching him get out of bed and walk naked to the window, Hannah thought he was the sexiest man that ever existed, those big brown eyes, muscles and slightly curly hair in the nape of his neck making her tingle with desire. Reading her mind, Ben returned to bed and kissed her. "Let's forget what I just said. Remember what I promised earlier?

I'm going to prove to you I'm a man of my word." Pulling him down to her, Hannah quickly realised she had no reason to doubt him.

It was early afternoon when, finally getting their act together, they rang reception to order a late brunch of coffee and croissants.

"We'd better put something on so as to not embarrass whoever brings it up," Hannah said, pulling on a pair of leggings and a t-shirt.

"Aren't Swedes supposed to be pretty laid-back about that sort of thing?"

"That's a myth – most of us are actually quite shy."

"Can't say I noticed where you're concerned!" Ben teased, playfully pinching her left buttock. Making love to her was the significantly most fulfilling experience he had ever had. With her hair scraped back from her face, no make-up, he thought Hannah looked more beautiful than anyone he'd ever seen.

"I can't wait to marry you, darling, you want to as well, don't you?"

Taken aback by the direct question, she was about to respond when their food arrived. But Ben wasn't going to give up that easily, and repeated his question after they finished their meal.

"Shouldn't we spend more time together first?" she asked.

"I disagree." Ben was adamant. "A decade and a half without you is more than enough. I want us to spend the rest of our lives together."

"But it's not that simple, neither of us lives in the same city."

"We'll figure something out. It's been years since I had a proper Christmas."

It was pitch black and snowing heavily when they returned to their room some hours later, soaking wet after chasing one another outside in the snow.

"I'm the happiest I've ever been," Ben whispered, helping her get undressed.

"Me too," Hannah replied, changing into a thick white robe. Coquettishly she twirled its belt, asking, "Is there anything I can do for you, Mr Isaacs?" Her voice provocative, she continued to tease him as she sauntered towards him, pouting.

"If you don't stop doing what you're doing, I've no option but to make love to you right here and now." Ben's eyes were dark with desire, as he caught the belt and pulled her to him.

"You're always the one insisting practice makes perfect," she cooed, following him into the bathroom and slipping out of her robe. Both stepped naked into the shower cabin, hot water cascading down their bodies as he started massaging soap onto her legs, thighs and breasts. His fingers explored every part of her body until her legs felt like jelly and he lifted her up so that her legs were straddled around his back, feeling him urgently push inside; their bodies so close only suds came between them. Hannah called out his name, hands urging him to push deeper until neither of them could hold back, both abandoning themselves to each other. She felt tears of happiness mingled with soap and water.

When again she could speak coherently, she murmured, "My parents left a message saying they're expecting us to dinner."

Turning to look at her, a contented smile on his lips, Ben groaned.

"I was looking forward to drying ourselves in front of the fireplace."

"We'll do it later – for me – please?"

"I'd do anything for you, my love," Ben whispered.

Hannah sighed and prepared to leave, suddenly thinking of something. "What will we say happened to the bathroom floor?" They'd dried it up as best they could but it was still wet.

"I'm sure they'll figure it out for themselves," Ben replied, grinning.

Later, at her parents' house, they'd finished their meal when Walther reminded them it was time to give one another Chanukah gifts. Sure enough, there was a stack of parcels on the living room table.

"But I've nothing for you!" Ben exclaimed, mortified he'd forgotten about it.

"You already gave us that wonderful book about Picasso," Zadie reminded him.

"And I received this beautiful bracelet," Hannah added, smiling down at her wrist.

Their gifts that year were particularly fragrant; a bottle of Charlie for Zadie, L'Air Du Temps for Hannah, and Walther's favourite aftershave, Old Spice.

"This is for you, Ben," the latter said, handing him a small, soft package. "We hope you like it. Unwrapping a pair of black suede gloves, Ben thanked them, exclaiming:

"It's what I've always wanted, how did you guess my size?"

"My wife never gets it wrong. I always leave her in charge of my suits, shirts and socks!" Walther answered, kissing Zadie's cheek.

That night was just as successful as last time. Acutely aware of his imminent departure, Hannah and Ben opted to spend the last days on their own, talking at length about the future.

"We'll see each other as often as we can, little one," Ben kept assuring her, yet both knew it was easier said than done.

Celebrating New Year's Eve and the beginning of 1993 with her parents, they drank champagne and ate canapés with smoked salmon and Gorgonzola cheese. Zadie suddenly asked if they wanted to stay the night in Hannah's room.

"You're a couple – Walther and I really don't mind at all."

Turning to look at each other, Ben replied, "Please don't take offence but I'd feel better returning to the Inn."

"I might have guessed – Zipporah reminds me often enough you're the perfect gentleman," Zadie replied, smiling at them.

Aware Ben and her parents had been discussing something between themselves, Hannah was on the verge of asking what it was when Ben approached, looking deep into her eyes. He took her hand.

"I can't leave without asking: I want us to get engaged. Your father already agreed to us getting married. Please say you will and make me the happiest man on the planet, little one."

Stunned they had succeeded in keeping such a thing from her, Hannah felt tears of happiness well up in her eyes.

"I will," she whispered, her voice breaking.

"Be my fiancée or wife, Hannah?" Ben asked, looking tense.

"What do you think? Both, of course!" Bursting into tears of joy, Hannah threw her arms around his neck.

"I got you a little something to mark the occasion," Ben said softly, placing a small black velvet box in her hand. Everyone watched her open the lid.

"Oh my God! It's the most exquisite ring I ever saw!" Shaped like a rose with tiny diamonds covered in gold, it was a perfect fit. Urging her to read the inscription, Hannah's voice shook when reading it out loud:

"'For H – the love of my life now and forever – B'. I'm at a loss for words . . ."

"I've something to confess," Ben said, smiling. "Had it not been for your mother kindly offering to assist in finding the right ring for you, none of this would have happened. As soon as she saw it in a local jeweller's and described it to me, I knew it would be perfect for you."

"In fact, Ben never saw it until now – he trusted me to get you something special, sweetie." Dabbing at her eyes, Zadie didn't reveal it had cost a small fortune.

Turning to look at her father, Hannah asked, "I gather you were in on it as well?"

"Of course! So were your brother and Lena – Ben made us promise we'd keep it from you, my darling." In just a few minutes she and Ben had made his and Zadie's dreams come true.

Overwhelmed by the evening's event, Hannah felt happier than ever before, yet miserable her fiancé was leaving the next day. Seeing how upset she was, Ben asked them all to join him and his family for Easter and the Jewish Passover.

"As much as we'd love to meet them, Zadie and I already booked a trip to Paris. You'll be much better off spending time on your own," Walther assured them. Getting ready to leave, Ben asked them to keep an eye on Hannah for him.

"You're always welcome to visit. This is your home too, now," Zadie replied, glad her glasses hid the tears in her eyes.

Ben and Hannah said their goodbyes, with Ben embracing them once more and expressing how grateful he was for everything they had done for him.

"You're the nicest people I ever met," he told them as the Steins closed the door to the snow, privately wondering how the two of them would cope being apart.

★

Having settled their bill at the guesthouse, Ben watched Hannah pack in silence.

"Let's not drag this out," he said, feeling just as miserable as his beloved. "We'll part outside the airport,"

"It's probably for the best," Hannah replied, too upset to think straight.

"Promise you'll call if you need me – we'll start planning our wedding at Easter."

"That's months away! I want us to be together all the time, not just a few weeks now and then!" she cried, incapable of pretending she was okay. They'd been inseparable for two weeks – tonight was their last night.

"I'm not leaving you like this. Collin will understand." As Ben reached for the phone, Hannah put her hand on his.

"People depend on you – you mustn't let them down."

"I don't care! As soon as our contract with the Westbrooks expires, I'm selling my share of the business."

"Why won't you let me come to you instead?" she asked. "You know it makes perfect sense."

"I can't let you sacrifice everything that matters so much to you, my love. We'll work something out – I give you my word." Seeing her so upset and forlorn tore him apart.

Finishing the last of their packing, all they had left was to make love until the early hours of the morning. Unable to sleep, Hannah reluctantly woke him up, knowing that it was time to leave for the airport.

"Please let me stay a few more days, until you're feeling better, giving us the chance to discuss the future."

"I'm okay. The quicker you leave the sooner we'll see each other again."

"I mean what I said – I'll even learn Swedish – We're moving here to live, darling!" Ben joked, trying to lighten up their mood. They somehow managed to shower, dress, even have some breakfast in the small cafeteria downstairs, before slowly making their way to Malmö Airport. When they parked outside, Hannah suddenly started to cry.

"I'm going to miss you so much," she said, holding onto his sleeve.

"That's it! I'm not leaving you like this, Hannah," Ben told her, feeling awful.

"No, I'll be fine – let's get this over and done with – just call me when you arrive."

"You're quite sure? Please catch a cab; you can pick the car up tomorrow. The thought of you driving back on your own in this state scares me." It had stopped snowing – the first signs of spring filling the chilly air.

"Don't be silly. Peter's coming over tonight, he's bound to cheer me up."

All too soon, the moment they both dreaded had arrived. Kissing her one last time, Ben got out of the car.

"Never forget how much I love you, little one. Just look at your ring," he told her, eyes caressing her face. They hadn't had the opportunity to buy him an engagement ring as per the Swedish tradition, agreeing he'd purchase one later in plain gold with her name engraved in it.

"Please go before I change my mind!" Hannah whispered.

Exchanging one final look through the car window, Ben mouthed the words, "I love you," turned and walked briskly through the large revolving doors, disappearing inside. Hannah sat there for a while, quietly contemplating everything that had happened, then eventually began the journey back to Limhamn where her mother awaited her.

"I never knew I could hurt this much," she cried in Zadie's arms.

"It's not forever – you and Ben will soon be together again, sweetie".

For his part, it took Ben every ounce of strength to board the flight, and he spent the entire journey wishing he'd stayed. He told her as much when calling her later that day.

"Just remember, I'm only a call away if you need me, little one."

That night, tossing and turning and unable to sleep, Hannah couldn't stop thinking of him when Zadie called up to her room, announcing Melanie was on the phone.

"I'm sorry I woke you up," said a familiar friendly voice, "Ben's just called – you two sure sound as miserable as each other."

"It's so good to hear your voice! I miss our conversations."

"Congratulations on yours and Ben's engagement; I can't wait to see you married. Whenever he tells me how much he misses you, I keep reminding him of all the time you spent apart. Surely another few months won't make that much difference?" Listening to her, Hannah suddenly knew what she had to do.

"No. I'm returning to him and London. It hurts too much having to part and say goodbye."

"There's really no other way? I'd hate to see you giving up on everything you care about."

"Sadly, not at present. It's not forever – Ben's just as keen to live here as I am."

"Zipporah will be over the moon! Shall I tell her or will you?" Melanie's excitement was clearly evident down the phone line.

"It's probably better coming from me – mind you, Ben will take a lot of convincing."

"I can't wait to invite you both to dinner. In case you're wondering, I'm not pregnant yet . . ." Hannah detected a hint of sadness in her voice.

"Is there something you're not telling me?" she asked, her heart skipping a beat.

"I miscarried a while back, it's not a good sign at my age. Saying that, a close friend just gave birth to her first baby, she's in her mid-forties so I guess there's hope for me yet . . ."

"I'm so terribly sorry for both of you. Why didn't you confide in us?"

"Hey, you've your own problems to deal with. We've hardly seen each other since the wedding. It'll be such fun to meet and catch up!"

Vowing to keep in touch more often, Hannah went back to bed; a million thoughts whirling round her head. Now she'd made the decision to move back, all she had to do was tell everyone.

The mere thought of it brought tears to her eyes.

CHAPTER FIFTEEN

1993

WITH THE EXCEPTION of Linus, everyone at school congratulated Hannah on her engagement. Seeing the resentment in his eyes, she decided to have as little to do with him as possible until late one afternoon, when an angry group of parents informed her he didn't monitor their children's progress.

"How could you forget something so basic and fundamental? It's not as if I've not told you off in the past!" Hannah was furious, her face flushed red.

"Don't I know it? You're always on my case about something."

"I wouldn't have to be if you knew your job," she snapped.

He'd returned after the Christmas break looking even more obese but what concerned her the most was the smell of alcohol on his breath, making her think Mary ought to be informed.

Linus aside, in less than a month she and Ben would be reunited. Having booked her flight, she was slightly disappointed his parents wouldn't be there to meet her.

"Mum's absolutely livid with Dad for booking a holiday without consulting her. They want me to tell you how sorry they are and how much they're looking forward to meeting you in the future."

She wanted to tell him she'd return before too long yet decided to wait till she arrived.

When the happy day arrived, Ben turned up at Heathrow Airport an hour early. Spotting her walking through Customs, he ran up to her and scooped her into a warm embrace. They kissed passionately then, taking a step back, he surveyed her appearance. With a new short hairstyle, the fringe falling down part of her face, and wearing a denim dress, bangles and cowboy boots, she was even more beautiful than he remembered. Ben wished they were alone.

"You look great, but much too slim!"

"I missed you too much to eat," she explained, tingling all over at the sight of him in black jeans and blue shirt, his hair slightly longer at the neck.

"You're sure that's all it is, darling? Peter mentioned some guy giving you a hard time at work?"

"I wasn't aware you're in contact."

"We're not. He told me the first time we met at your parent's home at Christmas."

"Well, it's all over now – my brother's sometimes too protective of me," Hannah lied, adamant Linus wasn't going to come between them.

"If that guy or anyone else so much as looks at you in the wrong way, they'll have me to answer to," Ben said, his eyes narrowing. Putting her suitcase in the boot of his car, he asked if she wanted to spend a few days with her grandmother.

"Would you mind terribly? Mamma's worried she's keeping something from us."

"I'll miss you, but it's for the right reason."

The minute Zipporah opened the door, both Hannah and Ben knew something was wrong. Realising there wasn't much point in lying to them, Zipporah reluctantly admitted her GP had diagnosed her with angina.

"Don't look so upset. I'm perfectly fine as long as I don't forget to take my tablets. Heart problems are apparently quite common in people of my age. Let's go into the kitchen for coffee and apple cake."

But Hannah was too shocked to eat. She could tell her grandmother had lost even more weight since they last saw each other; her normally robust appearance replaced by thin arms and legs adding to her already frail demeanour. Just as concerned, Ben asked if there was anything they could do for her.

"You can start planning your wedding. Once I see you married off, I can die a happy woman."

"Please stop talking like that! Don't you remember telling me how much you want to be around to see your great grandchildren? I wish you'd told us you were ill – we have the right to be informed," Hannah reproached her, close to tears.

"I didn't want to upset your mother, besides, Dr Anderson's fairly confident I'll be fine."

"I'm not taking your word for it!" Seeing the doctor's number on the fridge, Hannah left to call him from her grandmother's bedroom. She'd barely introduced herself when Dr Anderson confirmed her worst fears.

"Mrs Friedman's an extremely independent lady used to doing things her way. She's alright for the time being but I'm not ruling out the possibility of residential care in the future. Between me, my nurse and the carer, we have everything under control at present." Thanking him for his time, Hannah promised to keep him updated. She returned to the kitchen, a grim expression on her face.

"From now on, you're doing exactly as you're told! Dr Anderson made it very clear you must have plenty of rest and remember to take your medication." Worried Hannah wouldn't cope on her own, Ben offered to stay the night.

"It won't make a difference. I'll keep you informed of everything."

"You know where I am if you need me – just call day or night." Kissing them goodbye, Ben quickly walked out the door before changing his mind and dragging her with him.

The next few days were spent ensuring her grandmother got plenty of rest, even going so far as to cook her favourite dishes in the vain hope they'd help restore her appetite. Hannah took great delight in watching Zipporah finish her meals.

When it was time to leave her, Hannah had arranged the number of hours and days the carer and nurse would be checking up on her so that she'd always have someone with her.

"Let me stay a few days longer, Ben won't mind – I'll call him right now."

"You're doing nothing of the sort! My carer's already on her way and Dr Anderson's popping in tonight."

Zadie had called the previous night, offering to come over and care for her mother but Zipporah wouldn't hear of it, telling her she was perfectly capable of looking after herself and would keep them informed of everything.

"Alright Granny. I'll take your word for it – Ben's number's in your phone book, don't hesitate to call if you need me." Kissing her grandmother's soft cheek, the scent of Arpège brought back a flood of fond memories; sufficiently enough to repeat her initial offer to stay a few more days. "Ben knows how much I worry about you," she added.

Opening the front door, a determined look in her eyes, Zipporah almost pushed her granddaughter out into the corridor.

"Go to your fiancé – I certainly would in your shoes!"

When she saw Ben standing next to his old Bentley outside the petrol station, Hannah threw her arms around his neck, telling him how much she'd missed him.

"Me too – knowing you were so close yet not being able to touch and hold you in my arms . . ." Entering his flat half an hour later, Hannah noticed new cushions on the sofa and paintings on the walls in the living room.

"I see you took my advice," she said, following him into the bedroom where they immediately made love – their lovemaking even more passionate than last time. Finally falling asleep in each other's arms, neither woke up until late afternoon.

"How about I make us an omelette?" Ben yawned and stretched. Watching him pull on a pair of faded jeans and jumper, and walk barefoot to the kitchen, Hannah wished they didn't have to get up. "Please help make us a salad. There's a French stick in the bread bin by the sink." With her tousled hair and smudged make-up, Ben thought she looked like an angel – albeit a very sexy one with her bare legs draped seductively around the high stool at the kitchen bar, an oversized t-shirt falling off one of her shoulders.

"Will you please stop looking at me like that?" he asked.

"If I don't – what'll happen then?" she whispered, walking up to him and burying her face in his neck. "Let me help make us an omelette," she mumbled, her lips brushing his.

"You know I can't resist you when you behave like that – please stop or we'll never get to eat," Ben replied, his voice full of desire for her as he squeezed her left breast.

"Did you hear me complain? Another performance of what we did earlier is all I need to satisfy my hunger!"

Laughing out loud, Ben put his arms around her and kissed her. "Will you please do as you're told?" he asked, pouring them some red wine and slicing the bread. Watching her eat, he suddenly asked, "Is it as good as your father's?"

"Almost," she teased, one foot wandering up his thigh.

"Seeing as he's the master of omelettes, that's good enough for me. Your grandmother's right; we ought to start organising our wedding." Sipping her wine, Hannah reached for his hand.

"I'm returning here to live. There's nothing you can say or do to change my mind."

"I somehow knew you'd say that but I can't let you give up on everything you worked so hard to achieve." Sighing, Ben went to the sink to rinse their plates.

"Don't you want us to fall asleep and wake up together? I need to be with you, I'm assuming you feel the same . . ."

"I'm not a selfish man." He turned to look at her. "You've too much to lose, Hannah."

"I'm doing it for both of us! Besides, Collin needs you to be around a while longer."

"Collin's my friend and associate. You're my future wife."

"Can't you see? I want to be with you. Anyway, who will make sure Granny does what she's told? She needs me now more than ever."

"You've an answer to everything I say, haven't you? Of course I want you here with me all the time. Saying goodbye hurts too damn much – but what if you start resenting me for giving up on everything at home?"

"That will never happen. I'll miss my family and friends . . . most people would but it's not indefinite. You said as much as well."

"Will you please discuss it with your family first?"

Pointing to her hair, Hannah smiled and shook her head. "There's a reason I'm a redhead – my mind's made up! All I have to do now is set the wheels in motion."

"And whatever I say won't change your mind?"

"Absolutely not. I'm afraid you're stuck with me, Mr Isaacs."

Exasperated yet delighted she was returning to him, Ben kissed her lips. "Alright! But nothing's changed. We're definitely making a life for ourselves in Malmö in the future."

"I'm glad you finally see sense. Why don't you focus on finding a special place for us to live? This place is nice but it's not *ours*. I want us to start afresh."

"Lots of Swedish people live south of the river – there's a Swedish school in Barnes. Perhaps you could apply for a job there?"

"I don't think so. While in London, I'd much rather work in a British school. How about Richmond? It's where your office is, right?"

"Yes, we're close to the town centre and park."

Delighted he agreed with her, Hannah asked, "Did you forget what you promised me earlier?"

"I've not got the faintest idea as to what you mean," Ben lied. Seeing the outrage in her eyes, he laughed out loud. "As if!" he joked, then carried her back to the bedroom where they proceeded to make love until the early hours of the morning.

"What's stopping you from moving back?" Zipporah asked, when they were halfway out the front door.

"My family and work," Hannah replied, thinking she ought to tell her parents first.

"I'm your grandmother, my days are numbered – it's a miracle I'm still alive!" She dabbed at her eyes.

Ben went up to Hannah, asking privately, "Why can't you share the good news with her?"

"She's incapable of keeping it to herself."

"What are you whispering behind my back?" Zipporah looked from one to the other.

"Only that you'll be seeing me a lot sooner than you think," Hannah blurted out, forgetting to think it through first.

"I knew it! You're coming back to me, aren't you? It's the best piece of news I've had in a long time!" she cried, clapping her hands, the old familiar spark returning to her eyes. "You must stay and celebrate the good news – my carer's just delivered a freshly baked apple cake, it's nearly as good as how I make it myself."

Leaving half an hour later, Hannah reminded her to not tell anyone.

"You worry too much. What do you take me for – a gossip?"

Now Hannah and Ben had both agreed she was returning in the summer, neither of them felt bad saying goodbye outside the airport and Terminal 3. Sitting in his car, their arms around each other, Hannah suddenly felt a shiver run down her spine.

"What's up? You look as if you've seen a ghost."

"We're so happy, what if someone or something comes between us?" she asked in a small voice.

"Whatever gave you that idea?" Ben kissed her. "You and I are forever, it's written in the stars."

As soon as she saw their downcast faces waiting for her at Copenhagen Airport, Hannah knew Zipporah had already spilled the beans. Putting her case in the car, Walther said, "If that's what it takes to make you happy so be it, my darling."

"We're having the ceremony in Malmö and the synagogue," she told them, hoping it would cheer them up somewhat.

"That's wonderful – we'd better start looking to find you the perfect dress, sweetie." Zadie tried her best to sound happy.

That night Ben called with excellent news.

"I think I found us the perfect house. It's close to my office and Richmond Park. I'm making an offer first thing in the morning. Are your family terribly upset with me?"

"Of course not! I told them we're getting married here and that we're returning to live in Malmö in the near future."

"Good! Listen to me darling; if, for any reason, you decide to change your mind, I'll understand – just let me know before I sign the deeds of the house."

"I'm not changing my mind," Hannah replied in a firm voice.

"Great. I'll start the ball rolling, shall I?"

"One more thing: is it very expensive?"

"The house? Don't worry about it – I can easily afford to buy it."

"That's not the point. You must promise to put it in your name only or I'm not living there."

"Let's talk about it later. I'll call in the morning – Collin sends his best wishes." Ben didn't have the slightest intention of complying with her demands. As far as he was concerned, buying her a house was nothing compared to what she had sacrificed to be with him. The place in Richmond was just the start of what he had in store for her future.

Telling her family was hard enough but informing Mary somehow felt much worse. They'd finished discussing the curriculum when the latter asked, "You've made the decision to leave, haven't you?"

"I'm sorry but yes – yes, I have. Ben's buying us a house in Richmond, south west London." Finding it hard to meet Mary's eyes, Hannah shifted in her seat, looking around at the familiar office. The stuffy cramped room no longer bothered her as much as it had in the beginning of her employment; dishevelled rooms and books being an integral part of the school.

"And there's nothing I can say or do to change your mind?"

"Nothing whatsoever – my family's not best pleased either, but they're good at hiding it from me."

"Well, as much as I hate to say it, Ben's a decent person."

"One in a million!"

"Have you thought about what you'll do over there? You're much too intelligent to stop teaching."

"Once we're settled in the house, I'm sure I'll think of something."

Shaking her head, Mary frowned. "The British are such a conservative lot. I may know of someone interested in meeting you. Sally and I often bumped into each other at conferences several years ago. Although not as advanced as this school, I seem to recall hers is located somewhere south of the River Thames."

"I can't let you help find me a job! Nothing will ever compare to this place – I'd be nowhere if it wasn't for your guidance."

"Nonsense. Everything you've achieved is down to one person: you!" Rummaging through the drawers of her desk, Mary found what she was looking for. "You'll never guess where Sally's school's located . . ." There was a distinct hint of triumph in her voice.

"Where is it?" Hannah asked, frowning.

"It is in Richmond of all places – if that's not destiny, then I don't know what is."

"That's insane! Are you quite sure?"

"See for yourself if you don't believe me." She put a file under Hannah's nose and watched the latter browse through it.

"You're much too good to me," Hannah said, reaching for Mary's hand.

"I'm certain you needn't be reminded of having to work through your notice period," Mary barked, quickly covering her eyes with her glasses. "You're the best teacher I ever had," she added, her voice the softest Hannah had ever heard. "I'll call Sally right away shall I?"

As she closed the school gate behind her, Hannah saw her colleague Annie approaching, asking if they could talk. In her mid fifties, busty, with short blonde hair and blue eyes, she and Hannah had hit it off from the start.

"I've decided to hand in my resignation – my mother's too ill to cope on her own and I'll not admit her into a nursing home!" Annie admitted.

"I'm sorry to hear you've such a lot to deal with – do you recall what I told you about my father's friend? He was also diagnosed with Alzheimer's."

"That's the reason I confide in you – you're the only person who understands what I'm going through. I've no sibling to share the responsibility – it's not fair. I work all day then care for my mother. We need to make the most of whatever time we've left together," Annie cried.

"Mary will be distraught to lose both of us – Ben's buying a house for us in South West London."

"That's wonderful news! I'm so happy for you both. I need to tell you something though, please don't be upset." Wringing her hands, Annie informed her that Linus had told their colleagues the two of them were in love. "There's obviously something wrong with him."

"Oh, not again! I can't tell you the number of times I warned him off. The man's an imbecile and the only reason I'll be glad to leave."

"Try to not think about it. He's simply not worth the aggravation. Will you let me organise a farewell do? We can't leave without saying goodbye," Annie said, a hopeful look in her eyes.

"I really don't think it's appropriate, given the circumstances. I'd much rather leave without a fuss."

"What if I get together a few people we really like?" Annie was desperate to have something to look forward to other than waiting on her mother.

"Alright . . . But nothing fancy – just a few drinks and snacks."

"Great! I'll start planning it right away – and Hannah? Would you mind us staying in touch?"

"Of course not! Will you do something for me? Before you hand in your resignation, I want you to call Social Services. I've a feeling they can help put you in contact with people who can care for your mother."

Time passed quickly and suddenly her last day at the school arrived. Celebrating the time she had spent with them, Mary thanked Hannah in front of everyone. Surrounded by children, colleagues and parents, she knew Budding Stars would continue to live in her heart, but it was time to move on, looking forward to her future with Ben. For the last time she watched the children playing around her, admired their paintings on the walls, and was grateful for the many cards and flowers bestowed on her. Finally Hannah joined Mary to say goodbye in her office.

"Will you let me hold your position for a couple of years?" Mary asked.

"It's not fair on the children, they deserve someone permanent."

"Can't say I'm surprised. I guess there's always a time and place for everything in life. Please keep me posted on your life in London; I need to know you're safe."

"Wild horses couldn't stop me." There was a big lump in Hannah's throat.

"This place won't be the same without you. Take good care of yourself."

"I'll keep you updated on how things go with Sally. She sent me a card saying how much she's looking forward to our interview. I can't thank you enough!" Embracing one last time, Hannah could tell Mary was just as upset as she was.

Closing the door behind her, she decided now was as good time as any to pick up her things in the classroom. On entering, she immediately regretted her decision seeing Linus pacing the room, an angry look in his eyes.

"Why did you choose him over me? What's that bastard got that I haven't?"

Terrified he'd lash out at her, Hannah felt months of resentment build up inwardly. But this was her last day; she'd be damned if she'd let him ruin it.

"Ben's everything you're not."

"You fucking little bitch! First you pretend to care about me then make it off with that shit behind my back!"

Gathering her boxes, Hannah looked at him with contempt in her eyes.

"You so much as come near me again, I'll report you for assault. Furthermore, I'll see to it you never set foot in this or any other school again, is that clear?" She was shouting now, her eyes blazing.

"I'm sorry I spoke to you like that . . ." Linus muttered, scared she'd act on her words. "Why couldn't you have loved me instead of him?"

"When will you get it into your thick skull I'm not your girl-friend? Now get out of my way!"

"What's up?" Zadie sensed there was something wrong. "Was it hard saying goodbye to everyone, sweetie? Given time, you'll realise it was the right decision."

"I guess I never knew it would be so difficult to leave them all behind."

"Perhaps what I'm about to tell you will put a smile on your face. Guess who's joining us for dinner tomorrow night?"

"He's booking a cab to pick him up so you don't have to," Walther added, entering the kitchen. As Hannah registered their words, a big smile spread across her face.

"Ben's coming over to see me?" she asked, the incident between her and Linus firmly at the back of her mind.

"That's right. Are you sure you're okay? Walking in the door you looked as if you'd been crying, sweetie." Zadie felt convinced she was hiding something from them.

Aching to confide in them, Hannah told them everything. Their faces dropped in horror.

"That man's a lunatic! Mary must ensure he never teaches again!" Walther's face was contorted in anger, livid someone dared to verbally assault his child.

"I'm reporting him to Mary in the morning. After that, it's down to her. Please don't tell Peter and Ben," Hannah pleaded with them, asking if the latter mentioned where they'd be staying.

Zadie had left them to answer the phone, but now she returned, replying, "Why don't you ask him yourself? Ben wants to talk to you."

"Hi little one – I can't wait to see you! How about I book us a room at The Savoy? We'll invite your family for a meal before I leave on Sunday night."

"What's wrong with staying at the Inn? It's much more intimate – I never heard you complain last time!" she teased, vividly recalling everything they did.

"Since you're putting it like that, how can I refuse? The Inn it is! We'd better make the most of it."

Meeting at the guesthouse the following afternoon, Hannah turned up in a summery dress, sandals and flowers in her hair just as his cab pulled up outside the gate. She smiled to see him, still of the opinion he looked like a cross between Sean Connery and George Clooney, wearing a dark suit and blue shirt.

"You look adorable!" Taking her into his arms, Ben asked if her parents were expecting to see them anytime soon. "I was hoping we'd get some time to ourselves first . . ." he said hungrily.

"They're alright. They asked me to tell you we're welcome any time . . . It's Midsummer's Eve tonight."

"Of course! Hence the flowers in your hair."

As they walked hand in hand to reception, Lisa greeted them with a big smile.

"I got you the same room – let me know if there's anything you need," she said, handing them the key.

As he unlocked the door to their room, Ben whispered, "I'm

not sure I can wait much longer, Hannah – I've missed you too damn much!"

"Me neither," she replied, aching to be with him. Pulling her onto the bed, Ben started to help her remove her clothes then watched as she positioned herself onto his lap.

"How would you feel if we were to conceive a baby?" he asked in a soft voice.

"That's impossible – I'm on the Pill, remember?" she replied, feeling him push inside of her, urging him to thrust deeper until they exploded and collapsed on the bed.

"Can you imagine what he or she would look like?" He repeated his question.

"Let's call her Ella if it's a girl. Do you suppose she'll inherit my hair and your eyes?"

"Maybe. All I know is that no other child will be as loved and cherished."

They were on their way to Limhamn when Hannah asked if Ben had remembered to put his name on the deeds of the house.

"We'll talk about it when you're over, my love. Right now all I want to do is focus on the present."

Feasting on meatballs, gravad lax and several types of herring from the traditional *smörgåsbord* laid out in the garden, Ben joined Hannah and her parents watching the sun go down in the early hours of the morning; the blue sky and rainbow taking his breath away.

"I've never seen anything as beautiful," he told them, wishing he'd brought along his camera to immortalise the event.

Saturday was spent taking him to all the places she couldn't show him last time. Starting with Mary's school, Ben commented on how different it was compared to British schools.

"Some of them are pretty run down, others confined to derelict halls," he told her, admiring the big building and environment in one of Malmö's best areas.

Strolling to Limhamn Harbour to watch the boats sailing on the Öresund water, Hannah confided that this was the place she went to whenever she needed to be alone.

"I can see why – it's so incredibly beautiful and peaceful down here."

Chatting companionably, they followed the coastline into Central Malmö, with its sandy beaches, clean streets and pavements. Ben asked if she wouldn't miss leaving it all behind to live in London.

"This is the perfect place for us to live and start a family, little one."

"I agree, but only when the time's right for us both." She steered him in the direction of Malmö's oldest café, Hollandia, on the pedestrian walk near the station. There they ordered egg-and-prawn open sandwiches and a giant chocolate mousse gateau to share between them. Hannah took great pleasure in watching her fiancé devour it, a contented smile on his lips.

"We're lucky we're not having dinner at my parents' to-night . . ."

"I have the greatest respect for your mother's and grandmother's culinary skills, but this is absolutely delicious!" Ben took in the picturesque scenery inside and out of the tiny, pretty room.

As they walked back to Limhamn, Hannah told him about Mary's friend, Sally.

"Whatever job you take, it'll not compete with Mary's. None of this is comparable to living in London," he replied, gesturing towards everything around him.

"This is a big part of who I am but I'm quite looking forward to our future, aren't you?"

"Of course I am! I just think we should live here sooner rather than later. I'm in my forties; not a young man anymore."

"So that's the reason you're so philosophical?" she asked, kissing him.

"Maybe, but mainly because I want you to have everything you so richly deserve."

He'd already paid for their room at the Inn and booked his cab to the airport when they arrived to have lunch at The Savoy with her parents. Looking stylish in a Chanel suit and chunky gold bracelet, with perfectly styled hair and signature glasses, Zadie informed them Lena and Peter had been unable to join them due to a prior engagement.

"They send their love and wish you a good flight back, Ben."

"It's our 40th anniversary this year and my 60th birthday – hence the reason today's lunch is on me," Walther announced as a uniformed waiter led them to their table in the centre of the iconic venue with its high ceilings, crystal chandeliers and oil paintings on the walls.

"You can't! This is my chance to show how grateful I am," Ben complained, turning to Hannah for support.

"You're most welcome to return the favour when we come to visit you in Richmond," Walther replied, refusing to discuss it further.

"Will you at least let me foot the bill for the wine and champagne?"

"Absolutely not!" Walther replied in a firm voice, indicating the matter wasn't up for discussion.

Talking and laughing throughout the meal, everyone agreed the Sunday roast with Hasselback potatoes and Béarnaise sauce followed by rhubarb-and-apple pie with custard were well worth waiting for. Toasting Hannah's and Ben's future, Zadie asked Ben to take extra good care of their daughter.

"You're family now, Ben," Walther said, shaking the other man's hand. Parting outside the magnificent building a few minutes' walk from the station, Zadie told them they were catching a cab home.

"The two of you need time to yourselves," she said, kissing them goodbye.

Both Hannah and Ben agreed it was best to say their own goodbyes at the Inn, with Hannah assuring him she had plenty to organise before going back to London later that month.

"I'll be counting the months, weeks and days till you're with me, my darling." Kissing her one last time, Ben picked up his suitcase and headed for the door. After one last look at each other, his footsteps echoed down the corridor. Before she too left, Hannah made a point of thanking everyone at reception for making them feel so welcome, following his example.

Later on, while Hannah was busy making a list of things to bring with her, she was interrupted by her friends calling to say goodbye.

"I'm so happy for you!" Rosie gushed, adding, "But I still feel the move's unfair. I wish you weren't the one always having to give up on everything you care about."

"You're wrong, Ben's always putting my needs first." Digesting her friend's comment, Hannah was deep in thought when Sanna called half an hour later.

"Rosie says I'm much too adaptable – do you agree with her?"

"No, I don't! You and Ben belong together. He's the best thing that ever happened to you. Forget what Rosie told you – you know what she's like whenever she gets some idea into her head."

She spent the last days in the company of her family, eating in some of her favourite restaurants and visiting the harbour to watch the boats bathed in sunshine. Zadie repeatedly reminded her of the fact they were only a short flight away should she get homesick.

"We're always here for you, sweetie."

"I know, but it won't come to that," Hannah replied, wishing they could say their goodbyes there and then instead of at the airport the next day.

Accompanying her to the Check-In counter, Peter gave her a bear hug, promising he'd keep an eye on their parents for her. "You just concentrate on your wedding, sis," he said in a muffled voice. Hannah turned to her sister-in-law, thanking her for everything.

"But I've not done anything?" There was a puzzled look in Lena's eyes.

"Yes you have – I've never seen my brother so happy."

"I hope you and Ben are just as blessed," Lena replied, touched by the sentiment.

Saying goodbye to her parents, Hannah picked up her bag, took one last look at them, waved and disappeared into the crowd of people around her. Trying her utmost not to cry, she started to focus on the man awaiting her at the other end and all that life had in store for them.

CHAPTER SIXTEEN

A CCEPTING THE HOUSE as a gift on the condition its deeds be transferred to an eventual offspring, Hannah's expectations of living in it during the next couple of years looked likely to be more than fulfilled. Despite the fact there weren't any beaches and harbour like at home, she instantly warmed to the neighbourhood. Falling in love with the commons, vicinity of Richmond Park and River Thames, and buzzing town centre where Ben and Collin had their offices, she and Ben decided to furnish it in a mixture of modern from IKEA and antiques found in local bric-a-brac shops. Thinking the eclectic mix of furniture, blue and yellow kitchen curtains a welcome change to the usual net curtains, they spent most of their time in the sunny kitchen and reception area, inviting friends over for a meal then retiring to the small conservatory in the back garden.

Upstairs there were two large bedrooms, one of them a combined study and guest room where Zipporah spent the night approximately one weekend a month, expressing delight in the peaceful surroundings. The cafés and restaurants particularly endeared to Richmond Park, not to mention the beautiful deer.

It was on Hannah's mind that Zipporah's health might prevent her from travelling to Malmö to attend the wedding, so she arranged a meeting with Dr Anderson. He advised they postpone it a while longer, ensuring she'd be sufficiently well to board a flight.

"Perhaps you wouldn't mind relocating it to London? At her age, there are no guarantees."

Confronting Zipporah with the possibility, the older lady insisted she'd be fine. "Your dear parents are so looking forward to planning it; just give me another few months to recuperate sufficiently."

Only a ten-minute walk from where she lived, Hannah's initial interview with Sally Giles resulted in the latter offering her a full time position at the small church where every morning and afternoon equipment was laid out then disassembled, with the hall resembling a sauna during the summer, and freezing cold during the winter. A far cry from Budding Stars, Sally's Heroes relied almost entirely on charity, Hannah's main concern being that the teachers only contributed with their individual skills as opposed to working as a team. She also noted that the parents were unused to participating in activities promoting the pupils' physical and mental wellbeing.

Ben's parents, Rebecka and Michael Isaacs, were eager to meet their son's fiancée. Living close to Melanie and Matthew in Hendon, they shared a house with their youngest son Stephen, who was in his early thirties and following in his father's and older brother's footsteps, studying to obtain a law degree at Cambridge. Ben's twenty-six-year-old sister Zoe also lived there, her aspiration being to become a model or actress.

Both Rebecka and Michael were semi-retired from their careers; hers a popular and sought-after secretarial agency, his a successful established law firm for which Ben and Collin had worked until branching out on their own. Conscious of how much they doted on their oldest child, Rebecka's invitation to Sabbath dinner reduced Hannah to a nervous wreck. She invited her grandmother to come with them for moral support, but Zipporah politely declined, insisting they first become acquainted with her granddaughter.

Wearing a blue velvet dress, kitten heels and subtle make-up, Hannah started to panic the moment they parked outside the impressive two storey house.

"What if they disapprove of me?" she asked Ben as he helped her out of the car.

"They'll love you just as much as I do," Ben assured her, squeezing her hand and walking up the path to ring the doorbell.

"What if you're mistaken?"

"It's not an option," Ben replied in a firm voice, just as a tall blonde with identical dimples in her cheeks to his answered the door.

"You're even prettier in the flesh!" she exclaimed, hugging them both. "I'm Zoe – we've been dying to meet you!"

Hannah felt a flood of relief engulf her, noticing how different they looked, Zoe with her Scandinavian colouring versus her own petite frame and Mediterranean appearance. As they were putting their jackets on an antique chair in the big cloakroom, Ben's parents came up to greet them. Rebecka had the same blue eyes and blonde hair as her daughter, hers worn in a flattering short page. In smart black trousers and blouse, she could easily have been mistaken for being her daughter's older sister. Michael was slightly shorter than Ben, both sharing the same strong features

239

and intense brown eyes. He looked very handsome in a dark-blue suit, white shirt and tie.

Telling her how much they'd looked forward to meeting her, a tall fair man with the same colouring as his mother and sister, walked up to them.

"Hi, I'm Stephen. Ben's been talking about you for years: now I know why!" He offered to show her around the house. Hannah was under the impression she had entered the pages of *House & Garden* magazine, the gold and beige décor and spacious rooms making her feel she'd been transported to the French Riviera. Twenty minutes later, they had dinner in the combined living and dining area, surrounded by family photographs on the walls and side tables. Rebecka served a starter of chicken soup with dumplings and Challah followed by coq au vin in rich wine gravy. For dessert there was scrumptious chocolate cake with fruit salad, everything tasting wonderful.

"Ben's told us about your grandmother and mother's culinary skills. I can't thank you enough for making him feel part of your family," Rebecka said to Hannah, once more expressing gratitude for the beautiful yellow vase she had given them, its designer famous for her extraordinary glass work and jewellery all over Scandinavia.

"I love your ring – it looks exactly like a rose." Turning to her son, Rebecka added, "I never knew you were such a romantic!"

"Well, now you do. Only the very best for the woman I love." His eyes sought out Hannah's, indicating the evening was a total success.

Saying goodbye a few hours later, tears of happiness brimming in her eyes, Rebecka told Hannah how delighted she was her son found someone so special. Taking his son aside Michael repeated her words: "She's a lovely woman – inside and out."

"I never imagined I'd be this happy and fulfilled," Ben replied, touched by their response to his fiancée.

In the following months, Hannah and Rebecka frequently met up for lunch in Hendon or Richmond, reminding her of how much she wished Zadie could join them.

Happily Walther and Zadie were finally able to visit at Passover. Assuming the Steins and Isaacs would have little in common, both Hannah and Ben were surprised at how many things bound them together; similar interests such as travelling and literature, not forgetting the same core values. Complete contrasts appearance wise, one tall and blonde, the other tall and dark, Rebecka and Zadie instantly warmed to one another, neither of them willing to compromise on issues close to their heart.

"You're just like 'The Iron Lady'!" Michael told Zipporah, who was also able to join them.

"I'll not be compared to anyone! I'm quite unique as I am!" the older lady joked, making everyone laugh.

Taking Hannah aside into her bedroom, Rebecka confided in her how lucky she was to have a grandmother.

"Mine's been gone for decades; Michael and I lost most of our family to the Holocaust or illness. Engaging with the Jewish community gives me a sense of belonging."

Later, when Hannah drove her parents to the airport, Zadie told her how much they'd enjoyed staying at their lovely house.

"Let's hope your grandmother's soon well enough to travel and attend your wedding, sweetie."

A few days after her parents' visit, Ben told Hannah that he had set up a meeting between them, Collin and his wife Karen, and

Vanessa Westbrook, thinking it important since he and Collin had recently extended their contract with the Westbrooks.

"Don't let Vanessa's hard exterior put you off her – she's actually rather nice once you get to know her. For some obscure reason Mel and Dad detest her, please don't take any notice of them." Ben said, thinking fleetingly of the crush Vanessa had had on him at Cambridge and how she'd opted out a few months prior to graduation.

When he'd told her of his plans for his and Hannah's wedding, she'd retorted, "Just another one biting the dust, I hope she's worthy of you giving up your freedom for."

"Hannah's everything I want in a woman – I've not a clue as to how I managed to live without her for so long!" he'd responded, somewhat put off by her reaction.

Recalling how Melanie had once referred to Vanessa as a "snake obsessed with Ben", Hannah called Karen, asking her opinion of the American.

"Assuming Collin and Ben weren't in partnership with them I'd personally have nothing to do with her," she said. "That woman's much too opinionated for my liking."

On the actual day of their introduction, Hannah felt a foreboding sense of disaster. She took extra care to look presentable, genuinely wishing she hadn't consented to meeting the woman everyone loathed. It took almost an hour to drive to the bistro in Primrose Hill, where they met the Hendersons. The bistro was packed with people sitting at tables so close to one another, they couldn't help eavesdropping on their conversations from their position in the centre of the room. It was a sunny May afternoon and Hannah thought Karen looked extremely uncomfortable in a printed maternity dress.

"I bet Vanessa's late as usual!" Collin grumbled, concerned his wife's health was being compromised by the American.

"We'll give her another few minutes before ordering." Ben sighed. He wore a dark suit identical to his associate's.

"But I'm starving! Karen's exhausted from the heat – we promised the babysitter we'd return in a couple of hours." Collin signalled for the Head Waiter to take their orders. Everyone opted for Steak Béarnaise with French fries and red wine.

"This tastes wonderful! I wonder if Vanessa mixed up the dates?" Hannah hoped she was right – by the sound of it, the spoilt American probably came up with a better offer than meeting up with them.

"I'm exhausted! The babysitter's bound to wonder what's keeping us so long – personally I'm relieved not having to listen to that woman's bragging and nonsense," Karen told them, fuming Vanessa had the nerve to keep them waiting. About to reply, Ben noticed a tall blonde in her thirties wearing a tight fitting leather jacket and skirt enter the bistro. She nodded at some people on her way towards them.

"Hi guys! Sorry I'm late but Daddy insisted we have a chat," she said in a thick American accent.

"Some of us have a job to go to in the morning!" Collin snapped at her.

"Oh, stop giving me such a hard time. I'm here now, aren't I? Wouldn't you agree, handsome?" Vanessa looked at Ben, before seating herself between him and Hannah. She turned to the latter. "I gather you're the lucky woman marrying him? I'm very pleased to make your acquaintance." Her ice blue eyes were dark with resentment.

Melanie and Michael are right, Hannah thought, *Vanessa's not the sort of woman to accept defeat.*

"I feel as if I know you already seeing as Ben's told me everything about you," Vanessa added coldly.

"Only good things I hope?" Hannah asked, aware that everyone was staring at them. Unexpectedly, Vanessa turned her back.

"Where's that waiter? I want to order something from the menu." Judging by her bored expression, it was obvious she didn't rate their chosen venue. "I can't believe you're getting hitched!" She turned to Ben.

"You'd better! Hannah and I are relocating to Sweden in the near future – it's such a wonderful place to live and raise a family."

"Is it really?" Looking them up and down, Vanessa started to laugh.

"What's so bloody amusing? That we're getting married or that we're moving?" Ben had had enough. "I'm crazy about this beautiful lady! Do you have a problem with that?" Perhaps it was a figment of her imagination yet Hannah could have sworn the American flinched.

"This heat's getting to me! Daddy's chauffeur had to pick me up earlier or I'd have collapsed in the street."

"You're not fooling me. You were obviously involved in a spot of 'afternoon delight' hence the inability to be on time!" Ben hissed, fed up with her behaviour.

"I confess! There are moments when a woman simply can't help herself!" Vanessa giggled, resembling an adolescent girl. "Your fiancé's a very special man," she said to Hannah, simultaneously touching Ben's hand.

"Lay off! We're friends – nothing more."

"Don't I know it? I'm very happy for you both."

No you're not. You're gutted he's mine, not yours, Hannah thought, watching Vanessa order ice-cream and a glass of white wine. Standing up, Collin announced he and Karen were leaving.

"It's been nice meeting you, Hannah – we'll get together after the baby's born," he said, completely excluding the American.

Watching them walk away, Vanessa burst out, "At last! I thought they'd never leave. Isn't it wonderful we get the table to ourselves?"

"We're leaving as well," Ben declared, livid she had behaved so badly.

"But I've not finished my wine!" Vanessa replied in a subdued voice.

"You've two minutes to do it."

Repulsed by her attitude, Hannah listened idly to her rambling on about her boyfriend when Ben cut her short.

"I'm going to pay the bill – I sure hope you're capable of being civil to my fiancée while I'm away."

Watching him leave, Hannah asked, "Would you mind explaining your role in Ben and Collin's agreement with your father?"

"Of course not! One can't assume a nursery teacher has an understanding of these things. The best way of describing it is to liken me to a spouse, keen to promote her husband's career."

"I see . . . I was under the impression you're just a sleeping partner?" Hannah feigned a smile. Watching them from a distance, Ben knew in his heart that Mel and his father were right: Vanessa still harboured feelings towards him. Ignoring Hannah's question, Vanessa smiled at them, saying she'd had a great time. "I'm off to the Ladies'," she said, walking in the direction of the toilets at the back.

"I'd better do likewise." Hannah sighed heavily. "It'll take us at least an hour getting back."

"I wish you'd wait till she's gone."

"Don't be silly, she's hardly going to attack me in the Ladies'!"

Leaving him, Hannah was astonished to find Vanessa awaiting her outside the cubicles.

"How dare you humiliate me in front of Ben?" the American hissed, a furious expression in her eyes.

"That wasn't my intention."

"You deliberately set out to ridicule me!"

"I'm sorry you feel that way but I didn't." Hannah's heart was racing in her chest.

"If you ever do that to me again . . ." Reeling with anger, Vanessa roughly took hold of Hannah's right arm

"Let go of me!" Hannah cried, wincing in pain.

"Ben belongs to *me* – I loved him first!" Vanessa shouted, tightening her grip. "He'll never marry a nobody like you."

"B-Ben's onto you," Hannah stammered, sobbing, her arm hurting so much she was in agony.

"You're lying! Ben's only concern is that I'm out of his league. Tell me something: are you as frigid as you look? Ben deserves a real woman." Tears blurring her vision, Hannah somehow managed to break free of Vanessa's grip, wishing she had the strength to wring her neck. "Ben's mine! You'd better watch your back. He's the real reason I'm part of my father's deal." Before Hannah could respond, Vanessa threw open the door and ran out. Crying, Hannah splashed cold water onto her face and arm, and reluctantly returned to the restaurant, her pale face and swollen eyes alerting Ben to the fact something had happened.

"What on earth did she do to you?" He was concerned she was about to faint.

"Get me out of here! We'll talk in the car."

Feeling the remaining guests' eyes on them, Ben held her close, wondering why he never saw Vanessa leaving, assuming she used

246

the back entrance. In the car, he helped to put on her seatbelt, and listened to her story. His eyes turned dark with anger.

"How dare that bitch lay a finger on you!"

The minute they arrived home and entered the hall, he requested she pull up her sleeve.

"It's black and blue!" he whispered, seeing the damage Vanessa had caused. "She'll pay for what she did. Collin and I are annulling our part of the contract!" His voice broke, thinking how stupid he'd been to believe Vanessa was his friend.

"You can't, seeing as you already signed a document," Hannah cried, certain the Westbrooks well and truly had him and Collin under their thumbs.

"I don't give a damn! She's not getting away with it."

"Please don't act before you've thought it through! So much depends on that agreement. Karen's having another baby . . ."

"Can you find it in your heart to forgive me?"

"This isn't your fault! Tell that father of hers you're only dealing with him, not his daughter from now on. Perhaps asking my GP to refer me for an x-ray will help to put the message across?"

"That's not enough. She should go to prison for what she did to you!"

"Continue talking like that and the tables may be turned on you and Collin!"

"To hell with them! My father's only too willing for us to continue working with him."

"What if he's affected as well? Between them, Vanessa and Ronald Westbrook are capable of ruining you."

"Why didn't I see this coming? I've been an idiot not listening to Mel and Dad."

"You're not responsible for Vanessa's actions."

"You believe me when I tell you there's never been anything between us, don't you, little one?" Ben asked in a low voice.

"The thought never crossed my mind!" Feeling his arms around her, careful to avoid her arm, Hannah told him she was calling her GP. As expected, he sent her for an x-ray, confirming she hadn't suffered a fracture yet was advised to not work, thus avoiding pupils accidentally causing more complications. When she confided what had happened to Sally, the latter warned, "You'd better keep a low profile where that bitch is concerned . . ."

"Poor Hannah!" Collin exclaimed. "Vanessa loathed her the minute she discovered you're getting married. Unfortunately, our legal team tell me there's not a lot we can do to get out of that contract. Unless, of course, Hannah decides to sue her . . . Had this happened to Karen, I'd have killed her!" Collin watched Ben slump in his chair, hands over his face.

"Hannah says she's fine . . . But I know she isn't."

"Things aren't as bad as that, surely?

"Meanwhile that bitch is hiding behind her father, both relying on neither of us taking action against her."

"Let's set up a meeting with Ronald. Wouldn't it be great if the old bastard decides to let us off the hook?"

After her father found out about the incident, Vanessa was consumed by the fear that he'd cut off her monthly allowance, perhaps even disown her altogether. Conscious of him being in his study getting ready for a meeting, she put a comb through her hair, forcing herself to knock on the door.

"Who is it?" Ronald shouted. He watched his daughter enter, a sheepish expression on her face.

"You – how dare you show your face? What's your excuse this time?" he bellowed, pacing the room furnished entirely in antiques. Coming to a halt, he smoothed the fabric of his striped grey suit, the same shade as his hair.

"Collin called last night. What the hell possessed you to attack Hannah Stein?" Without pausing to hear the answer, he continued, "You're your mother's daughter alright, never ceasing to disappoint me!"

Regretting approaching him, Vanessa looked around her, thinking the room was as sterile as their relationship. What hurt her the most was his constant referral to her mother, a woman so desperately unhappy, she'd seen no way out but to kill herself, leaving her child at the mercy of a man incapable of showing respect or affection.

"I'm sorry . . . I'll do whatever you ask of me to put things right between you and Ben," she mumbled, eyes fixed on her shoes. "What did I do to make you hate me so much?" Her voice faded to a whisper. As always, he'd reduced her to a nervous wreck, the tough exterior hiding a broken spirit – a skill he'd refined over the years.

Ignoring her, Ronald glanced at the framed photos on his desk. There they were: himself as a young man with Lily, his bride, standing beside him, as plain and feebleminded as their offspring. Only the colour of Vanessa's eyes proved they were related.

He'd been desperate to have a son and heir, but Lily had failed him miserably by giving birth to a daughter. Realising he didn't care for her, she started to withdraw from everyone around her, a series of public outbursts resulting in him taking action to divorce her, forcing her to sign a document agreeing to never come near him and Vanessa. Ultimately this led to her untimely death by suicide when her little girl was four.

Each time Vanessa asked about her mother, Ronald told her Lily was a selfish, weak woman and that she was much better off without her. It wasn't until she turned eighteen and accidentally bumped into a former maid, that the ugly truth was revealed to her. Seriously depressed, Lily had slashed her wrists in the bath one night, her body only discovered the next morning. Vanessa made a mental note to research her mother's condition.

Irrelevant of how handsome he was, Ben had made her feel special the moment they were introduced at Cambridge, so much so that she started to gain confidence, turning herself into a glamorous woman, desperately in love with the man she believed was her destiny and camouflaging the fact she was still painfully insecure on the inside.

Now she was petrified Ben would disappear from her life, Vanessa swallowed her pride, asking her father, "Tell me what you want from me?"

"I demand you write a letter of apology to Ben and Hannah, then show it to me prior to sending it. Your feelings are of no concern to me." Ronald slammed the door in her face.

A few weeks later, standing in Ben's office wearing a frumpy black dress and no make-up, Vanessa was acutely conscious of her father's eyes on her, his attorney Tim Clancy watching over them.

"I was a fool to think you're my friend! Please leave, I can't bear the sight of you!" Ben commented in a low voice – Hannah's bruised arm fixated on his mind.

Willing him to forgive her, Ronald omitted to tell her Ben was the perfect candidate to head his businesses, perhaps even assist in giving him what he craved: a grandson and an heir, while also taking her off his hands. Should his burning wish materialise, he'd have plenty of time entertaining his mistresses in the south of

France and New York, both places a far cry from the Primrose Hill mansion he shared with his daughter. *I shall make him an offer he can't refuse,* he thought. *This will propel him to leave the Stein woman and marry Vanessa instead. Ben's no fool; he's perfectly conscious of how affluent I am, owning the most sought after real estate, hotels, restaurants and casinos around the world.*

"I'll make sure she behaves, this will never be repeated. Please convey our sincere apologies to Hannah."

Humiliated beyond words, tears of indignation stinging in her eyes, Vanessa nodded her approval. She avoided Ben's gaze.

"If you ever come near Hannah and me again, I'll personally ensure you're thrown into prison," Ben said to her, eyes dark with anger.

"I won't," Vanessa mumbled, loathing her father with every fibre of her being.

"You signed a legally binding document – I'm sure neither of you gentlemen need reminding of the repercussions should you decide to breach its terms and conditions?" Ronald's attorney commented.

"Right!" Ronald's face broke into a grin. "I'm relieved we've put this unfortunate incident behind us – giving all of us the opportunity to focus on our professional relationship."

"Are you quite finished? I believe it's my turn to talk now. Collin and I demand a legal document dictating that Vanessa is forbidden to enter my home and this office. Do I make myself understood?" Ben demanded in a menacing tone.

"Certainly – Tim will see to it immediately," the American replied, thinking his gesture of goodwill would benefit him later.

Glaring at Ben and Collin, Tim Clancy seated himself in the far corner of the office, handing them a document ten minutes later.

"Be so good as to sign it in my presence," he said coldly.

"Well, it's been a pleasure doing business with you, gentlemen!" Ronald declared. "We'll no doubt be seeing a lot more of one another in the near future." He led the way out of Ben's office, Vanessa and the attorney following closely behind.

"I knew you'd find a solution to all of this! A few more years won't make much of a difference," Hannah said when Ben told her of the day's events.

"Perhaps you're right – the sight of Vanessa grovelling to me in front of everyone should be enough . . . if I didn't know better, I'd pity her having a father like him, dictating her every move . . ." Adopting a bright tone, he abruptly changed the subject. "Did I tell you our secretary Eve recommends I learn Swedish prior to us moving to Sweden? She, her husband and young son moved here three years ago. Seeing as she's a qualified solicitor, we're thinking of promoting her to partner."

Downing a glass of scotch, Vanessa tried to figure out a way to get close to Ben. Having discovered his number in her father's desk, she decided that calling Hannah to apologise for what she did to her was her best option. She answered immediately.

"It's Vanessa – please listen to what I have to tell you before hanging up. I'm so utterly ashamed of the way I treated you the other day. Let's meet face to face so I can apologise in person? How about I take you out to lunch?" Vanessa kept her voice soft and unthreatening.

"You and me meeting up for lunch? You've a nerve thinking I'm interested in anything you have to say!" Hannah replied, slamming down the receiver. When she told Ben, his face turned red with anger.

"How dare that woman ignore my order? She calls again and I'll place a restraining order against her!" he shouted, exasperated that Hannah was at the receiving end of Vanessa's wrath.

Driving home after visiting Zipporah later that week, Hannah realised she didn't have the ingredients to make dinner. Deciding Brent Cross was her best option, twenty minutes later she parked outside John Lewis and rushed into the ground floor and Marks & Spencer, checking she'd not forgotten anything on her list. She was queuing at the till when she had the distinct feeling someone was staring at her from behind. Turning, she found herself staring into Mark's eyes. Inexplicably pleased she'd bothered to wear a nice dress, open-toe sandals and make-up, her first thought was how much he'd aged. His hair was receding even more than she remembered.

"Hannah! I don't believe it. You're just as pretty, have you been visiting your grandmother?" he asked, same husky voice, looking her up and down.

"I've no time to talk – Ben's expecting me at our house in Richmond, we're setting a date for our wedding!" Hannah revealed, angry with herself for confiding it to him.

"You deserve to be happy. Petra and I split up a long time ago . . . Marrying her was the biggest mistake I ever made." Mark's eyes clouded over. What he really wanted to tell her was how much he regretted losing her.

"And the baby?" Hannah asked, thinking she couldn't care less.

"Maruschka's living with her mother."

"I guess all of it happened for a reason . . . Ben's the best thing that ever happened to me, we're so very happy together."

"There's something I'd like to run by you – please agree you'll meet up for a couple of hours."

"Why would I even contemplate something as ludicrous as that? I've no interest whatsoever in anything you have to say!" Hannah snapped at him.

"I accept you're still angry with me for everything I did to you but come on, I was an immature kid acting on my hormones."

"Whatever . . . as far as I'm concerned all of it's over and done with. Goodbye Mark." Hannah asked herself yet again what she'd seen in him all those years ago. As she walked away from him into the busy mall, Mark called after her.

"I hope Ben knows he's a lucky man? There's a small Italian café behind Waitrose in Richmond. Please meet up with me, I'll not continue bothering you if you do." He explained that he had a small office on Richmond Green selling second-hand furniture. Hannah whirled around.

"Get it into your head I've not the slightest wish to meet you!" she shouted, upset to discover he worked so close to where she and Ben lived.

"My dad's just died – he was very fond of you."

"I'm sorry to hear it, he was a nice man."

Watching her disappear among the crowds, Mark reluctantly walked in the opposite direction to where he had parked his car outside Fenwick department store.

A few months later, with the episode firmly at the back of her mind, Hannah was busy paying at the till of her local Waitrose, when she heard a familiar voice.

"It must be fate bringing us together like this!" Oblivious to everyone staring at them, Mark repeated his request they meet up. Exhausted after a hard week's work, all she wanted to do was to get away from him.

"I already told you I'm not interested in having anything to do with you," she said in a low voice, walking out onto the pavement.

"Let me carry those bags, they're much too heavy for you".

"Do I have to spell it out to you?" Hannah felt like slapping him. "I'm not interested!"

"Please! It'll only take a short time, I'll not bother you again . . ."

"Oh, alright! Anything to get you off my back for good."

"Does that mean you'll see me?"

"It's the only and last time," Hannah replied, already regretting succumbing to him.

"Remember the café I mentioned earlier? We'll meet up this coming Wednesday at 5pm," Mark suggested, his ill-fitting brown suit only accentuating the pallor of his face and bloodshot eyes.

"I'll think about it," she snapped, worrying he'd follow her home and discover where they lived. Unknown to her, Mark had long since found out this information, having accidentally spotted her walk home from work, and following behind in his car.

Returning to his own empty, cold house in Stanmore, Mark loosened his tie. *I'll never give up on us getting back together, baby*, he thought, deciding to leave the dishes in the kitchen sink until the morning in favour of driving to his local pub.

Equally determined to rekindle her and Ben's friendship, Vanessa was nursing a glass of red wine in her bedroom. Having rejected an ex-lover's invitation to meet up for dinner, she was desperately trying to find a solution to the problem that was named Hannah.

Wednesday arrived much too soon. The sky was cloudy and there was a slight drizzle of rain. As she watched Ben waving goodbye to her from his Bentley, Hannah wished she had never agreed to meet up with Mark. Still, she felt safe in the knowledge that what Ben didn't know wouldn't hurt him. Walking the short distance to the café and seating herself at the entrance, watching people pass in the mews outside, Hannah was oblivious to a group of businessmen staring at her legs. A young waitress came up to her, enquiring if she wanted something from the menu. Quarter past five and still no sign of him. Livid he had treated her like that, Hannah settled for a cup of coffee and croissant and was about to ask for the bill when he rushed in, a flustered expression on his face.

"I'm sorry I'm late! Some jerk of a client called just as I was leaving the office," Mark said, seating himself beside her.

"Spit out whatever's on your mind; I've no time to waste."

"Let me order something first – I'm sure you recall I'm not keen on having breakfast and lunch!" he said, flashing her a smile.

"You're mistaking me for someone who cares," she hissed, while he ordered scrambled eggs on toast. She was convinced the red Toyota parked halfway up the pavement belonged to him and recalled the times she'd footed the bill, yet he thought nothing of splashing out on himself. Absentmindedly she compared his shabby suit and thinning scalp with Ben's immaculate appearance.

"You're looking great as usual," Mark told her, reaching for her hand.

"Don't!" She pulled away. Suddenly she was repulsed by his mustard-coloured shirt and thin gold chain. She reminded herself he was stuck in a time warp.

"It sure feels good having no one to answer to but myself!" he boasted, omitting the fact he was up to his eyeballs in debt. "So what's the secret to you looking so young?"

"Good genes and the love of a wonderful man!" It felt wonderful seeing his jaw drop whilst chewing his food, mouth open wide.

"You have to admit I've not changed much either?"

"If you say so . . ." She had no intention of boosting his inflated ego.

"Is that all you have to say?" Mark asked, a hurt expression in his eyes.

"You're twenty minutes late yet expect I engage in small talk?" Hannah hissed.

"You're sure Ben's the right man for you? Or are you just getting back at me for what I did to you back then?"

"How dare you of all people question my relationship? He and I love each other, a word you don't know – much less its implications."

"Sorry I asked! He's obviously all I'm not." Angry with himself for upsetting her, Mark put aside his greasy plate, smiling at her. "I'm a different person – all my dreams went up in smoke when I lost you, baby."

Hearing him referring to her in that way made her even more upset. "You're clearly doing alright, judging by that car." Her voice was dripping with sarcasm.

"It's leased on the company – Dad left everything to my mother. Can you imagine how I feel having to take orders from her?"

"Nothing's changed then! You're still under her thumb – I've heard enough, I'm leaving."

"Don't! I've a reason for wanting to see you ."

"Spit it out."

"Since Petra and I divorced, all my birthday and Christmas cards to Maruschka have been returned to me – it's as if I don't exist," Mark whispered, his lower lip trembling.

"That's nothing to do with me. Are you paying alimony?"

"Of course not! It'd only end up in Petra's pockets."

"And you're wondering why she wants nothing to do with you? Perhaps Social Services can bring you together, preferably before Maruschka forgets she has a father . . ."

"They're adamant not to interfere, not even permitting I go there to visit."

"You're seriously telling me you know where they live?" She couldn't believe it. He'd duped her into seeing him yet not even contributed to his own child's upkeep!

"I wanted to see you – you're the only person I can talk to."

"You're a liar and cheat. Come near me again and Ben will hear about it." Pushing past him to pay her bill at the counter by the door, Hannah stormed outside, angry with herself for thinking he'd changed for the better.

Upset she'd refused to listen to him, Mark followed her out into the mews when a young waiter came running after him, giving him his bill.

"I'm sorry – it must have slipped my mind," Mark muttered, handing him a £10 note, just as a passing traffic warden put a ticket on the screen of his car, the £50 penalty notice causing him to swear loudly all the way back to Stanmore.

Angry that she'd been so easily tricked and taken advantage of because of her good nature, Hannah threw her arms around Ben's neck the minute he entered the kitchen.

"I can't wait to marry you!" she cried.

"Me neither – what's up? It's not Zipporah is it?" I know she's not improved much, we'll find a way to sort everything out, little one."

Six weeks later Melanie and Matthew had their biggest wish come true: the birth of their twin boys, Teddy and Monty. Exhausted after a 48-hour labour, Melanie expressed gratitude that Hannah and Ben visited her in hospital by asking if they'd agree to be godparents.

"Matt and I can't think of anyone better suited to the job," she said.

Looking at each other, both simultaneously replied, "Yes, please!" They agreed it was the simplest decision they'd ever made.

In the spring of 1998, Sanna called telling them she and Roger had a daughter they named Julia, weighing nearly one stone. "I'd never have managed had it not been for Roger's support. Despite gaining an awful lot of weight, we're already planning the next!"

But the biggest piece of news came from Rosie, who had married Marcel at a Paris registrar office, spending the wedding night at The Ritz.

"He talked me into it," she said, having long since put her parents' bitter divorce behind her. When Hannah mentioned she'd bumped into Mark, Sanna and Rosie urged her to stay away from him.

"His daughter's well rid of him! Is Ben aware of the two of you meeting up?" Rosie asked.

"No, he'd only get upset. I'm not having anything to do with him."

"Mark's nothing but trouble. You'd better watch your back."

The three of them somehow managed to spend a weekend in Copenhagen celebrating twenty years of friendship, each looking almost the same as back then. Sanna complained she hadn't lost any weight since her baby was born, yet kept picking food off her friends' plates, including the time Hannah's parents invited them to dinner in Limhamn.

Some time later, Hannah was on her way back to London to visit Zipporah when Dr Anderson left a message saying he wanted her to get in touch.

"I'm concerned Mrs Friedman's not responding to the medication as well as I hoped. We'd better start preparing for the worst case scenario."

"Are you telling me she's dying?" Hannah whispered, voice trembling.

"I don't wish to speculate . . . she's not in pain, only exhausted. I persuaded the carer and nurse to extend their shifts – both said they'd be happy to." Conveying their conversation to Ben, it was obvious he was just as upset, judging by the look in his eyes.

"There must be something we can do – how about seeking a second opinion?"

"Dr Anderson's been talking to several specialists. They're of the same opinion; ensuring she gets plenty of sleep and rest."

"I'll inform everyone the wedding's been relocated to London – we'll give her some time to rest up and get used to the idea." But when they told her, Zipporah sat straight up in bed, shaking her head,

"I'm not permitting you to postpone your wedding! Don't take any notice of me. Stick to your plan." She was painfully short of breath.

CHAPTER SEVENTEEN

1998

LIFE PASSED BY without further trauma, it was only another six months until the contract with Ronald Westbrook expired, leaving Ben free to sell his share of the firm. During this time, Melanie and Matthew frequently invited them to dinner and to play with the twins, who at one year old looked adorable with dark curly hair and dimples in their cheeks.

"The two of you will make great parents! Getting married and starting a family are the best decisions I ever made," Matthew confided in Ben.

Listening to him, conscious of the fact they had to wait while always being so considerate to everyone else, Ben yet again wished they were able to get on with their lives.

Popping into his local Waitrose on his way home, Mark noticed a sexy, tall blonde staring at him from behind the magazine counter. Having witnessed his and Hannah's heated conversation several weeks ago, Vanessa had been eavesdropping on them, certain he held the key to her problem. She was still banned from coming close to Ben's offices and her father never missed an opportunity to belittle her, even going so far as saying he and Ben talked about it, delighting in giving her all the gory details.

"You're aware of how much I look up to you, Ben. It's not a secret I've no one to succeed me, ensuring everything's taken care of for future generations. Despite the fact Jews marry among themselves, I'm certain we can come to a mutually satisfactory arrangement." Ronald smiled, thinking, *And I'll get that useless daughter of mine off my hands and perhaps even a grandson into the bargain!*

Stunned he had the nerve to proposition him, Ben's eyes narrowed.

"You're clearly deranged if you expect me to marry Vanessa! She's your only heir – no one else. All I feel for her is contempt – Hannah's the only woman I love. Leave this minute or I'll make you!"

Vanessa felt as if she'd been stabbed in the heart, cringing in a corner of his office.

"Can I talk to you? I'll not take up much of your time," she asked now, following Mark carrying his shopping bags out onto the pavement.

"Why? What is it?" he snapped, thinking that although she wasn't exactly ugly, he was rather pushed for time.

"I'm not crazy if that's what you're thinking. You and I have a mutual friend. Hannah Stein's engaged to someone I've known for a long time; his name's Ben Isaacs." Mark stopped in his tracks, watching her closely. "I saw the two of you having a conversation in this shop a while back."

"What's it to do with you?"

"Seeing the two of you got me thinking. My name's Vanessa Westbrook, you probably heard about my father Ronald? He's in partnership with Ben and his associate. Years ago Ben and I were close, long before Hannah turned up on the scene. Let's cut to the chase – I'd like to buy you a drink. It'll be to both our advantages. We've a lot more in common than meets the eye."

Impatient to return to Stanmore, Mark glared at her. "I disagree! What the hell makes you think I'm interested in anything you have to tell me, lady?"

"You're looking as thirsty as I am – let me buy you a drink at The Ship. It's only a ten-minute walk from here," Vanessa replied, ignoring his little outburst.

"You're not listening! I'm not interested in anything you have to say." Mark continued to walk away from her.

"Your car's parked in the same garage as mine down the road, right? Let's put our shopping in the boot of our cars and meet outside Waitrose in five minutes."

Uncertain as to why he complied with her demand, Mark nodded, thinking he should trick her into waiting for him then leave. But the vision of her pert bottom and sexy long legs as she walked ahead of him was rather alluring. *She's sexy and she knows it . . . I'd love to know what's underneath that flimsy black dress of hers*, Mark thought, then instantly regretting taking an interest. It was Hannah he loved and wanted, not some cheap tart men used then discarded, only too easily dispensed of and cast aside. Still, curiosity getting the better of him, Mark did as she asked, following her to the pub in the high street opposite Dickins & Jones. There a large crowd of people were celebrating someone's birthday, talking and laughing so loudly both Vanessa and Mark regretted not going somewhere else.

"You look like a Guinness type of guy to me. Get us somewhere to sit while I buy the drinks, I won't be long." She returned a couple of minutes later with a pint and glass of white wine. Mark, who had so far sat in silence, could take it no longer.

"Cut the bullshit and tell me what this is about, lady!"

"What's going on between you and Hannah?" Vanessa asked, watching him gulp down his pint and wipe his mouth on his sleeve.

"You're thinking we're having an affair? Sorry to disappoint you. Hannah and I had a fling years ago."

"Was it serious?" Vanessa's voice shook. This was more exciting than she'd hoped.

"You could say that, so much so we were planning on getting married."

Vanessa couldn't believe her luck – it was obvious how much he still loved her.

"Before you continue asking me questions, I need to let you know it was my fault we split up," Mark continued. "I couldn't keep my trousers up – Ben's the only man for her. Anyway, what's this got to do with you?" His instincts told him Vanessa was no friend of Hannah's.

"Ben and I met at Cambridge. He's way out of her league!"

"But you're not? Those two are in love – you'd better accept it. I have."

"I'm not a fool! All I know is that we're made for each other, in every possible way," she added in a seductive tone.

I bet Isaacs is the only guy she can't buy, Mark thought to himself.

"I can tell you still care about her," Vanessa whispered, reaching for his hand.

"Hannah was the best thing that ever happened to me. I was an idiot not realising it at the time." Mark pulled away from her angrily.

"Those two aren't married yet . . ."

"I've heard enough of your ranting, lady. I'm off."

Desperate for him to stay and hear her out, Vanessa played her trump card.

"If you let me, I can be of great help to you, Mark."

Thinking she was coming onto him, Mark slammed his fist on the table.

"What the hell's making you think you've anything to offer me?" People were watching now, intrigued by his outburst. So as to not attract further attention to himself, he put his jacket on and started to walk out.

"Don't be silly! I don't fancy you . . . Tell me, what's your line of work?" Relieved yet somewhat hurt she wasn't attracted to him, Mark stopped in his tracks.

"Nothing much. I'm buying and selling old furniture and office equipment – not an exciting venture, nowadays."

"It needn't stay that way. I've numerous connections looking for that sort of thing."

"What's your price? You're not doing it out of the goodness of your heart, are you? That's assuming you've got one to begin with . . ."

"I like the way you're talking. So: let's talk business!" She flashed him one of her seductive smiles, revealing a set of even white teeth. Mark knew instantly what she was after.

"Hannah wants nothing to do with me. My hands are tied."

"Bullshit! You can help me in numerous ways . . . I scratch your back, you scratch mine, get it? Then both of us get what we're after: me, Ben, you, Hannah."

If it weren't for the fact that he desperately needed someone like her in his corner, Mark would have cut his losses and left there and then. He shook his head.

"You're clearly not the man I took you for! Throwing in the

towel without a fight?" Vanessa teased, her cold blue eyes mocking him.

"Exactly what type of man's that, then? Someone like your old man?" Mark had heard Ronald Westbrook stopped at nothing to get what he wanted. Those two were cut from the same cloth – judging everyone by their financial worth.

"My father's a bully. Living with him taught me how to survive, irrelevant of circumstances." For a split second, she almost sounded human, but then the old Vanessa resurfaced. "Hannah Stein can rot in hell! Has it occurred to you Ben's only her consolation prize? He's incredibly good-looking, not to mention successful. She'd be a fool to pass him up.".

Listening to her, Mark wondered if she could be right. Could Hannah still be harbouring feelings for him?

"What's your price?" he repeated, their eyes locking.

"We'll take this one step at a time. Patience is a virtue, trust me on this." Smoothing her dress, Vanessa raised herself off the chair, certain he fancied her. After all, most men did. But that's as far as it ever went. She blamed her father for it – he'd never loved her so why would anyone else?

"However long it takes, I always get what I want in the end." She leant across the table, giving Mark a great view of her ample cleavage.

"Even if it's a lost cause?" he asked in a thick voice, suddenly extremely turned on in spite of himself.

"Especially then! All it means is that I'm having to work a lot harder to achieve it, which to my mind makes it so much more exciting – wouldn't you agree?" Her tongue brushed her lips.

"That's it! You're not wasting any more of my time, lady. It's a pity your offer comes at such a high price. London's inundated with single men – go find yourself a husband among them!"

"Perhaps I already did? You're free and available, right?"

"Not for the likes of you! Where I come from, it's the men doing the running – not the other way round."

"What a shame – you sure look as if you could do with some-one like me in your bed ..." Raising an eyebrow, Vanessa continued, "Stop playing games. You and I need each other. How else will we get the people we want? Call when you're ready to talk! I meant everything I said earlier, you'd be pushed to find anyone with my contacts. All I ask in return is your cooperation – surely that's not too much, considering you're in a tight spot?"

Leaving him a card with her number on it, Vanessa put her jacket over her shoulder, blew him a kiss and left.

Having lost his appetite, Mark tried and failed to sleep that night, memories of Hannah flooding his brain. Finally he passed out from exhaustion, grateful it was Saturday the next day. Not that it made the slightest difference; people weren't exactly queuing up outside his office.

Sleeping just as badly, Vanessa felt confident he'd come round to her way of thinking, the thought of continuing to live under the same roof as her father much too scary to contemplate. *If it weren't for Bernie, I'd have no one to lean on*, she thought. Her father's chauffeur and general assistant had almost immediately seen through her tough facade, both recognising a kindred spirit in each other, their rough exterior concealing a soft interior. Both had endured a difficult childhood; in Bernie's case physical and mental abuse. Yet each time he told Ronald how much he liked his daughter, his employer laughed at him.

"Bernie, my old friend, you're much too nice for your own good. That girl of mine's nothing but trouble; I curse the day she was born!" Deciding to keep his thoughts to himself until retiring

– at which point he'd let him know what he thought of him – Bernie Harris kept a low profile, only opening up whenever Vanessa was around. Six-foot-four, bald and muscular, people mistook the ex-boxer for being aggressive and volatile, but nothing could be further from the truth. To Vanessa he was the father figure she never had, the kindest, most caring friend a girl could wish for. Had it not been for his childhood sweetheart Angie, Bernie was convinced he'd have ended up behind bars. It became evident only a few months into his employment how hell-bent the old bastard was to destroy his daughter, breaking her bit by bit until she crumbled; or as Vanessa kept telling him: "My mother's weakness was that she loved him – it destroyed her and I'm next in line."

It didn't take long to find out where Mark worked. Fed up with waiting for him to call her, Vanessa decided to come to him instead. *It ought to be me living there, not her,* she thought, parking at a side street close to the common then walking towards his office in Parkshot. Seeing the old, derelict building, not too long ago much sought after, Vanessa pushed the bell to the front door, hearing someone approaching on the inside.

"What the hell are you doing here?" Mark shouted when, by jamming her high heel in the doorway, Vanessa forced her way in.

"I've something I want to run by you!" she said brightly, flashing him a smile.

"You've got five minutes to talk, after that you're out the door." He'd decided to not take her up on her offer, convinced it would do him more harm than good being associated with her.

Taking in the surroundings, tacky old desk, single chair, scattered shelves and paperwork on the wall and floor, Vanessa turned to look him in the eye.

"I've been thinking about our little conversation the other day."

"I've not."

Vanessa took off her coat. Wearing a tight-fitting black skirt and a transparent blouse, revealing a black lacy bra underneath, Mark thought she looked like a prostitute. The sweet scent of her perfume made him queasy.

"Seems to me you and this place are in urgent need of my help. The rent alone must be crippling."

"That's right," Mark replied, too exasperated to lie.

"Then why won't you let me be of help to you? All I ask is that you meet me halfway." Seated in the only ugly black chair, crossing and uncrossing her legs, Vanessa noticed Mark's eyes were glued to her stockings. Unknown to her, he'd accumulated debt after debt, his only viable solution being to declare himself bankrupt.

"These contacts of yours, how come you know of them?"

"Let's just say I've met some interesting characters since moving to London."

"Nothing too dodgy I hope?"

"Mark, we're both conscious of the fact you're in no position to make demands – do what they ask and you'll be fine!" she replied, eyes narrowing. "Do we have an understanding?"

"Perhaps . . ." That crazy American bitch had him exactly where she wanted – by the balls.

"Wise decision! I'll get the ball rolling at my end. In return, you have to come up with a solution to my problem and figure out how to get close to Hannah. Call me before the week's up – that'll give you another few days before this place goes up in smoke!" Putting on her coat, Vanessa walked slowly to the front door. Mark's eyes remained glued to her body. Smiling, Vanessa blew him a kiss, slamming the door behind her.

Unless I come up with a plan to get Hannah to meet me, this place and I are over! Fed up with his mother's constant nagging, Mark downed half a bottle of whisky and wiped his mouth with his sleeve. Disregarding any legal implications of being caught driving under the influence, he drove all the way back to Stanmore where after yet another sleepless night, he picked up the phone and dialled Vanessa's number.

"Meet me at The Swan in Richmond tonight. I've got something to tell you." Mark proceeded to steady his nerves with several pints prior to turning up at 8pm. Vanessa was waiting for him at a table by the entrance.

"I hope for your sake I've not come all the way for nothing!" She was wearing another little black number that stirred up something inside of him.

"Hannah knows I've not seen my estranged daughter for years. I'm going to call her, asking her to help me get in touch."

"Excellent! I knew you'd eventually find a way."

"She'll help put in a good word for me with Social Services," Mark said, grimacing at the idea of being confronted with them.

"You're not keen on seeing her, are you?" Vanessa recognised his sort only too well. Just like her father, Mark's only concern was for himself, no one else.

"Kids cost a hell of a lot of money! I never pretended to be 'Father of the year' . . ."

"Who gives a damn as long as you and I get what we want?"

"I'll give it my best shot," Mark snapped, furious she took that tone with him.

"I know you will. This is what you're going to do: as soon as Hannah's agreed to meet you, call me so I can arrange for my photographer friend to be present. Just ensure you make it look as if the two of you are having an affair, I'll see to the rest! Those photographs will be sent to Ben, I'm sure you can figure out the rest. If you let me down, there'll be hell to pay!"

Watching her leave the pub, Mark kept telling himself he'd be doing it not only for himself but for Hannah as well. He arrived home an hour later and Annuschka came out of the kitchen to greet him, cup of tea in one hand, laundry bag in the other.

"I've cleaned and left a casserole in the fridge. Don't forget to heat it up later in the oven."

"I never asked you to . . . thanks all the same!" Mark muttered, the mere thought of digesting her food as revolting to him as Vanessa.

"I'm pleased you paid those overdue bills, son. Continue this way and we may yet get close. I want to meet my granddaughter!"

"That's impossible. Petra didn't leave a forwarding address."

"She's our flesh and blood – we've every right to be part of her life!"

"I'll make some enquiries." Mark wished she would leave him alone.

"You'll do more than that, unless, of course, you wouldn't mind being left out of my will?" Annuschka replied, walking out the door.

Livid that she'd threatened to disown him, Mark was about to go after her, but the phone rang. It was Vanessa, offering to give him Hannah's number.

"I've got it!" he shouted, wanting to wring her and his mother's necks.

"Great. Pretend you genuinely want to talk to her face-to-face. I'll await your call. Don't let me down!"

Ignoring her, Mark decided to turn up unexpectedly outside the derelict church hall and intimidate her into seeing him again. Putting on a pair of faded, much-too-short jeans and denim jacket his father had given him when he turned twenty-one, Mark drove back to Richmond where, parking his Toyota round the corner of the quiet street, he proceeded to walk the short distance towards the drab church. There he waited for her to exit the building. At 4:15pm, he spotted her. She was accompanied by some colleagues and parents; children talking and playing all around.

"What a pleasant surprise!"

"What brings you here?" Hannah was startled to see him coming towards her from across the street. "I hope you're not stalking me," she added. He noticed her face was devoid of make-up.

"What do you take me for? I just came out of a meeting in the building next to yours," he lied, thinking she looked lovely in a shirt and jeans, her hair blowing in the wind.

"You'd better not be stalking me. If you are, I'll tell Ben!"

"There's no need – I've been contemplating some of the things we discussed last time."

"Well, I haven't."

"Maruschka's apparently tried calling my mother, yet Petra insists I have nothing to do with her."

"I made it quite clear I'm not interested in this," Hannah replied, walking away from him.

"But you're an expert on these things."

"I'm not some social worker! Ask Social Services to reopen your file."

"They won't. All I ask is to be part of her life!"

"Your ex obviously doesn't want you near her . . ."

"Please – it's not for my benefit – only my daughter's."

"No, Mark. My mind's made up. Go harass someone else." Desperate to get through to her, Mark blocked her way, begging her to listen to him. "Get out of my way!" she shouted.

"Can't you see how upset I am? Or is this payback for what I did to you back then?" Regretting saying too much, Mark put his hands up. "I was out of order talking to you like that – I've no right asking anything of you – all I want is to see and spend time with my little girl."

Remembering how manipulative he was, Hannah continued to walk. "Forget I asked! I obviously mistook you for someone who gives a damn . . . You'd better pray she's not getting too damaged by what I put her through!" It was his last chance to reach her, hoping she'd be too compassionate to turn him down.

"I'd only be doing it for her – is that clear?"

Relieved she succumbed to him, Mark beamed. "Thank you! You'll never know how much it means you're on my side." His eyes brimmed with crocodile tears.

"You realise I'll have to inform Ben – he and I don't keep secrets from each other."

Worried Ben would see through his lies, Mark persuaded her there wasn't any reason to confide in him. "I only want your advice."

"Perhaps you're right. Ben's not exactly a fan of yours, is he? I'll think about everything you told me and call in another couple of weeks."

It suddenly dawned on Mark that Social Services would update her on the fact he still didn't pay alimony to his daughter. "Should you decide to contact the social worker assigned to the case, confidentiality dictates you won't be given any information," Mark commented, breaking out in a cold sweat.

"You may be right. Anyway, I'll try putting in a good word on your behalf, saying you'll do anything to be part of your child's life?"

"If you think that's going to help . . . Yes, of course! I'm very grateful."

Watching her disappear in the direction of her and Ben's home, Mark wondered if his plan would work.

Having breakfast in the oversized sterile basement kitchen, with Bernie bringing her toast, eggs and tea, Vanessa smiled when questioned why she looked so happy.

"Isn't it obvious to you? I'm in love! Ben's the perfect antidote to being depressed."

"But he's not your boyfriend. He and his fiancée are setting a date for their wedding," Bernie replied, feeling awful he was the bearer of bad news.

"Did my father tell you any details of their contract?"

"I've not a clue. He keeps everything to himself – why don't you ask him?"

"You're perfectly aware he wants nothing to do with me – I'm banned from going near Ben's offices." Her face contorted in anger.

"Perhaps that's not such a bad thing now Ben's ceased to be part of your life?"

"I'll never give up on him! Had it not been for that woman, we'd be together. Tell your wife I'm sorry you had to come in today because cook's having a day off. I'll make it up to you." It was the side to her Bernie loved and recognised – something only he got to see. "Actually, take the rest of the day off, my friend. I really don't know how I'd have coped without you." Vanessa once again thanked God for sending him her way: the closest thing she'd ever had to a father and friend.

Ronald suddenly appeared from his study. "I can tell you're up to something," he snarled, "it's written all over your face."

"You know nothing about me!" She'd had enough of his bullying. "Ever since I was born, all you do is order me about." Astonished by her own ability to answer him back, she continued. "I'm exactly the kind of daughter you deserve! Selfish, disrespectful and devious – a carbon copy of you! In fact, there's only one thing separating us: I've got a heart whereas yours is made of stone."

"You're right there – I don't love you. Just like your mother, you're a burden to me. All I care about is that you're civil to me . . . or I may seek out someone else to bear me a son and heir!"

"Do that and I'll make you pay." She had never loathed him as much as she did there and then. A tiny voice inside her head warned her of the fact she had neither money nor qualifications – should he decide to act on his words, she'd be left destitute. "I'll go look for some other place to live, shall I?" she asked, clinging to her dignity.

"By all means. But understand this: I'll not be paying for it. Isaacs doesn't give a damn about you. It's thanks to you those two refuse to extend our contract."

"They'd never have anything to do with you if it wasn't for me!"

"Nonsense! Neither of them would look twice at you if it wasn't for my money and connections." As usual, he'd succeeded in reducing her to next to nothing, belittling everything she said and did; yet she wasn't about to give him the satisfaction of showing how much she hurt. *I'll find someone to get me pregnant – it'll make him beholden to me instead of the other way around*, she thought, leaving the room to call Mark.

"Did you get to talk to her?"

"Yes – Hannah's calling me in a couple of weeks."

"If you're lying to me ... if what we're planning doesn't work, we'll move on to plan B."

"Meaning?" Mark asked, fearing the worst.

"Never you mind. Make arrangements to meet." She didn't bother telling him Enrico, her photographer friend, was part of the 'paparazzi'. They'd frequently bumped into each other at numerous celebrity functions. After she'd instructed him the pictures must seem genuine, as if Mark and Hannah were carrying on behind Ben's back, Enrico dared to ask if she'd be willing to pay him a bonus in addition to their arranged fee.

"Of course! That's if you're willing to make me disclose your addictions to sex, gambling and drugs," she replied, reminding him she had enough information about him to ensure he went to prison.

"I can't talk long – my pupils are awaiting me in the hall." Hannah was calling from the school. "Social Services are adamant it's your job to convince your ex you're genuine about getting to know your daughter. I did my part; the rest is down to you. Please don't contact me again."

Afraid she couldn't be persuaded to meet him, Mark replied, "I want to discuss it with you in person."

"That's not what I agreed to." She'd been worried sick Ben would find out about it.

"Please, I beg you, if this fails I'll never set eyes on her again!"

"Alright. We'll meet up at the same café, this Tuesday at 5pm – don't be late."

"Try finding a table where I can see you – I can't tell you how grateful I am to you." Pleased with himself, Mark hung up, then dialled Vanessa's number. She must have been sitting by the phone given the fact she answered on the first ring.

"I did what you asked, Hannah's agreed to see me," he said, giving her the details.

"I'm impressed. You must demonstrate how pleased you are she's been helping you get together with your daughter. I've described the two of you to Enrico. He's tall and dark, hair in a ponytail, dressed in leather; you can't miss him. Just imagine: we'll soon get the people we love . . ."

Mark kept telling himself Hannah was bound to forgive him when she realised they were destined to be together. *I'm not losing you again – you belonged to me first!*

Tuesday afternoon soon arrived and with it butterflies at the pit of his stomach. Steadying his nerves with several pints, Mark was halfway out the door when Vanessa called, reminding him of the details.

"Screw this up and you know what'll happen!" were her final words.

Parking in Parkshot, Mark immediately spotted the sleazy-looking photographer walking towards the café, camera safely tucked away inside the pocket of his leather jacket, the black trousers leaving nothing to the imagination. Both men nodded, silently acknowledging each other. Entering, Mark found a table at the door. Turning up a few minutes later, wearing a short denim skirt, blouse and pearl necklace, Hannah informed him she only had half an hour to spare.

"Ben and I are invited to a friend's house for dinner," she explained, putting her shoulder bag and jacket on the chair between them.

"Can I get you something to eat or drink?" Mark asked, signalling for a waiter and ordering a glass of red wine for himself.

"No, thank you."

Pulling his chair closer to hers, he reached for her hand, kissing each finger.

"What the hell are you doing?" she shouted, her voice drowned out by the noise around them.

"I just want to show you how grateful I am," Mark lied, putting a hand over his eyes, as if to indicate they were arguing about her not being free to be with him.

"Let's go outside to talk. I can't hear myself think in here!" Downing the rest of his wine, Mark casually put his arm around her shoulders as they walked outside.

"I really appreciate everything you did for me. What if Petra doesn't believe me?"

"She'll have no option but to let you see your daughter."

Mark looked around him. The photographer was nowhere to be seen. "You must know how I feel about you. You're all I can think of, baby." He lunged for her, lips touching hers.

"Get off me! Ben's the only man I love! I never felt this way about you – not even back then." Tears of anger stinging in her eyes, Hannah knew he'd tricked her again. "Come near me again and I'll make sure Ben knows about it!" she cried, pulling up the collar of her jacket, the steady drizzle of rain washing away her tears as she ran away from him, oblivious of the silver Jaguar parked further down the street. Sitting behind the wheel, clasping the camera catching the perfect shot, Enrico wondered why Vanessa was so keen to destroy that pretty redhead's life.

Perhaps when she sees that photo, she'll change her mind and add a bonus on top of what we agreed, he thought to himself.

★

A week later, Hannah decided to pass the French patisserie close to their house to buy bread and croissants for the weekend. There she noticed a familiar figure sitting by herself at a table in the corner of the café, her face covered in a magazine.

"Hello, Eve. May I join you? We've not had the opportunity to get acquainted since you started working for Ben and Collin."

"I've no complaints; Mr Isaacs' been very good to me. I'm sorry but I have to leave – my family expect me." Hair framing her heart-shaped face, Eve abruptly raised herself.

"Did I offend you in some way? All I ask are a few minutes of your time."

"Please, Miss Stein . . . this has nothing to do with me."

"What are you talking about? Please be so kind as to explain."

"It's late – my best wishes to Mr Isaacs." Clutching her bag, Eve resolutely walked out the door, Hannah following closely behind asking why she behaved in such an odd way.

"Please tell me if I did something to offend you?"

"I've something I think you should take a look at," Eve replied in a subdued voice and slight accent, her face and neck flushed red with embarrassment. From her bag she pulled out a large brown unsealed envelope addressed to *Mr B. Isaacs, Richmond Solicitors*.

"Why are you showing me this?" Hannah whispered, scared to look at the contents.

"Please take a look," the discreet PA replied, watching her pull out one photo after the other. A total of five, each showing her and Mark kissing and holding hands in and outside of the café on the common.

"Who sent them? Has Ben seen them?" Hannah felt as if she were about to faint. Her face completely drained of colour. Seeing her so upset, Eve knew without a shadow of a doubt she'd been right to show them to her, convinced someone deliberately set it up to look as if she and that man were having an affair.

"Mr Isaacs insists I go through his mail prior to giving it to him. I was inside the patisserie pouring through his letters when I first came across those pictures. My immediate thought was I must show them to you. I'm sorry you're having to concern yourself with this – I'm sorry I doubted you," Eve said in a gentle voice, touching Hannah's arm.

"Who'd do something so despicable? Ben's everything to me, I'd never willingly do anything to hurt him . . ." Slowly Hannah put two and two together. "Did . . . did Ben mention my introduction to Vanessa Westbrook?"

"You're referring to the incident in the restaurant?"

"This is her doing! The pictures have her name all over them. What will I tell Ben?" Tears streamed down her face.

"Does he know you and that man are in contact?"

"Mark? Ben knows of him but not the fact I agreed to meet him. Mark asked me to help him reunite with his daughter . . . I should have known he'd stoop to this! What if there are copies all over London?" Privately, she wondered, *How did those two bump into one another?*

"My gut instinct tells me they were meant for Ben's eyes alone. He's their main objective – you're the target."

Too upset to talk, Hannah's hands were shaking so much that she dropped the pictures. They fluttered to the ground, Eve picking them up and putting them back into the brown envelope, which she handed to her.

"You must stay calm. Mr Isaacs is a sensible man, I'm sure he'll believe in you." Eve bid her farewell, then as an afterthought, added, "Make sure you tell him before she does!"

★

"What's wrong – it's not Zipporah is it? Oh little one . . ." Ben wondered why his fiancée looked so pale.

"Not yet . . . I've something to show you. You must promise me you won't jump to the wrong conclusion!"

"We'll talk about it later – what's for dinner? I'm starving."

"No, it can't wait. I want to show it to you *now*!" Hannah persisted, leading the way into the living room where the pictures were on display on the table.

Scrutinising the five pictures, Ben too turned pale.

"Eve gave them to me – she wanted me to see them before you did." *What if he doesn't believe me? What if he thinks Mark and I are lovers?* Desperate to explain the truth, Hannah sobbed: "That piece of shit persuaded me to meet him twice, asking me to help him reunite with his estranged daughter. The naive fool I am I said yes. Someone tampered with those photographs."

Seeing her so upset, Ben wrapped his arms around her.

"The idea of you and him? It never even crossed my mind. You're simply incapable of doing something like that. Trust is a wonderful trait but not where the likes of Mark are concerned." He paused for a moment. "Are you thinking the same as I am?"

"I'm certain Vanessa put him up to it! What if she sent copies to clients?"

In another month Collin and Ben's contract with Ronald was due to come to an end.

"If that's the case, I'll call an emergency meeting telling everyone exactly what the Westbrooks are like," Ben assured her, a grim look in his eyes.

Chapter Eighteen

"Consider yourself lucky our agreement is coming to an end!" Ben's voice was full of contempt as he watched the American scrutinise the photos laid out on his desk.

"We'll put it behind us . . . that is, unless you prefer to compromise your career?" Ronald's tone was smug, as he internally vowed to punish Vanessa for everything she had done to ruin things between himself and Ben.

"You're in no position to lay down the law with us! We're no longer dancing to your tune." Ben unintentionally knocked the desk, causing the pictures to fall down on the carpet.

"I'll personally see to it Vanessa is taken to task."

"Really? What will you do to her this time? Withdraw her pocket money? Please leave my office now!" He opened the door pointedly.

"Don't take that tone with me!" Ronald's voice was laced with menace.

"I'll take that as a threat, shall I?"

"Take it as you wish!" The older man marched out into the foyer, where Eve offered to help him with his coat. "I'm perfectly capable by myself," he snapped at her, angry things had come to a head between himself and Ben.

"As you wish sir – I wish you a pleasant evening," Eve replied, suppressing the urge to laugh out loud.

Later that afternoon, Ben invited his secretary into his office. "Please sit down – I've been meaning to talk to you, Eve," he said, pulling out a chair for her. "My associate and I are very pleased with your work; so much so we're considering promoting you to full partner as soon as our enterprise with Ronald Westbrook is terminated."

"That's extremely generous of you both! My husband will be so pleased." Eve was clearly overcome. "I took the liberty of suggesting to your partner we should put those pictures somewhere safe – where no one can get to them."

"You're quite right. I'll see to it myself. As a token of how much all of us value you, Hannah and I reserved a table for you and your family at Bertorelli's in Knightsbridge and tickets to see *Les Misérables* at The Palace Theatre tomorrow night. I want you to take a couple of days off."

"That's too generous! I'd have done exactly what I did regardless."

"We know that – sometimes actions speak louder than words."

"Take me back as fast as you can!" Ronald told Bernie. I've got a bone to pick with Vanessa!"

"Is there something I can do?" Bernie asked, concerned Vanessa was in for a hard time. Watching his boss staggering out of the car and up the steps to the front door, it was evident just how much he'd aged in the past year, probably to do with his and Vanessa's bickering.

"I've been much too lenient with her – no wonder she's turned out just like her mother," Ronald muttered, adamant to do things his way.

"I'll bring in your case, sir. It's much too heavy for you." Bernie thought the old bastard was a fool for not realising wealth and success had no meaning unless shared with someone who loved him.

"What am I guilty of this time?" Vanessa asked in a sarcastic voice, after being summoned to her father's office.

"I've seen those damned pictures! You went too far this time. I demand you get rid of any negatives and apologise in person to Ben and Hannah. If not, I'll ensure you're left destitute!"

"Those pictures are all there is – why are you always so keen to think the worst of me?"

"Don't you dare question my judgement of you! Ben's repulsed by your conduct."

"But I love him, Daddy! Please help me make everything alright."

Due to her own foolish behaviour, Vanessa had ensured Ben wanted nothing more to do with her. God alone knew what punishment her father had in store for her.

Tossing and turning in his bed, struggling to visualise his and Hannah's future, Mark was interrupted by the phone.

"You ruined everything!" Vanessa shouted. "I ask you do one thing right and you screw up!"

"Listen to me, lady! I warned this might happen. Did you listen? Of course not! Because of what you did, Hannah will never speak to me again." Mark was so upset that he wished she were there with him, if only to wring her neck.

"My father's demanding I apologise to them – can you imagine how that feels? When I'm finished with her, Hannah will regret the day she was born."

"Suit yourself. I wish I'd had the sense to not get involved with you and your crazy scheme."

"You listen to me, creep. I know all there is to know about you; things you don't want out into the open – especially not where that mother of yours is concerned!"

"You dare drag her into this . . ."

"Shortly my father, Ben and Collin are having their last meeting – I'm not permitted to take part."

"My heart bleeds for you!"

"This is what you're going to do: call Hannah and grovel, tell her you're sorry for what you did, that you and I bumped into each other and I forced you to help split them up."

"I'll do no such thing. Tell your 'connections' I'm not scared of them. I did my bit – this is where it ends." Mark wasn't prepared to spend the remainder of his life being at her beck and call.

Ignoring him, Vanessa continued, "Tell her we're an item, having quite a lot in common. As soon as they come round to the idea of an 'us', they'll drop their guard, thinking we're no longer a threat to them."

"You're insane! People as crazy as you ought to be in a straitjacket." Mark realised he was perspiring all over.

"You're fortunate I'm not a sensitive person! Unless you do as you're told . . ." Vanessa didn't bother to finish her sentence.

"If, and I stress, *if* your crazy plan works, what then? You're seriously thinking those two will ever fall out with each other?"

"When she sees him in a compromising position with me, she'll have no choice but to leave him!"

"You're even more sick than I thought." The room started to spin.

"Make her believe we're an item. My father's off on a trip to the Big Apple after that meeting, I'll turn up unexpectedly as soon as the coast is clear. Knowing Ben as well as I do, he's bound to linger and finish off some document. I'll plead with him to have a farewell drink with me, put a couple of Rohypnol tablets in his glass . . . I'm sure you can figure out the rest."

"That's sick! Those damn photos can get us into prison!"

"Don't be so bloody stupid. Who's to know? I'll leave no traces. Besides, I love the guy, remember?"

"I'm having nothing more to do with you. We caused enough damage as it is."

"Suit yourself, mummy's boy. You'd obviously much rather look over your shoulder for the rest of your miserable life. Get Hannah to love you again! So much so she'll be looking to cry on your shoulder when she finds out about Ben and me. I'll give you the details nearer the time, meantime you and I need to work on our so-called 'chemistry'," Vanessa purred.

"No way – I won't stoop to having sex with you!"

"Calm down – I'm not keen on it either." Oddly enough her comment hurt his male pride.

"You're serious about setting it up to look as if you and Ben are having an affair?"

"Of course! She's all yours after that."

"Leaving Ben free to marry you instead?"

"That's right. Unless, of course, you can come up with an even better idea to getting what both of us want; not to mention the small detail of boosting your so-called business . . ." She knew full well he couldn't afford to reject her.

★

Desperate to get all of it out of the way, Mark dialled Hannah's number, fingers shaking so much he had to put the phone down and try again. Busy preparing dinner, Hannah answered thinking it was Melanie wanting to talk to her about the twins' latest development.

"Please hear me out! There's something I need to talk to you about."

"What does it take to make you understand I want nothing to do with you?"

"What I did to you was despicable. Vanessa left me no option, saying she'd destroy my business, but everything I told you about Maruschka was true. I'd never lie about something like that."

"I don't believe a word of it! How dare the two of you mess with our lives?"

"What I'm about to tell you may come as a surprise but . . . Vanessa and I are dating. The future's looking good."

"Of course you are!" They clearly had something else up their sleeves. "Tell her Ben and I hope you rot in hell!"

"You probably disagree, but Vanessa and I have quite a lot in common – most importantly parents who are incapable of showing affection." He may as well have read the words out loud from a script.

"Don't call again. The two of you in love? Don't make me laugh!" Hannah slammed down the receiver before he could say another word.

Later that evening, Mark met Vanessa at The Swan to discuss their next move. As he told Vanessa about his conversation with Hannah, she shrugged her shoulders.

"It's rather funny – you and me? Mind you, most men would jump at the idea to have me for a girlfriend." She complied with her father's order, sending a letter of apology to Hannah and Ben, and not expecting a reply.

"Let's quit before someone gets hurt," Mark pleaded, hoping she'd see sense.

"Fine by me! I'll spread the news to our mutual friends then, shall I?"

"You wouldn't dare." Imagining what it would do to him, Mark asked, "If I agree to this, will that be the end of it?"

"Of course! I'm not the Mafia . . ."

Getting out of the bathtub looking forward to a quiet night in front of the telly, Mark was about to open a can of beer when Vanessa called saying she was on her way to him.

"I should be with you in half an hour – it's high time we get properly acquainted . . ."

Too stunned to reply, Mark put on some clothes just as her cab pulled up outside his house. In heavy make-up, peroxide blonde hair and high heels, she got out of the cab, telling the driver to come back for her in a couple of hours. Walking towards the front door and pushing the bell, Vanessa surveyed the yellow brick estate, ugly front garden and net curtains, thinking, *Who the hell would stoop so low as to live here?* Mark opened the door.

"You can't just barge in without asking first! I've put the heating on in case you're cold – let me take your coat."

"Don't bother, I'll keep it on a while longer. This place's awfully dark." Barely over the threshold, she had already succeeded in insulting him, eyes falling on his top, commenting, "Yellow's not your colour, it makes you look ill." She followed him into the drab, sterile living room, which housed a beige sofa and a small table, with no paintings or photos on the walls. *He's in desperate need of a good dentist and hair stylist*, she thought to herself.

"I'm sorry my home's not to your liking – please feel free to leave!" Mark told her, taking the bottle of red wine she brought with her and fetching a couple of glasses from the kitchen.

"This tastes great! Did you make some food to go with it? Smoked salmon with watercress salad would suit nicely!" she joked, starting to laugh.

"What's so bloody funny? Give me your coat. You look ridiculous wearing it indoors – perhaps you're embarrassed at what's beneath?" Mark attempted to belittle her. Instead of answering him, Vanessa simply got up and sidled up to him putting a hand on his crotch, her long red nails stroking the fabric of his trousers. Shocked, yet incapable of pushing her away, Mark groaned.

"You've not come for *that* . . ."

"I disagree." She pushed him onto the sofa and climbed onto his lap. Too turned on to resist her, Mark's hands found their way beneath the coat.

"My God – you're naked!"

"That's not strictly true . . ." Slowly she unbuttoned her coat, revealing nothing but a skimpy corset, black suspenders and stockings, bringing back memories of when he was in his late teens, visiting prostitutes in Soho. Unzipping his flies, Vanessa asked, "What have we got here? Looks like we have plenty to amuse ourselves with!"

Watching her head moving up and down, Mark thought she was every bit as good as the hookers he'd frequented, knowing exactly how to please him. Wiping her mouth with one hand, Vanessa put her legs on either side of his back, buttocks slightly raised, making it easier for him to enter, each thrust bringing them closer to the edge as, moaning, both climaxed. His flies were still undone when she bent to kiss him, fingers and tongue causing another erection.

A while later, they lay spent in each other's arms.

"You obviously enjoyed it as much as I did."

"It'll never happen again!" Mark replied, angry with himself for so readily succumbing to her, while begrudgingly admitting she was the best lay he'd ever had.

"I wouldn't be so sure about that if I were you," Vanessa teased, a wicked smile on her lips. Too turned on to protest, Mark watched her stroke him until, beyond caring, he indulged in what could only be described as an orgasmic feast.

"What the hell are you doing to me, lady?" he asked in a thick voice.

"Me? Giving you a taste of paradise, that's what! How can something so pleasurable be so bad?"

"It isn't." She took off her corset, black suspenders and stockings, then lay down on the grey carpet, legs wide apart, her black stilettos waving at him to come join her on the floor. Mark ripped off his clothes, throwing caution to the wind.

"I sure as hell hope you're using protection!" Mark whispered, too far gone to care.

"What do you take me for? A bloody virgin?" Vanessa replied, omitting to inform him she'd only just started to take the Pill. Seeing her lying there beneath him looking so abandoned, her body brushing his, Mark felt another stirring in his loins.

"This sure beats food!" she said, raising herself off the floor, completely oblivious to his eyes on every part of her anatomy. "We're damned good together, Mark. It's a pity neither of us has feelings for the other."

"My heart belongs to Hannah! This ends here and now."

"It's not as if they'll find out about it." Her words made sense to him. As much as she meant to him, Hannah wasn't as exciting as Vanessa between the sheets.

Later, sorting out their scattered clothes on the floor, Mark watched her getting dressed, her dishevelled hair and smudged make-up making her look somehow vulnerable.

"The driver's been waiting outside for well over an hour," he said, helping to put her coat on.

"Don't worry, I'll make it worth his while!" Vanessa replied, flashing one of her seductive smiles.

Trying to make sense of what happened between them, Mark didn't get to sleep until much later, images of what they did haunting him throughout the night. Calling him the next day, Vanessa announced she was coming round again that night to discuss what she referred to as 'Ben's office party' then put the phone down before Mark had the opportunity to tell her he'd rather they meet somewhere neutral so as to not end up in bed. A small part of him was already regretting things had to end between them when Hannah and Ben came to their senses.

Calling for a take-away at his local Chinese restaurant and popping into his local pub to buy a bottle of wine, Mark let her in at 8pm.

"What if this blows up in our faces?" he asked immediately, dispensing with any pleasantries.

"It won't. After I've spiked Ben's drink with Rohypnol, he won't know what's hit him . . ."

"If you're wrong, we could go to jail."

"You're a terrific lay, Mark, but I'd rather you left the planning to me. You must tell Hannah you're worried I've not returned to you and ask her to meet you at Ben's office."

"Seeing you and him like that . . . It'll devastate her!"

"That's the whole point. It's our last chance to break them up."

"And you're quite certain that drug won't cause permanent damage?"

"It'll only make him drowsy. I'd never go so far as to risk his life!"

"Then let's get it over and done with. The sooner those two return to us, the better."

They were in the entrance saying goodbye when someone turned the key in the lock. Letting herself in, Annuschka Copeck stared at them open-mouthed.

"You never told me you'd have a visitor at this time of night, son!"

"What the hell do you think you're doing? It's almost 1am in the morning. I told you, you have to call first!"

"I'll come and go as I please – this house is mine – not yours! Anyway, I brought your shirts and laundry." Thinking he behaved like an adolescent, not a man, Vanessa felt Annuschka's pale-blue eyes on her. "Aren't you going to introduce us? Your father and I brought you up to have manners!"

"Mark and I were discussing work. I'd better be on my way – my cab's waiting outside."

"So I've noticed! What's your interest in my son? Mark's just a salesman – nothing else." Annuschka thought the blonde standing in front of her looked vulgar.

"I won't bore you with the details. It's been nice making your acquaintance," Vanessa replied, certain this woman wasn't the kind of person who'd take no for an answer. "We'll talk in a couple of days, Mark," she said, walking outside to her waiting cab.

"Well, she's certainly unlike any other woman you ever met, son," Annuschka muttered.

"How could you embarrass me like that?" Mark shouted at her.

"I refuse to make an appointment to see my own son in my own house!"

"This is *my* house! What goes on inside is none of your business."

Taking no notice of him, Annuschka started emptying the bag of laundry at the bottom of the stairs. Walking upstairs to his bedroom and seeing the state of the bed, her worst suspicions were confirmed: those two weren't colleagues but lovers.

"I demand you call me before barging in!" Mark screamed at her, eyes dark with anger.

"Your father left this place to me! The deeds are in my name – not yours."

"Perhaps you'd rather I look for another place to live?"

"Anyone with an ounce of respectability and dignity would run a mile where her kind's concerned. It'll never last – her sort never do."

"Unlike Hannah you mean? You're the real reason she left me!" Pacing the room, Mark repeated what he'd said earlier.

"How will you afford it? You're hard-up as it is. If it weren't for your father's and my generosity, you'd not have a roof over your head."

"I won't let you treat me like this – you'll eat your words once the tables are turned and you're in a nursing home."

"You're threatening your own mother? I demand you pack your things and leave this minute. No child of mine addresses me like that!"

Regretting he'd said too much, Mark put his hands up. "I spoke out of line – we've done nothing but argue since Dad died. I'm sure we'll find a way to compromise."

"You're hoping I turn a blind eye to what you said? As for that woman, I don't know where to start!"

"She's just a bit of harmless fun, mother."

"You're my flesh and blood and I'm ashamed of you."

"You're so much better than me? Was that the reason Dad preferred working all hours so as to escape your nagging?" The words came out of his mouth before he had the chance to think.

"When I think of the things we sacrificed to raise you . . . I'm an old woman yearning to spend whatever time I've left with my grandchild. Do these belong to your 'girlfriend'?" Picking up a pair of lacy black panties off the floor, Annuschka handed them to him, adding, "I'll return in the morning. As for your father, let's just say he wasn't what you thought he was."

"What's that supposed to mean?"

"I'll explain if and when I feel like it!" An angry look in her eyes, Annuschka turned and stomped downstairs, slamming the door behind her.

"My Father's expecting you," Vanessa declared later that week.

"Won't he take offence if we're seeing each other?" Mark asked nervously.

"Of course! It'll be to our benefit if he talks about us to Ben."

"But I don't wish to meet him!"

"Then we'll come to you instead. Get your lazy bum over here now," Vanessa ordered, reminding him who was boss.

Putting on one of his brown office suits, shirt and tie, and ensuring his shoes were polished, Mark drove to Primrose Hill and parked his red Toyota at the corner of the affluent street. The spectacular mansion stood out from the rest of the properties. Scared her father would see straight through him, Mark ran a hand through his hair and pushed the bell of the large black door. He heard footsteps approach from the inside.

"You're Mr Mark Copeck, right?" A tall, muscular man in his sixties with a bald head asked. Not waiting for an answer, he lead the way into a enormous hall with huge crystal chandeliers and gold statues of tigers and wolves standing against the walls.

"Mr Copeck's arrived, sir," Bernie announced as Mark followed him into what looked like a ballroom entirely furnished with antiques, paintings by Picasso, Matisse and Constable on the walls. Just as he began to break into one of his cold sweats, Vanessa arrived to greet him.

"This is Mark, Daddy – we're in *love*," she declared, proving it by kissing Mark's cheek.

Stocky with silver grey hair and ice-cold blue eyes, wearing a black evening suit and spectacles at the tip of his nose, Ronald scrutinised the man in front of him.

"Aren't you the man in those pictures?" he barked. "Ben showed them to me. It's your fault he wants nothing to do with me!"

Sick with nerves, Mark reached for his hand, eyes fixated on his shoes. "It's an honour to meet you sir."

"What the hell's going on?" Ronald ignored Mark's out-stretched hand. "First the Stein woman, now Vanessa!"

"Hannah's just an old friend – it's your daughter I love."

"Don't you mean my wealth?"

"Daddy . . . *please!*" Vanessa interjected. "Mark and I regret everything we did."

"What good's that to me and Isaacs? In love? Don't make me laugh. Your so-called friend here's only interested in whatever he can lay his hands on. Well, I've got news for the pair of you: you'll not squeeze a penny out of me."

Listening to him, Mark felt certain Vanessa wasn't on his list of priorities. Astonished her own father addressed her in such a derogatory manner, Vanessa repeated how much they regretted causing Ben and Hannah to get upset.

"Your boyfriend's not a patch on Isaacs," Ronald said to his daughter, then turned to Mark. "I demand you leave immediately! You never cease to disappoint me, Vanessa."

Watching her behave in such a submissive way around her father, Mark suddenly knew why Vanessa had turned out the way she did. Following her into the hall, her expression downtrodden, Mark said, "Don't listen to him! He's nothing but a bully. Lots of men would love for you to be their girlfriend – all you have to do is find the right guy."

"I already did! It's high time my father showed me some respect," Vanessa replied, her eyes avoiding his.

"You're sure this plan of yours is the only way?"

"There's no turning back now."

Parking outside his own house – a mere shack compared to hers – Mark had a sudden flash of despair, certain something awful was about to take place. Remembering Vanessa's face when her father shouted at her, he thought, *You're more damaged than I was led to believe.*

Driving into Knightsbridge to attend a meeting, Ronald asked Bernie if Vanessa had confided in him about Mark.

"Your daughter's personal life's her own, sir – perhaps they're in love?"

"Don't be such an idiot! I instructed my legal team to investigate him – it emerges he's not paid a penny in alimony to his daughter. I was right all along. That jerk's after one thing only: my fortune!"

Having arranged for a caterer to deliver sandwiches, beverages and cakes to the office, Ben watched Ronald seat himself and completely ignore Eve. He declared Tim Clancy was present to ensure everything was above board.

"You're quite certain this is the end of the road for us, gentlemen?" Ronald asked, his eyes glued on Ben.

"Without a shadow of a doubt," the latter replied in a firm voice.

"It's not because of what Vanessa did to you and Hannah?"

"It obviously had some bearing but Collin and I wish to proceed on our own, giving our clients the excellence they deserve."

"What a pity. I was looking forward to our continuing success – especially where you're concerned, Ben."

Slightly put off that he wasn't of as much interest, Collin kept his mouth shut, focusing on the fact neither of them would have to dance to that man's tune anymore.

"I've nothing more to add," Ben replied. "Eve, please be so good as to witness our signatures – Mr Westbrook is leaving." Glaring at him, Ronald signed the document laid out before him.

"It's been a pleasure doing business with you both. My offer's still on the table, should you decide to take it, Ben." Seeing the look of contempt in the younger man's eyes, the American walked out, his attorney in tow, without so much as a "goodbye".

"When's your flight due, sir?" Bernie asked, as he drove them towards the airport.

"I've plenty of time yet. Keep an eye on Vanessa for me – my PA will get in touch about when to pick me up." He didn't mention he'd be staying at his penthouse on Park Avenue, his 'Madame' assuring him she arranged for a group of 'accommodating' young girls to cater to his demands. *If only my useless daughter would behave and give me the grandson I crave,* Ronald thought, convinced it would complete his existence.

"It feels wonderful having that bastard out of our lives," Ben told Collin, as they wrapped up the day's event. "Did I tell you

Vanessa's dating Hannah's ex, Mark? Those two are as bad as each other – a perfect match!"

"There's someone for everyone I guess. So what makes you so special Ronald's determined to have you working for him?"

"Isn't that obvious? Think yourself lucky he's hassling me, not you. I hope I never set my eyes on either of them again," Ben replied, letting out a deep sigh of relief.

"Don't stay too long – does Hannah know you'll be late?"

"Yeah. Tomorrow's Saturday, we'll crack open a bottle of champagne – I've some paperwork to read for Monday's cases."

"Rather you than me, mate. Karen's forbidding me to come near the office over the weekend. We're taking the boys to Richmond Park to watch the deer on Sunday." Collin saluted his friend on his way out. Ben stayed late until 10pm and was about to leave when he heard a noise coming from the entrance.

"Who's that? We're shut. Please return on Monday morning," he called out, considering using their direct line to the local police station.

"It's only me – I've come to say goodbye to you," a woman replied, appearing on his doorstep with a large bag in her hand.

"Get the hell away from me!" Ben shouted. All he wanted was to spend the rest of the night at home with Hannah, looking forward to the future. Brushing past him, heart racing inside her chest, Vanessa put down a bottle of expensive red wine on the counter.

"Leave and take that with you," Ben ordered, eyes blazing.

"Please hear me out! Since you never replied to any of my letters, I made up my mind to come here asking if you'd at least share a farewell drink with me. I can't bear us parting like this!" There were tears brimming in Vanessa's eyes.

"You're not my friend. I was a fool thinking you'd be happy for me. Had I known what you're really like, I'd have washed my hands of you long ago."

"I blame my father for the way I turned out ... Mark's changed me for the better," Vanessa lied, moving a step closer to him.

"You and that idiot? It's poetic justice fate's brought you together," Ben replied, glaring at her.

"Please believe me when I tell you I genuinely wish you and Hannah all the best."

"Is that all? My beautiful fiancée's waiting for me at home." His words were like a knife deep inside her heart.

"One drink is all I ask – a sign we're getting on with our lives," Vanessa begged him, succeeding in squeezing out a few crocodile tears.

Trying to figure out if she meant it, Ben's thoughts turned to all the fun they'd had in Cambridge then back to his and Hannah's future and everything they had to look forward to.

"Perhaps you're right ... I've cut all ties with your father. We should do the same. I'll call Hannah to let her know I'll be delayed for half an hour."

"Why? Mark's awaiting me as well – you'll be home in no time." Vanessa was nervous she'd talk him out of staying. "Just relax and make yourself comfortable while I tend to the wine."

"Don't take too long. I wish to spend the rest of the night with my future wife." A tiny voice in his brain warned Ben he'd made a terrible mistake in agreeing to her suggestion. Kicking off his shoes, he loosened his tie and sat down on the couch, images of his and Hannah's wedding springing to mind.

Reassured Mark knew what was expected of him Vanessa set her plan into action, pouring wine into two glasses from the kitchen cupboard, and adding a couple of Rohypnol tablets to his. Stirring the wine with a finger, she made a mental note to clear up any traces.

"This wine's great," she said, walking back into the office and handing him his glass. "Here's to us!"

"You're right, it does taste great." Ben emptied his glass in less than a minute, eager to get home to Hannah.

"Can I pour you some more? There's plenty left in the bottle."

Putting a hand over his glass, Ben shook his head. "I've had enough – I hope you and Mark will be happy together. Life's complete now I've someone to share it with."

Listening to him mentioning that woman's name made her skin crawl. *Hannah this, Hannah that . . . she's all he can think of!*

"Thanks for the wine. I'm off home!" As he stood up, Ben felt the room spinning around him.

"What's up?" Vanessa asked, feigning concern.

"Nothing a good night's sleep won't put right . . ." But as soon as he tried to walk, his legs buckled beneath him.

"You looking as if you're about to fall!"

"What the hell's happening to me? It . . . feels as if I'm . . . drugged . . ." Seeing her through a haze, the ice-blue eyes penetrating his, Ben knew he should have listened to his gut instinct. "What . . . what did you put into my drink?"

"I can't let you marry her! Can't you see how good we are together? I've loved you since we first met. Daddy will give you anything you want."

"You . . . bitch! Get your . . . h-hands off . . . m-me . . ." But as much as he tried to get past her, his body wouldn't obey.

"It won't harm you – only prevent you from making the worst mistake of your life."

Hating himself for being so gullible as to trust her, Ben tried to tell her as much, the words spilling out of his mouth slurred and incomprehensible.

Vanessa laughed and pushed him down on the couch. His head was throbbing so much he wanted to scream. Pleased everything was going according to plan, Vanessa started to undress, and turned her attention to Ben, unbuttoning his shirt, struggling to remove his trousers until he was naked except for his shoes, tie and underwear. Returning to the kitchen to wash their glasses ensuring she left no traces of her deception, she came back into the room and sat down next to him. A contented smile on her lips, she wished someone was there, taking a picture of them.

She's setting it up to look as if we're having an affair – Hannah can't see me like this!

As Ben made another attempt to stand up, Vanessa pushed him back onto the couch and pillow, her scarlet lips hovering above his face.

Answering the phone on the second ring, Hannah felt certain it was Ben informing he was on his way, the voice at the end of the line making her see red.

"I warned you to never contact me again!"

"I'm sorry to disturb you so late," Mark said. "Has Ben returned to you?"

"What's it to do with you?"

"Vanessa's attempting to make amends with him – what if something terrible happened to either of them?" Pretending to be frantic with worry about her, Mark suggested they meet outside Ben's offices in another ten minutes.

"Vanessa gave me the address a while ago."

Not bothering to ask the reason, her only concern being Ben's welfare, Hannah put the phone down and grabbed the keys to the brand new Volvo he'd given her for her recent birthday. Driving as fast as she could to Richmond town centre, she parked outside the main entrance. After waiting fifteen minutes for Mark to turn up, she made the decision to go in on her own, praying nothing had happened to the man she loved. Walking through the front door and seeing a dim light coming from his office, Hannah took a deep breath and went into the dark room

The sight meeting her eyes made her freeze to the spot. An anguished cry escaped her lips as she saw them lying next to one another on the couch. Shaking off her stupor, she walked up to them and reached for his arm, noting the smell of alcohol on his breath. The rug barely covering their bodies fell to the floor.

"She . . . s-spiked . . . my . . . d-drink!"

But the marks on his face and neck provided proof they were lovers. Pulling away from him, all she could think was, *He told me he loved me – this can't be happening to me – not again!* It was the second time someone she loved and trusted betrayed her. Numb with pain, Hannah ran into the toilet, making it just in time to wretch over the basin.

"What the hell's going on? You look as if you're about to faint!" Mark had come in unannounced, feigning shock as Vanessa approached them in her skimpy underwear, heels and throw draped casually around her shoulders.

"I'm sorry you had to find us like that." Her eyes searched Hannah's. "I only came here to say goodbye . . . one thing led to another . . . I tried telling him Mark and I are together."

Emotionally drained, Hannah forced herself to stay calm, her only thought, *You did this! Staging every detail – Mark's just an accomplice. Why couldn't you have seen through her, Ben? After everything she did to us* . . . Too distraught to keep her feelings to herself, she lashed out.

"You set this up!"

Vanessa laughed out loud, her eyes full of loathing and contempt.

"None of this would have happened had you known how to satisfy him!"

Finding the strength from somewhere, Hannah went up to her, raised her arm and slapped her hard in the face. The ugly red mark she left was not unlike the one Vanessa had inflicted on her arm.

"I've wanted to do that for a long time!"

"You bitch!" Vanessa hissed, splashing cold water onto it, wishing she could get away with murdering her.

"Stop it!" Mark shouted, standing between them. "I was worried sick about you! Look at yourself. You're practically naked!"

"I don't care. Ben and I are in love! There's not a thing either of you can do about it."

"You're not seriously telling us you and he are lovers? I demand you tell me how long this has been going on!" Mark was screaming at her now, desperate to keep up the pretence.

"It only started tonight – Ben's always loved *me*, not her!"

As they continued to fight, Hannah went back into the hall. Ben staggered towards her, his body swaying, the words coming out of his mouth horribly slurred.

"I . . . swear . . . I n-never . . . l-laid a fin-ger . . . on . . . her!"

What was happening to them? In less than a few hours their lives had been turned upside down.

"I know she staged it. What I don't understand is why you didn't see through her?" Hannah's voice broke just as he collapsed in a heap on the floor, eyes pleading with her not to leave him.

"No. No! I can't deal with this right now – sober up before return-ing to me!" she cried, stepping over his body on her way out.

Following behind, Mark reached for her hand, offering to drive her home. "You're in no state being on your own," he whis-pered.

"Don't come anywhere near me! All of this is down to you and Vanessa!" Hannah shouted, tears blurring her vision.

"This isn't how it's supposed to be! Ben's the villain in this – not me. You're just upset. Things will look a lot better in the morning," Mark mumbled, glaring at Vanessa.

Debating if she should stay to ensure he was alright, Hannah made the decision it was probably best for her to leave.

"If anything happens to him, I'll make sure you're held respon-sible!" she sobbed, running out the door. Crying all the way home, she was amazed no one noticed how fast she was driving.

"If your reckless behaviour causes repercussions . . ." In all the excitement, Mark forgot that Ben was eavesdropping on their conversation.

"We're fortunate I copied my father's key. How else would we succeed in doing what we did?" Vanessa told him to carry Ben into his office and onto the couch, the small rug covering only part of the latter's body.

"I'll repeat my question: are you absolutely sure those tablets won't harm him?"

"Of course! I often take them when I can't sleep."

"But not with alcohol, right?"

"It makes no difference. Apart from a nasty hangover, Ben won't know what hit him."

"Ben knows you drugged him. What if he decides to get

himself medically tested? I'll not go to prison because of you!" Mark was breaking into one of his sweats.

"If that happens, it'll be my word against his," Vanessa reassured him, exasperated with his questions.

"Another thing: you told me Hannah would turn to me for support, but you should have seen her reaction when I offered to take her back. She can't stand the sight of me – much less my touch."

"Give her time to get to grips with the situation. After tonight, she'll never trust him again."

"Stop kidding yourself! Those two only have eyes for each other. Not even a vicious snake like you can change it."

"Maybe that's true but you're much too involved now to walk away . . ."

"Just watch me! I'm cutting you out of my life, lady. Tell your so-called friends if they come near me and my mother, there'll be hell to pay."

Running into the empty, dark street, Vanessa following closely behind shouting obscenities at him, Mark managed to get rid of her by disappearing into the darkness of the night, raging in the car all the way back to Stanmore.

Returning inside, making sure she didn't leave any incriminating evidence, Vanessa went into Ben's office. She watched him toss and turn, shouting Hannah's name, completely unaware of her presence.

"I only did it so we can be together," she whispered, kissing his forehead. Looking at him one last time, she closed the door behind her.

Falling into bed not bothering to undress, Hannah cried so much her pillow was soaked with tears. The incessant ringing of the phone woke her a few hours later. Pulling the cover over her face to drown out the noise, all she could think was, *I'll have to tell everyone we made a mistake and that the wedding's off.* Suddenly a small voice inside of her alerted her something happened at home. Jumping out of bed, holding the receiver so tight her knuckles turned white, she shouted, "Who is it?"

"It's me, Dr Anderson. I've been trying to get hold of you for a long time. I'm sorry to have to inform you your grandmother has suffered a heart attack. Please get here as quickly as you can."

"Is she still alive?" she asked, crying so hard, he could hardly hear her.

"The ambulance is on its way. Between us we'll do everything we can to save her." Dr Anderson withheld the fact he didn't hold out much hope she'd survive.

Sobbing so much she doubted her own ability to drive yet hell-bent on getting there as fast as she could, irrelevant of traffic police along the way, Hannah told herself she had to call her mother, giving her the bad news.

Please God: don't let Granny die! she prayed, getting there in less than half an hour due to hardly any cars at that time of night. Parking outside the entrance, she rushed in, taking the lift to the third floor, all the while praying she wasn't too late. Dr Anderson opened the door as soon as he heard her footsteps in the corridor.

"Is Ben with you?" he asked, taking in her tear-stained face.

"We had an argument – I've come on my own. Please take me to my grandmother!"

"I've something I need to tell you first . . . let's go into the living room." Seated next to her on the couch, arm around her shoulder, the kind GP looked into her eyes. "It's with deep regret I have to inform you Mrs Friedman passed away before the ambulance arrived. There wasn't anything anyone could have done to prevent it. I'm so very sorry for your sad loss."

Slowly registering his words, Hannah got up from the couch. The room was spinning around her.

"Sit down and put your head between your legs while I get you some water. You've had a terrible shock."

I'm too late. Why didn't I answer the phone on the first ring? Hannah blamed herself for not being there in time. Returning with a glass of tap water, Dr Anderson repeated there wasn't anything either of them could have done.

"Regardless of you being present or not, the outcome would have been exactly the same."

Sipping her water, Hannah turned to look at him. She smiled through her tears.

"I'm so very grateful she had someone with her when she died. Please convey my sentiment to the carer. I'll never forgive myself for not having the opportunity to say goodbye and tell her how much I love her . . ."

"Your grandmother knew that," Dr Anderson patted her hand. "This was the best way for her to go – no more lingering on, awaiting the inevitable. You ought to have someone here with you. Is there perhaps a relative or friend you want me to call?"

Tears falling into her mouth, Hannah whispered, "There's no one else – only me."

Taking her hand into his own, Dr Anderson smiled at her.

"Mrs Friedman was one of a kind. Always a nice word for everyone, despite everything she endured – the Holocaust, being widowed and raising a child on her own."

"She'll continue to live inside our hearts – I'll never forget her. Her heartfelt laughter . . . Always telling me life's for living."

"Hannah," the doctor said gently, "I wish I could stay, but I've a full schedule in another couple of hours. I will, of course, return to help organise everything." He was referring to releasing the body and subsequent funeral.

It was almost 6am. Acutely conscious of the need to inform her parents, Hannah's head hurt as she tried focusing on the present.

"Your grandmother repeatedly expressed how happy she was you and Ben are getting married. I sincerely hope whatever's come between you can be resolved."

Closing the door behind him, Hannah went into her grandmother's room. Sitting on the side of the bed, she gazed at Zipporah's rigid body beneath the cover. Hands clasped, eyes shut as if she were asleep; the sound of birds singing outside the window. Bending to touch her soft cheek she whispered, "I'll never forget you, Granny, forgive me for not being here when you needed me the most."

Incapable of holding back the tears, Hannah grieved all the losses she suffered that night.

CHAPTER NINETEEN

E YES SQUEEZED SHUT to protect them from the sun streaming through the office blinds, Ben rubbed his head, groaning.

Hannah was here . . . I have to talk to her, tell her nothing untoward happened between Vanessa and me, he thought, recalling the shocked expression on her face. Head exploding, mouth dry, the events of the previous night vividly returning to him in lurid detail, he dialled the number of the local minicab firm, asking them to send out a car. Throwing on his clothes, he stumbled over his shoes on the floor and staggered into the kitchen to pour himself a glass of tepid water. *I must get myself checked out for drugs.* Putting down the glass on the sink, Ben noticed an empty sachet on the floor by the bin, but his head was too fuzzy to read the small print. Putting it in his jacket pocket, he went outside to the waiting cab.

"Looks as if you overdid it last night, sir," the driver commented.

"I'm fine!" Ben snapped, relieved they sailed through the empty early morning streets.

Watching him stumble up the path, the driver called, "See you later, mate," lingering while he unlocked the front door.

"Please let me explain, Hannah . . ."

To his chagrin, the house was empty, lights out; the only evidence she had been there being the crumpled sheets on her side of the bed. *How will I be able to continue if something happened to her?* Grimacing at his blotched face and dishevelled hair reflected in the bathroom mirror, Ben tried to figure out where she could be. *She'd surely have left a note if Zipporah was taken ill – I'll call Mum and Dad.*

Busy making breakfast, Rebecka picked up on the first ring.

"It's me, Mum. I've just come back from my office and Hannah's nowhere to be seen. Have you and Dad heard from her?"

"Not since last week . . . Why did you stay the night at the office?"

"We'll talk about it later, I'm sorry I disrupted your breakfast."

When she told her husband about it, Michael had the same response,

"How come he didn't return home until now?"

"I bet they fell out over some stupid misunderstanding," Rebecka said, adding, "Mothers feel these things."

Where is she?

Remembering how Mark had pretended to be in shock seeing him and Vanessa in a compromising position, Ben went through Hannah's bedside table, finding an old diary with his number in it. Dialling it, Mark answered just as he was about to give up.

"If it's you, Vanessa, consider yourself dumped!" Mark's words were slurred, his jaw dropping when hearing who was calling him. "I don't know where she is."

"Stop lying! If something's happened to Hannah, you and Vanessa will pay!"

"I've not seen her since she ran out of your office." Mark slammed the receiver down.

9am and still no sign of her.

Forgetting he'd been drugged, Ben took a shower to clear his head, twenty minutes later stepping into his Bentley, determined to comb the streets of Richmond, searching for her. After driving around for hours, with no trace of her whereabouts, Ben parked his car outside the local police station.

"I want to report my fiancée as missing," he told the elderly officer at reception.

"Sorry sir, unless she's been gone for twenty-four hours, there's not a lot that can be done."

"Someone spiked my drink last night . . . I've not seen her since then . . ." Ben tried his hardest to sound coherent.

"I see, sir. Please be so kind as to fill out this form, giving as many details as possible. Based on what you've just told me, I must insist you consent to a blood test."

"But I'm a solicitor – my office is in the high street!"

"The same rules apply to everyone, sir."

"What if she's seriously injured? Lying unconscious in some clinic?"

"All in good time, sir. If the test's negative, you're free to leave."

I'm done for – Vanessa made sure of it!

Asking him to breathe into a tube, the officer pricked his finger for blood, minutes later commenting, "You're way above the limit, sir. I've no option but to place you in a cell. Coming forward of your own free will is in your favour."

Hours later, after being released from the small cubicle, the same officer informed him Hannah hadn't been admitted to any local hospitals.

"Thanks for finding out," Ben muttered, relief flooding over him.

"I bet she's waiting for you at home, right as rain. I'll have an officer drive you back."

"Is it too late to get myself checked out for drugs, officer?"

"It depends on the drug. The hospital's bound to let you know."

"I'm sorry I snapped at you"

"It's quite alright sir, we get all kinds in here."

When the officer dropped him off, his Bentley parked at the station, Ben noticed Hannah's car in the open garage. Fumbling with the key to the front door, he found her slumped in a corner of the kitchen floor, crying.

"You've got to believe me when I tell you nothing happened! Vanessa and Mark set me up! I've been held in a cell at the police station having been found guilty of having drugs in my system thanks to that bitch spiking my drink. I went there to report you as missing – Hannah, say something, please!"

Her refusal to meet his eyes set off alarm bells in his mind. Sitting next to her on the floor, Ben gently touched her face, willing her to look at him.

"Granny's gone . . . I arrived too late to say goodbye to her!" she sobbed, eyes full of pain.

Oh God, she has every right hating me for not being there for her . . .

"Oh little one, I'm so sorry, you must be devastated." His thoughts turning to the woman he had viewed as family, Ben felt tears sting his eyes as he cradled Hannah in his arms. The anguish she carried inside erupted when he picked her up into his arms and carried her into their bedroom, where he watched her cry herself to sleep.

When she stirred next to him in the early hours of the morning, he asked if there was anything he could do.

"It's too late to give a damn," she hissed, turning her back to him.

"I know I shouldn't have trusted her . . . But that's my only mistake!"

"To you, maybe – how could you succumb to that woman? Why wasn't Collin with you?"

"Karen planned a picnic in Richmond Park . . . I should have had the sense to leave as well. It's probably too late to get myself checked for drugs . . . I found this on the floor by the bin in the kitchen at my office, Vanessa most likely forgot about it." Ben showed her the packet on his bedside table. Hannah shook her head.

"I guess that's it, I'll have to take your word for it." Her voice was flat.

"Please don't get this out of proportion, Hannah! Your grandmother would have been so upset seeing us like this."

"Leave her out of this! Granny loved and trusted you."

Moving closer to her, Ben mumbled, "I was wrong saying what I did . . . you need time to get everything into perspective."

"Why was Vanessa permitted to have access to the office? You told me her father banned her."

"That's right. I already told you she and Mark staged everything – she knew he'd be away on some business trip."

"Like I said earlier, I'm having to take your word for it . . ."

"Meaning what exactly?"

"Figure it out for yourself – this isn't the time to discuss it."

"You'll not give me the benefit of doubt?"

"Is that really so strange? Especially now Granny's . . ."

"I never doubted you when I saw those pictures of you and Mark!"

"There's no comparison. We weren't discovered naked!" Hannah was too hysterical to think straight.

"It's best I sleep on the sofa in the living room . . . you need to focus on the funeral."

"Quite!"

At the breakfast table the next morning Hannah glared at him when he once more asked if there was anything he could do.

"Perhaps you'd prefer I don't attend her funeral?" he asked bitterly.

"Granny would want you to be present!"

"That's not what I asked. Do *you* want me there with you?" It was her chance to put things right between them, but she stayed mute, idly watching some children play on the street outside, thinking fleetingly of their time at the Inn. "Let me clarify what I just said: perhaps you don't want me anywhere near you? Would you prefer we don't go through with our wedding?"

"You know how I feel about that woman. As for us getting married," Hannah's voice sank to a whisper, "I just don't know!" She hated herself for being so unreasonable.

Nodding, Ben quietly left her to it.

Zadie arrived the day before the funeral and checked into a local guesthouse. Virtually unrecognisable in a plain black dress, veil and hat, she helped Peter, Lena and Hannah pack Zipporah's effects and decide what to ship to Malmö. The following day was gloriously sunny, just the way Zipporah liked it, and she was buried in the same Golders Green graveyard as Ella. Sanna, Rosie, Melanie and Matthew were among the guests at the reception afterwards, the former flying in especially to mourn the woman they had all loved.

"How are you bearing up, my darling?" Walther asked, watching his daughter standing at the window in the kitchen. "Your grandmother, her Russian friends, Ella . . . They're all gone now."

"I'm alright . . . just trying to come to terms with the idea I won't be seeing or talking to her again," she mumbled.

"You're so much like her; the same fiery red hair and zest for life! Have you and Ben set a date for the wedding?"

"We've not had the time, what with everything that's happened . . ." Hannah's voice was muffled as she wished she could confide in him.

With everyone expressing their heartfelt condolences, Peter persuaded Zadie to join in just as the Rabbi's wife came up to them with a bag of delicacies.

"My culinary skills don't come close to Mrs Friedman's," she said, taking Zadie's hand, her kind eyes telling them how loved Zipporah had been.

"My mother would have been very touched you left your busy schedule to be here," she cried, dabbing at her eyes beneath the glasses.

"Zipporah was so looking forward to attending Hannah and Ben's wedding!" Rosie exclaimed, thinking it odd they were standing in opposite corners of the living room.

"She'll no doubt be present in spirit," Melanie said.

"Mrs Friedman always had something nice to say about everyone. I shall miss her very much," Dr Anderson commented, filling everyone in on the details of her passing.

Leaving early so as not to miss their flights, Sanna and Rosie asked Hannah if she and Ben were alright. Thinking now wasn't the time to fill them in on the details, she came up with a white lie, saying they were just upset.

"You must let us know if you need us," Sanna offered, when saying their goodbyes.

Having a similar conversation, Rebecka reminded him of their phone conversation on Saturday morning.

"Hannah's angry I wasn't there for her when Zipporah died, Mum . . . I hope we can work it out."

Following his sister into their grandmother's bedroom, Peter asked, "Are our parents correct thinking you and Ben have fallen out?"

Fed up with bottling things up, Hannah blurted out what happened that ill-fated night. Peter was aghast.

"Ben wouldn't betray you, sis! You're permitting that despicable woman to come between you."

"You want me to continue as if nothing happened?"

"Of course not, only that you don't put all the blame on Ben."

"He was perfectly conscious of what she's capable of, yet he still put his trust in her."

"Ben made a mistake! You know I love you, but there are moments when I could throttle you, Hannah. Stop putting everyone on a pedestal! Everyone's fallible – including you."

"No . . . He's shown another side to him. I'm not sure I know him anymore," Hannah replied, digging in her heels. Shaking his head, Peter searched her eyes.

"Ben wouldn't let you down, sis – did you conveniently forget how loyal he was to you after what happened with Mark? You wouldn't have coped as well without his support."

A few days later, offering to be of assistance to his estranged fiancée, Ben caught her staring at him. Hannah's expression was hostile.

"I'm grateful but everything's under control," she snapped.

"You treat me as if I'm some monster! My only mistake was trusting someone I shouldn't."

"How do you think I felt seeing you both like that?"

"Terrible! I would too if the roles were reversed. Thinking she wanted to make amends was stupid and naive but that's all it was."

Hannah walked away from him into their bedroom, refusing to acknowledge his presence. Trying to focus on some TV programme, Ben gave up, returned to his office and spent most of the day staring at a file on his desk.

That night lying alone in their bed, hating how things had turned out, Hannah thought, *Why am I finding it so difficult to put what happened that night behind me? Peter's right, my expectations are too high – if I continue the way I am, I'll risk losing him.*

Devoting most of her spare time to assisting her parents and brother clear up Zipporah's flat and get it ready for the future tenant, Hannah picked a couple of items to remember her grandmother by, leaving the rest in boxes for her family to ship to Limhamn. Answering a knock on the door, Ben stood there in front of her.

"Hannah, will you marry me? I want us to set a date for the wedding."

Willing herself to be civil towards him, she let out a big sigh. "I need more time."

"That's a cop out! You're perfectly conscious of how much Zipporah was looking forward to our wedding; this is about you not trusting me. I love you, Hannah, but you're hell-bent on letting one lousy stupid error of judgement destroy what we have."

"Give me time to get over it . . ."

"Why? You already made up your mind that I'm not trustworthy."

"I do trust you!"

"So what's the problem?"

"I don't understand how you could have let that woman manipulate you."

"I'm sorry I let you down when you needed me the most, darling. I wish I could turn back time but I can't." It was no use attempting to convince her how sorry he was for being a gullible fool. When Hannah made up her mind about something, that was it. "I'll not marry you unless you believe me!"

"I agree, let's not involve my family."

Gutted that was all she had to say to him, Ben whispered, "You've obviously concluded I'm not to be trusted – my feelings apparently don't count for much!"

"I know you love me but I've more important things on my mind. I'm grateful you attended the funeral."

"Where else would I be?" Ben left without further discussion.

Saying goodbye to her family at the end of the week, everyone agreed it was for the best that they book a cab to Heathrow.

"I'm sorry you and Hannah are going through a difficult time," Zadie whispered in Ben's ear.

"She won't forgive me for something that happened on the night Zipporah died. Peter's most likely filled you in on the details."

"Yes he did . . . that woman sounds deranged! As for Mark . . . where do I start?" Turning to Walther, she asked if she could stay for a few extra days. Her husband assured her he'd be fine, having Peter and Lena visiting him.

Insisting she leave, Ben turned to look at Hannah, hoping she'd agree with him.

"Please stay! I need to talk to you about the night Granny died . . ."

Later, she confided in Melanie, Sanna and Rosie about that night, and Rosie shook her head.

"If you and Ben can't work things out, what hope is there for the rest of us?"

Unpacking her things in the guestroom at the house in Richmond, Zadie offered to prepare dinner. "It'll give you time to talk things through. You must view me as a guest – let me help with whatever needs doing."

"Your mother's right, we need to talk," Ben replied, having had enough of tiptoeing around her, blowing hot and cold. They went into the small conservatory and sat next to each other on the settee.

"I'm sorry I gave you such a hard time," Hannah said, taking his hand. "I hate us arguing all the time. We've been through too much to let someone like Vanessa come between us! I never stopped loving you . . . not even after what happened that night."

"You and me Hannah – it's all that matters." Smiling, Ben threw his arms around her. "We'll get through whatever life throws at us as long as you trust me." Nodding, Hannah looked at him, her eyes stinging with tears.

"With my life – always."

"Am I forgiven for being such an idiot as to put my faith into that woman?"

"Only if you forgive the way I behaved towards you."

Nodding simultaneously, both went into the kitchen where Zadie was busy laying the table, thanking her for making them see sense.

"I didn't do anything, but I'm delighted you sorted things out between you," she told them, giving both a big hug.

★

After taking her mother to Heathrow at the weekend, saying their goodbyes then returning home, Hannah suddenly thought, *I don't recall the last time I had a period, could I be pregnant? No, surely not. I've had irregular periods most of my life.* She put it out of her mind.

But over breakfast one morning in the conservatory, birds singing outside the window, Ben took a closer look at her.

"You're looking very pale and tired, Hannah, I wish you didn't have to work so hard at that school."

"Stop fussing," she replied, secretly thinking what he told her made sense.

"I want you to make an appointment with your GP."

"What for? I probably caught a bug, there are plenty around."

"Unless you do what I ask, I'll book you in with a private doctor."

"Alright . . . as long as you stop nagging."

Privately Hannah acknowledged that she felt nauseous most of the time and had lost weight, despite having a ferocious appetite. It was all too easy to blame it on the stress of losing her grandmother. Checking her diary, Hannah's suspicions were confirmed when she realised she'd not had a period since February. *I could be three months pregnant!* Aching to give Ben the news, she decided to wait until seeing her GP.

"You're worse than all Jewish mothers put together!" she joked, feeling his lips on hers. As she ran out the door, he offered to come with her to the surgery later that day.

"There's no need."

"I love you baby, you're all I care about."

I'm pushing forty – Ben's in his late forties . . . This could be our last opportunity to have a baby.

★

"I can't find anything wrong with you, Miss Stein – it's most likely down to stress. Things are bound to get better given time," Dr Henry advised, after examining her that afternoon.

"I forgot to mention I've not menstruated for three months . . ."

"I see. You do look somewhat tired and lethargic – I'll get the nurse to run a few blood tests and call with the results at the end of the week."

Relieved he'd found nothing wrong with her, Hannah popped into a nearby café, ordering coffee and croissants with jam, and eating it all in no time. Out of the blue she felt the urge to vomit, making it just in time to the toilet at the back of the café. Beads of perspiration prickling her skin, she quickly settled the bill and returned home to splash cold water on her face. *I'm alright now . . . what's wrong with me? One minute I'm hungry – the next throwing up!*

She decided to confide in Ben. His eyes turned serious.

"The results are taking too long to come through, if only I'd got you a private consultant!" However, later that night, Dr Henry called to confirm the results had come back normal.

"Seeing as you've not menstruated for several months, as a precaution I'll refer you to a gynaecologist."

Ben insisted he would accompany her to meet Dr Stone in nearby Barnes the following week. The stylish gynaecologist asked him to take a seat in the waiting room, saying she'd call for him after examining Hannah. Ten minutes later, seated at the opposite side of her desk in the office, she surveyed the couple with her grey eyes.

"I'm pleased to tell you you're having a baby! Hannah's three months pregnant – it certainly explains her symptoms."

Ben slowly registered her words.

"She's not ill . . . only pregnant?" He was over the moon at receiving such wonderful news.

"Precisely! My congratulations to both of you."

"But we're not married yet," Hannah whispered, a million thoughts going through her mind.

"Is that of concern to you?" the consultant asked in a gentle voice.

"It ought not to be, seeing as we're planning our wedding," Ben replied on her behalf. Suddenly everything he wanted came true at once: Hannah, the wedding and having a baby. Pushing aside a pile of papers on her desk, Dr Stone turned to Hannah.

"I'm concerned you've not put on any weight. You're tiny . . . My nurse will run a few blood tests, we'll take it from there." Scared the baby was at risk, Hannah asked if it was stress causing her to feel so lethargic. "It's too soon to tell – I'll call with the results in a few days."

Feeling anxious, Hannah followed behind her and Ben into the laboratory when a wave of dizziness and nausea overwhelmed her so much, the walls felt as if they were caving in on her. Luckily Ben caught her in his arms before she hit her head on the floor and helped carry her back into the examination room, placing her gently on the couch.

"I'm sorry to be such a nuisance," Hannah cried. "What's happening to me?"

"Don't be. It's better you faint here and all the more reason we get to the bottom of why you're feeling so lethargic. I must stress you don't work and get plenty of rest," Dr Stone told her, eyes warm and concerned.

"I give you my word she'll not go anywhere," Ben said, too shaken to fathom the implications of what had just happened.

The next few days passed in a blur, following much the same pattern: hunger then nausea and vomiting every time she had something to eat. Adamant he wasn't leaving her, Ben told Eve and Collin they'd caught a bug, and he was taking some time off until further notice.

"Have you set a date for the wedding?" Zadie asked over the phone one night, thinking it odd they hadn't yet make a decision.

"Would you mind awfully if we do it in the autumn instead? It'll give us time to wrap things up at our end."

"If that's what you want," she replied, certain something wasn't right.

When Dr Stone called at the end of the week, requesting they come to her surgery to discuss the results of the tests, Ben had a premonition something wasn't as it should be. He kept his thoughts to himself, holding Hannah's hand.

"It's as I suspected – you're anaemic. Have you been haemorrhaging?"

"Not to my knowledge . . . why?"

"No spotting of blood?"

"No, only discomfort in my lower back and abdomen." Hannah sounded frightened.

"Bleeding can be difficult to detect. I'll write out a prescription of iron tablets – let's hope they'll boost your energy levels. Try to get plenty of rest."

Lucky for them, the tablets seemed to do the trick, helping to improve her appetite so much she was able to hold down her food.

"I wish you'd tell your parents! They're probably worried sick we've not called."

At work, Sally told Hannah to take as much time off as she needed to get rid of the bug she'd caught.

"Call if you need me – the children send their love."

Telling friends and family much the same, Ben told Rebecka she mustn't visit or risk catching the flu.

"You don't *sound* ill . . . Collin tells me you're working from home." Rebecka was suspicious; making a mental note of telling Zadie next time they talked.

"We're redecorating part of our house," Ben lied, praying she would stop asking awkward questions.

After another scan and examination, Dr Stone assured her everything seemed fine, including the tests.

"Did you tell your family you're expecting a baby?"

"I wasn't sure it would be safe but now you're telling me the baby's fine, we may as well share the happy news!"

"Go ahead! Would you like to know the baby's sex?"

"Why don't we wait and see – it'll be more exciting," Ben intervened, privately unable to shake the same foreboding sense of disaster looming inside of him.

That evening both took turns telling everyone they were expecting a baby.

"How wonderful!" Zadie cried. "I'll be a grandmother for the third time!" By now, Lena and Peter had two boys, Sebastian and Nicklas. "Would you like me to be there with you, sweetheart?"

"Perhaps in the near future – Melanie and Rebecka constantly threaten to come round!"

"They're not your mother, I am," Zadie replied in a low voice.

"How could I forget? This baby's very lucky to have you!"

"Just you wait until you hold it in your arms – it's the best feeling!"

★

On the other side of town, Vanessa examined herself in the bedroom mirror, disgusted by what she saw.

I'm huge! Seven months pregnant . . . the gynaecologist thought I was lying, claiming I never had a clue, but how could I have missed it? I'm regular as clockwork!' Deep down she'd suspected as much yet refused to admit it, even when her clothes became too tight. *I eat like a horse, not even plagued by morning sickness. Daddy has no idea seeing as I wear loose fitting clothes. If he did, he'd have a fit!*

They were in the kitchen having dinner when Ronald looked her up and down, thinking she looked awful.

"Why do you insist on wearing such ugly clothes?" His face was twisted in repulsion.

"You've not got the faintest idea of what's fashionable, baggy clothes are all the rage!"

"It's not becoming on someone of your size," he snapped, hiding behind his newspaper, too put off to look at her.

Reluctantly accepting Ben wanted nothing more to do with her, Vanessa had kept a low profile, contemplating calling her connections and ordering to cut off all ties with Mark. *It serves him right for treating me so badly*, she thought, ignoring her father's rambling.

"You're not listening to me! Are you deaf as well as fat?" he yelled, glaring at her.

"What are you on about? Spit it out – I'm on my way out!"

"I'm selling part of my company to the shareholders. After my solicitor's legal team have dealt with the financial aspect, I'm setting up a trust fund for my grandson."

"What grandson? You've not got one!" Vanessa shouted. "I'm your daughter and heir!"

"You, you, you! You ruined my chances with Ben; the two of

you could have been married, giving me the grandson I so badly crave!"

"You seriously thought Ben would leave her for me?" Vanessa shouted, oblivious of Bernie and cook eavesdropping on them.

"Seeing as you're incapable of providing me with what I ask, I've no option but to find someone who can. All I ask is that they give him my surname."

"You're insane! Who in their right mind would comply with something so ludicrous?" Her face turned white as a sheet.

"Quite a few – if the price is right!"

"Why are you doing this to me? Everything you own is mine! I sure as hell earned it." Recalling his cruelty towards her mother, Vanessa suddenly thought of something. *I'm pregnant . . . I'll let him think the baby's Ben's, then ensure Mark never finds out or he'd do whatever it takes to rob me of my inheritance.* A devious plan was taking shape in her head. *Ben and I were discovered lying naked on his couch – that's almost six months ago . . . I'll say it's premature. This is my only chance to make sure I'll get what's owed me: the man I love and my father's fortune! If Ben requests a paternity test, I'll refuse, saying it might harm the baby. Once we're married, he'll stop asking questions . . .* She turned to look at her father.

"I'm sorry you feel this way, especially as I'm six months pregnant with Ben's child."

"You're as crazy as your mother!" Ronald barked at her in disbelief. "Ben's washed his hands of you – he can't bear the sight of you, much less father a child!"

"Says who? You?" Vanessa willed herself to not let him get to her. "I'll let you into a secret, shall I? After your last meeting with him and Collin ended, I went there, offering to make amends and asking if he'd join me having a drink for old times' sake."

"Despite the fact I forbade you to come near him?"

"Ben soon changed his mind, telling me I was the only woman for him. We sorted out our grievances, ending up making love on his couch!"

"You did *what*? You're expecting me to buy this . . . this cock and bull story of yours? I offered Ben your hand in marriage, asking him to name his price – he turned me down! He laughed in my face, saying if you were the last woman on the planet, he'd rather die than come near you!"

Hurt by his words, Vanessa shook her head.

"Ben realised what he risked losing. We started to talk, reminiscing about the past – I'm sure you can figure out the rest!"

Taking a closer look at her, looking for signs she was lying to him, Ronald didn't know what to think. Could Isaacs have changed his mind after all? Was it possible he'd been secretly in love with Vanessa despite everything she'd put him and Hannah through?

"I was so happy when I found out I'm pregnant with our baby, Daddy, yet I won't ruin his and Hannah's future." This time round she got the reaction she wanted.

"Tough! Isaacs got you pregnant. That Jewish fiancée of his isn't our concern. When I think of how much I admired his integrity . . ." Ronald's eyes searched hers, still not convinced she was telling the truth. Vanessa met his gaze, determined not to blink. "If you're deceiving me, I'll disown you!"

"I'd never lie about something as important as this," she whispered, looking offended he'd even suggest it.

"If some loser knocked you up, I'd pay him off. But seeing as you're the mother, the baby's still my grandchild."

The die was cast. It was too late to change her story.

"Everything I told you is true – I swear it!" she said, watching his features soften, making him look ten years younger, as if a heavy burden had been lifted off his shoulders.

"When were you planning on giving me the news?" he asked, still unconvinced.

"Shortly. I was scared you'd force me into having a termination," Vanessa lied, bottom lip quivering.

"What on earth gave you that idea? You know how much I want this!"

"What if it's a girl? Will you be just as happy then?"

"She'll be my granddaughter, I'll raise her the same way I would a boy."

Phew – I'm off the hook for now, thought Vanessa. *This baby's the ticket to the life I always wanted! Ben's bound to forgive me when he sees how perfect we are together. I'll give him the good news very soon.*

"I'm sorry I kept it to myself," she said out loud. "Telling you would have spared us both unnecessary grief."

"Don't worry about it," Ronald replied, walking up to her and kissing her cheek. "Isaacs is clearly too ashamed to show his face."

"He said some awful things to me! I resigned myself to the idea of being a single mother . . ."

"It won't come to that. I shouldn't have criticised you earlier, I'm conscious of the fact it wasn't easy growing up without a mother." It was the first time he'd acknowledged his late wife's existence in this way.

"I was so scared and lonely after she died, Daddy!" Vanessa whispered, milking the moment for all it was worth.

"I can't get my head around it – a grandson to carry on my legacy! It's the best news. You turned my dream into reality. I'm sorry we argued so much. It'll be different once the baby's born."

Liar! You don't give a damn about me – only having someone to succeed you and that damn legacy of yours! she thought, loathing him more than ever. The odds were finally in her favour: she wasn't going to let him forget it.

"Who'll inform Isaacs?" Ronald suddenly asked.

"It's of no significance – those two are probably married."

"I'll take care of it. My PA will set up a meeting." Eyes narrowing, he asked, "You're certain he's the father? I demand you tell me the truth."

"Ben's this baby's father!"

"Good. Copeck's a loser. Let's pray Isaacs isn't married yet. Bernie came across some gossip about that woman's grandmother dying. I can't believe I'm to become a grandfather!" Ronald repeated.

"Only another three months," Vanessa replied in a cheerful voice, thinking, *No, Daddy – two to be precise!*

"I'll cancel all my social arrangements – this baby's my top priority."

"I'm very grateful you're not upset with me!"

"You're sure you didn't mix up the dates? Your mother wasn't as big with you."

"We're of a different build, Daddy."

"Of course . . . from now on Bernie's to do all the carrying and shopping."

"I'll call Ben as soon as I summon up the courage."

"Tell Isaacs we have a lot to discuss. You just concentrate on that baby!"

Closing the door behind her, Vanessa smiled, thinking, *You'll soon regret treating me the way you do . . .*

"Are you okay? I heard you and your father arguing." Bernie helped Vanessa with the seatbelt at the back of the limousine, driving her to Primrose Hill High Street.

"I'm pregnant! Daddy's over the moon to have a grandchild."

"That's great news . . . perhaps the two of you will get closer?" he asked, taken aback by her response.

"It's too late for that! Besides, this baby belongs to *me* – he won't treat it the way he treats me." Stroking her bump, her thoughts turned to Ben.

"You look fabulous – those pills clearly work!" Dr Stone told Hannah on leaving the surgery. "We'll book you in for a scan in the next few weeks, I want you to take it easy and rest."

"She's right – you're looking so much better, darling," Ben agreed. "There aren't many women in your condition who can wear a Diane Von Furstenberg dress when six months pregnant. Are you absolutely sure you'll be alright on your own? I'm only too happy to cancel my meeting."

"You heard the consultant! I'm looking forward to having you serve me breakfast in bed in the morning." They hadn't yet finalised a name for the baby, but were leaning towards Ella if it was a girl.

Tucking her up in bed, Ben kissed her mouth.

"Have I told you how much I love you, little one?"

"Several times a day!" she giggled, blowing him a kiss.

Hours later, eager to get back to her, Ben noticed her side of the bed was empty. Hearing her shout his name, he found her howling in the corner of the bathroom.

"Do something! *Please!* I'm losing it . . . I know I am!"

Panicked, Ben put his arms around her shoulders.

"Shh . . . try to calm down while I call Dr Stone. It won't take long . . ." Fetching a pillow from the bed, he put it behind her lower back. "Are you in a lot of pain? I should never have left you!"

"I felt this excruciating pain . . . it's over, isn't it? Don't lie to me!" she sobbed, face contorted in agony as he dialled the consultant's direct line on his mobile. Listening to him, Dr Stone ordered he immediately call for an ambulance.

"I'll be here, awaiting your arrival," she said, hanging up.

Seated next to her at the back of the ambulance, adjusting the oxygen mask over her face, Ben couldn't stop blaming himself for leaving her. *It's my fault if something happens to them,* he told himself, watching her lying there, petrified.

Hannah was wheeled into an examination room, a drip attached to her arm.

"I can't find an explanation to the haemorrhaging," Dr Stone said. "You'll have to stay the night so we can keep an eye on you. The baby's in a lot of distress," she added, lowering her voice so as not to cause further upset.

"Would you like me to call your parents?" Ben asked, struggling to compose himself.

"Don't! Mamma's been through enough, don't leave me – you're all I need!" Hannah's eyes begged him to make everything alright. Standing in the corner of the large, sterile room, Ben dialled Eve's number on his mobile.

Listening to him, the latter asked, "Is there something I can do to help?"

"Pray as hard as you can!" he whispered, eyes brimming with tears. Just then, the consultant attracted his attention. "Please tell me what's wrong."

"I'll be brutally honest with you: it's touch and go. I've asked one of the nurses to bring a mattress for you to sleep on."

Speechless, Ben nodded, not trusting himself to talk.

★

Sadly, the next morning Hannah haemorrhaged so badly the sheets were soaked in blood. Her eyes pleaded with the consultant to save their baby as they wheeled her straight into theatre. Not allowed to accompany her, Ben turned to watch the woman he loved disappear out of sight.

After what felt like an eternity Hannah returned to her room, face drained of colour, eyes blank.

"I'm so very sorry for your loss, Ben," Dr Stone said gently.

"Why did this happen to her – to us?" His big brown eyes were brimming with tears. She's born to be a mother . . . it's too cruel."

"Is there something I can do for you, sir?" the young nurse replied in a kind voice, checking up on Hannah.

"Not anymore," he replied in a broken voice, his only concern how to tell Hannah when she woke up from the anaesthetic. "Please ensure there aren't any babies around . . ."

"Of course – we're short of beds but not insensitive," the nurse replied timidly.

"Was it a boy or girl?" he asked the doctor.

"A girl . . . she died in the womb. I'm so very sorry."

Seeing her looking so small in the hospital bed, Ben vowed to spend the rest of his life making it up to her. Awakening from the anaesthetic, her eyes searched his for an answer.

"How are you feeling, my darling?" He reached over to smooth a strand of her hair from her face.

"It's gone . . . we lost our baby . . ." she cried.

"I'm so sorry, Hannah – more than you'll ever know."

Turning her head to look at the consultant, Hannah asked, "How long before we can try again?"

"You must give yourself time to grieve and heal."

"Thank you for everything you did . . ."

"Would you like to have a chat with a counsellor? It helps to come to terms with what happened."

"No! Tell me what went wrong," Hannah cried.

"It was probably nature's way of saying it wasn't meant to be . . . I know that's not much consolation to you."

"If I take extra care, will I get to keep the next one?"

"It's too soon to know, I'll inform your GP," the consultant replied kindly, visibly dismayed to hear a baby crying in the corridor.

"Can I pay for a private room?" Ben asked the nurse abruptly. Ten minutes later it had been dealt with, his eyes saying he'd not forget her kindness. Seated on the bed watching Hannah wracked with grief, Ben asked once more if she wanted him to call her parents. "Everyone's bound to be frantic."

"I can't bear the thought of everyone pitying me!"

"We'll have to tell them eventually."

"All I can think of is having another baby! You heard the doctor. Lots of rest and I'll be fine!"

"She also told you you're too weak to consider it right now."

They decided not to have a funeral for their dead baby, preferring to keep her in their hearts, naming her after Ella and Zipporah. Collin and Eve both expressed their deepest condolences. The latter dreading telling his wife, well aware of how much it would upset her.

"I'm so sorry, mate. You'd have made brilliant parents."

Each time Ben mentioned the wedding, pressing her for an answer, she kept repeating how much she wanted to have a baby and a fresh start. She'd been back home for almost a week when Zadie called.

"How come you're not answering any of my calls? There's something you're keeping from me. Why isn't the baby born yet?"

"Hannah's fast asleep – I'll tell her to give you a call in the morning," Ben lied, just as Hannah entered the room, shaking her head, indicating she wasn't in the mood to talk to her. Refusing to give up on her, Zadie phoned just as she was finishing her coffee, flashbacks of their baby assaulting her mind.

"I'm sorry I never called – I'll get back to you later – I'm extremely busy at work this time of year."

"You're lying! Sally told me you've been very sick lately . . . what's happened to the baby?"

"Stop worrying, everything's fine, I have to leave," Hannah whispered, blinded by tears.

As the weeks passed by without having a period, Hannah made an appointment to see the gynaecologist at her surgery in Barnes. Dr Stone examined her once more.

"You've some scarred tissue in your ovaries and womb; it could be the reason you're not ovulating."

"Is that the reason I lost the baby?" Hannah asked, heart in her throat.

"I didn't say that . . . Take my advice and get plenty of rest."

"That's easy for you to say – my biological clock's ticking!"

When they still didn't hear from them, Zadie became increasingly convinced something wasn't right.

"What if they lost the baby or it's seriously ill? Oh, Walther, it doesn't bear thinking about!" The Steins had been bedridden with a nasty bout of flu. Now they were impatient to recover and book a flight to London.

"You know what Hannah's like – always insisting she'll cope by herself," Walther said.

"I'll travel by myself . . . we don't want to cause them distress."

A couple of days after she visited the consultant, Hannah woke up in the middle of the night, exclaiming: "I think I've started a period, it's much heavier than usual!" Her eyes were hopeful.

"You look nearly as ill as last time!" Ben was worried sick. "I'm not taking any risks – we're calling the consultant straightaway." Once more, his gut instinct was telling him something was wrong.

Unfortunately, after examining her later that morning, Dr Stone confirmed his fears.

"It's not good news, Miss Stein. You're haemorrhaging again – so much so I've no option but to recommend a full hysterectomy. I'm so, so sorry."

Looking as if someone had passed a death sentence on her, Hannah felt the room spinning around her.

"This can't be happening to me!" she screamed. "I'm not going through with it! No . . . no . . . no!" She cried hysterically in Ben's arms.

"Please listen to me, darling, " Ben was crying too, not giving a damn what anyone thought of him.

"You're mistaken! My mother practically sailed through two pregnancies! I demand you refer me to another consultant!" she stammered between sobs.

"I wish I was wrong but sadly I'm not," Dr Stone replied. As Ben cradled Hannah in his arms, telling her he loved her, both heard the consultant mentioning adoption. "Age is the only barrier but there are so many children in desperate need of a good home. Having a child is not only about giving birth to it but also loving and nurturing it. Any child would be blessed to have you as its parents."

"I'm sorry I shouted at you," Hannah murmured. "Would you be so kind as to leave us alone for a couple of minutes?" Turning to look at the man she loved, fully aware of how much he wanted a family, she said, "I'm so sorry I failed you."

"What are you talking about? You could never let me down – not in a million years!" A nurse came in to give Hannah a sedative, causing her to feel drowsy and incapable of feeling anything. Meanwhile, Dr Stone took him aside.

"It's essential I operate on her in the morning. It's too late for transfusions – is there someone you can call to support you?" she asked him, grey eyes moist with tears.

"Hannah won't permit it – it's just me. I'm the one having to consent to the operation or risk losing her," Ben sobbed, tears streaming freely down his face.

CHAPTER TWENTY

1999

Flying into Terminal Three at Heathrow, Zadie pulled her coat tight, jet-black hair blowing in the wind while queuing for a cab outside. Giving the elderly driver her daughter's address, she looked out of the window at passers-by, cars hooting in the heavy afternoon traffic. It took almost an hour to arrive at her destination, the cab driver parking outside the pretty house in the quiet cul-de-sac and thanking her for the generous tip.

"Please don't take offence but you remind me of someone . . . got it!" He exclaimed in a cockney accent. "Jackie Kennedy Onassis or Jackie O, same classy appearance, hair and glasses."

"You're very kind – I'll take it as a compliment seeing as she's an icon. I'm visiting my daughter and future son-in-law hoping they'll not object I'm here . . ." Her voice was tense.

"They're fortunate to have you," the driver told her, opening the door to let her out, wishing his wife were as refined and stylish.

Her heart beating frantically in her chest, Zadie rang the bell. A curtain in the kitchen window flickered, followed by the sound of footsteps, door opening wide.

"Zadie!" Ben exclaimed, breathing in the scent of Charlie while embracing her. "What a lovely surprise! Guess who's on our doorstep, Hannah? I wish you'd let us know; I'd have picked you up at the airport. Did you leave Walther behind in Malmö?"

"We decided I should visit on my own," Zadie replied, just as her daughter joined them, throwing herself into her mother's arms. The sadness in her eyes and drawn face made her wish she'd listened to her intuition a lot sooner.

"I'll carry your suitcase into the guest room . . . the two of you need time to talk on your own," Ben said, hoping she'd succeed where he'd failed.

"You must tell me everything!" Holding her close, Zadie's eyes filled with tears. They sat at the kitchen table talking for hours, both crying when Hannah described every detail of the night she'd haemorrhaged causing the baby to die inside her, and the subsequent hysterectomy.

"Why didn't you tell us? We should have been here for you!" Zadie and Walther's child had been through hell yet neither of them had known anything.

"I'm so happy you came, Mamma!" Hannah cried.

"I still don't understand why you kept it from us . . ." Zadie mumbled, the full impact of what her daughter had endured slowly registering.

"Granny died not so long ago . . . I didn't want to cause more upset."

"You were wrong! I was here last time you needed me. This . . . This is an entirely different situation. You're not an island – we love you. Sharing your grief helps the healing process."

Ben joined them in the kitchen in the early hours of the morning

"I'm relieved you've had the opportunity to talk . . . I kept insisting she should tell you."

"It's water under the bridge now – let's concentrate on the present. You must tell me how I can be of assistance," Zadie replied, dabbing at her eyes with a handkerchief. Picking her bag up from the floor, she followed them into the conservatory, asking Ben if they could have some more time to themselves.

"I've something I need to tell her."

"That's okay, I'll be in the bedroom."

Sitting next to each other on the settee overlooking the back garden, watching the sun rising, Zadie's voice shook.

"Your father and I didn't deem it necessary you and your brother should know . . . but after finding out what happened, you may benefit from what I'm about to tell you."

"What is it? Are you or Pappa ill?" *Was it possible her parents were hiding something from her?*

"We're absolutely fine, sweetie! It's just . . . I know how it feels to lose a child," she said, removing her glasses, eyes full of pain.

"You lost a baby? When?" Hannah whispered, millions of questions entering her mind. "How come Peter and I never knew?"

"Yes, a little girl. You were too young to understand. Your father and I coped because we had the two of you to love and look after. I gave birth to a stillborn baby. Time passes . . . you try putting it at the back of your mind yet it never leaves you."

Peter and I had a sister we never knew existed?

"You and Peter were so young at the time – I'd no idea something was wrong! The consultant told me when I was six months pregnant . . . I had to go through labour, delivering a baby who had already died inside me. Your father had to cope in so many ways; comforting me, taking care of us all and working . . . to this day we still haven't talked it through properly. A few years later a close friend had a similar experience. It's more common than you think." Blowing her nose, Zadie continued, "Your doctor's right: it's nature's way of telling us something wasn't as it should be." She touched her daughter's face. "You and Ben love one another so much. Why don't you look into adopting?"

Thinking about the sister she had never had, Hannah felt bereft. A sister – someone to confide in besides her brother and parents, someone to share 'girlie' things with.

"How did you and Pappa move on?"

"We came to terms with it. You wake up one morning realising it's not the first thing entering your head. Having a good relationship helps enormously, just like you and Ben. I didn't need a hysterectomy, though. Do you begrudge him for giving his consent?"

"Not at all – he saved my life," Hannah replied in a flat voice.

"That man adores you, sweetie."

"Which is the reason I feel so bad! Ben has his heart set on having a family. What if he starts resenting me? I'm condemning him to a life without children," she sobbed.

"You mustn't talk like that! Ben loves you – you lost a baby, not each other." But despite Zadie's wise words, Hannah couldn't think straight.

When Zadie told Walther everything that happened, he immediately offered to book a flight to London.

"You must wait a while longer, having me here with them is sufficient for now . . . I promise to keep you updated." She didn't mention telling Hannah about the baby they'd lost all those years ago. When later that week, Walther was finally able to speak to his daughter and listened to her saying she'd failed them, he felt her pain almost as much as if he'd been there with her.

"Rubbish, you're always making us proud, we couldn't have wished for a better daughter."

Looking huge in a maternity dress her father insisted she wear, Vanessa felt bloated. She struggled to get up from a chair in the living room, acutely conscious of his eyes on her. *All I am to him is the hen that lays the golden egg,* she thought bitterly, recalling every cruel word he said to her. Unknown to him, she had less than a month before going into labour.

At her last scan, the sonographer had asked if she wanted to know the sex of her baby.

"What for? I'll soon find out!" she snapped, her only concern how to inform Ben he'd soon become a father. *Please let it be a boy! Daddy's bound to forgive my lies if I give him a grandson.*

Deep in thought, she heard Ronald come in. "You've not told Isaacs yet, have you?"

"I will when I'm ready."

"You're certain it's not Copeck's?"

"How many times do I have to tell you? Ben's the baby's father!"

Ignoring her outburst, Ronald walked up to the bay window in the opulent room.

"You and the baby will live here under my roof. As soon as you and Ben are married, I'm converting part of the house into a separate flat."

"You'll not dictate what I can and can't do!" Vanessa couldn't imagine living under his roof for the foreseeable future. "This is my child – not yours."

"I'm well aware of that small detail. But seeing as I'm the one footing all the bills, you'll answer to me!"

"And if we refuse?"

"Fine by me – but the child stays here with me."

"How could I forget? You never gave a damn about me – but now I'm carrying your grandchild, I'm the one calling the shots!"

Ronald stormed out and Vanessa spent the rest of the afternoon talking to Bernie in the kitchen.

"Is there someone willing to support you during labour?" he asked, petrified she'd have to cope by herself. Vanessa shook her head.

"There's no one . . . Only me." A feeling of despair overwhelmed her.

"I'll discuss it with Angie. She of all people knows what it's like giving birth, seeing as we've got five kids."

"You're much too nice to me! There's no need – the consultant and midwife will be there." No one had ever cared about her like he did.

"The offer's there if you change your mind."

Later, Ronald and Vanessa ate their dinner in silence, paintings of Monet, Constable and Renoir on the dining room walls looking down on them.

"I've something to discuss with you," she ventured at last. "You're to stay out of my personal affairs. The baby's my responsibility – you'll not treat him or her the way you treat me."

"Why the hell wouldn't my own flesh and blood want the life I carve out for them? Most people could never achieve what I leave behind: a legacy to be proud of! You just concentrate on giving birth and caring for it while it's an infant. Leave the upbringing to me."

"We're going round in circles." Vanessa rose unsteadily to her feet. "You'll do as I tell you!"

Refusing to comply with her wish, Ronald ignored her as she lumbered out. Returning to her bedroom, she changed into yet another maternity dress, flat clogs and plain cardigan somewhat concealing her bulging midriff and stomach. *I'd better get this out of the way,* she thought, asking Bernie to drive her to Richmond. "I'll explain later. Please get me there as fast as you can."

During the drive, Bernie watched her through the rear-view mirror, fidgeting with her hair in the back seat of the limousine, hands stroking her swollen abdomen. He helped her get out, saying he'd wait for her further down the street. "Best of luck!"

Vanessa thought of her unborn child, a sudden surge of emotion welling up deep inside of her. *Fingers crossed little one . . . if he wants nothing to do with us, we'll at least have each other.*

As it was her last day with them, Zadie busied herself packing her suitcase, inwardly thinking she ought to stay a while longer. Wearing a black and white Chanel suit, and a chunky gold bracelet Walther had given her for their twentieth anniversary, she told them as much.

"I'm feeling much better now, Mamma! Besides, Pappa's not used to you not being with him – Ben and I will be fine on our own."

"The two of you ought to book a holiday and get away from everything. Maybe it's time to start planning the wedding." Zadie was relieved Hannah had some colour in her cheeks.

"The timing's not right, we'll do it in the summer instead. It'll give us plenty of time to catch up." Zadie couldn't help but think it odd she kept postponing it.

"Is that your wish too, Ben?" she asked.

"If it were up to me? Hell no! I want us to move on with our lives but Hannah's right: it'll give her time to regain her strength." There was a hint of sadness in his voice.

"I understand – time's a great healer. You've the rest of your lives ahead of you," she said sadly.

"Why don't you continue talking in the kitchen?" Ben suggested. "There's someone at the door – I've a feeling it's Collin coming round for some paperwork. I'll book us a table in a restaurant before we leave for the airport." Shutting the door behind him, his face turned red with anger when he saw who was standing outside.

"What the hell are you doing here?" he spat, thinking Vanessa looked awful in an oversized frock and ugly clogs, greasy hair and no make-up.

"I'm sorry to disturb you on a Sunday, I've something to tell you . . . is there somewhere we can talk in private?" Words tumbling out of her mouth, Vanessa panicked, thinking she'd go into labour there and then.

"What the hell are you rambling on about?"

"This is what I'm talking about!" She removed her hand on the cardigan, revealing a swollen, protruding abdomen. "I'm pregnant with our baby, Ben!" She handed him a large envelope from her bag dictating Ronald's terms and conditions. Ben's eyes turned dark with anger, his face draining of colour.

"Liar! I never laid a finger on you! You're ready to give birth now . . . Tell Ronald that Copeck's that baby's father!" Ben unintentionally raised his voice.

"I'm sorry you feel this way. "Being the mother of your child I anticipated you'd be as thrilled as I am."

"Thrilled? Are you insane? I'd never so much as look at you even if you were the only woman on the planet!" Raising his voice a second time, Zadie and Hannah came out of the kitchen, the latter faltering when registering who was standing on their doorstep.

"*You!* How dare you come here . . . to our home!" she screamed, eyes glued to the other woman's bump.

"Please go back inside. We'll discuss this later," Ben pleaded with her, gently steering her in the direction of the conservatory.

"No! I demand to know what's going on!"

Taking off her glasses, Zadie focused on the dishevelled woman about to go into labour. "Haven't you caused enough damage? You heard my daughter just now! State your errand and leave."

"I never intended to cause upset . . . Ben's the father of my baby!" Vanessa blurted out, avoiding looking into Hannah's eyes.

"What did you just say?" Hannah whispered, turning to look at Ben. "How could you do this to me? After everything I endured . . ." An agonised sound escaped her mouth.

"Don't listen to her! She's a rotten, stinking liar! I'd never deceive you, *never!*" As Hannah fell sobbing in her mother's arms, Ben slammed the door in Vanessa's face.

"Unless I hear from you by the end of next week, my father will call you!" she shouted through the door. "The two of you have things to discuss." She turned and walked slowly back to the limousine, easing herself into the back seat. "Oh, Bernie, I think I've ruined someone's life! Daddy's bound to kick us out into the street when he finds out Ben's not the father of my baby."

"He'll do no such thing! That baby's his grandchild."

"Why do you always give me the benefit of doubt? I don't deserve it. Or you."

"Because I know deep down you're not a bad person – only misunderstood."

"I'll . . . I'll be the best mother I can be."

"I never doubted it."

★

"You must tell him you trust him! If Ben says nothing happened between them, you must take his word for it," Zadie told Hannah. They were in a local café after the former had decided to extend her visit by another week. Walther assuring her he was fine, only missing her, seeing as they usually never spent a minute apart. "Ben told me about her mother committing suicide when she was a child . . . she's bound to have mental issues too."

"Are you taking his side?" Hannah asked in a low voice.

"He's telling the truth! You know as well as I Ben's incapable of something like that, drugged or not."

"Can't you see how painful this is to me? Knowing that woman is capable of something I'm not? She has the one thing I crave more than anything: a baby." Hannah's anguish was palpable.

"Perhaps it's just an unfortunate misunderstanding, sir?" Bernie asked, driving his employer to Ben's offices.

"Vanessa lied to me! I was over the moon when she told me he's the father!"

"Don't be too hard on her, sir, she's about to go into labour. I'm sorry things turned out the way they did."

"So am I, Bernie, so am I." Watching Ronald dragging his feet to the main entrance, Bernie couldn't help thinking he'd aged at least ten years.

"I summoned you here to sort this mess out," Ben declared, pulling out a chair for the American to sit on. Their dark suits and grim expressions indicated neither of them was about to budge an inch. Telling Collin about Vanessa's latest stunt, the former had shaken his head, asking if there was anything she wouldn't stoop to.

"Your daughter's unborn baby's nothing to do with me," Ben insisted from across the table. "I demand a paternity test."

"She assured me you came on to her." Ronald's eyes narrowed.

"Your daughter's prepared to do whatever it takes to destroy my life! Copeck's most likely the child's father. He'll be only too pleased to be part of both their lives; that guy will do anything to get his hands on your fortune."

"Copeck? That parasite's not coming near me and my grandson!"

"I gather the two of you have met, then?" Ben's voice was dripping with sarcasm.

"Now you listen to me, Isaacs! There'll be no testing. No one's jeopardising that baby's life. Vanessa told me all about what happened between you that night."

"Did she also tell you she spiked my wine? This little charade stops here and now. Vanessa's at least nine months pregnant! My attorney will be contacting you very soon. Should you refuse to comply with my wish, I'll see to it she ends up in prison . . . Who'll care for the baby then? I've nothing more to say to you. Please leave this instant!"

"Did you manage to sort it out, sir?" Bernie enquired the moment Ronald stepped inside the car.

"Does it look that way to you?"

"No, sir, you look extremely upset. I hope you and your daughter don't have another argument . . ."

"*Argument?* Are you a comedian as well as an idiot?" Ronald screamed at him, not saying another word throughout the rest of the journey back to Primrose Hill.

"What are you accusing me of this time?" Feeling the baby kicking inside her, Vanessa slumped into the antique armchair in the study, awaiting his reply.

"Ben demanded we meet. He wants a paternity test! You lied to me – your own father!" Face pale, lips trembling, Vanessa knew she'd been found out. "Can you imagine how I felt taking orders from some Jew? Tell the truth for once in your miserable life!"

"You and Ben met up behind my back?"

"Your story didn't add up! Isaacs is madly in love with that fiancée of his. You and your baby are of no consequence to him."

"Why do you believe him, not me?"

"Because we know you're a pathological liar!" Vanessa caressed her stomach.

"So, is this a lie too?"

"No, it's the outcome of your cheap fling with Copeck. You couldn't even be bothered to use contraception!" His eyes were furious.

"I love him, Daddy! Please forgive me for lying to you." With just another few weeks until the baby was born, the last thing she needed was another confrontation.

"You're an embarrassment. What will we do now? I'll inform Isaacs he's off the hook . . . the man's an attorney for Christ's sake! What the hell possessed you? You've turned me into a laughing stock." Listening to his ranting and raving, Vanessa had suddenly had enough.

"To hell with you both! What do you want from me? I'll not grovel to you!"

"I demand you show me some respect."

"And if I don't? What will you do then?"

"You'll be very sorry indeed!" For all she cared, he could rot in hell.

"Really? This baby's mine – we don't need you."

"Isaacs knew all along Copeck's the father," Ronald repeated, trying to get his head around it.

"I'll never tell!"

"I'll ask Clancy to check him out."

"Be my guest, I couldn't care less. I wish you were dead instead of my mother." She left him standing there, shaking with fury.

"Consider yourself damn lucky I'm not having you thrown out into the street!" That was too much to ignore and Vanessa returned to have it out with him.

"Lucky? You still don't get it, do you? Without me and my baby, you have nothing, you stupid old fool." Now Ben was lost to her, the baby was all she had left.

"Are you threatening to cut me out of my grandchild's life?"

"You'd better believe it! Go find some whore to bear you a grandson."

"What if I do just that?" Ronald's tone was menacing.

"Go ahead! I'll view it as a lucky escape." Suddenly the tables had been turned in her favour. *Damn her*, Ronald thought. "Nothing you do or say will make the slightest difference," she said, laughing at him.

"Not even the fact you and the baby need never go without money or worry about anything for the remainder of both your lives?"

"You're spinning me a yarn! Tim Clancy's just as rotten and corrupt as you are."

"I'll see to it he draws up a contract stipulating your terms and conditions."

"That's not good enough! Try coming between me and my child and you won't see us for dust. We'll move somewhere you can't find us." It felt great watching him squirm; even better standing up to him.

"I'll arrange it straightaway," Ronald whispered, clutching his chest.

"Your only concern is for the baby."

"Who else? You'll both continue living here under my roof throughout the remainder of my life!"

Listening to him, Vanessa contemplated telling him to get lost. *Can we do it? Spend years in a home devoid of affection?* she wondered. "What if my answer's no?"

"Even someone as stupid as you knows better than to cross me!"

"You've had your say . . . it's my turn now! You're to treat me and my child with respect, is that clear? I'll have the freedom to come and go as I please. Most significantly, I'll have the final say in anything to do with my child's upbringing. Take it or leave it." She'd never seen him in so much turmoil.

She knows how much I crave a grandson! "You'll get what you want, Vanessa!"

"Good. I knew you'd eventually come round to my way of thinking. Just one more thing: in the event of you passing away prior to his or her eighteenth birthday, I demand I'm named legal guardian."

"No grandchild of mine will entertain the notion of passing up on following in my footsteps. Is that answer enough?"

"I demand everything in writing."

"Of course – I'd not expect anything less of you." There was nothing more to discuss.

Burying his head in a file on the desk, Vanessa left him to it, a big grin on her lips. *I'll humour her for the time being*, Ronald thought. *My main objective is to ensure Copeck's not informed about the child. I'll instruct my legal team to handle it.* He dialled Tim Clancy's direct line.

★

Reconciling the fact her mother had a point claiming Ben would never lie to her, Hannah expressed gratitude by giving her a gold necklace from both of them.

"You shouldn't! I'm your mother – it's only natural I care about you!"

Zadie looked amazing in another Chanel suit, eager to reunite with her husband. She kissed them goodbye at the airport, secretly thinking: *Something's bothering her . . . I hope she's not contemplating doing something she'll regret.*

A few days later, Ronald returned home after a business meeting in Knightsbridge to an ambulance parked at the front of the house, two men carrying Vanessa out on a stretcher. He rushed towards them, shouting, "What's happened?"

"I'm in labour, Daddy . . . if I'd known it would be this painful . . ." Vanessa screamed, reaching for his hand.

"Stop making such a spectacle of yourself! Women give birth all the time – so can you," he snapped, distancing himself from her. "I'll join you at the hospital later. Bernie will accompany you." Bernie was left reeling, thinking it should be the other way round.

"Are you sure you don't wish to stay, sir?"

"Whatever for? You're here, aren't you? I'm surplus to requirements."

Positioning himself next to her in the ambulance, Bernie stroked Vanessa's hair, reminding her he was there for her.

"You must promise me to look after the baby if something happens to me!" she cried, the contractions becoming much stronger and excruciating.

"Nothing's going to happen to either of you. Your father's meeting us at the hospital."

"To hell with him! He'd much rather I die so he gets to keep the baby! Ohhhhh . . . I'm in agony, Bernie!" Delirious with pain, Vanessa's nails dug into his hand.

That man's a vicious bully. Had it been my daughter lying here instead, I'd never have left her side, Bernie thought, swearing inwardly.

Having been informed about their imminent arrival, the consultant, nurse and midwife instructed the ambulance men to take Vanessa into one of the examining rooms further down the corridor. Attached to a monitor, Vanessa shrieked, "Well, what are you gawping at? Give me something for the pain . . . blast you all!"

Taking ages to examine her and measuring how far gone she was, the gynaecologist was on the verge of a nervous breakdown. It was hard not to order her to shut up as she called them all the names under the sun; the midwife convinced she was just a spoilt brat used to getting her own way.

At some point, Ronald entered the room, seeing his daughter lying there looking scared and shouting obscenities. *Please God, give me a grandson to carry on my legacy,* was his only thought as he paced the room.

"You need your strength to bring this one into the world," the midwife told her while the consultant explained to her father what they were doing. Ronald demanded he was present at the birth or they wouldn't receive the large donation he'd promised them. Taking time from his busy schedule, the consultant, a middle-aged, tall, fair man with glasses, returned to tell Vanessa everything was as it should be.

"Try breathing in and out," he said, in a soothing tone.

"Do it yourself!" she hissed at him, having long since given up on being civil – her only wish to get it over and done with.

"Why don't you and your friend have a break? We'll keep you posted on any progress," the nurse suggested, thinking it odd Bernie was the one supporting her.

"I'm not abandoning her!" he told her, voice adamant, mopping her brow.

After almost twenty-five hours in labour, Vanessa at long last gave birth to a healthy baby boy weighing in at one stone. Touching his face, fingers and toes, watching him lying in her arms, snuggling up to her breast, all she could think was how good it felt. *The way I felt about Ben doesn't compare to this . . . I'm in love, deeply and irrevocably with my son! Welcome to the world my darling, precious Jake!* Flooded with postnatal hormones and the happiest she'd ever been, Vanessa looked at the baby, her eyes shining.

"I told you it'd be fine," Ronald whispered, thinking this was his proudest moment.

Turning to look at Bernie, Vanessa asked if he'd consent to being Jake's godfather.

"I'd never have coped without you."

Frowning, Ronald heard Bernie reply, "It'll be an honour!"

"This is the best news. I'm very grateful to you, Vanessa," her father added.

"Say hello to your grandson, Daddy . . . We need to sleep now; it's been a long day." It felt surreal lying there with her baby in her arms.

"It's nice to see how well you're bonding so well," the midwife commented, thinking they'd been wrong, mistaking her for someone who didn't care. *Looks like this little chap's got himself a winner in her.*

"I'm sorry I said those thing to you," Vanessa apologised to all present. "It was the pain talking, not me."

"It's all in the past, love."

"Well, I don't know about your father but I'm in serious need of sleep! See you later," Bernie whispered, kissing her cheek.

This is the start of a new life, Vanessa thought, relishing the idea of having someone to love and care for. *I'm not alone anymore . . .* was her last thought before she and her newborn son fell asleep, faces touching.

CHAPTER TWENTY-ONE

2000

IT WASN'T UNTIL Jake was six months old that Vanessa finally did what she'd vowed to do: write a letter of apology to the man she no longer loved.

Dear Ben, my once special friend,

Whilst writing this my beautiful son's sleeping in his cot next to me. Please find it in your heart to forgive me for everything I put you through.

Yours sincerely,
Vanessa

Squealing with delight every time his mother picked him up, Jake's little face lit up when she talked and sang to him, reading him the stories she herself enjoyed as a child. *I wonder if my mother did the same with me?* she thought. *Depression's awful . . . There's so much more that can be done these days.* She planned to look into it later.

In truth, motherhood had changed Vanessa inside and out. Swapping to a more feminine look, her former tight-fitting clothes had been replaced by dresses in soft shades. She was breastfeeding

Jake in the nursery adjacent to her bedroom when Bernie popped his head round the door, asking if she was planning on having dinner with her father.

"Cook's kindly offered to bring up a tray."

"Good for you. I was wondering, Vanessa, how do you feel about employing a nanny?"

"No way! Apart from us and Cook, no one's permitted to come near him. Daddy's scared we're too close."

"I'm glad you're showing him who's boss . . ."

"Jake's my only priority – no one will ever come between us!"

Meanwhile, business was going badly for Mark. Threatening to increase the rent and insisting people were queuing up for the premises, his landlord gave him one month to cough up or get evicted. It was all too clear that unless things started to improve, he would have no option but to declare himself bankrupt.

With only a few clients left, he even contemplated calling Vanessa, begging her to reinstate him with her contacts and offering them an even bigger discount.

At the end of July, Ronald made numerous business trips, camouflaging the fact he was seeing his mistresses in the Hamptons and French Riviera, and giving Vanessa and Jake the house to themselves. As they enjoyed a late breakfast in bed one morning, Bernie came up with the idea of asking Cook to pack a picnic basket.

"You've hardly been out since Jake's birth! We'll drive to Richmond Park; Cook will make us sandwiches."

"I'm not convinced it's such a good idea. What if Ben or Mark see us?"

"I thought you put everything behind you? Please . . . Jake will love the deer."

"You're right, they're of no concern to us."

Parking outside a café at Robin Hood Gate, they watched Jake bounce up and down in the buggy every time a bird or deer passed by.

"Are you planning on telling Mark about Jake?"

"He'd only attempt to steal his inheritance."

"What if someone finds out he's the father and tells him?"

"No one knows except us, I'll cross that bridge if it comes to it." She was determined no one would come between her and Jake. Laughing at Jake's attempt to catch a flying bird as they headed back to the car hours later, Vanessa noticed two familiar faces staring at them. She alerted Bernie, telling him it was Annuschka and Mark, Bernie persuading her to stay calm and asked her to let him push the pram.

"They'll think we're a family enjoying a day out in the park," he said, regretting convincing her to come to Richmond Park was a good idea in the first instance. But it was too late for regrets, as Annuschka's suspicious eyes fell on the pram.

"Look, Mark, it's Vanessa . . . she's not fit to be a mother!" Helping to clean his office earlier that day, she'd talked her son into taking her to the park and café. "Let's approach her!" she continued, grabbing his arm.

"You're making a fool of yourself and of me," Mark whispered, embarrassed to see Vanessa again.

"How nice to see you again! I never knew you have a baby, when was it born?" Annuschka's eyes were glued on the infant beneath the cover.

"Our baby's not your concern!" Bernie replied abruptly, fairly certain they didn't buy he and Vanessa were an item. Ignoring him, Annuschka pushed closer.

"Leave us alone!" Vanessa shouted when in one swift movement, Mark's mother pulled off the cover, eyes wide in jubilation.

"I knew it! That baby's the spitting image of Mark and his father, even the same cleft in the chin!"

Woken up by the noise, Jake opened his eyes and began to wail. Picking him up, Vanessa shielded his face with her hand. "This is your doing!"

"Come near him again . . ." Bernie warned, returning the baby to the pram.

"That baby's our flesh and blood – you've no right keeping it from us!" Annuschka shot back, her eyes glued on the small creature neither of them had known existed until moments earlier.

Pushing the pram as fast as they could towards the car, Bernie whispered, "You must tell your father, he'll find a way of keeping them out of your lives."

"It's not that simple, Bernie! Mark won't give up now he knows he has a son. He'll use him as his meal ticket!" Vanessa began to cry, adding, "Perhaps I'm wrong . . . Jake has the right to know his father . . ."

"Listen to me. That guy's a loser, failing at everything he touches. His daughter's living proof of it."

"What the hell possessed you?" Ronald barked when they relayed the story back at home. "If Bernie wasn't such a damn good driver, I'd give him the sack."

"Please help us, Daddy!"

"You're an idiot!" Fetching his diary, Ronald paged through, looking for a phone number. *I ought to have dealt with it from the start, but I suppose now is as good a time as any. I might have guessed that daughter of mine would give me cause for concern. She's just like her mother: pure poison! That child belongs to me!*

*

Meanwhile, Mark was also deep in thought. *Vanessa's probably worried sick. Did she really imagine I wouldn't find out? She must have tried to pin it on Ben seeing as she drugged him that night . . .* He drifted off to sleep on the living room couch, still fully clothed, jumping up when the phone rang at 6am.

"Who is it?" he grumbled down the receiver. His face went pale when Ronald Westbrook summoned him to his office at 7am.

"This is the address . . . you'd better be there!" he said, hanging up.

So he knows about us bumping into Vanessa and the baby! I wonder what he wants? Putting on a brown suit, shirt and tie, all washed and ironed by his mother, Mark was eating a banana on his way out the door when it dawned on him. *Why didn't I think of this before? It certainly paid off meeting Vanessa . . . She's welcome to that baby, but only after paying me a fair sum to stay out of their lives – it's not as if her old man can't afford it! Once he's out of the way, I'll demand to be part of their lives.* The only snag was his mother – she'd never stand for it. *So what? I'll be rich, getting a place as far away from her as possible.*

Greedily imagining what he'd do with all the money, Mark suddenly thought of something. *What if Ronald's found out about the creditors? Perhaps it's for the best I seek legal advice? Nah, it's too damn expensive!* Deciding he'd call their bluff by not turning up, Mark settled in front of the television, idly tuning into some breakfast show just as the phone rang a second time.

"Don't you dare stand us up! My client ordered you to be here an hour ago." The voice on the other end of the line was ice cold.

"What's it to you? Mr Westbrook's perfectly aware what this is about."

"You shouldn't have said that. If you're not here within an hour, we'll send someone for you. The choice is entirely yours.

We've sufficient evidence to ensure you go to prison: considering you've not paid tax for well over a decade, refused to pay alimony to your daughter and had dealings with dubious people in the recent past, you're looking at a long stretch!" The line went dead.

Shaking like a leaf and perspiring so much he had to change his clothes, Mark got ready to leave. He drove quickly towards Park Lane and Ronald's offices, praying he wasn't being caught on speed cameras. Parking around the corner from the luxurious premises, he was met by a tall, dark man in his late twenties declaring he was ten minutes late. Together they took the lift to the sixth floor, then Mark followed him through a corridor covered in modern art, and into a large room where two men awaited him.

"I resent being blackmailed!" Ronald's eyes were just as cold and blue as he remembered. The other man stood up. He was tall, balding and in his late forties, with glasses at the tip of his nose.

"My client's right! I'm Tim Clancy – Mr Westbrook's attorney – we spoke earlier. Now Mr Copeck, Mr Westbrook's an extremely generous man . . . so much so he's offering you a one-off sum in return for your never coming near his daughter and grandchild. Should you decide to reject the money, our offer will be withdrawn and not repeated. In addition, your creditors and Inland Revenue will be informed of your misdemeanours." He handed Mark a document and stepped back expectantly. Mark tried reading the small print, conscious of their eyes on him.

"You're seriously expecting me to sign this . . . this shambles of an agreement? £50,000? My son's worth at least a million!" Eyeing him up and down, Clancy swore.

"You're a cocky little shit, aren't you?"

"My attorney's right! Unless you sign it, the offer will be immediately withdrawn and you leave with nothing," Ronald commented between gritted teeth, an evil expression in his eyes.

"What'll you do if my son finds out about it? How will you deal with it then, Mr Hot Shot?" Watching their faces turn red, Mark reached for the pen on the table, fully aware they'd not succumb to his threats. He signed the offensive piece of paper. "There – satisfied now? I don't know how you can sleep at night!"

"That's easy. We're not the ones selling our child," Clancy replied, throwing the cheque at him.

"Try not to waste all of it on booze," Ronald mocked him, roaring with laughter.

I sold my own son for a lousy fifty grand! What kind of man does something like that? Someone who's desperate. I'll have nothing left when I've paid my creditors. After paying the cheque into his account, Mark went to his local pub to drown his sorrows, returning home well past midnight. There was his mother, rummaging through a kitchen drawer.

"Where have you been? We need to discuss how best to handle the situation with Maruschka and this new baby!" Annuschka didn't even know her grandson's name yet was determined to get to know him. Listening to her, Mark lost his temper.

"Get the hell out of my life! You're a fine one, preaching to me on how to deal with my children. Dad had a lucky escape dying!" Froth was building up at the corners of his mouth.

Face drained of colour, Annuschka picked up her bag, left the kitchen and slammed the front door behind her, oblivious to her son sobbing his heart out at the top of the stairs.

Passing his parents' house on the way home from a meeting in Central London, Rebecka persuaded Ben to join her for tea.

"Tell me to mind my own business, but I need to know if you're alright, darling? It can't be easy knowing you'll never have a child of your own."

"It isn't . . . Hannah refuses to adopt, end of," Ben replied sadly.

"How come? There are so many children badly in need of a good home. Aren't you of the same opinion?"

"Hell yes! But I respect her wishes. Many couples are in the same situation. I'm too old . . . you and Dad had better pin your hopes of becoming grandparents onto Zoe and Stephen," he said, a wistful expression in his eyes.

"Hannah's on the mend, son. Should either of you wish to talk about it, you know where I am," Rebecka commented, her voice trembling.

Meanwhile, Hannah had met Melanie for lunch in Hendon and was now at her house, playing with the twins. Melanie had the distinct impression Hannah was distancing herself somewhat, smiling absent-mindedly each time she commented on something. *She'll never experience the joys of motherhood . . . Going so far as to pretend what happened has no bearing on the future, refusing to adopt . . .*

"You're always welcome to visit, you know."

"You're very kind, Ben and I are extremely busy, let's meet up in the New Year," Hannah replied, avoiding her friend's eyes. Later, watching her disappear in her Volvo, Melanie told herself she was imagining it. *They've each other to lean on – I'm seeing ghosts where there aren't any!*

Calling a couple of weeks prior to Christmas, Rosie announced she would be visiting for a few days.

"Sanna and I are concerned about you – we've not heard from you for a long time."

"You needn't be! We've had a lot to do at work . . . You must stay here with us."

"Great! It'll give us time to catch up."

What if she finds out what I'm about to do? Hannah wondered, switching off her mobile.

Together Ben and Hannah watched the snow falling in the garden, eating prawn cocktails, her mother's recipe of roast beef and potato gratin followed by chocolate mousse. Ben smiled at her warmly.

"You look beautiful in that green dress – it matches your eyes."

"You're always so nice to me . . . I'm not sure I deserve it," Hannah replied in a small voice, pretending to be searching for something in a kitchen drawer, her eyes filling with tears.

"What's up, little one?" Ben asked, coming up to kiss her on the lips.

"Oh, you know how sentimental I get at this time of year," she joked, feigning a smile. "I spent the entire day reminiscing about Zipporah and Ella. I'm pleased we named our baby after both; they'll continue to live in our hearts forever."

Blowing out the candles on the table, Ben pulled out a bottle of red wine from the fridge. "How about we have an early night?"

"That's a great idea." Forcing herself to sound cheerful, she couldn't help thinking they'd better make the most of whatever precious time they had left.

"I love your new hairstyle," Hannah said when Rosie arrived, looking stunning in a lacy blue dress, heels and make-up – the epitome of a successful entrepreneur.

"Thank you! That dress you're wearing . . . didn't it used to belong to your mother?"

"Yes, she gave it to me years ago saying the green colour goes well with my hair." Leaving them to talk in the kitchen, claiming he had some work to do, Ben told Rosie how happy they were she wanted to spend time with them in their home. Half an hour later, they sat together, sipping their wine.

"There's something you're keeping from me. Is it about the baby?"

"We'll never get over losing it . . ." Hannah sounded evasive.

"You're up to something! I can tell just by looking at you – spit it out, you'll feel much better afterwards," Rosie persisted.

"I want to but I can't! Please don't make me."

"You're beginning to scare me! I'm not leaving until you confide in me." Hannah sighed.

"After losing the baby and having a hysterectomy, something died inside of me. All I can think of is having another yet I'm so conscious of the fact I can't." Tears welling up in her eyes, Rosie held her close.

"Sanna and I were so happy you're on the mend . . . why can't you adopt?"

"We're too old . . . Plus I prefer we have our own child," Hannah cried, clinging to her friend.

"Other countries aren't as discriminating, you know, you'd love it like you would your own. What's the problem?"

"There isn't, only me! Is it really so wrong wanting to have a baby with the man I love?"

"Of course not, sweetheart, but it's no longer an option. Why can't you find it in your heart to love someone else's? You keep saying you want to teach because of your love for children yet won't accept one unless you've given birth to it . . . Sounds like hypocrisy to me."

"You've no right criticising me! Just because you're not maternal doesn't mean I can't be," Hannah snapped, pushing her away.

"Calm down! I've a habit of shooting my mouth off. I'll do whatever it takes to help you."

"That's just it. You can't! Ben and I are so very happy, now. But how long before he starts resenting me? His eyes light up whenever Melanie's twins are around! He's born to be a father."

"Oh, Hannah. How long have you been thinking like this? Sanna and I should have been here for you! What else are you keeping from us?" Rosie asked, certain this was just the tip of the iceberg.

"Ben thinks I'm alright but I'm not!"

"Time's a great healer, the two of you have such a lot to look forward to . . . the kind of love most people search a lifetime for."

"Can't you see? I'd give anything to have his baby! Just because I can't doesn't mean someone else couldn't . . ." There. She'd said it. The truth was out in the open and Hannah felt a mixture of relief and sadness on seeing her friend's shocked expression. "You can't tell him . . . please don't!"

"And watch you make the worst mistake of your life? Leaving won't solve anything – except cause more misery! He loves you, for Christ's sake!" Exasperated, Rosie's voice rose an octave.

"I'm not leaving until the end of the week," Hannah whispered, burying her face in her hands.

"How kind. You listen to me, Hannah Stein! If Sanna or I planned the same, you'd do your utmost to stop us. I'll be damned if I'm going to let you go through with it." What was meant to be a relaxing time between two friends had rapidly turned into a battlefield.

"Please say you don't hate me. I need your friendship more than ever."

"Tell me something: how will you live with yourself, knowing it'll break his heart? At least have the guts to tell him!"

"I'll manage somehow. Telling him won't change how I feel; Ben deserves to have his own child."

"That's exactly why you ought to adopt."

"It isn't the same . . ."

Rosie took a deep breath. "Whenever you get something into that head of yours, you're like a dog with a bone!"

"Will you tell him?" Hannah asked, wringing her hands.

"I ought to! But, no – I'll not be the one breaking his heart. Didn't it occur to you you're all he wants?"

"I'll take that risk if it means he gets what he deserves . . ."

Having lost their appetite both helped clear up, returning the barely touched Caesar salad to the fridge.

"I'll leave first thing tomorrow. Don't worry, I'll come up with some plausible excuse." Rosie shook her head. "What will you do? Return to live with your parents, ask Mary to give back your job?"

"Something like that."

"You've thought of everything then." Rosie's tone was hard and unforgiving.

"You're awfully upset with me, right?"

"Bingo! I think you're an idiot for throwing away your best shot at happiness. For what? Some crazy notion you know what's best for Ben? Well, you don't! I'm so bloody livid, I wish you never confided in me!"

"That makes two of us," Hannah mumbled.

"What'll happen to this place? Ben gave it to you."

"It belongs to him; I'll transfer the deeds."

The foreseeable future held nothing but pain and loneliness.

The next day Rosie thanked them for having her and Ben carried her suitcase to the cab waiting outside.

"Did you have a row?" he asked, looking puzzled.

"Of course not! Marcel's eager for me to join him at The Ritz in Paris." She sounded cagey. "Take very good care of each other," she whispered, avoiding looking at her friend. Swiftly she got into the cab, shouting "Happy New Year!" over her shoulder.

"She's something else isn't she?"

"That's Rosie all over!" Hannah replied in a shaky voice, heart sinking inside her chest.

It didn't take long for Rosie to spill the beans. "That's it! I'm booking a flight – someone has to prevent you from making the worst mistake of your life!" Sanna shouted, getting straight on the phone to Hannah.

"Don't bother! I wish I'd kept my mouth shut, now all I do is worry one of you will tell Ben before I can."

"The two of you spent years apart! They really should have offered you counselling, it helps put things into perspective."

"Really? Who do you think you are, telling me what I should and shouldn't feel?" Hannah screamed.

"There's not much point trying to talk some sense into you when you're like this – Rosie and I are here for you, day and night."

Meanwhile, staring at some file on his desk while absentmindedly Googling something on the web, Ben couldn't shake off the feeling something was wrong. *Why was Rosie in such a hurry to leave?* He decided work would have to wait until the morning. He was going home to talk to Hannah.

Seeing him looking so forlorn as he came through the door, a troubled expression in his big brown eyes, Hannah intuitively knew he suspected something was wrong.

"Why won't you set a date for our wedding – is that the reason Rosie left?"

She's right; I have to open up to him. I owe him that much. Too scared to look into his eyes, Hannah turned to him.

"I can't marry you, Ben," she whispered. "You've the right to meet someone who can give you what I can't. Rosie decided to leave when she found out."

Stunned beyond comprehension, Ben slowly walked up to her.

"This is a joke, right? We're the same people . . . Nothing's changed between us! I love you, Hannah!"

"None of this is your fault," she said, keeping her distance.

"You're sick if you think a child will substitute for losing you!" Ben replied, tears spilling down his face as he realised she meant what she'd said. "We'll talk when you've calmed down . . ."

"I'll not change my mind!" She refused to look at him.

Ben slammed his fist on the kitchen table.

"Let me get this straight. You're leaving . . . Abandoning me so I can meet someone who'll give me a child? Can't you hear how ludicrous that sounds?"

"Given time you'll see I'm right . . ." Suddenly she sounded entirely different from the woman he knew and loved.

"Bullshit! You're dumping me – us! Please don't do it . . . I beg you!" Seeing his eyes so full of despair, Hannah trembled, tears blinding her vision. "You're the only woman I contemplated having a baby with! I should have realised you've not recovered. I'll get the best therapist . . . Anything except this – this lunacy!"

"I'll not waste more of your life."

"So when things are great, we're fine but not otherwise – is that it? You're jumping ship. What if the roles were reversed and I was taken ill? You wouldn't leave me – I know it!"

"This isn't the same . . . you're clutching at straws."

"No I'm not! I thought we were happy. I was obviously deluding myself."

"Let's not make this harder than it already is. I'm leaving the day after tomorrow. It's for the best."

"For whom? You're walking out of my life for good, leaving everything we have behind; me, this house – our future!" Crying tears of anger and despair, Ben knew it was too late to reach her, not caring that she was seeing him at his most vulnerable. *She's like a machine! It's almost as if she's already left me . . .*

"You must remove my name from the deeds of this house. Unless you object, I'd like to keep a few items to remember us by, leaving the rest behind." Internally, Hannah was astonished at her own ability to remain detached.

"I won't let you do it – not without a fight!" Feeling as if he'd been transported into some horror movie, Ben abruptly left her standing there, frozen to the spot.

Emotionally drained after yesterday's revelation, her face pale and drawn, Hannah lay the finishing touches to their meal consisting of smoked salmon, eggs Florentine, champagne on ice in the fridge. She was even wearing his favourite dress. *It's our last night together,* she thought, a big lump in her throat. Ben came into the kitchen and put his arms around her.

"Forgive me for shouting at you, Hannah. I was terrified you had already left . . . you smell nice, L'Air Du Temps, right?"

"Mmm – and yours is Pour Homme?"

"Some things never change," Ben whispered. Hannah took a moment to appreciate how handsome he looked in a dark suit, shirt and tie, speckles of grey in his hair. *I'll miss everything about him: the man, lover and friend . . . especially his kindness and generosity.* Picking at the food, both too distraught to eat, Ben raised his glass.

"Happy New Year, darling, may many more come our way . . . you're leaving me aren't you, little one?" Hearing him referring to her by that name brought fresh tears to her eyes.

"It's too late . . . if none of it had happened . . . but it *did*!" she cried, watching his eyes cloud over.

"What makes you so damned certain you know what's best for me? I'm not like you! I can't switch my feelings on and off on demand. I'm sleeping on the couch in the living room."

"If that's what you prefer, I'll not stand in your way . . ."

"I'd have brought down the sun, moon and stars if I thought it'd help change your mind. I want you gone first thing in the morning," he whispered, eyes full of pain.

"I'll finish my packing . . ." Hannah's voice faltered as she ran into the bedroom. She threw herself on the bed, tears soaking the pillow. *Why am I doing this? If only our baby was alive! How will I continue living without him?* Due to her own decision to leave, the sun had disappeared from her life.

After staring for a while at the blank paper on the desk in the guest room, Ben began to write:

My darling Hannah,

Forgive my cruel words earlier. They were said out of anger. You're my reason for living – I'll never stop loving you.

Ben

Leaving it there for her to read in the morning, Ben decided to drive round the block to clear his head. Returning in the early morning hours of New Year's Day, he heard the muffled sound of sobs coming from the bedroom. It tore him apart so much that he left once more, cruising the neighbourhood, thinking: *Why did it have to come to this?*

★

"I'll never forgive myself if something's happened to him!" Hannah cried, reading his note. She decided now was a good time as any to call her brother.

"What's up, sis? You sound as if you're crying."

"Ben and I are over . . . it's my decision to leave. Our parents don't know yet, will you pick me up at Copenhagen Airport? These are the flight details . . ." Peter was still in bed, with Lena stirring next to him. He rubbed his eyes.

"Of course! I don't believe it . . . How's Ben taking it?"

"Badly," she whispered, switching off her mobile.

Seated at the desk in the guest room, pen and paper in front of her, Hannah wrote:

> *Dear Ben, love of my life,*
>
> *Please forgive me for leaving you. It's the only way.*
> *Try remembering the happy times we shared – I will.*
>
> *With all my love,*
> *Hannah*

The cab driver carried her cases to the car while she took a final look around the house she fell in love with the moment Ben had described it to her. *This is it! I'll never see either again.* Brushing away the tears spilling down her face, she picked up her handbag, locked up and threw the key into the letterbox.

"You can't leave without saying goodbye, little one," she heard Ben whisper behind her. Running into his arms, she watched him smile through his tears.

"I'll never love anyone the way I love you, Hannah," he said, tears mingling with hers, registering every detail of her face.

"Yes, you will! You're always with me in here." Gesturing to her heart, Hannah disentangled herself from him and climbed into the backseat of the cab, her final words: "Be happy!"

Ben stood there, numb, watching her disappearing from his life.

CHAPTER TWENTY-TWO

2001

THE MINUTE HE saw her at the airport, her face pale, eyes red from crying, Peter drew Hannah in close, neither of them speaking for a moment. He carried her suitcases, realising their mother had been right in thinking she kept something from them.

"I had to leave," she cried. "I had to set him free to get on with his life!"

"You're wrong. Ben will never stop loving you, sis – baby or no baby."

They drove across the Öresund Bridge towards Malmö and Limhamn, both lost in their own thoughts.

Peter and their parents would spend the whole of the following year helping her to move on. Hannah had been back for six months in early June, when she received an unexpected parcel. Staring at the pieces of jewellery she left behind, she read the attached note in its familiar handwriting.

My darling Hannah,

Wear them and think of us.
With my undying love,

Ben.

All she could do was lock herself in her room, listening to the haunting voice of Karen Carpenter singing 'Solitaire'. The lyrics resonated with how she was feeling and she wondered if leaving him was the biggest mistake she'd ever made.

Over the next couple of years, Hannah settled quietly into old routines at home and school, where Mary had welcomed her back to Budding Stars with open arms. One day Hannah was suddenly left in charge when Mary unexpectedly caught pneumonia and was admitted to hospital. Visiting her every day after work, Hannah was deeply concerned and asked the young consultant why she wasn't improving.

"At her age, things could go either way," he mumbled, shrugging his shoulders.

When nearly a month passed with no improvement, Hannah took her old friend's hand in hers, asking how she was feeling.

"You'd better prepare yourself for the worst," Mary whispered. "I am!" Her head fell back onto the pillows. Taken aback by her comment, Hannah turned to look at the nurse standing there watching them, shaking her head. Discussing it with Annie later that week, her colleague's eyes filled with tears.

"I can't imagine this place without her," she said, just as Hannah's mobile rang.

"Miss Stein? It's Gustav Petren, Miss Ohlsson's solicitor. Can you come to my office at 10am?" The steady voice gave her directions of how to get there.

"What's happened?" Hannah started trembling, panic building up inside.

"It's best we talk in person."

"I'll be there." Rushing out of the door, she said to Annie,

"You'll have to look after the group of children awaiting me in my classroom."

"I hope it's not bad news?" Annie shouted after her. Hannah drove as fast as she dared towards the block of offices in Central Malmö, forcing herself to stay calm. Ten minutes later she found herself sitting opposite a tall, bespectacled middle-aged man with light-blue eyes and grey hair.

"It is with deep regret that I have to inform you Miss Ohlsson died in her sleep during the early hours of this morning. I'm very sorry for your loss." Handing her a document, Gustav Petren asked her to read it so that he could help with any questions she may need answering.

My dear Hannah,

When you receive this letter, we'll both know that my life is over. You helped turn Budding Stars into a school I'm proud to leave behind. There's no one I trust my life's work with apart from you and I'm convinced you will safeguard it for future generations!

May God always be with you.

All my love,

Mary

Tears blurring her vision, Hannah was momentarily at a loss for words.

"I don't believe it," she cried, clutching the document.

"Miss Ohlsson was determined you succeed her." Petren asked her to sign it, confirming she was the new owner. Shaken to her core, Hannah left his office a few minutes later, promising to be in touch later that week, thinking, *Oh Mary! You'd so much faith in me – what if I fail you?*

A few weeks later, she moved into the small flat above the office. Still in mourning, her thoughts turned to the funeral and everyone who had paid their respects. Hannah and Annie were busy discussing next term's curriculum, the latter mentioning the possibility of offering Linus his former position. Upon discovering how badly he behaved towards Hannah, Mary ordered him to leave; yet the parents and children still missed his presence.

"Is he working in another school?" she asked her colleague.

"Rumour has it he's doing odd jobs and helping his parents renovate their farm."

"Please ask if he would like to do a trial period for six months – we'll take it from there."

Back in London, Melanie regularly had Ben over for dinner and to stay the weekend. She was still angry her friend had left in such a callous, cowardly fashion.

"She caused you to get ill! My God, Ben, does she even know about your panic attack?" she said, meeting him in a café in Primrose Hill one day.

"Please don't refer to her like that. I should have known she wasn't over the loss of our baby . . ."

"You'll be telling me next you'd have her back," Melanie muttered, the image of him shaking in a corner of his living room just as vivid as if it happened yesterday.

"You're right. I should have realised she was putting up a front," Ben replied, eyes empty, looking like a shadow of his former self.

"I don't believe what I'm hearing! Your mother's of the same opinion; Hannah's a selfish, heartless bitch, cutting you out of her life as if you never existed!" But however many times she told him, Ben couldn't stand the thought of them bad-mouthing her. Seeing him so withdrawn, Melanie leant over to kiss his cheek.

"Matt and I worry about you," she said, in a kinder voice.

"You've got to understand I'm the kind of man who only loves once. She's all I want."

"But you've so much to offer! You're letting that woman ruin your life."

"What bloody life?"

"I can't listen to you talking this way. It's been two years! I know you deliberately avoid socialising, so let's at least have a drink together at The Flask in Highgate, 8pm tomorrow . . . for me?" She was always there for him whenever he needed to talk.

"Okay . . . for you," he heard himself reply. Her eyes lit up.

"Great! See you then."

Instantly at ease at the pub they referred to as their second home the following evening, Ben and Melanie were chatting about nothing in particular, when Melanie set down her glass.

"An old friend just walked by. Will you excuse me while I go and say hello?"

"Be my guest! It's not as if I've got anything else to do . . ."

"I thought it was you!" A leggy, tall blonde with high cheek-bones and big blue eyes embraced Melanie warmly.

"I'm so glad to see you again! I bet you're a model, look at you: as stunning as I remember," Melanie declared, privately thinking it odd she'd hardly changed.

"We'll meet up for lunch soon," the blonde suggested, impeccably groomed in white jeans and Lurex top, showing off her long slim legs and toned arms.

"That'd be great! There's someone I think you should meet . . . He's sitting over there."

"I'll have to take a rain check because a friend's invited me to dinner in Belsize Park."

"It won't take long . . . just one drink! No one's ever on time nowadays!"

"Alright. You talked me into it."

As they approached his table, Ben looked at the statuesque woman flashing a smile, showing even white teeth, thinking she had the bluest eyes he'd ever seen. She reminded him of a young Grace Kelly – same frame and delicate features.

"This is Annabelle Clarkson. She's an old friend; we've not seen each other for years." Melanie stood up, enabling Annabelle to squeeze in between them.

"Pleased to meet you," said Ben, shaking her hand. You're bound to have a lot to catch up on . . . I was just leaving."

"Don't be such a spoilsport!" Melanie interrupted, her eyes telling him how rude he was.

"I guess another hour or so won't make a difference. Let me get us some wine." Ben headed for the bar.

Watching him walk away, Annabelle thought he looked like her type of guy: tall, dark and handsome with impossibly big brown eyes. *There's an aura of vulnerability about him*, she told herself, unaware an idea was taking shape in Melanie's head.

"I'm sorry I was so rude earlier." Ben excused himself, returning with a bottle of red wine and pouring them each a glass.

"Don't worry about it! Everyone has their moments – I do as well." Informing them of her job as sales rep in a department store in Kensington, Annabelle added, "I recently divorced my ex . . . you could say we were a match made in hell!" Although she laughed loudly, inwardly she was wondering why she was telling this to a complete stranger.

"How long did your marriage last?" Ben asked in a kind voice.

"Ten years. It took a long time to admit to myself I was fighting a losing battle, imagining I could turn him into a loving, faithful husband," she said, eyes clouding over.

"I'm sorry you got such a raw deal." Ben's eyes met hers, thinking they had something in common, both losing the people they loved.

Getting to her feet, Annabelle thanked him for the wine, saying she'd better leave or risk incurring her friend's wrath.

"It was nice talking to you Ben. I hope you find a way of getting over whatever's troubling you."

Taking her hand in his, Ben replied, "Ditto, take good care of yourself."

"She's a terrific girl," Melanie said, watching her leave, blonde hair cascading down her back. "Don't you think?"

"She's certainly very attractive . . ." Ben was distant, his only wish now being to get out of there and into bed.

"That's all you have to say? Belle's stunning! I'm green with envy . . ."

"Don't get any ideas, Melanie."

"A beautiful woman enters your life and you're not even tempted?" His old friend pretended she was outraged.

"Not in the least! I'm certain Miss Clarkson's perfectly capable of organising her own love life."

Pretty soon, Annabelle appeared at every dinner he was invited to at Melanie and Matthew's house. Ben had to admit to himself how much they seemed to have in common; same favourite places to eat and drink, theatre, cinema and books. When Melanie remarked to her husband how well-suited they were to one another, Matthew let out a big sigh.

"I wish you'd stop interfering in Ben's life. The poor guy's not ready to move on. I've a feeling he never will be and he won't thank you for meddling in his life."

"You've no idea what you're talking about. Ben and Belle – even their names fit perfectly!" Melanie refused to discuss it any further.

Meanwhile, wanting to get to know her better, Ben invited Annabelle to dinner in an Italian restaurant not far from her home in Muswell Hill. Over dinner he politely made it clear all he wanted from her was her friendship, seeing as both of them enjoyed each other's company so much. About to thank him for a nice evening, Annabelle stopped and looked him in the eyes.

"I don't wish to pry . . . It's just that it baffles me you're single. Mel told me you split up from your fiancée years ago?" Sensing he wasn't willing to talk about it, Annabelle touched his hand across the table. "I'm sorry, please ignore my question."

"We were planning on getting married . . . my heart is hers forever," Ben told her, withdrawing his hand.

"What if someone came along to change your perspective? The right woman may be closer than you think . . ." Having spent so much time together in the last few months, Annabelle knew she was in love with him – she hoped he'd feel the same.

"Oh, Annabelle. I'm sorry I misled you . . . You're an incredible woman. I do hope we can still be friends?"

"What if I agree to both? It's so refreshing encountering a man who carries his heart on his sleeve, someone with integrity. We're attracted to each other, Ben, same core values and interests, no strings attached: what do you think?" Her greatest hope was that he'd eventually get over his ex.

"You'd settle for a relationship based on respect and friendship? Are you certain you can handle knowing I'm in love with someone else?" It was absurd even contemplating such a thing but he was fed up with being alone and miserable, always dwelling on the past.

"Yes to both. We're only given one life, Ben. Let's make the most of ours together!"

And that's how it started. Things progressed slowly between them; meeting up for a drink, then a meal, eventually spending the night together at each other's flats. Although compelled to make love to her, Ben felt guilty betraying Hannah and never expressed any feelings or words of endearment. In time Annabelle started to resent it, yet was too scared to mention it in case he left her.

After Hannah had been the owner of Budding Stars for three years, the school went from strength to strength. The year 2006 saw parents queuing to apply for a vacancy, while the borough suggested she should expand, in which case they were only too willing to make a large donation. However, Hannah was adamant that everything should stay the same; the school a safe haven for children with learning difficulties, not some extension to satisfy the hard driven politicians of Malmö.

After discussing it with Annie she made up her mind to offer Linus his old job. *I hope I made the right decision*, she kept thinking, knowing that even her own parents disagreed.

"I can't put my finger on it but I don't trust that man," Zadie had said after coming face-to-face with him outside the school gate. "It's the way he looks at you . . . Promise you'll be very careful whenever he's around."

As Hannah came out of her office one late January afternoon, Linus passed by carrying a pile of books, causing her to jump.

"I wish you wouldn't sneak up on me like that!"

"I didn't mean to scare you," he said. "Some colleagues asked me to fetch these for tomorrow's assembly." He would use just about any excuse to be close to her.

"I didn't hear anyone mention it. See you in the morning."

"I know you're busy . . . Would you like to meet up for a drink? I've come across this little café serving nice food, it's only a short walk from here." Angry he persisted in pursuing her, Hannah looked him square in the eyes.

"You know my answer!"

"Perhaps some other time . . . Did you decide to return home after splitting up with that boyfriend of yours?" Linus continued, remembering some colleagues mentioning it years ago in the staff room. Livid with him, Hannah dropped her bag.

"I warned you numerous times to stay out of my personal life!" she snapped, walking quickly towards the lift to take her upstairs to her flat.

Spending a weekend together in February at Hannah's flat, Sanna looked at Rosie, exclaiming, "What did you do to your face?"

"Botox's great! My clients expect I look my best. At my age I need all the help I can get," she replied defiantly. "You ought to give it a go!" She was barely able to smile.

"No way! You look weird with those pouty lips and no wrinkles," Sanna replied, not in the least concerned she was getting on, preferring comfortable clothing to the latest trends.

"That's because you're a social worker, surrounded by people not taking any pride in their appearance," Rosie hissed, face still blotchy and red after her recent treatment.

"You can think I'm a slob all you like, it's far more preferable than being stretched to oblivion!" Sanna retorted, fully aware their friend had long since 'caught the bug' and there wasn't much either of them could do to change it.

"Stop bickering!" Hannah interrupted. "The world's so different to when we were young. Everyone's living in 'cyberspace', kids aren't capable of stringing together a sentence . . . God alone knows how it'll end!"

Celebrating Hannah's forty-sixth birthday at the house, Zadie repeated what she'd first told her years ago.

"A career's no substitute for a happy life!" Her eyes betrayed her concern, as she wished for the hundredth time her daughter could find someone and be as happy as Lena and Peter.

Everyone except Zadie was fast asleep when the phone rang at midnight. Busy laying the table for breakfast, she picked up the receiver, her face turning pale when she heard who was calling.

"I'm sorry I woke you up . . . I forgot the time difference," Ben said in a low voice, apologising for calling so late. "Is Hannah there with you? I want to congratulate her."

"She's gone to bed. Ben, it's wonderful to hear your voice! Are you and your parents well?" she asked, wishing things could have been different.

"Everyone's just fine . . . Please say hello to everyone from me."

"Please hold on a moment while I tell Hannah you're on the phone," Zadie told him, uncertain as to how her daughter would react. Running to the small passage and knocking on Hannah's door, she announced: "Ben's called to wish you a happy birthday, I can't believe it!"

Sitting straight up in bed, Hannah whispered, "Is he okay?" Her heart was racing.

"Seems like it, yes. Don't make him wait! I can't believe he's actually calling to talk to you!"

"I can't . . . Tell him I'm grateful but it's no use . . . it's best we don't stay in touch." *If I hear his voice, I'll not be able to keep my distance!*

"You're wrong! This could be your only chance to put things right!"

"No. It's too late . . . we've both moved on."

"I never thought I'd say this, but I'm ashamed of you, Hannah!" Zadie said, anger rising inside of her. "Despite everything you put him through, Ben still loves you. Can you imagine what it took him to call you?"

"I just can't . . . Please try to understand!" Hannah cried, burying her face in the pillow.

"Why won't she come to the phone?" Ben asked, devastated she'd refused to talk to him.

"I'm so sorry . . . There's nothing I can do to make her," Zadie mumbled, tears brimming in her eyes. With nothing left to say, she hung up.

Standing in the entrance of his flat, Ben stared at his phone.

I can't continue like this! There's more to life than this . . . this vacuum. The time has come to move on. He'd loved her for decades. *If we'd never met, Annabelle would be perfect for me. Unless I start letting her into my heart, she'll leave and then I'll have no one.* Making a mental note to call her in the morning, Ben went to bed, Hannah's face haunting him in his dreams.

"Are you inviting me to dinner? But you told me you wanted a break . . ." Annabelle was so much in love with him she would settle for anything just to have him in her life.

"I had a lot on my mind – don't bother dressing up, you're perfect just the way you are." Thrilled he'd finally seen sense,

Annabelle had tears of joy in her eyes. His friendship wasn't enough anymore; she needed him to love her, not only as a shoulder to cry on.

At six, Jake was already a small person with opinions of his own; his and Vanessa's bond a far cry from hers and Ronald's. Watching him and his friend Eric playing around her in the kitchen, she couldn't help wishing they lived somewhere else. *He's a mixture of me and Mark, my hair colour and his cleft in the chin . . . The girls will go crazy for him – who could resist those deep-blue eyes?*

Always seeing the best in everyone, Jake loathed his mother and grandfather arguing. At seventy, 'Grandpa' walked with a stick, his eyes as cold and calculating as ever, hair completely white yet just as thick, constantly complaining his daughter wouldn't let him near his grandson unless she was present to supervise.

"You're keeping him from me!" he'd accused her, reminding her of their agreement. As if reading his mother's mind, Jake went up to her asking, "Why haven't I got a dad just like my friends, Mom?" He preferred the American spelling and pronunciation.

"Your dad left before I knew I was expecting you, honey." Vanessa was stunned he kept asking despite her repeatedly telling him they'd split up before she'd found out she was expecting a baby.

Leaving his friend to play by himself, Jake seated himself on her lap.

"Grandpa says Grandma was crazy . . . is it true?"

"No, it's not!" Vanessa sighed, livid Ronald deemed it appropriate to badmouth the woman he'd treated so appallingly to his grandson. "Your grandmother was ill . . . it's called manic depression or bipolar. It's a terrible condition causing people diagnosed with it to be sad and upset a lot of the time."

"Are you sick too, Mom?"

"Of course not. Neither are you." Jake took a moment to register what she'd told him.

"Grandpa told me he'll give away his money to someone else if I refuse to work for him."

Damn him! How dare he intimidate my son?

"Listen to me Jake, you're free to do as you wish – I'll make sure of it!"

"Thanks Mom, you're the best!"

"You must forget what Grandpa told you. You're too young to start thinking about the future."

"Are you okay, Mom? Your eyes look sad . . ."

"Sad? Me? How can I be sad when I have you? I can't believe you're so grown up. You'll soon be taller than I am!"

"Yeah . . . I'm very strong!" Jake giggled, flexing his upper arms until both cried with laughter. No matter how bad she felt, he always put a smile on her face. *Daddy's hell-bent on dictating our lives,* she thought, telling Jake they'd have dinner in the nursery after his friend had gone home.

Later that evening, when Jake was fast asleep in his bedroom, Ronald came knocking on the door.

"Why didn't you and your mother join me downstairs for dinner?" he demanded gruffly, scaring his grandson.

"I'm sorry, Grandpa . . ."

"Get dressed! We need to talk, man to man."

"But I'm asleep! Can't it wait until tomorrow?"

"No it can't. I want to tell you about my businesses."

"But . . . but Mom told me you can't make me work for you!" Jake was suddenly concerned his mom might not have told him the truth. "Bernie!" he shouted, scared his Grandpa would make him.

Running upstairs thinking something happened to him, Bernie swept him up into his arms, oblivious of Ronald glaring at them.

"Why are you so upset? Most kids your age would jump at the idea. Your mother had no right telling you you can do what you like!"

"I d-don't want to w-work for you!" Jake wailed, tears streaming down his face, his little hands beating his grandfather's chest.

"Stop it at once! I don't know what's got into you!"

"I'm calling Vanessa – Jake's not going to calm down unless she's here with him," Bernie snapped at him, furious Ronald would treat his own grandson this way.

"You'll do nothing of the sort! Unless you obey me, I'll . . ."

"You'll give me the sack – is that it?" Bernie yelled, a grim expression in his eyes, no longer giving a damn about the consequences. "I've had enough of you bullying everyone!" he shouted, daring to look his employer in the eyes.

"Why are you screaming? You woke me up . . ." Taking in the scene, Vanessa walked barefoot towards her son, who was crying hysterically in Bernie's arms. "You'll regret this!" she spat at Ronald, helping Bernie to calm Jake down. "Your Grandpa and I have something to discuss, be a good boy for Mom and return to your room. I'll be with you shortly." Taking him back to bed, Bernie offered to read a bedtime story.

"How dare you treat my son this way?" Vanessa hissed at Ronald the minute the door shut behind them.

"He's my grandson! We have an agreement."

"Let me remind you once and for all: if you persist in treating him this way, I'll take him away from you and this house."

"Even if I cut you both out of my will?"

"You know what? Go ahead, Daddy! I've something far more valuable: my son. He's priceless!"

"You'll not abide by our contract? You owe me Vanessa, that's an end to it." Glaring at each other, Vanessa took a step closer to him.

"I'll make sure everyone knows how you treat us. You're *nothing* to me!" Her eyes were dark with anger. "Go knock up some whore! You imagine I don't know about them? They're the reason you're travelling to the States and France. Let some bastard manage your precious company!" Scared she'd act on her words, Ronald swiftly calmed down.

"I hear you. I'm sorry I frightened Jake, I'll apologise in the morning."

"Oh, I've not finished with you yet! I demand you sign over half of your assets to me, the other half in a trust fund for Jake when he turns eighteen – take it or leave it." It was her way of ensuring she was in control of their future.

"Alright! But only on the condition that he doesn't get it until he's twenty. In the event you get married, your eventual spouse will *not* get access to my money. Unless both of you stay here in my house until Jake's eighteen, you'll lose your share or what's left of it." Praying he'd soon be dead, Vanessa nodded.

"We've got ourselves a deal. Tell Clancy I demand everything in writing."

"You sold your son for a measly fifty thousand!" Annuschka sobbed, her eyes swollen from crying.

"Who told you?" Mark whispered, certain she'd never find out.

"A friend's daughter does some administrative jobs for Tim Clancy and his associates. She happened to listen in on some gossip, and came across a copy of your agreement with Ronald Westbrook."

"They left me no option! My creditors would have hounded

me to my grave . . ." Mark mumbled, an agonised sound escaping his mouth.

"You're telling me those two intimidated you to sign? We'll find a way to reverse it!"

"It's too damn late! I've agreed to never have anything to do with either of them."

"Your father would be turning in his grave." Annuschka wrung her hands.

"You've not yet told me what you meant when you said there was more to him than met the eye."

"It wasn't supposed to come out! You're always putting the blame on me for everything that goes wrong . . . Your father was a womaniser . . . You're his son, alright! I put up with it for decades, keeping the family intact. Abandoning my dreams, everything. You should have seen me back then: so full of life . . . your father made certain I lost my confidence."

Listening to her, Mark recalled the times his father had worked 'overtime' yet reeked of booze when he came in the door. Looking at her, with her tightly permed hair and stooped back, he suddenly put his arms around her.

"You should have confided in me. Forgive me for all the things I said to you . . . But you're suffocating me with your constant attention."

"I'm only doing it because I want what's best for you. Your father was everything to me . . . We made up in the end . . ."

"I used to think he was so damn perfect! Everything I'm not: decent, kind, moral. A pillar of the community — had I known that he was cheating on you . . ."

"It's water under the bridge. I'm relieved you found out. You must start acting responsibly, though. Your children need you to be part of their lives, a proper father."

For the first time since he was a child, Mark felt something resembling affection towards the mother he had resented for so long. Annuschka Copeck was human after all.

She's right . . . I made such a mess of my life! It's high time I face my demons.

So a few days later, Mark took a little trip.

"You're certain we're talking about the same people: Hannah and Ben?" he asked the elderly neighbour whose garden was adjacent to theirs. She eyed him suspiciously.

"I told you already! Those two left years ago, such a nice, refined couple. Always offering to help carry my shopping. The couple living there now don't even bother to say hello."

It was New Year's Day, 2007. As they sat enjoying lunch together, Annabelle looked meaningfully at Ben.

"Why don't I live here instead of my own flat? It makes perfect sense seeing as we're spending most of our time in Primrose Hill." Trying to find the right words, Ben shook his head.

"It's not such a good idea. You know how much I enjoy your company, but . . ." She knew the score, and she deserved better than a man still hung up on his ex-girlfriend. Moving around the table to be closer to him, her long hair brushing his face, Annabelle spoke softly.

"I'm willing to give it a go. You're fond of me – that's enough for now."

"Is it really? What if you're wasting your time?"

"We'll take it one day at a time," she whispered, too much in love with him to walk away and return to her flat in nearby Muswell Hill.

★

Busy organising boxes in the closet in her flat, Hannah had a sudden change of heart. Fingers shaking, she dialled the number for Ben's flat in Primrose Hill. A woman answered on the third ring, repeating "Hello?" then hanging up.

It's probably his new girlfriend . . . I blew it. If only I'd talked to him when he called me . . . Now he's met someone, just like I wanted, she thought, convinced they were finished.

Invited to Sabbath dinner at the Isaacs' house in late February, Annabelle praised the food, saying she loved the chicken soup with dumplings.

"You'll have to teach me how to make it!" Rebecka's eyes lit up. "Mum's a terrific cook," Ben interrupted. "Hannah, her mother and grandmother made the most amazing dishes! I never tasted anything like it . . ."

"Please excuse me." Annabelle's face drained of colour and she abruptly left the table. Following her into the kitchen, wishing he'd kept his mouth shut, Ben put his arms around her.

"That was unforgiveable. I don't know what came over me. Friends again, please?"

"I can't go back in there. Please tell your parents we're leaving."

Joining them in the large foyer while Annabelle said goodbye to Michael, Rebecka turned to her son.

"Annabelle's a lovely girl! You'll lose her if you're not careful. Tell her you're sorry for raking up the past."

"She knows how I feel about Hannah, Mum! I tried so hard to get her out of my mind but I can't and never will."

"That woman adores you. You've either got to make it work or go back to how things were before you met her."

"You know as well as I do Hannah's the only woman I love."

"Then you must set her free! It's the least you can do."

"I can't go back to being lonely and miserable . . . I just can't."

"So start afresh!" Walking up to their guest, thanking her for the bouquet of flowers she brought them, Rebecka told Annabelle how nice it was to get to know her and invited her to come again.

A couple of months later, Annabelle introduced him to her parents, Dorothy and Joe, the latter taking him to one side saying his daughter was a 'daddy's girl' and adding, "You must treat her right or answer to me!"

Proud people with a passion for nature, Joe was an insurance broker, Dorothy a housewife looking after their pretty house in the Cotswolds. An only child, Annabelle was everything to them.

"We're so happy she's finally settled down with the right man," Dorothy said, serving them homemade cakes in the small living room, filled with memorabilia of Annabelle's childhood. "Belle tells us you're Jewish; she's never brought back anyone of another faith."

"Do you consider it a problem?" Ben asked, bemused she'd even mentioned it.

"Not in the least, only it's different to what we're accustomed to."

"What Mum's saying is we're not acquainted with your faith, darling, yet willing to adapt, wouldn't you agree, Dad?"

"I couldn't have put it better myself. You're part of our family, Ben – it's only fair we take an interest."

They'd been living together for six months when lying in bed one Saturday morning, Annabelle turned to look at him, saying, "I love you and wish you'd reciprocate. A woman needs to know she's loved."

His stomach in knots, Ben replied, "Surely you must know by now how fond I am of you?"

"But I want you to tell me!"

"I just did!"

"I want you to tell me you love me."

"You're being unreasonable. Love's just a word . . . Actions speak louder than words."

Looking into his eyes, Annabelle nodded, thinking it would have to do for the time being.

Keeping his head down so as to not cause an argument, Linus purposefully bumped into Hannah outside her office.

"Annie's asked me to supervise the builders mending the roof of the patio. I said I'd check with you first," he mumbled, secretly admiring her hair and legs.

"Fine by me. Yesterday's rain and storms caused some damage."

"How about we grab something to eat later? I know you don't want us to meet up but what's the harm? We're colleagues!" His tone was cheerful, hoping she'd accept.

"You know the answer."

"Please! Just once. I won't tell anyone . . . but I will keep asking until you say yes." He dared to look her in the eyes.

"Oh, alright! But only on the condition you stop pestering me. Let's meet outside the main entrance in a couple of hours. I'll come find you when I'm finished." She immediately regretted succumbing to him.

After waiting patiently for her meeting to come to an end, Linus suggested they go to a local café a few minutes' drive from the school.

"I'd better change. Is 7am alright with you?" she asked, heart sinking in her chest.

"I'll find us a nice table." Linus was delirious with joy she'd relented to him

Hours later, in jeans and no make-up, Hannah turned up at the cosy bistro. She sat opposite him, ordering a turkey sandwich, while he asked the waitress to bring him a large portion of spaghetti bolognaise and a pint of beer.

"I'm starting my diet tomorrow," he said, fully aware he needed to shed at least two stone. "How come you're not willing to further expand the school?" he continued, mouth full of food.

"Mary was opposed to it, I'll not do anything she'd disapprove of."

"I'm sorry I brought it up," Linus looked sheepish. "It won't happen again."

"I'm sorry. I didn't mean to snap at you. You've done a lot for the school."

"You're not just saying that?"

"No. We appreciate your hard work. I'd better leave – I've an early start in the morning." Pushing aside her plate and thanking him for the sandwich, Hannah reached for her coat on the stand behind them.

"I'm always available to you!" Linus commented, grinning.

Working late nearly every night leading up to Easter, Hannah was finishing off a report when she heard a knock on the door.

"It's only me . . . Do you fancy coming out for a drink?" Linus asked, red in the face.

"We agreed the other night was a one off. Please don't ask again."

"It's only a drink – I enjoy talking to you."

"We're colleagues, that's all! You and I are not part of one another's lives and that's how it'll stay." She stood up and switched off the lights. "It's time to go home, please lock up before you leave." She pretended she didn't see the look of disappointment on his face.

One week later, Hannah arranged to meet her brother for lunch at Malmö's popular fish restaurant, Johan P. She'd barely ordered when Peter announced: "We need to talk, sis."

"Is it something to do with our parents? I've not seen them for some time. Whenever I offer to come round, Pappa puts me off . . . It's as if they're hiding something from me."

"I agree. I'm worried about Mamma. I can't put my finger on it, but she's been very forgetful lately, as if in another world."

"Can you give me an example?"

"We arranged to meet at Café Hollandia; you know how fond she is of that place. She never turned up! I sat waiting for hours. Concerned she'd had an accident on the way, I decided to call home. Pappa answered, saying she was fine and telling me they were having a late lunch. I didn't mention we'd arranged to meet."

"They're getting on, you know. Perhaps it just slipped her mind?"

"Mamma would never miss an appointment with her children."

"Do you suppose Pappa's hiding something from us? If so, we'd better find out what it is."

"There's something else. I went there to fix something in the garden and I was shocked to find our father unloading the dishwasher! Mamma's usually the one dealing with domesticity."

"Maybe the cleaner was ill or on holiday?"

"Nah, something's wrong. I think Pappa's helping Mamma get dressed – she looks immaculate but something's missing . . . A woman's touch."

"If what you're telling me is true, we'd better get to the bottom of it. It has to be serious for them to not confide in us, their own children." Hannah's eyes were full of fear.

"Let's hope it's not dementia. Do you recall Pappa's old friend, Dennis?" Peter asked. Hannah had to agree; it was the first thing that sprang to mind.

Taking turns visiting their parents, helping with shopping and cooking, Hannah and Peter met up to compare notes in Hannah's office a couple of weeks later. Both were equally upset.

"Mamma's very forgetful. She forgot my name when I helped her get dressed and apply make-up," Hannah said sadly.

"What if it's the onset of Alzheimer's disease? She may as well be dead if that's the case . . ." Peter thought out loud. "We'll have to continue checking up on them. I can't believe how much her memory's deteriorated in just a few months."

Zadie was the centre of their family. If she was diagnosed with the same condition as Dennis, they all had a long painful journey ahead of them.

CHAPTER TWENTY-THREE

2008

As the weeks and months passed, Hannah and Peter's fears were confirmed: Zadie forgot the simplest things including recalling where she put something, the names of those dearest to her and simple tasks like laying the table for breakfast. This alternated with having moments of being her usual self, causing them to think they were mistaken, only to discover she was just as disorientated a while later.

When Hannah pleaded with her father to book an appointment with a neurologist, Walther shook his head.

"What's the point of having some specialist confirm she's suffering from dementia? When Dennis was diagnosed, your mother said she'd rather die than end up like he did."

"Research is more advanced these days . . . There's medication available that helps to slow down the progress of the disease." However hard she tried to convince him, Walther refused to listen. "I understand you're scared, Pappa, but you know as well as I: it's for the best."

"What you propose makes sense but if it's the same condition as my poor friend's, then it's only the beginning of the end!" Visibly shaken, Walther was unable to continue.

"Nobody's expecting you to decide right now. Why don't you take a nap while I help Mamma get undressed?" Putting an arm around his bony shoulder, Hannah was devastated to feel how much weight he'd lost.

"There you are! We must hurry or we'll miss our flight!" Zadie exclaimed, seeing them enter the bedroom, clothes scattered everywhere.

"Let me help you get ready for bed – I'll sort everything out later." Hannah purposefully kept her voice calm, willing herself to not cry. Face crumpling, Zadie put a hand over her mouth as she attempted to recall what was on her mind, yet she was incapable of finding the words.

"What are those clothes doing on my bed?" she asked, suddenly angry.

"I'll sort it later . . ." Hannah soothed her as if talking to a child. Her father lay silently on his side of the bed, staring up at the ceiling. As Hannah helped her mother remove her make-up and brush her teeth, Zadie had a moment of clarity.

"I'm sorry you're having to witness this . . ." It seemed she was at least conscious of something not being as it should.

"That's alright, Mamma," Hannah whispered, a big lump in her throat. "You're always there for me whenever I need you. It's only right I return the favour."

Much to his children's surprise, Walther changed his mind the following week, agreeing to make an appointment with a reputed neurologist. Prior to the meeting, Zadie was required to take a number of tests with her GP, who then referred her to a specialist. A few days later the Steins found themselves seated in the comfortable, airy waiting room. They were talking amongst themselves when a stocky, bearded man in his forties came up to them.

"I'm Dan Sholtz, please call me Dan. Why don't we have a chat in my office?" The Steins instantly warmed to the consultant's gentle manner, following him into another pleasant room. They sat in a semi-circle opposite him, Zadie holding hands with Walther, admiring the photographs of smiling children on Dan's desk.

"The people in the photos . . . are they your family?"

"Yes, my wife and kids. May I ask you a few questions?" Dan responded, smiling at the striking-looking woman in front of him.

"Be my guest!" Zadie suddenly sounded so normal that everyone in her family wondered how someone so alert could be so ill.

"Did you dress yourself or did someone help you?"

"I can't remember," Zadie said, turning to look at her husband. "I think Hannah helped me."

"Is that right?" Dan asked the pretty redhead.

"Yes, but my mother chose what to wear."

"Excellent!"

"What makes you say that?" Peter intervened, a puzzled expression in his eyes.

"It's a sign things aren't progressing," Dan replied hesitantly, not willing to cause concern. He turned back to Zadie. "Which part of your daily routine is the most difficult?"

"Recalling where I put things," came the immediate answer.

"I'm sorry to have to inform you it's part of your condition. There's no easy way of putting it: unfortunately you're in the early stages of Alzheimer's disease. The test results confirm it. I'm sorry to be the bearer of such bad news. Would you like me to give you some time to yourselves?" Dan clearly felt just as much empathy with the Steins as with all his patients.

Taking a deep breath, Walther replied, "We're alright . . ." At a loss for words, he squeezed his wife's hand.

"With all due respect, you look exhausted. Let me arrange for you to have someone to look after Zadie so you can get some rest."

"There's no need. My children take turns to visit and stay the night."

"I see . . . Still, please ensure you have regular check-ups with your GP, it's in both of your best interests." Dan really wanted to add that this was just the beginning of a gruelling and merciless condition.

"I'm going to give you a prescription of tablets which will help slow down the symptoms of the disease. Unfortunately we have yet to find a cure."

"Are there any side effects?" Zadie asked.

"Yes; nausea and exhaustion. But that's on an individual basis and may not apply to you. The tablets will improve your memory, vocabulary and help simplify daily life."

"Aren't I the lucky one!" Without warning, Zadie's personality switched.

"I sympathise with your anger and frustration. Please do ask any questions: I'm here to help."

"How long will this 'wonder drug' work?" Now her voice was frail, as the full impact of what he told her slowly registered.

"It's difficult to say and I don't wish to speculate, Mrs Stein." No matter how well she looked on the outside, Dan knew how bad she felt inside.

"Please call me Zadie . . . I've a feeling we're going to see a lot more of one another." She further managed to express herself without difficulty.

"Certainly, Zadie. But only if you call me Dan."

"You're a nice man, Dan. I appreciate your honesty. Please in-dulge me by answering my next question. Will I have to go into residential care?" Listening to her, Walther put his face in his hands.

"There is a possibility of that happening, yes. But let's not focus on that now, instead on the present."

"It's ironic," Zadie said, removing her glasses and looking up at him. "My mother lived well into her nineties and even uprooted herself from Stockholm to London when she was in her seventies. Yet here I am, struck down with the illness that will eventually rob me of my life." Her eyes were full of despair.

"Alzheimer's is not always hereditary. Yours is, in my opinion, atypical. Have you led a stressful life?"

"That's just it, my life's been wonderful so far . . . except for losing my father when I was very young." She'd forgotten about the stillborn baby. "So what's the verdict, Dan? How long before I rely on my family for everything?" Her eyes searched his.

"Every case is unique. But you'll gradually deteriorate in the near future." His patients always asked the same questions, essentially wanting to know how long they had to put their affairs in order.

"How about the unlucky ones, Dan?"

"My advice is that you take every day as it comes and enjoy life to its full potential. I'll not deceive you – you are deteriorating, but it's too early to envisage to what extent."

"Looks like this disease is going to beat me one way or another!" Zadie gazed around at her family.

"You made the right decision to see me now as opposed to waiting," Dan said, in a bid to offer some reassurance.

"My final question is this: how long before I succumb to my condition? Please be honest with me."

"Approximately eight to ten years after diagnosis."

"I appreciate your honesty, Dan," Zadie replied, smiling at everyone. Unknown to them, she had no intention of becoming a burden to them. Things were already bad enough. *I'm going to have to make some important decisions before I get too ill,* she thought.

Asking the nurse to schedule the next appointment, Dan shook hands with the four members of the Stein family. "Please don't hesitate to call with any questions and concerns – I'm always available to you," were his last words, as he thought to himself he'd never come across anyone as gutsy as Zadie Stein.

But sadly for all concerned, Dan's prescription didn't turn out to be the 'miracle' they had hoped for. Instead Zadie belonged to the category of patients whose illness progresses rapidly, almost to the extent of losing her vocabulary, causing her grandsons to wonder why she no longer recalled their names. Time after time she would get up in the middle of the night and wander around outside in the street, neighbours bringing her back. Walther, Hannah and Peter took turns to ensure the front door was locked and the windows bolted.

"I'm concerned about you, Walther," Dan said during a surgery visit. "Have you considered sleeping in another room?"

"Zadie and I never spent more than a few nights apart . . . Unless I'm there next to her, she'll get anxious and disorientated." Walther's tone was flat and dismissive.

"Will you at least see your GP?"

"There's not much point." Walther shook his head. "I'd much rather go in the same direction as my wife." Hannah couldn't help but burst into tears.

Indeed, every time his family told him how dangerous it was for him to neglect himself, Walther ignored them, closing his mind to everything they said. Even Zadie tried to reason with him in moments of lucidity.

"You're not listening!" she protested when trying to make arrangements for their future. "Sooner or later you're going to have to come to terms with the fact I'm terminally ill! I'd be better off in care . . ."

"Nonsense! I'll sell this house and find us a flat in Central Malmö, close to all the restaurants, shops and cafés you like," he told her, ignoring her concerns.

"You're the one talking rubbish – I'm living on borrowed time. If I can face up to it, so should you." Zadie was deeply upset by his refusal to accept the situation.

"I will never accept it – *never!*"

"Not even when you've no choice?"

"Not even then! Oh . . . Why did this have to happen to you . . . to us? No. I married you for better or for worse. I'll not abandon you."

"But you must prepare yourself for when I'm no longer able to live here," Zadie cried, clinging to his arm.

"How can I? You're my everything!" He looked at her lying there next to him in their bed, every bit as beautiful as when they first met. "Your disease can't tear us apart. It just can't. We're still the same people inside!"

Unknown to Walther, Zadie found a moment when her family weren't present to ask Dan Sholtz if he could recommend a place for her to live.

"My family are all I care about. I'll not have them caring for me when I'm at my worst! It'll break my heart to move to an institution but it's my only option." Her brown eyes were full of despair.

"I've decided to change your medication. Let's see how we get on with that for a while and then talk about this later," Dan replied, thinking Exelon might prevent further deterioration in the next few years. "Wouldn't you rather discuss it with your family first?"

"Walther's refusing to accept my condition. He understands alright but won't talk about it. Please let me have a list of places available to me. I have to be prepared when the time comes and I can no longer live at home."

A few night's later, as they fell asleep in each other's arms, Walther whispered, "We've just made love; I can't get my head around the fact you're ill. Your new tablets are much better than the previous prescription." Their passion didn't rely on anything but the special bond they'd shared for decades, something that didn't need words, only their own unique language.

"Will you do something for me?" Zadie asked.

"Of course. Anything at all."

"Hannah's not happy . . . That school's no substitute for love! I've decided to write to Ben, telling him about my illness and that Hannah still loves him." She'd kept Ben's old address in her diary just in case it came in handy one day.

"You can't! Hannah will be very upset if you interfere in her life."

"You must give me your word you'll continue corresponding with him when I'm too ill," Zadie persisted, ignoring his comment. Seeing her looking so upset, Walther immediately agreed. "She'll thank us for it one day," Zadie said, as sleep began to enfold her. "Don't forget to invite the Isaacs to my funeral . . . I want Ben to be there for her . . ."

Busy making rhubarb pie with custard sauce, Jake's favourite pudding, Vanessa and Bernie were discussing Ronald's recent outburst, the latter complimenting her on being such a wonderful mother.

"You're too kind. The truth is I'm nothing without him. Please see to it the pie doesn't fall apart in the oven while I change into something else." Pleased her father was in a meeting with some associates in London, Vanessa couldn't wait for her and Jake to have the evening to themselves. Passing the window in the foyer on her way upstairs, a familiar figure on the pavement outside suddenly caught her eye.

"Bernie, please take a look!" Climbing two steps at a time, Vanessa whispered: "It's Mark! Jake mustn't see him. I told him his father left me not knowing I was pregnant ... What's he doing outside our house? My father got rid of him years ago!" She trembled in Bernie's arms.

"If he's come to stir things up, I'll see to it he leaves and never returns!"

"Why are you upset, Mom?" Jake asked, coming towards them on the way from his room.

"Please go back to your room – I'll call for you when dinner's ready!" Vanessa shouted, terrified he'd catch a glimpse of Mark.

"But I'm starving, Mom."

"Aren't you and Eric playing together later?"

"Yeah, we are ... I'd forgotten about it. Can we play at his house?"

"I'm not sure it's such a good idea. You've got homework to do." *What if Mark already knows which school he attends?* "Call Eric and ask him over for dinner – he loves rhubarb pie just as much as you!"

"Awesome! Thanks Mom, you're the best!" The nine-year-old had nagged her into getting him a mobile among other gadgets so as to not feel excluded from his friends' lives.

At that very moment, seated in his black Ford outside, holding the steering wheel so tight his knuckles turned white, Mark swore out loud.

"You'll not keep him from me any longer, Vanessa! Now's not the right time but I'll return – you can bet your bottom dollar on it!"

A few weeks later, Vanessa was carrying in her shopping bags, when she noticed Mark's car at the front of the house.

"I'll not be bought off this time!" Mark had at long last faced up to his demons. He got out of his car, slamming the door and walked towards her. Vanessa prayed Jake would stay safely out of the way in his bedroom, upstairs.

"How dare you threaten me after what you did?" she hissed.

"Your old man and his corrupt lawyer pushed me into a corner; I've every right to be part of my son's life!"

"I get it." Vanessa's eyes narrowed. "The money we paid you wasn't good enough, so you've come back for more! Well, you listen to me: you're not getting another penny. Is that clear? No one forced you to sign that document. Jake's *my* son – you'll never be part of his life!"

Only too conscious of his misdemeanours, Mark put his hands up.

"I had to get those damn creditors off my back! You left me no other option by ordering your connections to not have anything more to do with me. What will you do when our son starts asking questions about me? Jake has the right to know his father and grandmother. I bet the old bastard's happy he's got a grandson to carry on his name and legacy. You're not fooling me, Vanessa – we're both conscious of the fact you're only in it for the money!"

"Jake doesn't have a father. You lost that privilege when you sold him! Nobody wants you Mark; it's high time you accept it.

Get the hell away from us or I'll report you for trespassing. Good-bye and good riddance!" As she began to close the door, Mark changed his tactic, placing his foot in the doorframe.

"Can't you see how difficult this is for me? I was wrong saying those things . . . I've no right to criticise you – everything I did was wrong. But a boy needs his father. Please let me make it up to you both," he begged.

"You don't give a damn about my son – only his inheritance!" Vanessa screamed, pushing him away.

"I'll not go until I've seen him and introduced myself!" Mark shouted, when a small boy with blond hair and big blue eyes suddenly appeared, interrupting them.

"Why is that man shouting at you, Mom?"

"Jake! You weren't supposed to find out this way. That man's your father . . . I know I told you he'd disappeared from our lives . . . his name's Mark, Mark Copeck. But he's only here because we're rich!" She cradled him in her arms, just as Bernie, who was wondering what all the shouting was about, joined them.

"You! How dare you come here to this house?"

"All I ask is that you let me talk to my son! Would you like to get to know me, Jake?"

"Can I, Mom? I'll tell him to leave if he upsets you . . ."

"Go ahead, I'm right here." Vanessa had no intention of leaving them on their own, terrified Mark would snatch him from her. Holding onto his mother's hand, Jake moved closer.

"Are you really my dad?" Tears stinging in his eyes, Mark bowed his head.

"I'm sorry I hurt your Mom . . . Vanessa, please let me in so we can talk properly."

Stepping aside to let him into the large foyer but no further,

Vanessa got the impression Mark meant what he said. "I'm watching you like a hawk," she warned.

"Are you a criminal?" Jake asked, noticing they had the same cleft in their chin.

"No, I'm not – would you like us to get to know each other, Jake? I've waited such a long time to meet you!" Mark turned to look at Vanessa, who reluctantly nodded her agreement.

"Thanks, Mom! I'll only talk to you if you don't upset her," Jake added, pointing a finger at him. "Do I have siblings?"

"A sister . . . her name's Maruschka, but I've not see her for years," Mark replied, eyes sad.

"Can't you find her like you found me?"

"I doubt she wants to have anything to do with me."

"That's awful! Don't you have anyone who cares about you?"

"My mother, your grandmother . . . she can't wait to meet you." That was too much for Vanessa, who interrupted.

"Please go upstairs to your room Jake. Mark and I need to talk."

"Must I? Can't I stay a while longer?"

"Perhaps another time." Jake took one last look at the man whose eyes were glued on him, before running inside.

"My Mom's the best in the whole world! It was nice talking to you."

"I'm sorry I behaved so appallingly," Mark said. "He's a credit to you."

"Unless you genuinely want to get to know him, please stay away from us! My son's everything to me." Vanessa kept her voice low in case Jake was eavesdropping on them.

"Please let me spend time with him. I'll never be as special to him as you are but I want to make amends . . ." Reaching for her hand, Mark instantly pulled back when seeing the look of contempt in her eyes.

"I'll consider it. Goodbye Mark."

Closing the door behind him, Vanessa took a deep breath. *Daddy will hit the roof when he finds out about this.*

They were on their way to the park a couple of days later when Mark turned up just as Vanessa and Jake were driving off in her blue station wagon.

"I was going to call first but I lost my nerve, convinced you'd hang up. Where are you going?" "Parliament Hill." Vanessa was furious he hadn't called to ask her permission to come round and visit, but she kept her voice light so as to not upset Jake. "Seeing as you're here, you may as well come along."

"Awesome!" said Jake. "Can Eric join us?"

"Perhaps next time." After watching him climb into the car and backseat, Vanessa turned back to look at Mark. "Jake's capable of something I'm not: forgiveness. If you upset him . . ."

"I won't! All I ask is that you give me the opportunity to prove I've changed." He wanted to tell her how much he respected her for being such an exemplary mother to their son but the words stuck in his throat. "I like your car . . . is it new?" he asked instead, desperate to clear the tension between them.

"Grandpa didn't want her to buy it!" Jake intervened, singing along to a melody on the radio.

The old bastard's still controlling her, Mark thought to himself, dropping the subject.

Not long after, they stood at the top of Parliament Hill, admiring the view of London while Jake played with his kites, which were flying high up in the sky.

"I'll call next time – not just turn up," Mark said abruptly.

"Jake was waiting for your call. You let him down!"

"I was scared . . . You made it abundantly clear I've no place in your lives." Vanessa took a moment to reply, watching her son looking so happy, dancing around with his kites.

"Put one foot wrong and you'll never see him again. Jake and I are very close. You'll not come between us."

"I wouldn't dream of it! I said it before and I'll say it again: he's a credit to you, Vanessa."

Listening to him made her feel good about herself. *Bernie and Mark both agree I'm a great mother* . . . "Go join him! I'll wait here for you," she said quietly.

"You mean it? You'll let me spend time with my son?"

"Everyone deserves a second chance." *He's different . . . almost as if he's lost his zest for life. I bet that mother of his has something to do with it!*

Running up the hill towards her twenty minutes later, helping one another carry the kites, laughing and talking, Mark mouthed the words "Thank you."

"You should have told us you were coming, Dad! I was waiting for your call," Jake mentioned on the way back to the car.

"I was scared you'd changed your mind about wanting to see me. But I'm very glad I decided to come along; today's been great!"

Running ahead of them to the parking lot, Vanessa turned to look at Mark.

"You're much too slim . . . are you ill?"

"Hell no! I'm just not as young as I used to be. Anyway, you're looking great. I like your new hairstyle – it suits you. Are you over Ben?"

"Yes, I am . . . I wrote him a letter of apology a while back but haven't heard from him. My life began when Jake was born. We'd better make a move, I'm dropping him off at a friend's house."

"Can I see you both again . . . soon? I promise to call first."

Interrupting them, Jake ran towards them shouting, "I'm glad you made up!" then continued playing with his kites.

"Kids! Can you remember how it felt not having a care in the world?"

"Not really. My mother killed herself when I was younger than Jake is now."

"I'm so sorry! I don't recall you telling me about it."

"I wouldn't have. You and I never had that kind of relationship. But Ben knew."

"Why did she do it?" Mark asked softly.

"Being married to my father drove her to it." Vanessa wondered why she was opening up to him about something so personal.

"How is the old so-and-so?"

"Still alive, controlling everyone's lives!"

"Why are you letting him – surely it's not about the money?" Mark frowned, struggling to keep his feelings in check.

"My father's determined Jake succeeds him. He's hell-bent on showing him the ropes as soon as he turns eighteen or he'll see to it that we end up with no money or a roof over our heads." She omitted telling him about the Trust.

"That's despicable! And if Jake wants no part of it, what then?"

"We'll cross that bridge when we get there. Jake's caring and artistic. Somehow I can't visualise him being interested in my father's company. He's much too genuine and kind to be a bully! So . . . are you still in love with Hannah Stein?"

"What's the point? She and Ben are probably married with kids . . ."

Why did I ask about Hannah? Vanessa wondered. *Whom he dates is none of my concern.*

"Will you let me introduce Jake to his grandmother?" Mark asked.

"No disrespect but I'm not convinced she's a good influence . . . you are the way you are because of her . . ."

"I agree to an extent but we've sorted out our differences now. Please?"

"I'll think about it."

Leaving that day, Mark kept thinking how much she'd changed. *Vanessa's the mother of my son . . . but I'm in love with Hannah . . .* he told himself, unable to shake off the strange mix of feelings stirring inside of him whenever she appeared before his eyes.

"I demand you come into my office this minute!" Ronald barked the next morning when they were getting into the car.

"Can't you see I'm busy driving Jake to school?" Vanessa's irritation was obvious.

"Let Bernie take him. You and I need to talk." Reluctantly agreeing, Vanessa dragged her feet into the stuffy, sterile room.

"How come you're permitting Copeck to spend time with you and Jake?" her father shouted, red in the face.

"Mark's changed! He wants to be part of our son's life."

"Bullshit! The man's a loser and fraudster. I paid him off on the condition he'd stay out of our lives!"

"Are you quite finished?" Fed up with his patronising attitude towards her, Vanessa remained calm. "Don't meddle in our lives! Jake has every right to get to know his father."

"You've changed your tune – perhaps you've forgotten our agreement? Don't be such an idiot! Jake's all I care about. I'll not have that loser interfering in his life! I agreed to your terms . . .

Please feel free to leave if things aren't to your liking. But Jake stays here with me – that imbecile's not coming near him. If you let him, I'll, I'll . . ."

"Do what exactly? What will you do to me if I disobey?" she teased.

"I'll strip you of everything you have!" Clutching his chest, Ronald struggled to get up from his chair, breathing heavily. "Would you like me to call an ambulance?" Her tone was icy.

"There's nothing wrong with me . . . I've years left. It's hearing that man's name that causes me to get this upset."

"Mark has every right to get acquainted with his son."

"How come you're all of a sudden defending him?" Ronald's eyes narrowed. "Perhaps the two of you picked up from where you left off?"

"You're nothing but a crude, vicious bully. Jake's already seen your true colours!" Vanessa sneered, slamming the door on her way out.

"Why is Grandpa always so mean to you, Mom?" Jake asked later that day.

"He wants us to have nothing to do with Mark," she replied, burying her face in his hair.

"But we can still see him, right?"

"Of course! Your grandfather can't stop us."

"Why does he always shout at you?"

"I guess he's just old . . ."

"But you're his child, he ought to be nice to you!" Loving the fact he was standing up for her, Vanessa shook her head.

"It's not that simple. Your grandfather needs us to care for him. It's the reason we're living in his house." It was a lie, but she was not willing to involve him in their conflict.

"But it's you I care about, not him!" Jake persisted.

"Listen to me, honey: just because he and I don't get along doesn't mean the two of you can't. Just don't let him bully you into doing something you're not willing to do."

"Must we really continue to live here when he's so nasty? You're always upset when he's around."

"Upset? How can I be upset when I have you? It won't be forever, honey."

She didn't tell him they had no other option. They could either stay put or risk losing everything.

Vanessa had long since agreed to Annuschka meeting her grandson. The old woman's eyes brimmed with tears when the meeting finally took place at Mark's house.

"Her food's not as good as yours, Mom!" Jake commented when driving home, thinking it tasted burnt. He'd been too polite to mention it to her. Embracing him, Annuschka had cried tears of joy.

"I'm so happy Jake's back in our lives! All you have to do now is locate Maruschka. I won't rest until she's back where she belongs!" Expressing how grateful she was to him, Annuschka handed Mark a signed document.

"It's the deeds of the house – I signed it over to you, son."

"I don't know what to say . . ." Mark's eyes were moist with tears.

"You've changed for the better since becoming part of your son's life. Please ensure Maruschka's found and I'll die a happy woman indeed."

Unfortunately, neither of them was conscious of Ronald harbouring a devious plan he was convinced would rid him of the Copeck family once and for all.

★

"You're . . . not . . . listen . . . ing to . . . me!" Zadie shouted at them one hot afternoon in May 2009.

"Mamma, please! What are you trying to say?" Hannah was exasperated. Her father looked on silently, too exhausted to intervene.

Between school and looking after her parents, Hannah hardly found any time for herself. She was incapable of recalling the last time she'd enjoyed a good night's sleep. Having lost most of her vocabulary, and now requiring constant supervision and care, Zadie had an awareness she was running out of time. Coming up to her, Walther held her close.

"We're listening to you, my darling." He thought about how much weight she'd lost; she was skin and bones.

"Dan . . . s . . . foun . . . nd . . . me . . . a pl . . . ace . . . to li . . . ve!" Gesturing at her forehead, she was desperate for them to comprehend. Face crumpling, Walther shut his eyes.

"I'll not listen to this."

"Loo . . . ok . . . at . . . m . . . ee! It's . . . my . . . life . . . my . . . de . . . cis . . . ion," she cried.

"I'm not listening to you!" He repeated, swaying on his feet.

"What's wrong, Pappa? I'm calling an ambulance!" Tears spilling down her cheeks, Zadie tried catching their attention and succeeded in getting them to look at her.

"Thi . . . s . . . is . . . the . . . rea . . . son I . . . can . . . t . . . stay . . . he . . . re!" Turning to look at her, Walther's voice trembled with emotion.

"You've made up your mind you're leaving me? Tell me when!" The man she had spent half of a century with was truly broken.

"I can . . . t . . . rem . . . emb . . . er, ask . . . Dan!"

"Dan found you a place to live? You prefer living in an institution? They may be capable of giving you the care you need, but what about love?" Walther cried. Stumbling, his wife made her way up to him, her steps painfully slow.

"You can't see . . . me like . . . th . . . is! I've not los . . . t my self . . . res . . . pe . . . ct and pri . . . de!"

Suddenly everything she had tried to tell them made perfect sense.

"Please don't leave me . . . I beg you!" Walther sobbed, turning to his daughter for support. At that moment Peter ran into the kitchen, wondering why they were arguing.

"Mamma's just told us Dan has found her a place to live . . . Pappa nearly collapsed earlier."

After helping to calm down his mother and moving her into bed, Peter asked Hannah to join him in the library. There, sitting next to each other surrounded by their parents' extensive collection of books, she burst into tears.

"I don't know how much more I can take . . . It's too awful for words!"

"I've Lena to support me, but you've got no one, sis . . . I know how much you're still hurting over Ben. Tell me how you're feeling."

"Sad, empty, devastated . . . I try to avoid thinking about it! If I do, I'd lose my mind. I was wrong to leave him, Peter." It was the first time she'd admitted it to anyone apart from herself. "Linus called earlier, offering to come round to do some gardening or anything else that needs doing," she added, seeing the look of disapproval in her brother's eyes.

"He just wants to get close to you."

"You're wrong! Linus knows full well I've no feelings for

him." Ben was the only man she loved. No one could fill the void he left behind.

"We'll employ someone, I guess until then it makes sense he does the odd job ... You're mistaken about him though; that man's only concern is how to best impress you."

"I apologise for causing you to get upset," Dan told them at the surgery the following evening. "Zadie asked me to help find a suitable place. Villa Springview is the best of its kind and close to where you live. You ought to make an appointment to view the premises. The supervisor, Roland Svensson, has a particular interest in patients with dementia. He's also one of the nicest people I've ever come across – he'll be only too pleased to show you around."

As they left, Hannah told Peter she'd join them at the house a while later.

"I need some time on my own," she explained, looking drawn and pale. "Limhamn's harbour's the perfect place to unwind."

Half an hour later, sitting in her car with the windows wound down, she inhaled the smell of rain and fresh air. Her reverie was interrupted by a voice calling her name.

"What brings you here at this time of night?" Linus asked. His van was parked behind her car. Hannah regarded him from behind the open window.

"Perhaps you found out from Annie ... my mother's been diagnosed with Alzheimer's disease ... it's terminal."

"I don't know what to say, that's terrible! Is there anything I can do for you?" It struck her then how kind he was offering his support despite the way she'd treated him lately.

"It's a lot to take on board."

"You don't have to talk about it unless you want to. I'm always here for you."

"You're very kind ... Let's keep this between you, me and Annie."

"Scout's honour," Linus replied, thinking this was the perfect opportunity to get close to her. "Are you sure you don't want me to drive you home? I can deliver your car in the morning."

"That's sweet of you but I'm on my way back to spend the rest of the night at my parents' house."

From then on Hannah saw a different side to him. Increasingly she agreed to meet up for a drink or meal, extending to weekends and after work, meeting at the gate. She would listen to his stories about growing up with a volatile mother who never missed the opportunity to ridicule him, somewhat explaining why he turned out like he did.

Over the summer Zadie gradually withdrew from her family, her eyes blank and vacant whenever they tried getting through to her, the normally well-groomed woman they all knew and loved turning into a shadow of her former self, hair grey and limp.

My beautiful, vivacious mother's dying before our eyes, that wretched disease is robbing us of her! Watching her father assist her into bed, her trademark glasses on the bedside table, and gently putting her book to the side seeing as she could no longer read, Hannah thought, *We have to suppress our own feelings of despair and put our parents' needs before our own.*

Visiting Villa Springview for the first time took all of them by surprise. Roland Svensson looked different from what they'd expected: tall, muscular and bald, with big tattoos on his arms and neck, and a ring in his left earlobe, Hannah guessed he was in his forties as they listened to him explaining how his own parents had both succumbed to dementia.

"Their demise inspired me to become involved with people just like them. I bet you expected a woman to run this place?" he asked, telling a few jokes. The Steins all agreed he was kind and considerate with a wicked sense of humour, Zadie's face lighting up as she listened to him, her eyes scrutinising the spacious room and adjacent bathroom reserved for her. The sunny back garden, combined large kitchen and dining room made Villa Springview feel as if they were in a private house, not an institution.

"We encourage everyone to bring with them a few personal items and pictures, making it less traumatic and easier to adapt. I personally advocate regular piano and reading sessions – hence the Steinway & Sons in the main foyer. Above all, no one's referred to as patient, only client."

Leaving an hour later, everyone agreed: Villa Springview wasn't as scary as they'd been led to believe, even Walther admitting to the fact Roland Svensson was one of the nicest people they'd ever met.

Several weeks later, insisting they chose what they wanted from her personal belongings whilst she was still alive, Zadie, Hannah and Peter spent days sorting out old letters, photos and clothes.

It feels strange accepting she wants us to pick the things we want the most before she's gone, Hannah thought, close to tears when receiving her mother's favourite Pucci dresses. Hovering in the background, adamant he wasn't part of it, Walther retired to his study, only returning when he was certain they'd finished. But a few weeks later, busy putting up paintings by artists they'd first discovered when travelling to Paris, Walther had to admit her room at Villa

Springview had turned out nicely, furnished with her favourite pieces from the house.

Visiting one weekend prior to Zadie's departure, Sanna and Rosie were invited to stay at the house in Limhamn.

"How do you feel, Zadie?" Rosie enquired, pretending they didn't notice how ill and frail she was. Eyes blank, the former continued humming a tune no one recognised.

"You've no idea who we are, have you?" Sanna whispered. "We're Hannah's friends, Sanna and Rosie." She stroked her soft cheek, big brown eyes searching hers.

Struggling to mouth the words, Zadie replied, "You're . . . pret . . . ty!" Then her eyes became vacant.

After spending twenty minutes attempting to get through to her, both admitted defeat, resigned to the fact their dear friend had no recollection of them.

"I had no idea she'd deteriorated so much," Rosie said on the way to the airport on Sunday night.

"We'll probably never see her again . . . You'd think I'd be used to this sort of thing given my profession. But Zadie's different . . . I feel as if my heart's been ripped out of my chest!"

"She's been such a big part of our lives."

"You must let us know if you need us, Hannah. Please forgive me if I'm unable to attend the funeral . . ." Sanna mumbled, unwilling to bid Zadie goodbye.

"Thanks for coming. You mustn't feel pressured into coming again . . . I won't hold it against you," Hannah said, her friend's words ringing in her ears as she drove back across the bridge to Malmö.

"Are you available to meet up this weekend?" Linus asked a week later, after Zadie had moved into Villa Springview.

"Pappa's very upset . . . perhaps another time." *Damn – I should have turned him down!* Hannah knew she didn't owe him any explanations. Linus would never be more than a friend and colleague.

"All the more reason I help you out," he persisted, hoping she'd change her mind.

"Perhaps you're right. Mamma's spending next weekend at home. Come round for an hour or two – I'm sure Pappa will be pleased." Hannah told herself he was harmless. But the moment Zadie spotted his van outside, her eyes grew dark with resentment. Reaching for Hannah's hand, she began to mouth some words.

"Don't. Bad . . . man . . . Get . . . rid!" She was visibly upset.

She's clearly worried about him being here . . . I'll ask him to leave. Hannah went outside, explaining to Linus how ill her mother was and that it was best he picked up his tools and left. Her eyes fixated on him as he walked past her to the front door, Zadie wished there was something she could do to prevent her daughter getting too close to that man.

"Isn't it nice coming home, my darling?" Walther commented, pulling her close. "Hannah's right to get Linus to do the things I can't." Zadie grabbed his arm urgently.

"You must . . . tell Be . . . n abou . . . t it!"

"You're asking me to tell Ben about this? But he's already made it very clear he's with someone!"

"You . . . prom . . . ised!"

"Don't upset yourself, we'll do it together . . . you and me, I'll find a pad and pen." Ensuring she sat comfortably in her armchair, Walther was halfway to the study when the phone rang in the kitchen.

"Did I catch you at an inconvenient time?" Rebecka asked, calling to find out if Ben was right about Zadie being ill.

"We're alright, just getting older than everyone else!"

"Ben told me he'd received a letter from Zadie – how is she? Michael and I often think of you both."

"There's something you should know, unfortunately it's not good news. Zadie's been diagnosed with Alzheimer's disease. She's living in a special place catered to people with dementia."

"That's awful! We're so very sorry for you both."

"There's not a lot to be done about it . . . How's Ben?" Walther sounded tense.

"He's fine . . . he's living with a nice lady we're extremely fond of." She wanted to add "unlike your daughter" but it wouldn't have been appropriate under the circumstances.

"I'm glad to hear it. Thank you for calling, it's always nice hearing from you. Give my best to Michael . . ." Walther replied, heart sinking in his chest. So Ben had found someone else. *This will break Zadie's heart,* he thought, staring at the phone. He sighed, then pulled himself together. "That was Rebecka wanting to know how we're doing. I'm afraid she told me Ben's in a relationship, my darling."

"No! He can . . . n't!" Zadie cried, making him wish he'd kept it to himself.

"But you knew already? Ben told you as much in his letter."

"He's not . . . in love . . . with that . . . woman!" she replied, suddenly finding it easier to get the words out, thinking Rebecka was wrong saying what she did. *She's still angry with Hannah for leaving him!* After six months at Villa Springview Zadie's speech and ability to dress and undress herself had improved to the extent that she even managed to comb her hair, aided by her carer. "Time's running out . . . Hannah needs me!" were her last words before falling asleep in her husband's arms that night.

★

422

"You should have told me Zadie's ill . . . Rebecka delivered the news the other day." Melanie called the following morning just as they were having breakfast in the kitchen.

"Mamma was diagnosed a while ago. I didn't think you'd ever want to speak to me again, not after what I did," Hannah replied, stunned to hear her old friend's voice after so long. "Peter and I take turns staying over . . ."

"Oh Hannah – I'm so sorry I gave you such a hard time. Why couldn't you have confided in me? I thought we were friends! I'd have been there for you if I'd known how upset you were! Please forgive me for being so insensitive . . ."

"Is Rebecka still angry with me?" Hannah was holding back her tears.

"Yeah . . . Ben was in pretty bad shape for a long time. He had to be admitted to hospital after suffering a severe anxiety attack, the doctor told him it was brought on by stress . . ."

"Oh no!" Hannah's heart leapt into her mouth. "Is he alright now? All of it's my fault!"

"He's okay." Melanie omitted telling her about Annabelle.

"I'm not surprised Rebecka hates me – I would as well in her shoes." Too upset to talk longer, Hannah thanked her for calling, promising to keep in touch. Yet she knew she wouldn't. *Our lives are so different now . . . perhaps I should have asked her about that woman answering his phone . . .*

Ending the call, Melanie dabbed at her eyes and dialled Ben's number, asking if they could meet up later.

"What's up? I can hear it in your voice!" he replied, busy parking his Bentley in a side street. "I'm on my way home . . . spit it out . . . you're sounding as if you're crying!"

"I'd much rather talk to you face to face," Melanie sobbed.

"Is this about Zadie? She sent me a letter telling me about her condition. I couldn't believe it . . . not *her*; she's too good to get struck down with Alzheimer's disease . . . Who told you?" Ben was suddenly suspicious, wondering if she and Hannah kept in touch behind his back.

"I can't remember. Maybe Peter, I'm not sure." *He's with Belle now . . . it's too late for him and Hannah!*

"Zadie wants me and Hannah to get together again! It's typical of her to be so concerned. Unselfish till the end . . ."

"Is that what you want as well? Are you still in love with Hannah?" Melanie asked, holding her breath.

"You already know the answer to both questions."

"What about Belle? I thought the two of you worked things out?"

"Perhaps if I'd never met Hannah . . . But she needs me now more than ever! There's nothing stopping us now . . ." Suddenly he realised it was destiny bringing them together again.

"Except Belle . . . she's in love with you! Don't do this to her – please!"

"I'd be doing her a favour. She knows I don't love her. No. It's now or never . . . before I'm in too deep." He was too old to waste any more time living up to Annabelle's and his parents' expectations. Just thinking what Hannah must be going through made him even more determined to be there for her. *You must be beside yourself, little one, dealing with what's happened to Zadie.*

"Hannah left so you could start afresh and start a family of your own! Belle's younger . . . the two of you could be very happy together."

"Hannah's wrong! You all are! All I want is to spend the rest of my life with the woman I love. Belle's not that woman and she never will be."

"You don't even know if Hannah's involved with someone!"

"I don't care. All I know is that she loves me just as much as I love her. The last thing I want is to hurt Annabelle but I've no option."

"Please don't go making any hasty decisions . . ."

"Haven't you listened to a word I've said? Zadie's confirmed Hannah's just as unhappy we're not together . . . My life's not worth living without her!"

"It's obvious you're hell-bent on doing things your way . . . at least tell Belle, you owe her that much," Melanie replied, regretting being the one bringing them together in the first instance.

Determined to confront her with it there and then, Ben was getting out of his car at the front of the property when he noticed Annabelle running towards him, hair dishevelled, cheeks streaked with mascara.

"I don't know how to tell you . . ." she cried, throwing herself into his arms and instantly making him feel guilty about wanting to end their relationship.

"Let's go inside," he mumbled, a million thoughts entering his head.

"My father's committed suicide! Mum found him hanging from the ceiling in their bedroom. He left a note saying he'd lost their savings in some insurance scam . . . telling her he was too ashamed to continue living . . . Begging for her forgiveness . . ." She was wracked by sobs. Stunned, Ben loosened his tie, falling into a chair in the kitchen. "Mum told me their solicitor's assured her she's not eligible for his debts . . . Oh, the shame of it! The entire neighbourhood's gossiping about it. All I kept thinking was, 'Thank God for Ben – he'll stand by me!'" She sobbed, sitting on his lap.

"Is Dorothy alright? She must be beside herself with grief," Ben spoke in a broken voice, his only thought: *I can't leave her now, not when she relies on me . . .*

"The GP gave her a sedative. Can you imagine how she must feel? She thought she knew him inside out . . . turns out she didn't! I used to think he was decent and honourable . . . I was wrong! How could he do this to us, leaving Mum and me to face the consequences?"

"Did you tell Mel?"

"Not yet. I wanted you to know about it first," Annabelle was close to hysteria as she fought to block the mental image of what her father must have looked like when her mother discovered his body.

No, I can't abandon her . . . not after everything she did for me. Joe's unforeseen demise had destroyed his and Hannah's only chance of being reunited.

Over the coming weeks and months Annabelle relied on him for everything: organising her father's funeral, carrying his coffin and inviting Dorothy to stay with them until they could find a flat for her nearby.

"You're a good man, Ben," she told him after another six months went by, her eyes still sad. "Mum's signed up to learn computer training, she's been offered a job at a dental surgery with the option of moving into the upstairs flat – looks like I'm the only one still grieving."

Annabelle omitted to mention she had discovered a letter from a woman by the name of Zadie Stein in one of his jacket pockets while sorting out clothes to send to the dry cleaner. Sitting in a heap on the bedroom floor, clutching it in her hand, Annabelle had wept for hours. *He must have received this before Dad killed himself . . . I never knew they kept in touch!* Eventually deciding she wouldn't confront him, she got up from the floor and returned the letter to his jacket pocket, vowing, *I'll not lose him to that woman's daughter!*

"I brought with me Ben's recent letter, my love. Would you like me to read it to you?" Walther asked, seated on the edge of Zadie's bed at Villa Springview.

"Please!" she managed to reply, eyes lighting up when hearing Ben's name; face falling when listening to him.

"He can't leave her . . . There's not much else we can do." Walther sighed afterwards, wishing he'd kept it from her after all.

I'll never give up on them, Zadie thought, weeping softly into her pillow, struggling to tell him he must respond on their behalf.

"If you insist . . ." her devoted husband replied, obeying her wish by expressing how sorry they were for his girlfriend's loss.

As her mother descended ever deeper into a world of her own, Hannah buried herself in work, only admitting to herself how depressed she was. *I'll end up having a nervous breakdown if this continues,* she was thinking to herself when Linus knocked on the door to the office, offering to take her out to dinner.

"I can't bear seeing you this upset! You're so beautiful," he gushed, without thinking it through.

"You're very kind, I certainly don't feel it," she replied, keen for him to leave. "All I need is a good night's sleep." She sounded more upbeat than she felt.

"Can't you see how much you mean to me?" Shyly Linus touched her arm.

"How many times must I tell you I'm not interested? Only as a friend."

"I'm aware of that," Linus lied.

"Good . . . please leave . . . I'll see you in the morning."

"Why won't you let me take care of you? As a friend I make a mean Spanish omelette!" Listening to him brought back memories of her and Ben having a late snack in their house in Richmond.

"Oh, alright! But you're leaving when we've eaten." She was too exhausted to cook. Half an hour later the aroma of omelette with leftovers from the fridge and toast made her realise how hungry she was. Hannah relished her food, thanking him for cooking for her.

Friends? I'll soon make her fall in love with me! Linus thought, feeling as if he'd been transported to heaven.

After reading Zadie's recent letter, Ben was on his way back from work, reflecting about the content. *Who's that jerk Linus she's referring to? I remember Hannah mentioned some guy she had some misunderstanding with . . .*

A year had passed since Annabelle's father died. Her mother was seemingly well and coping, moving into the flat above the dental surgery. *She's okay now, well enough for me to tell her we're over. Both of us deserve to be happy.* Parking down the road, Ben saw her approaching him, wearing a fitted red dress, her hair blowing in the wind.

"I've something to tell you," she said, bursting with excitement.

"Tell me now . . . I was looking forward to us having a relaxing evening and chat, is it to do with your mother?"

"She's fine! I made chicken casserole."

Perhaps she's been promoted at the department store?

"I'm taking a shower . . . we'll talk in a short while."

Joining her in the kitchen, surprised she'd laid the table with their finest glasses and plates, Ben ran a hand through his hair, wondering how he was going to tackle the subject of their break-up. Stalling for time, he poured them each a glass of wine.

"What was it you wanted to tell me earlier?"

"Let's eat while it's hot . . ." Belle replied, avoiding looking at him.

"Mmm . . . this tastes great . . . are we celebrating something?" he asked, praying she hadn't booked them into some fancy hotel.

"I'm pregnant with our baby, Ben! Isn't it wonderful?" She was beaming.

Putting down his glass, Ben abruptly stood up, a wave of nausea overwhelming him to the extent he had no option but to sit down again, face drained of colour. *Hannah and I will never be together . . . not now!* Pushing aside his plate, he let out a big sigh.

"When did you make the decision to stop taking the Pill?" Annabelle's face fell.

"You don't want it . . . perhaps you'd rather I have a termination?" she whispered, hot tears blurring her vision.

She's carrying the child Hannah so desperately wanted me to have! Unable to stop himself from recalling how ecstatic he'd been when the woman he loved had announced they were having a baby, Ben swallowed hard, pacing the room.

"I'm sorry I reacted the way I did . . . I need time to think. You mustn't tell anyone – not yet. No one can know about it – not until we decide what to do . . ."

"Mum knows . . . I had to confide in someone! After everything we've been through lately, I thought this would be wonderful news," she sobbed, tears streaming down her face and neck.

"Did you tell my mother as well?"

"No. I thought you'd want to."

"How kind of you!" There was no mistaking the resentment in his voice. Without knowing it, Annabelle had singlehandedly ruined his and Hannah's future. "I'm sleeping at my office tonight – we'll discuss this in the morning." He stormed out of the kitchen and Annabelle heard the front door slamming behind him soon after. As if in a trance, she started clearing the table, the enormity of what had happened between them slowly starting to register.

Falling into a restless sleep on the living room couch, she was woken up by the sound of his Bentley pulling up outside in the driveway. When he came in, his eyes were just as red and swollen as her own. *Screw him!* she thought, viciously. *This could be my only chance to have a baby. I'll raise it single-handedly if I have to!*

"I'm only six weeks pregnant – we don't need you in our lives!" she cried, not giving a damn about his feelings.

"I never lied about how I felt," Ben said gently as he pulled her close, hating himself for causing her so much pain. "You always knew . . ."

"Yes! I know you still love her. The stupid, naive fool I am I was hoping you'd fall in love with me! That telling you we're having this baby would change everything . . . I've been an idiot, thinking you'd care for me."

This is what Hannah wanted for me . . . a child . . . Mum and Dad will be delighted . . . Annabelle's a good woman, I've no right putting her through this . . . this torment! It's not the baby's fault I'm not in love with its mother.

"Please forgive what I told you earlier . . . we're keeping the baby." He tightened his grip around her.

"Are we? You'll not change your mind? Or blame me later? I'm so sorry I tricked you," she cried, clinging onto him.

"I'll not change my mind . . . All I ask is that we get married prior to the birth." The expression on her face was the only answer he needed.

"You're asking me to become your wife?" she stammered, fresh tears brimming in her eyes.

"I'm committed to you and our child."

"Aren't you going to kiss me?" Annabelle asked, deliriously happy.

"Of course I am. Come here . . ."

But as their lips touched, Ben couldn't help wishing it were Hannah standing there instead. *Stop it! You made your bed, now lie in it! Seeing as the woman I love is no longer available to me, this baby's all I have to live for. The only thing that will make my life worth living.*

CHAPTER TWENTY-FOUR

2010

Rebecka and Michael Isaacs and Dorothy Clarkson were the only people invited to witness Annabelle and Ben taking their vows at a registrar's office in London's Marylebone. They thought the bride looked spectacular in a Vivien Westwood off-white satin gown and matching shoes. The groom was solemn in a light-blue suit while slipping the ring on her finger, later announcing they would celebrate by having lunch at The Ritz, where they would also spend their wedding night.

Three months before their baby was due, Ben let his Primrose Hill flat to a young couple and purchased a two-storey house in Regent's Park. Closing his mind to images of his and Hannah's stillborn baby girl, he continued to convince himself everything would be alright. They were in the large back garden, busy deciding colour schemes for their five bedrooms and en-suite bathrooms when Annabelle's waters broke. She was rushed into hospital and endured a fifty-hour labour resulting in a C-section, Ben at her side throughout the ordeal. Afterwards, both marvelled at their six-pound baby daughter lying in her mother's arms, her mop of dark hair, plump cheeks and the cutest little mouth, shaped like a bud, instantly capturing her father's heart.

"Isn't she gorgeous? I can already tell Clara's going to be a daddy's girl!" Annabelle was ecstatic both at the arrival of their child and the creation of a special bond ensuring he'd never leave her. She pointedly ignored the small voice inside of her, warning she was deluding herself.

Ben began to cut down on his workload, preparing most cases at home. Michael and Rebecka both agreed he'd made the right decision to focus on his family, but privately thought, *He has everything a man could wish for except the woman he loves.*

The year passed quickly and soon they were celebrating Clara's first birthday. Annabelle snuggled up to Ben, both watching their tiny bundle of joy standing up in the crib, her eyes just as brown as her father's, with long dark lashes.

"Let's try for another baby," she ventured. "I don't want her to be an only child like I was."

Startled by the revelation, Ben shook his head.

"I'm too old, Annabelle; Clara's the apple of my eye. Besides, you're not going through another difficult labour." He had already made up his mind she'd not persuade him into having more children, preventing him from an eventual reunion with Hannah. "One child's enough. Clara already has so many people caring about her. Apart from us, there's her godmother, Mel, and the twins are like brothers to her." Although he recognised the disappointment in her eyes, this was his final answer.

Driving back after a meeting in Central London Ben passed his parents' home, popping in for a chat with Rebecka.

"Is everything alright between you and Annabelle?" his mother asked, seated in the cosy kitchen.

"Why do you ask? Did she say something to you?"

"She wouldn't confide in us . . . I sometimes think I was wrong talking you into staying with her, it's obvious you're not happy together."

"Shouldn't you worry about Zoe and Stephen instead?" Ben snapped, irritated she meddled into his personal life. "They're of mature age yet still haven't settled down."

"Perhaps . . . But unlike you, both are facing up to their flaws. Isn't it time you did some soul-searching as well?" Rebecka could tell he was upset.

"Belle wants us to try for another baby. I put my foot down, saying it's out of the question." His face was set in stone.

"She needs reassurance you'll never leave her . . . I know she's not your first choice . . ."

"You're correct saying that but what can I do? If I ask her for a divorce, she'll get custody of Clara. I can't imagine life without my daughter."

For once at a loss for words, Rebecka nodded, thinking her son was heading towards disaster.

"You must tell him how you feel," Melanie insisted when she and Annabelle had late lunch at her home in early spring.

"You're his best friend but I've no one to talk to. My mother's caught up with her new partner, Brian. They met at her bridge club; he's all she can talk about. Here I am, a woman with seemingly everything: handsome husband, beautiful baby, nice house . . . everything except . . ." She stopped talking.

"Except what?" Melanie whispered, knowing the answer.

"There's no intimacy between us. I know he still has feelings for her! I don't know how much longer I can cope."

"Yet he agreed to marry you! You and Clara are everything to him."

"Please, let's stop kidding ourselves. You and I know he only married me because I was pregnant . . . Ben's a decent man."

"Are you saying he's still in love with his ex?"

"I know he's fond of me . . . perhaps if we'd met first . . . But I'm fed up with tormenting myself, those two need closure. Ben told me about their stillborn baby. She left so he could meet someone giving him what she couldn't. All I am to him is a friend and the mother of his child." She twisted her wedding band round and round.

"Okay. I won't lie to you. They were in love – deeply. Ben was inconsolable after she left him but that's in the past. You and Clara mean the world to him. You'll think clearly after a good night's sleep. The two of you must be exhausted having a baby to look after at your age." Melanie tried to cheer her up.

"I wouldn't know seeing as we've not shared a bed for ages."

Damn it! thought Melanie. *They're both my friends. I don't need to hear this!*

"I've already been through one acrimonious divorce. Just imagining having to endure yet another fills me with dread."

"Surely things aren't as bad as that?" Melanie asked in a low voice.

"The man I love and father of my child doesn't love me, I'll not deny it any longer." Seeing her so depressed, Melanie reached for her hand.

"Take my advice: whatever happens between you and Ben, please don't drag Clara into your situation."

Ignoring the alarm bells in her head, Hannah told herself Linus was just a friend helping her get through the hardest time of her life.

I've no one else supporting me . . . Pappa's preoccupied with Mamma and Villa Springview, and as much as he wants to help, Peter has his own family and work, she was thinking, when out of nowhere Linus appeared at her front door, offering to make them something to eat.

"You know how much I appreciate your friendship but that's all it is," she repeated for the umpteenth time.

"I accept that . . . but don't you want someone to look after you?" he pleaded with her. Visualising having no one caring for her, Hannah burst into tears.

"Yes . . . No . . . Don't leave me! I value you as a friend . . . If that's not enough for you, please leave." Stunned she hadn't rejected him, Linus went up to her, touching her face.

"You'll never know how much it means to hear you say that . . ."

Placing a finger on his mouth, Hannah whispered, "As long as you understand I've no feelings for you, you're welcome to spend the night." *What's happening to me? I'm offering myself to a man I don't want!*

"You really mean it? I can stay the night?" Linus repeated in an incredulous voice.

"You may as well, seeing as it's late . . ."

Hannah wants me! I mustn't let her down by coming on too strong . . . She's tiny . . .

Leading the way into her bedroom, Hannah watched him turn off the light then start to undress himself. "Don't be shy," she murmured, wondering what on earth she was doing. "Neither of us is perfect . . ." Half of her wished she'd had the sense to ask him to leave, saying she'd changed her mind.

Less than ten minutes later Linus whispered, "I'll make it up to you next time!" After fumbling with her clothes and kissing her clumsily, he had been too turned on to not immediately push inside her. The main ordeal had been over in less than a minute.

"It's okay," she replied, feeling vulgar and exploited, and totally unaware he was thinking, *Hannah's mine at last!*

Covering his naked body with the sheet, Linus fell sound asleep, snoring next to her.

"Are you and Linus an item, sis?" Peter asked, watching him mow the lawn in their parents' garden.

"Sort of . . . he's there for me."

"That's enough for you?"

"Ben's no longer around! The past is over and buried – period." But Hannah's eyes were disturbingly blank.

"This could boomerang in your face. He's obsessed with you!"

"Linus knows the score. I've nothing to worry about where he's concerned."

"I'm aware you and Ben are over, yet I don't understand why you're settling for so little? You're beautiful, with so much to offer."

"Really? I'm a middle-aged woman with very little to show for myself except my career."

"You're selling yourself short, Hannah. Mamma would be devastated."

But Hannah wasn't to be swayed. Her depression allowed her to somehow fall into a detached physical relationship with Linus, even agreeing to him moving in with her. It wasn't long before he moved things around, claiming they were a couple. It was all too much for Sanna, who visited one week during early autumn.

"How can you bear to touch him?" She couldn't stop herself. "Look at his stomach . . . I've never seen anyone as ugly!"

"Are you suggesting I throw him out because he's fat? You and Rosie aren't exactly around to support me!" Regretting saying too much, Hannah apologised immediately. "I'm sorry. I'm lonely . . . Mamma's dying because of that stinking disease, Pappa doesn't take care of himself – Linus looks after me while I focus on my parents and school."

"You can employ someone to do that! Rosie and I wish we could do more for you, but our jobs and personal lives simply don't permit it."

"I've no right taking my anger and frustration out on you. No one understands how it feels watching your mother losing one faculty after the other. I've no idea if she even recognises me!"

After dropping her friend at Malmö City Airport, Hannah returned to the flat just in time to find Linus going through some boxes in her bedroom cupboard.

"Don't touch them – they're personal!" she shouted, putting back the pieces of jewellery and letters Ben had sent her. "So is this what you've been up to behind my back?"

"Of course not . . . let me help you put everything back," he muttered, red in the face.

"Not until I've had an answer! I'm not surprised you've never had a girlfriend. No one would put up with this kind of behaviour." She pushed him aside.

"You never told me you kept his gifts and letters!" Linus screamed, furious she'd kept it from him.

"Don't you dare raise your voice at me. I'm not the one caught out rummaging through someone else's personal belongings!" Flashbacks of his treatment of her years back suddenly returned to her mind. "We'll discuss it later. Please see to dinner while I put everything back," she told him, willing herself to stay calm.

"Are you still in love with him? Perhaps the two of you are carrying on behind my back?" His hands were clenched into fists.

How could I have been so desperate as to get myself into this? Peter's right, Linus is a vicious monster! "Continue like this and I'll have no option but to throw you out!"

Ignoring her, Linus moved closer.

"I'm still waiting for an answer . . . Are you still in love with him?"

"That's none of your business! Ben's my personal affair."

"Ben? I was right all along. You're still in love with that guy!"

"I'll not answer that."

"What am I to you, exactly? Someone to turn to when you're lonely?"

"I refuse to listen to you any longer. You've always known I've no feelings for you. I want you to leave immediately!"

Scared she meant it, Linus raised his hands. "I'm not leaving until you've calmed down. Please forgive me for causing you to get upset."

"You're behaving like an idiot. I want you out of here first thing in the morning."

Angry with himself for ruining everything between them, Linus left the room. Ten minutes later she heard the front door close.

I forgot to remind him to return the spare key, Hannah thought before at last falling asleep. An hour later she was woken by someone standing over her.

"We need to talk!" Linus shouted, slurring his words.

"I've nothing more to say to you, it's over," She was fed up with having to put up with his childish behaviour.

"I want us to make love," he demanded, something about his tone and way of looking at her making her freeze up.

HELENE FERMONT

"Leave me alone!"

But it was too late; pinning her down on the bed, Linus hissed, "I bet you never rejected *him*." His face was contorted in anger.

"What did you just say?" she screamed, breaking free from his grip, ordering him to leave her and the flat.

"You never gave a damn about me!"

Brushing past him, Hannah ran into the living room. Linus followed closely behind, dragging her down onto the couch when she attempted to push him away. Hannah had no choice but to watch him unzip the flies of his trousers, pinning her down with one hand, the other forcing her legs apart, ripping her nightgown in pieces whilst forcing himself on her until she cried in pain. *He raped me!* Hot tears spilled down her face as she lay there, gasping.

"Talk to me, Hannah, I never meant for this to happen! You've got to believe me." Linus's alcohol-fuelled anger was slowly subsiding.

"You raped me!" she screamed, sobbing so much he couldn't make sense of what she was saying.

"Don't be so bloody melodramatic, you're my girlfriend! We argued, these things happen."

Covering herself with the rug on the couch, Hannah jumped up, shouting.

"I don't love you! You're a vicious bully and a monster! Pack your things and leave before I report you to the police." *No one can find out about this . . . I guess I'm at least fortunate I can't get pregnant . . .* she told herself, as she rocked herself on the couch. Twenty minutes later she heard the sound of a key dropping through the letterbox.

★

"You're right, Linus and I weren't right for one another. we split up last night." Aching all over, Hannah prayed Peter wouldn't suspect something untoward had happened between them.

"He hurt you, you're barely able to move!"

"I don't want to talk about it, it's over."

But Peter was no fool; he was convinced she was keeping something from him. *I'll find out eventually. If that creep laid a finger on her, then his life's not going to be worth living!*

One month later in February, Hannah and Peter received a call from Villa Springview to say that Zadie had suffered a bad fall while trying to get out of bed. Leaving the school in Annie's capable hands, Hannah drove with her brother as fast as she could to the care home. They arrived at the same time as Roland Svensson.

"I just found out about it," he said, the concern apparent in his eyes. "Her carer apparently called in sick yet no one took it upon themselves to inform me. Rest assured I'm getting to the bottom of it, this sort of thing has never happened before."

Watching Zadie limping on one foot, her ankle sprained yet not in pain after they administered pain relief and sedative, both debated telling Walther.

"We've no option, he's bound to find out what happened to her," Peter said, dialling their father's number.

"I knew she'd be better off at home!" Walther ranted hours later. Roland had just offered to hold the fort while they returned home to sleep. "This is your fault!"

"He's just upset," Peter intervened. "We're relieved she's on the mend. Please don't blame yourself, you're all doing such a grand job the rest of the time."

Conscious of the fact she was gradually slipping away from them, Zadie willed herself to die thinking it would be a blessing for all of them, in particular the man whose eyes never left her.

Expressing how sorry he was she'd taken a turn for the worse, Dan Sholtz joined them later that day.

"Zadie's deteriorating much faster than I anticipated," he confirmed. "Please let me know if there's anything I can do for you."

The following day, despite being advised to stay away, Walther recognised two ladies from the book club saying goodbye to their old friend, both taken aback by how ill and frail she was, thanking her for everything she'd done for them then quietly leaving, tears in their eyes.

"You ought to get some rest. I promise to keep you updated if there's a change," Dan urged the Steins, fully aware she didn't have long to live.

"She's the kindest person I know, I can't bear seeing her in pain!" Walther's distress was apparent to all, even as he prayed inwardly it would soon be over.

"Mamma wouldn't want you to jeopardise your health," Hannah said. "Dan will call if there's any news." She looked down at her mother. "Mamma, I love you. Thank you for everything you did for me, there'll never be anyone like you."

They'd barely closed their eyes when the phone rang at 5am. One glance at his face confirmed the voice at the end of the line delivered the news they had dreaded for so long.

"It's over – no more pain and suffering," Peter whispered, holding her close to him, their tears mingling.

"Has Pappa been informed?" Hannah asked in a broken voice.

"Yes . . . he answered the phone before I did. We're all he has left; today's the start of the rest of our lives without her."

"Please don't leave me!" Annabelle pleaded, terrified he and Hannah would pick up where they left off years ago.

"Zadie's my friend! If you can't see why I have to be there, you're not the person I thought you were." Ben's anger spilled over into his voice.

"But isn't it sufficient your parents are attending her funeral?" The thought of him and that woman was eating her up inside.

"I'm leaving and that's the end of it!"

Watching him throwing clothes and toiletries into his suitcase, Annabelle suddenly recalled the letter she'd discovered long ago in his jacket pocket.

"It's too late . . . that woman's dead! We're your family now. You can't just abandon us." Seeing her so upset, Ben turned his back to her, irritation building up inside.

"I wish you wouldn't bring Clara into this. I'll return before she realises I'm gone." He was only away for the weekend yet she acted as if it was indefinitely. *She's so damn insecure. It's my fault. Annabelle knows I don't love her.*

"Why can't we come with you? Rebecka told me Sweden's beautiful this time of year."

"My answer's no! This isn't some holiday. I'm attending the funeral of an exceptionally dear friend! Now is not the time to make a scene."

"It never is!"

Briefly Ben wondered if he should cancel the trip, telling his parents they had to leave without him. *No way! I'll be damned if I'm letting her insecurity rule my decision. Why the hell did I marry her? I should have kept her as a friend, nothing more.* But if he had done that, Clara wouldn't exist.

"I bet you're dying to see Hannah again," Annabelle persisted, tugging at his jacket sleeve.

"I am *not* doing this now." Ben snapped, turning to look at her.

"Doing what exactly? Owning up to the fact there are three people in this marriage?"

"I thought we sorted everything out. You know how fond I am of you."

"No matter how hard I try, you'll never stop loving her," she sobbed.

"That's unfair! I know I'm not as demonstrative as I should be. Tell you what, let's go away on holiday. Tell me where you want to go when I return. I have to go, Annabelle. My cab's waiting outside; Mum and Dad are probably wondering what's happened given that we're picking them up on the way to the airport. Kiss Clara goodbye for me."

Ben sat by the window on the flight to Malmö City Airport, silently gazing out onto the clouds.

"How do you think he'll react to seeing Hannah again?" Rebecka whispered in Michael's ear.

"I'm not sure." He shrugged. "Let's hope it won't cause more friction between him and Annabelle."

The Isaacs had reserved two double rooms at The Savoy, Rebecka exclaiming on her arrival: "It's one of the most luxurious hotels I've ever seen!"

"Let's unpack then have dinner in the restaurant. I remember you telling us the food's wonderful," Michael suggested watching his son's face light up. Ben was transported straight back to when he and Hannah were invited to lunch to celebrate Walther's birthday.

It feels like yesterday. You must be in so much pain, little one.

In a plain black dress, with her hair in a knot, Hannah's eyes fell on her mother's coffin. *Oh Mamma, why did you leave us? I've never needed you like I do now. Leaving him was a terrible mistake.* Taking a deep breath, she took her place at the front bench, her father and brother on either side, and listened to the Rabbi putting forward his condolences, telling them he was there for them. Idly she thought how brave the Rabbi was after losing his entire family in the Holocaust, starting afresh when arriving in Sweden with the Red Cross.

Pappa's beside himself with grief. It's as if he's given up.

Ten minutes later, addressing the group of people paying their respects in the small Jewish chapel outside Malmö, Hannah told them how much her mother had doted on her family, literature and travelling, in particular to Lugano, finishing the Eulogy citing the famous Swedish poet Karin Boye's *Yes, Of Course It Hurts.* Barely able to hold back the tears when retiring to her seat, suddenly from the corner of her eye she spotted him in the middle row.

Ben! . . . Nothing's changed. I still love you just as much. Unknown to her he was thinking exactly the same, wondering if the man Zadie mentioned in her letters was present. *You look so forlorn . . . If only I could put my arms around you.*

After listening to Peter saying a few words about their mother, Hannah followed everyone outside into the cemetery. Her thoughts turned to Sanna and Rosie, who had called the previous night to apologise for not being able to attend. "Please don't blame yourselves," she'd replied. "I'd have felt exactly the same. Mamma wanted people to care for her when she was alive; she'd have understood."

As they threw soil on the coffin, Hannah's eyes filled with tears as she thought how she'd never see or talk to her mother again.

"How are you bearing up, little one?" The familiar voice hadn't changed one bit. "I've no words to express how sorry I am."

Hannah turned to look at the man standing behind her, his face etched in pain, fighting the impulse to throw herself into his arms.

"You came," she whispered instead, averting her eyes.

"Wild horses couldn't keep me away. Your father invited us. Mum and Dad are here as well. I so wish I could have been here for you."

"I wasn't aware you and Mamma kept in touch . . . The letters . . ." Her voice faltered, the pain in her eyes matching his.

"My parents are coming." Ben gestured to the elderly couple that in the not too distant past Hannah had viewed as part of her family.

As the Rabbi's prayers continued, Rebecka went up to them, putting an arm on Hannah's shoulder.

"You're too thin. Come here!" Their eyes locked briefly when kissing one another's cheek.

"Zadie was a true *mensch*. There aren't too many around these days."

"We're very sorry for your loss. Did Ben mention we're staying at The Savoy?"

"Mum thinks the food and rooms are wonderful," father and son said simultaneously, hoping to ease the tension between them somewhat.

"We'd better let them talk on their own," Michael said. "You must have a lot to catch up on." He steered his wife in the direction of the restaurant across the road.

"I'm sorry I can't invite you to the house. Pappa's not up to it," Hannah offered in a small voice.

"You mustn't worry about us at a time like this! Let me help you get through today, I'm here for you." He took her hand in his.

"You're too kind," Hannah mumbled. "I'm not sure I deserve it, not after what I put you through."

"Instead of dwelling in self-pity, I should have realised you were hurting," he replied, eyes searching hers.

She ached to ask if he was happy, perhaps married with the child she so desperately wanted to give him yet couldn't, but then Peter and her father joined them, thanking Ben for coming, the latter inwardly thinking how pleased his wife would have been to see him there.

"I wish it could have been under different circumstances. It's wonderful seeing you again," Peter said, shaking Ben's hand. He was looking forward to reminiscing about the past but now wasn't the right time.

"Please excuse me while I make sure my parents are alright," Ben said, giving them time to talk among themselves.

"He can't take his eyes off you, sis. Was Linus invited? I thought I saw him earlier."

"Of course not! Annie must have mentioned Mamma's funeral."

Hannah sat listening to guests' speeches in the restaurant, saying how special her mother had been. Ben sat next to her, his presence bringing back memories she had long since suppressed.

"Zadie mentioned a man," he murmured. "Is he the one you're having a relationship with?"

"Linus is just a colleague."

"If he laid a finger on you . . ." Ben muttered. Their connection was so tangible right there in the room, Hannah physically had to restrain herself to not let on.

"He has a few issues needing addressing. I'd rather we don't talk about it."

"Promise me you'll be vigilant where he's concerned?"

"Sure. Mary's school means everything to me."

"I know what you mean, work keeps me going," Ben whispered, touching her hand, neither bothering to eat the sandwiches on their plates.

"You've every right to hate me."

"Never! My only regret is that we can't go back. I was an idiot to let you go."

"I gave you no option. How come you've kept the house?"

"I gave it to you to do with as you wish, my unconditional gift."

Overwhelmed by his words and the day's events, Hannah slowly raised herself, asking, "Will you excuse me while I tend to my father? I wish you and your parents a safe trip home to London. Thank you for coming, I appreciate the gesture."

Sensing how scared she was of getting too close to him, Ben asked, "Zadie mentioned you called me at the flat?"

"Yes, some woman answered. Is she your girlfriend?"

"Annabelle?" He sighed. "She's been there for me ever since. We were married after discovering she was pregnant. I can't recall if I wrote about it to your mother." Registering his words, Hannah swallowed.

"I must have missed that bit. You have a child? I'm very happy for you both." Seeing how upset she was, Ben gently helped her return to her seat, her eyes moist. "Don't! Pappa needs me," she whispered.

"I wouldn't have gone through with it if it wasn't for the baby. Annabelle fell pregnant after losing her father to suicide. She's always known how I feel about you. I respect and care about her but I don't love her and I never will. I simply did what you requested. Now, because of your unselfish act of kindness, I have a beautiful daughter. You and Clara are all I want." He pulled out a photograph from his trouser pocket. Hannah's eyes filled with fresh tears on seeing the pretty little girl, identical big brown eyes to her father and curly brown hair.

"She's the most beautiful child I've ever seen! Are you planning on having more?"

"No way! As much as I adore her, Clara was an accident. Annabelle and I should never have married. As soon as our daughter's older, I'm filing for divorce." Feeling her eyes on him, a wisp of red hair brushing his cheek, Ben could control himself no longer. "My beautiful, precious Hannah! How I wish things were different. I so want to hold and touch you."

"You mustn't talk like that. You've a wife and child!" She kept visualising the little girl's face, pleased he'd found someone capable of giving him what she couldn't. "Listen to me, Ben. We've not seen each other for a long time, it's only natural we're nostalgic. I've moved on as well," she lied, feigning a smile. Looking directly into her eyes, Ben shook his head.

"You and I both know that's not true. My feelings are exactly the same: I love you and I always will. Perhaps you've resigned yourself to the notion we're over but I haven't! Zadie, bless her soul, knew we were meant to be together. My situation's complicated but I can deal with it."

Listening to him telling her what she longed to hear, Hannah smiled through her tears. "Not a single day goes by when I don't regret my decision to leave. But it's too late now. You must get on with your life and accept we can't be together. I have."

"I can't! You're everything to me. Nothing makes sense without you. I tried so hard to make it work, even to the extent of telling Annabelle we'll plan a holiday when I return. Have you any idea how I feel lying to my wife and the mother of my child?" He had never intended to put her on the spot, not today of all days.

Hannah stood up a second time and leant over to kiss his cheek, the familiar scent of his aftershave making her tremble inside.

"It's too late. Be happy," she whispered, not caring that people were staring at them. Desperate to not lose her again, Ben held onto her hand.

"We need to talk. Say you'll meet me at the hotel. Please!" he begged her, giving her a card with his mobile and room numbers.

"This isn't fair and you know it!" If they were alone, the inevitable would happen. He knew it too.

"I'll not touch you. We need closure."

"I can't. Leaving you changed everything between us."

Feeling almost as terrible as the day she left him, Ben persisted. "You know where I am if you change your mind." Taking the palm of her hand, he kissed it, then disappeared in the crowd of people leaving the café.

Blinded by tears, his words echoing in her head, Hannah looked around her, recognising the women from the book and French conversation groups, her father and brother in deep conversation with the Rabbi and Roland Svensson. Idly she noticed how forlorn her nephews looked, standing between their parents. *Pappa's suit's much too big. I have to get him home before he faints from exhaustion,* she thought just as he came up to her, pulling her close.

"Where's Ben? Was seeing him too upsetting for you, my darling? Your mother would have been so pleased."

"Oh Pappa! I've made such a mess of my life!" Hannah cried in his arms, ashamed it wasn't the other way round.

"It's alright. Rebecka confided about his wife and child, telling me he's not happy. It's obvious how much he still loves you. Listen to your heart, Hannah, and everything will fall into place. Children don't stay young forever. Grab every chance of happiness life throws at you! Love is what matters in the end. I should know. Tell him how you feel. If not, you'll regret it for the rest of your life." Walther's familiar scent of Old Spice made her cry even harder.

It took Hannah almost an hour to get ready, changing into a black Diane Von Furstenberg wrap dress, hand shaking applying make-up and brushing her hair. *I only just buried my mother yet here I am preparing to meet the man I love! A man with a wife and daughter. What am I thinking?* But then she recalled her father's words.

"Love is what matters in the end."

Running out of the flat, Hannah drove as fast as she dared into Central Malmö, parking a block away from The Savoy. A few minutes later she entered the magnificent building, passed reception and stepped into the elevator taking her to the third floor and his room. *There's no turning back now. He belonged to me first.* Locating his room at the end of the corridor, her hand still shaking as she knocked on the door. When she saw the look on Ben's face, she knew it had all been worth it.

"You came! I prayed you would," Ben gasped, shutting the door behind her. "You're stunning. I missed you so much, Hannah. Let me call room service. I bet you've not had anything to eat." But Hannah shook her head. Suddenly this didn't feel right after all.

"I was wrong to come here. Take good care of yourself."

"Don't! We'll go somewhere else."

"I can't stay. Please hand me my coat." She was crying now. Regardless, the same old electricity passed between them when he helped put her coat back on, his lips brushing hers. A sob escaped her throat.

"It's too late to walk away. I don't know how I lived without you for so long, little one," Ben pleaded.

"I feel the same way. Perhaps tonight's all we have?"

"We had it all, we can again." Standing close to the four-poster bed, Ben kissed her lips, switching on the light behind them.

"Don't. I'm not as young as I once was," she whispered, trying to shield herself with her coat and bag. Pulling her closer, Ben continued kissing her lips, face and neck, his hands caressing her beneath her clothes.

"I want to make love to every part of you. We've both matured, me most of all." The scent of Pour Homme taking her back to how they used to be, Hannah slowly started to relax, her inhibitions melting away with her clothes as their passion towards each other intensified. Ben pulled her down onto the bed, gently making love to her. The years of hurt faded as she felt him inside her, his body just as strong and firm as she recalled. "This is how it feels to be in love. I wanted you for so long," he whispered, bringing her to heights she'd almost forgot existed. After, tears stung her eyes as she lay sated in his arms, the sun streaming through the curtains announcing a new dawn.

"It's 7am. Your parents are probably wondering what happened to you," she said, snuggling up to him.

"This is our moment, little one. I'm starting divorce proceedings as soon as I return to London." He'd spent too long in a relationship he didn't want.

Showering in the enormous bathroom, Ben couldn't resist

making love to her a second time, both only too conscious the time to say goodbye was growing near.

"I can't leave, not now," he said when they were getting dressed.

"You mustn't file for divorce just yet," Hannah replied. "If you do, your wife will do whatever it takes to prevent it. I've seen too many children used as weapons."

"Don't you want us to live together? Annabelle can have whatever she wants. As long as I have you and Clara, I'm more than content. We'll finally get what we're owed. If only Annabelle and I had never met . . ."

"If you hadn't, Clara wouldn't exist. Your wife can't know about us, not yet." Putting her arms around his neck, Hannah kissed him on the mouth, exclaiming, "You'll never lose me again!" The sad expression in his eyes made her wish she didn't have to leave. "You've too much to lose. Unless Clara's part of your life, you and I will never work. She'll always come between us."

"You're telling me we have to put our lives on hold longer than we already have? I can't do it, Hannah. You're the woman I love!"

"We'll keep a low profile until your daughter's older. A few more years won't make much of a difference."

"I'll not hide my feelings!" Ben shouted, eyes filled with despair. They'd only just found each other again. All he wanted was to be with her. "That man . . . Linus, you must tell me what he did to you." Ben changed the subject, adamant she open up about it.

"Promise you'll not get upset?" Ben nodded and she sighed, slowly and painfully disclosing what had happened. "I'd never seen him like that . . . so vicious . . . After he found out about the jewellery and letters, he forced himself on me. I never stood a chance. He's too big and strong . . ." Her voice had sunk to a whisper.

"He raped you? When I get my hands on him . . ." Seeing how much talking about it upset her, Ben held her close. "What kind of person does something so despicable? Did he hurt you?" He'd noticed a couple of bruises on the inside of her thighs.

"I'm alright now. Linus knows what he did was wrong."

"I can't leave, not now I know what happened. Does Peter know?"

"Not yet. Please don't tell him. We've enough to cope with right now. Pappa can't find out."

"I hear what you're saying. That's it. I'm selling my share of the law firm to Collin. We'll get a nice place to live. I know how much that school means to you."

"Aren't you overlooking something? Annabelle won't let Clara be part of our lives! She's too young to travel by herself. We must wait until she's older."

"What you're saying makes sense. Return with me, then! The thought of that lunatic lurking about . . . You can stay at the house. I'll ask Collin to give the tenants notice."

"I can't abandon my family and school! Don't worry about Linus. I'm very vigilant where he's concerned. He'll never lay a finger on me again."

Room service arrived with coffee and croissants. Both ate in silence, focusing on the inevitable: saying goodbye.

"Always remember how much I love you, little one," Ben told her, nearly choking on the words.

"Promise me you'll not do anything to compromise your child?" Hannah kissed him one last time before running out the door, the expression in his eyes almost killing her.

Staring at the remainder of their breakfast, Ben pushed the tray aside. He started to pack his suitcase, not giving a damn about his parents' reaction when telling them they were reunited again.

Where's that lift? Hannah thought to herself, eager to get back to make sure her father was alright.

"I don't believe it!" Hannah looked up to see the lift doors open and Rebecka and Michael standing before her. She started to shake uncontrollably.

"I might have guessed you're the reason our son's been otherwise engaged!" Rebecka hissed, fully aware Ben had never stopped loving her.

"Don't be so hard on her," Michael interrupted, sensing how upset Hannah was. "They're both old enough to know what they're doing."

"Ben showed me a photo of your granddaughter. She's adorable. You must be very proud of her," Hannah whispered, painfully conscious of the fact they knew she and Ben had spent the night together.

"Your mother would have been ashamed of you." There was no mistaking the hostility in Rebecka's eyes. "Zadie was a lady! Our son's not available to you anymore. He has a wife and child."

"You think I don't know I'm the reason he's unhappy? What I did was wrong but I was ill! I'd just lost our baby and was being deprived of having another . . ." Hannah sobbed, stopping when she felt Michael's hand on her back.

"It's alright. We're aware how much you both love each other," he soothed, livid Rebecka was treating her so badly.

Mamma, I need you! Stepping into the lift, Hannah stood by herself in a corner, feeling Rebecka's angry stare on her. *She's petrified Annabelle won't let them be part of Clara's life.* Stepping out of the elevator, Michael turned to look at her.

"Take good care of yourself, my dear." With precisely one hour to spare before returning to pack their suitcase at the hotel, he steered his wife away from the situation.

The next day at the house, Hannah admitted to her brother and father that she and Ben had spent the night together.

"Your mother would have been thrilled!" Walther's eyes lit up. "She always knew you were made for each other."

"It's not that simple. Ben has a daughter."

But Walther refused to listen, thinking, *This is down to you, my love. I will soon be joining you.*

After they'd bid goodnight to their father, Peter requested they talk in the library, asking the question she'd been dreading.

"Linus assaulted you didn't he? Please don't deny it. I know I'm right." Listening to her pouring her heart out, Peter's eyes flared up. "I knew it . . . the bastard! You're moving out of that flat and in here with Pappa," he ordered, loathing the creep who had raped his sister.

CHAPTER TWENTY-FIVE

2011

I'M IN LOVE *with Mark despite everything that happened between us,* Vanessa found herself admitting, thinking how much he'd changed for the better.

"Maruschka's lost to me, probably married now, with kids," he mentioned when they next met up.

"Perhaps she'll look you up, Dad?" Jake asked.

"I doubt it. You're a good boy, always seeing the best in everyone." Jake was planning on being a teacher or veterinary surgeon.

"Must I work for Grandpa, Mom?" he frequently asked Vanessa, usually when going off to bed.

"You're to focus on the present! The future will sort itself out," Vanessa told him, wanting him to have all the things she didn't.

Inviting Mark and Annuschka to dinner one night not long after the latter was introduced to her grandson, Jake immediately went up to his grandmother, complimenting her outfit. "You look very nice in that pink dress, Grandma!" he said, embracing her. Blushing, Annuschka put a hand through her grey permed hair, telling him how much he'd grown. "You're outgrowing your mother!" she commented, praying Ronald wouldn't be joining them for dinner.

"Did someone mention my name?" Vanessa's father appeared, pretending he didn't notice the annoyed look in Annuschka's eyes, secretly thinking she was dressed like an aging Barbie doll. "Where's that son of yours?" he barked at her, voice full of sarcasm.

"Mark will be here any minute," she replied, tight-lipped.

"Is that right? You're quite sure he's not drinking in his local pub?" Joining them, Vanessa took a deep breath.

"Daddy, please try to be civil for once! I've made the effort to make tonight special. Cook's made Jake's favourite dishes."

"I never knew you were able to make so much as an omelette. Bernie told me you baked a cake." Ronald mocked his daughter, never missing an opportunity to belittle her, the devious expression in his eyes confirming he had something up his sleeve.

Minutes later, they were seated at the table in the dining room, pictures of ancestors and oil paintings on the walls around them. Mark smiled, his eyes hardening when seeing Ronald chewing on a piece of lamb, Annuschka complimenting Vanessa on the food, the latter's eyes glued on her father's next move. Unexpectedly, Ronald raised his glass.

"I found that daughter of yours, Copeck!" Everyone stopped eating at once. The table erupted into pandemonium.

"I warned you to not meddle in our lives!" Vanessa shouted, livid he'd disobeyed her.

"She's our concern – not yours!" Annuschka yelled, face red and flustered.

"That's not strictly true; she's my grandson's half-sister," Ronald replied smugly.

"You're to leave us alone – *now*!" Vanessa pointed to the door.

"There," Ronald said, taking enormous pleasure in handing Mark a note containing Maruschka's details. "Do you believe me now?"

"You knew how desperate I was to find her, I've been searching everywhere! You've gone too far. Mum and I are leaving." Mark pushed his chair back so violently it fell over.

"Please don't, not in front of Jake!" Vanessa pleaded with them to stay.

"Your father's meddling in our personal lives," Annuschka cried, following her son out of the door.

"Please go upstairs to your room, Jake. Your Grandfather and I need to talk."

"What's Maruschka got to do with Grandpa, Mom?"

"That's what I intend to find out," Vanessa replied in a low voice.

"But I was looking forward to dessert. Will you call for me?"

"Of course I will, honey." Head bowed, hands thrust deep inside his trouser pockets, Jake begrudgingly left them to it, angry his Grandfather had ruined everything.

"I located her mother. Turns out those two didn't keep in touch, funnily enough. She gave me her daughter's address and number. I thought you'd be pleased," Ronald lied, pretending to be offended they didn't appreciate his effort.

"What gives you the right to go behind Mark's back? Or should I ask – what's in it for you?" Vanessa was convinced he hadn't done this out of the goodness of his heart, seeing as he'd never had one to begin with.

"I'll not sit here listening to your accusations!" Ronald snapped at her, storming out.

I'll be damned if I can't find out what he's up to, Vanessa thought, calling her son.

"Who told you where I live?" Maruschka was about to close the door when Mark pushed his way in.

"You and I need to talk." He'd decided it was in his own best interests to just turn up or she'd not give him the time of day.

His daughter lived in a rough part of Clapham. It wasn't long before he noticed the squalor of her bedsit comprising one small room with in-built pantry, stove and fridge, dirty plates and glasses in the sink, clothes scattered on the floor and a single window overlooking the dustbins in the street.

"Hardly a mansion, wouldn't you agree? But then again you never bothered paying alimony!" Tall and skinny, greasy brown hair falling down her shoulders, Maruschka had the same cleft in her chin as him and Jake.

Steeling himself, Mark asked, "Did Ronald Westbrook tell you you have a brother? Jake's eleven and he's a great kid. His mother and I split up before he was born."

"You came all this way to tell me that? What makes you think I give a damn?"

"I understand your resentment towards me. Your mother wasn't exactly a saint either!" Mark snapped, pacing the ugly, cramped room.

"Don't you go blaming her! We don't see eye to eye about most things but that doesn't give you the right to badmouth her." Mark noticed now how upset she was, her lower lip trembling, eyes hostile. He felt ashamed of himself.

"I wasn't exactly a model father to Jake either. Once you get to know him, you'll like him."

"Why this sudden interest in me?" she asked suspiciously.

"By the time I owned up to my flaws, the years had passed and I was scared you'd reject me. Please let me make it up to you!"

"What if it's too late? Look at me! I'm twenty-seven for Christ's sake! Everything's your fault. I hated you for what you did to Mum and me. Always neglecting us!"

"Petra and I weren't compatible. You're the only good thing that came out of that marriage. I was just an immature irresponsible kid back then. Let me prove to you I've changed," Mark begged, wishing he could take her away from that dump.

"I'm not sure that's what I want anymore. You're living at the same address, right? I'll call if and when I'm ready to talk." Fiddling with her hair, eyes avoiding his, Mark wanted to tell her everything was going to be alright. It wasn't until he was sitting in his car that it dawned on him they hadn't touched; not even a handshake.

They had given up hope she'd call when two weeks later Mark's phone rang.

"I'm coming round later, 3pm okay with you?" Maruschka asked, not bothering to wait for an answer before hanging up.

"Who was it? You look like you've seen a ghost, son," Annuschka said, coming in from the garden.

"Maruschka's just called to say she's coming round. I've nothing in the fridge."

Overjoyed by the news that she'd finally get to meet her granddaughter, Annuschka replied, "Don't worry, I'll sort something out."

The only person still missing from my life is Hannah, Mark thought, vowing to get back the woman he'd lost.

When Maruschka stepped over the threshold, looking nothing like the drab, scruffy girl he'd met the other week, Mark's face dropped.

"You're gorgeous! Not at all like your father described," Annuschka blurted in her usual direct manner.

"Glad you approve of me, Granny. You've not changed. I like that red dress." Embracing the elegant woman with styled hair, make-up, pencil skirt and blouse with open toe shoes, Annuschka burst into tears.

"I'm so happy you've returned to us! I got you the delicacies you used to love when you were a child."

"I've already eaten but I wouldn't say no to a glass of sherry," Maruschka hastily replied, recalling only too well her grand-mother's inedible food. "This place looks just the same. Coming here bring back memories of you and Mum being at each other's throats," she said, her eyes on Mark.

"Would you like to see your old room?" he asked hopefully.

"Nah . . . the past's best left forgotten."

"Then why are you here?" Mark frowned, irritation bubbling up inside of him. "It doesn't seem like you're willing to make a go of this."

"Let's pretend everything's perfect, shall we? I cried myself to sleep for years after you and Mum split up. All my friends kept asking why I didn't have a father like them, someone who gave a damn!" she yelled, tears of anger spilling down her blouse.

"I hear what you're saying. The problem is I can't turn back time. You may not believe me but I never stopped caring about you."

"Bullshit! Mum sure as hell never let me forget that if it hadn't been for me, her life would have been so much better . . ."

"That's a vicious lie!" Mark faltered. "We were close enough to conceive you; she shouldn't have said those things. I messed up. All I ask is that you give me a break . . . please!"

"To hell with both of you! Seeing you again confirms how much better off I am without you." Slamming her glass on the kitchen sink, Maruschka ran out, not bothering to close the front door behind her.

"If this is what she's really like, we've had a lucky escape." Mark sat down heavily. "That girl never stood a chance with Petra for a mother." But Annuschka wasn't having any of it.

"When I think of how much I resented Vanessa at first, I know now I was wrong," she said. "Jake's turned out the way he is purely because of her. I'm ashamed of you, blaming an innocent girl!" Following in her granddaughter's footsteps, Annuschka stormed out, leaving him on his own.

Seated at the back of the bus bringing her home, Maruschka reprimanded herself for not telling them Ronald Westbrook had called late one evening a short while ago. Claiming her mother had given him her details, his brusque manner and American accent had caused her to instantly put up her guard.

"This is a once in a lifetime opportunity for you to earn a substantial sum, girl! How does £10,000 sound to you? You can move out of that dingy flat of yours for a start."

"Mum warned me you'd call one day. What do you want from me?" She was shaking like a leaf.

"That father of yours is looking for you."

"So what? I couldn't care less."

"My grandson's your half brother; he wants to meet you."

"What's it got to do with you?"

"Let's talk face to face."

"Go to hell!" Maruschka was about to hang up.

"Fifteen thousand pounds, it's my final offer – take it or leave it. Just imagine what you could do with that kind of money," he enticed her, hearing her catch her breath. "You'll get half up front, the rest when the deed's done."

"This is a joke, right? I wasn't born yesterday."

"We both know how badly you need that money. All I want in return is a few hours of your time, ensuring Copeck's out of my grandson's life for good. What will it be?"

Damn! I can't afford to turn him down. Even buying a lousy mobile's out of my reach.

"You've got yourself a deal on the condition I get £10,000 upfront in cash. If you trick me, I'll spill the beans!"

"I'll have it couriered to you straightaway. Meanwhile I want you to call your father, asking him and your grandmother to request my daughter throws a dinner party on the pretext you're dying to meet your brother. Get a piece of paper and pen, this is the address."

Maruschka needn't have worried about calling her father seeing as Annuschka beat her to it, contacting her the next day, apologising on their behalf for how things ended between them the other day.

"Thanks Granny, I'm sorry for the way I behaved. I want to meet my brother. Please arrange it with his mother at the house. Dad told me where they live," she lied.

"I'll talk to Vanessa, that's Jake's mother, as soon as I get off the phone and call back with the details. You must take a cab at my expense!" Annuschka replied, beaming.

All I have to do now is what's expected of me, praying Dad doesn't find out who's behind it! Maruschka's stomach was in a knot.

Laying the finishing touches to the table in the dining room, Vanessa reminded Cook to prepare the starter of salmon and avocado salad. Her face fell when seeing her father enter the kitchen.

"You told me you'd be in a meeting all night."

"It's cancelled. No one told me we're expecting guests."

"We're not – I am! Unless you behave, I'll get Bernie to serve you dinner in your study."

Eyeing her up and down, Ronald commented, "How come you're bothering with your appearance? Is it something to do with Copeck?" he teased, an evil glint in his eyes.

Hating him for seeing through her, Vanessa snapped, "You'd better not be up to something!"

Arriving on the dot of 7pm, Mark wore a black suit, starched shirt and tie, his mother looking very excited at the prospect of seeing her granddaughter again. Walking up to Vanessa, Mark thanked her for organising everything with such short notice.

"Maruschka and I argued. I'll explain later," he said, fidgeting with his jacket, a tense expression on his face.

Vanessa excused herself and went to talk to Bernie, ensuring everything was ready in the kitchen. She asked if her father had confided in him, but her old friend shook his head.

"I'm as mystified as you are. It's not like him to cancel a meeting."

"He's responsible for locating Mark's daughter, I'm certain it's not coincidental."

"Promise me you won't take offence, Vanessa. Are you in love with Mark?"

"Of course not! Whatever gave you that idea? Daddy's up to something, I know he is!"

Alone in the foyer, Annuschka asked Jake how he felt about meeting his sister.

"I'm excited, I only found out about her a short time ago," he replied, hands deep in his trouser pockets as usual, blond hair in a crew cut.

Smoothing the hem of her black skirt, Annuschka was about to say something when eyes full of horror, she noticed a tall girl enter, wearing a leather mini skirt, stockings and black lipstick.

"Hi everyone! Some bald geezer let me in. You must be my kid brother!" Maruschka gave Jake a big bear hug, his eyes glued on her spiky ankle boots. "Great to meet you, bruv!" She watched him distance himself from her intuitively.

"Do you and your Mom live together?" he asked, not sure what else to say to her.

"Nah. We've not met for years."

"I'd hate to live far away from mine. I'd miss her too much."

"You know what that makes you? A mummy's boy!" She roared with laughter.

"I'm not." Jake frowned, thinking she was mean.

Listening to them, Vanessa thought, *She reminds me of myself at the same age. I hope Mark realises how much she's hurting. I'm glad Jake's standing up to her, though.*

"I guess it's not your fault you love your mum," Maruschka muttered, avoiding eye contact with the boy. "I'm not close to either of my parents!"

"Not even our Dad? You'll like him once you get to know him – I do."

"Perhaps you're right. Time will tell."

She has no confidence whatsoever. Mark's got his work cut out for him, Vanessa thought.

Pretending they knew nothing of one another, Maruschka avoided looking at Ronald. Eating in silence, Bernie was clearing the table for dessert when Maruschka exclaimed, "Thanks for dinner; I really enjoyed it. It's a far cry from Granny's food! Did you taste it, Jake? Dad says it's awful!"

Seeing his grandmother's face crumple, Jake said, "Well, I think it's awesome, Grandma! Especially your chocolate fudge cake. It's nearly as good as Mom's rhubarb pie!"

"You're a good boy," Annuschka whispered, tears in her eyes.

Mouthing the words "Thank you", Vanessa couldn't help thinking, *My son's turning into a decent young man.*

"You'll apologise immediately to your grandmother!" Mark yelled, that muscle twitching in his cheek.

"Make me! Besides, you're a fine one to talk."

Eyes narrowing, Mark pushed his chair back and was about to walk up to her when Ronald tapped his glass to make an announcement.

"Maruschka's got something to say to us."

"I warned you, Daddy. Stay out of our business. I want you to get the hell out of here!" Turning to look at her, Ronald shook his head.

"This is my house. I'll not be told what I can and can't do!"

Struggling to hold it together, Annuschka and Mark exchanged a worried glance, watching Maruschka drain her wine. Slamming the empty glass down, she got to her feet, swaying slightly.

"I've come here tonight with the sole purpose of informing Jake what our father's really like."

Seeing the triumphant expression in her father's eyes, Vanessa immediately put two and two together. "It's for the best if you and Mark talk alone," she said aloud, fully aware of where this was leading.

"Why? We may as well get it out into the open!" The girl

raised a shaky hand to her mouth, inadvertently smearing black lipstick across her cheek.

"That's unless you've something to hide, Copeck?" Ronald interrupted, delighted everything was going according to plan.

Raising himself, Mark went up to Annuschka, taking her arm. "Thanks for having us, Vanessa. Mum and I are leaving and so is my daughter."

"I'm not going anywhere with you! Jake has every right to know the truth!"

"What's she talking about, Mom?"

"You mustn't listen to her, honey. Your grandfather put her up to this." *He's scared we're getting too close to Mark.* "Please go to your room."

"I'm not a baby – you can't make me!" Jake screamed, tired of being treated as if he were.

"Stop this now! We can work this out between ourselves," Annuschka wept.

But it was too late for second thoughts. Maruschka had already received two thirds of the money and she wasn't about to lose the rest.

"I'm sorry, Granny. Our dad doesn't give a damn about us, Jake! He never paid alimony for me. Mum and I didn't get a penny from him!"

Jake's eyes fixated on his sister.

"Stop this charade!" Mark was on the verge of exploding. "I'm your father. Ronald's had his fun. Let's get out of here and talk."

Crying hysterically, Annuschka reached for Maruschka's hand.

"Don't touch me!" she wailed, hearing Vanessa turn on her father: "How could you? She's just a kid. An insecure frightened kid! You'll pay for this."

"You really imagine Mark gives a damn about you and Jake?" Ronald shouted. "He's only in it for the money! No one's permitted to come near my grandson except me." But nothing he said or did to her had the slightest effect.

"Jake's *my* son, not yours! He doesn't give a damn about your bloody business. You'll not rob him of a life as well!" Vanessa's manner was firm, gaze unflinching. Turning to look at the girl, she asked, "Did my father put you up to this? Did he stage tonight's performance?"

"Of course not! It's all down to me. Listen to me, Jake, Dad doesn't care about us, only what's in it for him!" Grabbing her arm, Vanessa dragged her into the entrance.

"Get that bitch out of my sight!" She watched Mark carry her out into the street, kicking and screaming.

"You're poison!" he yelled. "Jake's in tears because of you! Couldn't you at least have spared his feelings? We're washing our hands of you." He left her lying there sobbing, regretting taking orders from that awful man.

In the end it was Bernie who persuaded Jake to go upstairs to his room, where he cried into his pillow, later turning up in his mother's room in the middle of the night, asking if he could sleep in her bed.

"Of course you can. I'm so sorry you heard those awful things. It's the reason I wanted you to leave us. Maruschka only said it because your grandfather instructed her to, honey."

"Is it true, Mom? Is Daddy only interested in us because we're rich?"

"No, he's not. Your father loves you very much. He and Maruschka have a lot to sort out between them."

★

469

Calling in the morning to apologise for his daughter's behaviour, Mark told her it was for the best they didn't see each other for a while.

"I understand. Just as long as you explain it to our son or he'll believe what she told him is true," Vanessa replied sadly.

"You're right thinking like that. It's the reason I wish to sign a paper dictating I'll have no stake in Jake's future inheritance."

Relieved he saw fit to do such a thing, Vanessa replied, "I'll ask my attorney to handle it. Thank you." She felt as if a heavy weight had been lifted off her shoulders.

"There's something else. I've no right imposing it on you but you're the only person I can turn to. Will you try talking to Maruschka? She'll listen to you." Stunned he wanted her to mediate between him and his daughter, Vanessa sighed.

"I don't know if it'll help but I'll give it a go. Give me her address and I'll see what I can do."

Later that week Mark signed the paperwork at her solicitor's office, stipulating Jake's money belonged to no one but Jake. Yet when Vanessa informed her father, the latter laughed out loud.

"More fool you for believing him! Copeck's just biding his time. He'll talk you into marrying him, insisting you don't bother with a prenup!"

"You disgust me. Forcing a young, defenceless girl into doing your dirty work? You have no integrity! Had it not been for Bernie, Jake wouldn't have calmed down. You'd better watch your back; your grandson's onto you!"

"Did my father ask you to come here tonight?" Maruschka asked, trying to close the front door when Vanessa forced her way inside.

"I was in the neighbourhood thinking we should talk."

"We've nothing to say to each other."

"Really? Ignore me all you like but I'll not leave until we've had a chat."

"Is that a threat?"

"You bet."

"You've no right barging in telling me what's right and wrong! Why don't you give your old man a hard time instead?"

"Daddy knows full well what I think of him."

"I was about to make myself something to eat."

"Great – I'm starving! It took ages to get here."

"Can't you eat at home?"

"Jake's at school, it's boring eating on my own. I don't suppose you know how to make scrambled eggs?

"I do."

"So what are you waiting for?"

Too stunned to contradict her, Maruschka cleared the shabby table, pulling out a pan from the cupboard.

"I've got no chairs. We'll have to stand up or sit on the floor."

"Fine by me. Hurry up, I haven't got all day!"

Watching Maruschka cracking a few eggs, adding salt and pepper then grated cheese, Vanessa was certain she was used to looking after herself from an early age. As they ate on the dirty floor, she said, "Jake's still upset. Please say you're sorry for the way you behaved."

"If I do, will you leave?"

"Only if you're genuinely sorry."

Taking a swig out of a beer can, Maruschka nodded. "Alright then. I'm sorry. That good enough for you?"

"Not quite! You have to mean it. Why do you hate your father?"

"I was upset and angry! You wouldn't understand."

"Try me. It wasn't so long ago when I was just like you, angry and hard on the outside, yet an emotional wreck inwardly. You and I have more in common than you think. I lost my mother when I was very young. My Dad never showed any affection towards me. It's the reason I tell my son I love him every day! Like you, I wasted too much time being angry and resentful. Unlike you, I had no one to turn to. This neighbourhood's dangerous for someone as young and pretty as you," Vanessa told her.

Shocked the immaculately groomed woman in front of her shared a similar background, Maruschka whispered, "I'm sorry I treated you so badly."

"Jake's been looking forward to having a big sister," Vanessa replied softly, reaching for her hand. "You must put the past behind you. I did when Jake was born. Talk to Mark! Give each other the chance to heal and move on."

"But I'm so ashamed of how I spoke to my granny!" Maruschka cried, biting her lower lip. "What if she dies and we don't get the opportunity to make amends?"

"Let them take care of you," Vanessa replied, putting an arm around her. "I'm here for you if you need to talk."

"I'll return the money your father gave me."

"There's no need, keep it and plan something nice."

Mark called Vanessa later that week, expressing how grateful he was she'd talked some sense into his daughter. Clearly delighted with the situation, he told her Maruschka had asked if she could live with him.

"I don't know what you did but it worked! We've a long road ahead of us but because of your intervention, we're heading in the right direction – you're a very special lady."

Ending their conversation, Vanessa smiled, thinking, *Mission accomplished*.

After dropping Clara off at his parents' house for the weekend, Ben looked at Annabelle from behind his paper.

"We need to talk." He watched her face drain of colour, a nervous expression in her eyes. "There's no easy way of putting it so I'll come straight to the point: I want a divorce, we're not happy together."

Room spinning, Annabelle registered his words, abruptly getting up from the couch in the spacious living room, tears stinging in her eyes.

"You couldn't stop yourself! To hell with us. She's the reason you want rid of me!"

"You've always known how I felt about her yet you chose to turn a blind eye to it. I never intended to hurt you. I respect you too much for that." He put a hand out to her but Annabelle pushed him aside.

"Did the two of you end up in bed before or after her mother's funeral? You're something else; a real class act! I trusted you. I thought you weren't like all the others," she cried, life as she knew it falling apart around her.

"I'm so very sorry, Annabelle. I tried to make it work. We'll have to come to some understanding about Clara."

"Did you consider her when screwing Hannah Stein? You sure as hell can't stand my touch!" Since returning from Malmö, Ben had slept in the guest room, saying he didn't want to disrupt her sleep when returning late from work.

"We'll continue this discussion when you've calmed down. None of this is down to you. You're a wonderful woman and mother to our daughter. But whatever happens between us, I'll always be Clara's father."

"Not anymore! You forfeited that right as soon as you got into bed with her!" Annabelle screamed, tears spilling down her mouth and neck.

"Don't be ridiculous. Did you forget I'm a solicitor?" Ben muttered, missing Hannah so much he positively ached inside. *She's right. Annabelle won't give up without a fight.*

"Don't you dare take that tone with me! I'm the innocent party in all of this." She wanted him to hurt as much as she did, their child her best weapon.

"I'll not listen to you when you're acting like this. We'll talk another time."

"There's nothing to discuss! I'm not subjecting myself to this humiliation. If you want to be part of Clara's life, you'll not bring this up again."

"You're insane. Please don't do this to us. Let us end our marriage in a dignified way."

Walking out of there, Ben thought, *She'll not succeed in turning my child against me.*

The next couple of weeks followed the same pattern: arguments, tantrums and tears. Ben moved into a rented flat and continued to try reasoning with her. Rebecka and Michael were caught in the middle, telling him Annabelle forbade them to spend time with their granddaughter unless she was there to supervise it.

"I'm sorry you and Dad are having to deal with this," Ben told his mother, having negotiated to see Clara for a few hours that afternoon. He watched her play with some toys, her big brown eyes so much like his own. Picking her up in his arms, wishing she was old enough to understand, Ben buried his face in her brown curls, whispering, "Daddy loves you, pumpkin, I'm always here for you."

"Sorry I'm late. Have you ordered something from the menu?" Melanie asked, rushing into the quaint café in Hendon town centre. She stopped a passing waiter, requesting a Niçoise Salad without dressing. "Belle called last night. She's a mess!" Sitting opposite Ben, she thought he looked awful; unshaven with dark circles beneath his eyes.

"I'm feeling pretty rotten as well. Counting myself fortunate I get to see my daughter a few hours here and there! Annabelle's determined to make me pay, no matter the consequences." He sipped his wine, too uptight to eat.

"Here I am, piggy in the middle as usual! I gather she's no idea we're meeting up?"

"Hell no. But whom else can I turn to? I'm at my wits' end. You're my oldest friend."

"You're quite sure this is what you want?" Melanie asked between mouthfuls of salad.

"Without a doubt. Hannah's all I want; you of all people know that."

"But Belle's my friend! You're all she's got. The two of you may not be perfect for one another but she'll never abandon you. We've been through this so many times. I thought you patched things up between you?"

"Hannah left me so I could meet someone who'd give me a child."

"What if history repeats itself? You'll have sacrificed everything for nothing! I'm Clara's godmother, my only concern is her."

"What's Matt's view on this?"

"Funny you should ask. He never bought the fairy tale of you and Belle. Turns out he was right! Tell you what, I'll try to get through to her but I doubt she'll listen to me . . ."

"You're the best. Thank you, Mel. The last thing I want is to cause the two of you to fall out."

The following day Melanie took one look at Annabelle, her eyes swollen, no make-up, limp hair, wearing a baggy jumper and jeans camouflaging her drastic weight loss and burst out: "What the hell have you been doing to yourself? You must pull yourself together for the sake of your child!" Invited to lunch at the house, Annabelle didn't bother to conceal the bitterness she felt inside, throwing herself in her friend's arms.

"My mother's deliriously happy with her partner, Clara loves attending nursery, but I can't function. My GP's advising I take time off work. He thinks I'm at risk of having a nervous breakdown."

"It's a miracle you're capable of caring for Clara! Listen to me, Ben was wrong in doing what he did but you have to face the fact he's not in love with you. I'd never want someone to stay with me out of pity. Take what he's offering, putting Clara's and your needs first. She deserves better than this."

"I might have guessed you'd take his side! What am I supposed to do? Let him walk all over me? I loved him for so long, I don't know how to live without him."

"You've no choice. Unless the two of you start talking, Ben will have no option but to take action. I want you and Clara to stay here with us. The twins will love it!"

Annabelle picked at her sandwich. "I'll think about it."

"And another thing. You're still angry with your father. Every time something bad happens to you, you bury your head in the sand, not wishing to deal with the situation. Well, I've got news for you, lady! Your father's dead and so's your marriage." She'd had enough of tiptoeing around her friend.

"Rosie and I couldn't be happier for you," Sanna said when Hannah divulged her news. "Our only concern is that he's married with a child. Do you know what that makes you? His mistress,"

"He'd have filed for divorce sooner or later; they're not right for one another."

"What's Walther's and Peter's take on this?"

"They're over the moon. Pappa's a mere shadow of his former self. You wouldn't recognise him."

"You must give him time to grieve and adjust. They were together for such a long time."

Walking into her parents' bedroom, Hannah froze on the spot, watching her father sort out the remainder of her mother's jewellery and clothes.

"Are you sure you're up to this?" she asked, eyes glued on the boxes by the bed.

"I've postponed it long enough. It's best I get on with it while I still can. You and Peter make me so proud, the things you said about your mother at the funeral. I worry about you, my darling; you've no one caring for you. Promise me you and your brother will always be there for each other. Don't look so concerned! I've had a wonderful life! Your mother made sure of it."

Why is he talking like that? "Is there something you want to tell me, Pappa?" she asked in a shaky voice.

"We've said it all," Walther assured her, continuing with what he was doing. Keeping an eye on him while helping to clear out the drawers and wardrobe, Hannah persuaded him to join her in the kitchen. They shared an omelette and then he asked her to assist him getting into bed. "I think I'll have a nap. It's been a difficult day."

"We'll figure out something nice to eat for dinner – you've an appointment with the heart specialist in the morning."

Looking vulnerable and frail lying on the big bed, Hannah went up to him, kissing his cheek. His hands cupped her face.

"Never forget how much your mother and I love you and Peter. Perhaps you and Ben can live here one day," he whispered, blowing her a kiss.

He's doing it again, talking as if it's the last time I'll see him. "I won't be long. Try getting some rest," she said, hurrying to the local shops in Limhamn. She returned an hour later, praying he was alright. Quickly she put the groceries in the kitchen and then ran into the bedroom.

"I'm back! Are you okay?"

There was something about the calm expression on his face and the way his hands were clasped on the duvet. She knew instinctively something was very wrong.

"Please say something . . . anything . . ." she cried, pulling down the duvet, feeling for his pulse. *I can't lose him as well, I just can't!* Sobbing hysterically, Hannah reached for the phone on the bedside table, fingers trembling as she dialled her brother's number. The words tumbled out of her mouth.

"Pappa's dead! We're orphans!" she cried, lying beside her father. And that is where, half an hour later, Peter found her curled up like a ball. Life as they knew it had suddenly ceased to exist.

"I booked a flight and will be with you later tonight, little one," Ben assured her, hearing the pain in her voice.

"What about Annabelle and Clara? Did she sign the divorce papers?"

"Not yet. You mustn't worry about it now. I'm so desperately sorry for your loss – Walther was such a fine man."

"I'd rather you stay put and not cause any further complications with your wife. Peter and I will cope on our own." However much Hannah hurt, she preferred him to sort things out at his end, enabling them to move on.

"We'll see each other tonight," Ben replied in a firm voice.

Within a couple of days the funeral came and went. Seeing Ben help carry the coffin, Hannah was relieved he'd insisted on being there for her. They were sorting out her father's belongings when Ben asked, "Why don't you come with me to London?"

"I can't. Peter and Annie need me," she replied, tears streaming down her face. Putting his arms around her, Ben held her close.

"I wish we could be together all the time, especially now when you need my support." Peter had his wife and kids whereas she only had him, yet because of his and Annabelle's situation he couldn't be the rock she needed.

"I so wish I could leave. Get her to sign those papers! Recent events have made me realise that life's just too short to waste." Touching her face, Ben looked deep into her eyes.

"I'll sort it, Hannah. I give you my word. I want you to find a way of being with me even if it's just for a short time." Kissing her lips, Ben pulled her closer, his suitcase already in the cab waiting outside. "Are you certain you'll be alright?"

"Yes . . . All I need to do is fetch a few things at the flat."

"I'd rather you wait and ask Peter to do it instead," Ben replied, kissing her one final time, lips lingering before reluctantly leaving her. Waving at her from the back seat of the cab, Ben dialled Peter's number on his mobile, asking the latter to make sure she was safe. "Hannah's on her way to the flat to fetch a few things. Please ensure that jerk's not lurking about!"

"Thanks for telling me. Have a safe trip," Peter replied, a worried expression on his face.

Busy unlocking the door, Hannah noticed someone coming up to her from behind.

"You didn't think I'd let you off the hook that easily, did you? I'm not leaving until we've talked!" Reeking of alcohol and slurring his words, Linus had most likely been drinking all day.

"Leave or I'll call the police!"

"Don't be silly, they've got better things to do than checking up on some hysterical woman," Linus spat at her, his stinking breath making her nauseous. Hannah pretended to fetch a couple of glasses from the kitchen cupboard, hoping she'd get the opportunity to call her brother and alert him to the situation.

"Would you like something to eat? It's dangerous to drive on an empty stomach."

"You're all I want! I want what lover boy's getting!" As Linus grabbed her arm roughly, Hannah winced in pain.

"Why are you treating me like this?" she screamed.

"Because it's time someone teaches you a lesson!" There was hatred in Linus's eyes.

He'll rape me a second time!

"You're sick! To think I actually stood up for you with Mary . . ."

He silenced her with a slap. "You little whore. I'll shut you up once and for all!"

Trying her damnedest to get away from him, Linus was much too strong, forcing her legs apart with one hand, the other pinning her down on the living room couch, ripping her blouse. His erection nudged against her thigh and he was about to push inside her when a voice shouted, "What the hell's going on?"

Taking in the ugly scene in front of him, Peter dragged Linus towards the hall, thumping him so hard, Hannah heard him cry out at the sight of blood coming out of his mouth.

"We were just fooling around," he muttered, attempting to raise himself off the floor. Sharply, Peter kicked him hard in the groin.

"That's for raping and assaulting my sister!" He turned to check on Hannah. She was sitting in a corner of the room, shaking. "If he's done what he did before, I'll wring his neck!"

"H-he almost s-succeeded, b-but nothing h-happened." She was trembling so much she could barely speak. Her blouse was ripped to pieces, and her lower lip bleeding.

"Watch that creep while I call the police!" Hearing a muffled sound, Hannah turned to look at Linus. He was wailing.

"I love you. Seeing you and him together at the funeral drove me nuts! Everything I do is for you, always you."

Listening to his pathetic excuses, Hannah felt nothing but contempt. Linus was extremely dangerous – a bomb waiting to explode.

It was midnight by the time two police officers finished taking statements, taking him with them, handcuffed.

"You saved my life!" Hannah sobbed in Peter's arms.

"He'll be forced into having psychiatric evaluation. I'll call Annie in the morning saying you came down with some bug. Let's go home."

Just before going to bed, Peter texted Ben about the night's events, ten minutes later reading his reply:

Thank God you came to her rescue, I should never have left her.

★

They were in the office, discussing Linus.

"Can't say I'm surprised," Annie shook her head. If Mary was alive, she'd have hounded him to his grave!"

"He told me his mother abused him, although that's no excuse for what he did. But that's the only explanation as to why he turned out the way he did."

"The children were crazy about him. What a terrible waste."

"Who knows? Given the right treatment and medication, he may eventually turn his life around. Others have." Hannah swallowed hard just thinking about what she needed to say next. "I've decided to return to London. Ben and I are getting on with our lives. You're the perfect candidate to succeed me, Annie. I'd never have coped without you these past few years. I'm leaving the school to you and all I ask in return is reimbursement for expenditure on recent refurbishment and extension of the premises." The building work was the best decision Hannah had ever made, because now Budding Stars was capable of meeting the demands of an ever-increasing waiting list and Mary's legacy of offering a safe haven for children with learning difficulties was ensured. Her announcement took a few moments to register, then Annie burst into tears.

"You're entrusting Mary's school to me? But she gave it to you," she whispered, not quite believing her ears. "I can certainly reimburse you for the recent work. Mum left me the house and enough money to live on for the remainder of my life. It's the least I can do!"

"Mary would have agreed with me: she valued you almost as much as I do."

"I can't get my head around it," she cried. "It's the best news I ever had! Mum, bless her soul, would have been very proud of me."

"We'll stay in touch. This school holds a special place in my heart."

A few months later, saying goodbye to colleagues, parents and pupils, Hannah witnessed Annie signing the paperwork in the presence of Gustav Petren. Clearing out the flat, leaving it as it was when moving in, she thought of the two things she had left to do: informing Peter he was in charge of their parental home and the task she'd postponed since Zadie died.

"Thank you for agreeing to come to my office." Ben stepped aside to let Annabelle in, the shock of seeing her looking so rough bringing tears to his eyes.

"Let's get whatever it is out of the way. Clara's waiting for me at the nursery." Her reply was ice cold.

"I want us to resolve our differences here and now. Our daughter's the innocent victim in all of this." Annabelle moved her chair as far away from him as she could without ending up in the corridor.

"I was always there for you," she snapped. "I gave birth to your child. And you? You returned the favour by corresponding with that woman's mother. Yes, Ben! I saw her letter. What kind of man stoops so low as to sleep with the woman who dumped him? You're obviously getting married?"

"I wish you'd calm down. Hannah didn't reject me. The way you're going on I'm surprised you've not ended up in hospital."

"Everything's your fault!" Jumping up from her seat, Annabelle reached over and slapped his face.

"What the hell did you do that for?" Ben shouted, touching his cheek.

"I'm sorry. I don't know what came over me," she cried, returning to her chair, face in her hands.

"I understand how hard this must be for you. But violence is not the answer!"

"You don't give a damn about us! Only her."

"I'll not dignify that with a reply. Please read my terms and conditions before signing." He handed her a document. Annabelle put on her glasses, browsing the contents.

"All I asked was that you loved and respected me. If I comply with this, what's in it for me?" she asked, removing her glasses and looking up at him.

"How do you mean? You're keeping the house, the money. What more do you want? I'm sorry I hurt you, perhaps you'll forgive me some day . . ."

"Would things have turned out differently if you'd never met her?"

"We've been through this over and over again!" Ben's exasperation was obvious.

"I need to know if everything we shared was a lie."

"I'm fond of you. You're the mother of my child."

Annabelle's eyes narrowed. "Okay . . . I'll sign it on the condition your girlfriend's not permitted to participate in our daughter's life. I'm not having her subjected to your sordid affair! My boss offered me a transfer to Macy's in New York. If I accept it, you'll never set eyes on her again! Take it or leave it."

"Why are you doing this?" Ben whispered, shocked she loathed him so much.

"Hannah stole you from me! Accept my terms or kiss your daughter goodbye."

"Alright! You win – this time. Just remember one thing: when Clara finds out about this, she'll hold it against you. You'll never succeed in taking her from me."

"You're mistaken. Our daughter's bound to side with me. I really loved you Ben. You broke my heart. That's the reason I'll never forgive either of you."

Half the battle was over. Ben had finally got what he wanted: a divorce. All he had to do now was tell the woman he loved she wouldn't be part of his child's life – the child she'd left him for. Yet when she found out about it, Hannah assured him it wasn't the end of the world.

"It's a small price to pay for the time being, seeing as we get to spend the rest of our lives together," she said, putting up a brave front.

"I'm proud of you," Melanie said when Annabelle called to share the news. "Now you can finally move on."

"It's on the condition that woman's never coming near Clara," Annabelle replied, angry Melanie always seemed to take Ben's side.

"You're pulling my leg, right? You know how much she means to him. Ben and Clara have a special bond."

"Those two betrayed me, Mel! We were doing alright before she reappeared on the scene."

"You were so happy together that you didn't share a bed?"

"Oh, I just can't do it, Mel! I can't let him have his cake and eat it."

When Melanie confided in her husband later that day he commented, "What did you expect? A miracle? Looks like Ben's bitten off more than he can chew. It's Hannah I feel sorry for, leaving everything behind. But at what cost?"

Hannah parked outside the neat one storey property at the outskirts of the city. After a moment, a pretty blonde woman in her thirties opened the front door.

"Can I be of assistance to you? My name's Suzy, I'm the society's administrator." Introducing herself, Hannah followed her into the large sunny kitchen of the Malmö branch of the Alzheimer's Society, part of a much bigger organisation in Stockholm with branches all over Sweden. They sat together at the round table, the aroma of freshly brewed coffee bringing back fond memories of breakfasts in Limhamn.

"I was about to take a break. Let me pour you a mug of coffee. I hope you're as partial to cinnamon buns as I am?" Suzy's voice was kind.

"I sure am! There's something I need to discuss with you. My mother passed away approximately eighteen months ago. Not a day goes by when I don't think about her . . ." Hannah stopped, suddenly close to tears.

"I'm so sorry to hear that, what was her name?"

"Zadie, Zadie Stein."

"Sounds familiar – I know! She used to run a book club and if my memory serves me right, a French conversation group. That's it! I remember her vividly. Dark hair, gold-framed spectacles and the biggest brown eyes I ever saw."

"You must tell me how the two of you met," Hannah exclaimed, feeling an instant connection between them.

"Granny brought me along one day many years ago. I was in awe of your mother's kindness and generosity. I remember she asked all kinds of questions about my favourite subjects at school, even offering me cakes and sweets. I take it you lost her to Alzheimer's? My grandmother was diagnosed in her eighties." Suzy's eyes clouded over.

"Mamma succumbed to it in her sixties. I'll never get over losing her and my father."

"Don't tell me he died from the same disease?"

486

"No, he didn't. I'm certain he died of a broken heart. They were so very happy together." Finishing her coffee and cinnamon bun, Hannah pulled something out of her bag. "Here. This is the reason I came. Please use it towards research." As Suzy took the cheque from her, she nearly fell off her chair.

"Are you sure? We've never received anything quite as generous as this before."

"All I ask is that you set up a trust fund in my mother's name, ensuring she's remembered," Hannah said, smiling.

"Please give me your details and I'll personally see to it you get regular updates," Suzy replied, in awe of the pretty woman whose eyes filled with tears when talking about her mother.

Half an hour later they said goodbye, and Hannah felt moved to give her a hug.

"Let's pray someone finds a cure preventing more people enduring the same fate as our loved ones." She'd spent Annie's reimbursement on an important cause, thus ensuring her mother's memory was kept alive.

"Are you okay, sis?" Peter asked the day she was leaving.

"I remember you asking the same question when Mamma and I were on our way to London in 1978," Hannah replied, taking a final look at her surroundings.

"You're right, Pappa and I came with you to Copenhagen Airport. Feels like yesterday," he said. Just for a moment, she was sure she detected the scent of Old Spice.

"I couldn't have wished for a better brother – you're the best."

"This is it, sis! You and Ben. Just like our parents predicted. I sure hope Ben's daughter can be part of all our lives one day."

"Will you manage looking after this house in addition to yours and work?"

"Stop worrying! Lena and the boys will help. Oh . . . why did they have to die, one after the other? Promise you'll not let anyone or anything stand in the way of your happiness, Hannah."

"I swear."

They had agreed it was for the best if she left on her own. The taxi was waiting outside. Embracing her, Peter whispered, "I've a feeling you'll soon return."

Watching her get into the cab, he waved until she was out of sight.

CHAPTER TWENTY-SIX

2012

The minute she entered the house in Richmond, Hannah felt at home. Their next-door neighbour wasted no time in complaining about the former tenant's inability to show respect.

"Not so much as a greeting . . . I almost forgot, someone came round enquiring about you. I can't recall his name. He said you had a history," she confided when Hannah helped carry her shopping inside.

"Can you describe him to me?"

"He's certainly not a patch on Ben! Balding on top, stained teeth and cleft in the chin. Beats me as to why someone as accomplished as you would give him the time of day."

"I get it! His name's Mark. I cut him out of my life years ago."

"That's exactly what I thought. I can't tell you how wonderful it is to see you again."

Waiting for Clara's return, Annabelle kept staring out the window. *Damn him! He's causing me constant stress,* she thought, chain-smoking, a habit she'd developed after they divorced. *Hannah's ruined my life! This house and the money in the bank can't make up for it. If it weren't for Clara, I wouldn't get up in the morning.* Hearing the sound of a car parking at the front, Annabelle straightened her skirt, catching a glimpse of herself, pale and drawn, in the mirror on the wall.

"What took you so long? I've been worried sick imagining all sorts!" Her words were aimed at her ex-husband.

"Look what I brought you, Mummy!" Jumping up and down with excitement, Clara handed her a brown paper bag containing freshly baked cookies. "Grandma helped me!" she added, grinning.

"How sweet. We'll have them for dessert. Dinner's ready, pumpkin."

"I want Daddy to stay and eat with us!" Clara replied, stubbornly refusing to let go of her father's hand.

"Can we talk?" Ben sounded strained. "It won't take long."

Eyes focused on her daughter, Annabelle shook her head, thinking: *You made your bed, now lie in it!*

"You must tell Mummy about the animals you visited at London Zoo," Ben said, watching the small girl stamp her feet.

"Don't leave me!" she wailed, tears spilling down her face.

"I bet Mummy's made you something special to eat." He picked her up in an attempt to calm her down.

"I want you to stay!" Clara screamed, wiggling around in his arms. Preoccupied with seeing her child in so much distress, Annabelle hardly heard Ben say she looked well.

"Are you alright?" he asked, hoping the animosity she felt towards him would soon cease. "Daddy can't stay, Clara. We'll do something fun next time!" Kissing the tip of her cute little nose, Ben gently put her down on the ground. She ran inside to play with her kitten, Rambles, temporarily forgetting what had upset her.

"I'm okay . . . you?" It was the first time she'd acknowledged his presence without sounding hostile.

"I'm fine . . . Delegating most of my workload to Eve and Collin."

"I'm considering returning to work but not until Clara's enrolled at nursery," she mumbled, looking away.

"That's wonderful! Let me know if you want me to look after her." *After the settlement I gave her, she need never work again.* "I hope one day we can resume our friendship." Too upset to respond, Annabelle watched him get into his car, then returned inside to her daughter.

Handing her a cheque for £10,000, Mark could tell by the expression on Vanessa's face how surprised she was.

"What's this for? I was under the impression you can't afford it."

"It's for all the birthdays I missed out on in our son's life. I owe you big time, Vanessa!" He didn't tell her it had been Maruschka's idea, seeing as she got to keep Ronald's bribe.

"You two fancy each other rotten!" she teased, watching his face turn red.

"You haven't a clue what you're talking about – Vanessa and I have a son, that's all." Finding work as a sales rep for a local estate agent, Mark had long since accepted he wasn't cut out to run his own business. These days his relationship with his immediate family was far less volatile. Annuschka even went so far as to employ a weekly cleaner, enabling her to spend time with her grandchildren who, despite their age gap, got along famously.

Listening to her telling him about the money Mark gave her, Ronald laughed out loud:

"More fool you for believing him. That jerk's out to impress you. Jake's twelve years old. It's high time you start honouring our agreement!"

Livid that he still ruled their lives, Vanessa called Mark to voice her concerns.

"We're always answering to him. I don't know how much more I can take."

"It's insane . . . isn't there something you can do to change it?"

"Not unless he's struck down with an incurable disease! I'm Jake's legal guardian until he turns eighteen. After that I can no longer protect him."

Putting her worries to the back of his mind, Mark's thoughts turned to Hannah, deciding to call her at the school in Malmö. A woman with a strong Swedish accent answered the phone, saying she was the new owner.

"Who are you? I don't recall Hannah mentioning your name," Annie said.

"Did she leave a forwarding number and address?" Mark asked, holding his breath.

"I'm not in the habit of disclosing personal details."

"But we go back such a long way . . ."

"If that's true, how come she didn't give it to you?" Annie hung up, memories of Linus entering her mind.

Swearing, Mark suddenly thought of something. *What if she returned to London?* He Googled Sally's Heroes to get the number. Sally herself answered the phone, immediately recognising his voice.

"I warned you not to call again! Hannah wants nothing to do with you!" Swiftly she slammed down the receiver.

Trying to work out how to best proceed, something suddenly dawned on him. *Why didn't I think of this earlier?* Locating the number of the estate agent managing the property in Richmond, Mark asked the salesman at the other end of the line if it was available to rent.

"Who wants to know?"

"I'm looking to invest in a house just like it," Mark said, ignoring the question. "Perhaps you wouldn't mind showing it to me?"

"I'm afraid that's not possible because we've been instructed to take it off the market a while ago."

"How come?" A bead of perspiration broke out on Mark's upper lip.

"The owner's returned to live in it. I can show you some other similar properties in the area, if you give me your details."

But Mark had already ended the call, thinking, *Hannah's come back to me!* The fact that she hadn't informed him did not even cross his mind. His mobile rang. It was Vanessa, wanting to invite him and Annuschka to dinner at the house.

"I'll have to take a rain check. Something's come up."

"It'll only be for a couple of hours, Mark. Jake's looking forward to it." Vanessa was conscious of not wishing to sound too eager. "Cook's making your favourite dish: rack of lamb, rosemary potatoes and mint sauce."

"Well in that case, how can I resist? Maruschka's out with friends, I'll pick my mother up on the way." *Richmond will have to wait until tomorrow.*

With her father safely away attending a meeting, Vanessa was relieved they had the house to themselves and dressed up for the occasion in a gold Lurex blouse, black skirt with side split, stilettos and perfectly applied make-up. After chatting with Annuschka about how well Maruschka had adjusted to living with her father, finding a job at a local chemist, she focused her attention on Mark. His eyes were vacant.

"A penny for your thoughts . . ."

"Sorry, I was miles away. You ought to put those fabulous legs of yours on display more often!" he complimented her, thinking she looked extremely sexy.

"Is there something you'd like to share with me?" They had recently opened up to one another about their lives.

"Such as?" Mark asked, watching her face turn crimson red.

"Your personal life's your own. Forget I asked. Can Jake and I visit you tomorrow? It'll be fun spending time together."

She wants us to get closer, Mark thought. "Sorry but I already told you I'm busy. We'll arrange something later."

He's keeping something from me, Vanessa thought.

"I promise to make it up to you," Mark repeated, feeling her eyes on him.

Afterwards, Vanessa confided in Bernie.

"Call it female intuition but I'm certain he's seeing someone."

"You've clearly got feelings for him," Bernie replied kindly.

"Yeah . . . I do, I've fallen in love with him yet I doubt he feels the same. Why else would he reject me?" She looked so upset that Bernie put his arm around her.

"What's keeping you? It's not as if the two of you aren't intimately acquainted . . . Jake's living proof of that! You must confront him."

"Oh, Bernie, what would I do without you? I'm too old to play games. I'll drive there first thing in the morning."

"Didn't you tell me he'd made other arrangements?"

"This can't wait any longer – I have to know where I stand."

"Good for you. And Vanessa? Should things not work out, just remember how special you are. Mark's an idiot if he can't see it."

After barely a wink of sleep, Vanessa jumped out of bed early the next morning. Willing herself to make an effort, she chose a low-cut dress, heels and make-up. Driving to Stanmore, she parked outside his house and sat in her car for a moment, applying another coat of lipstick. Noticing there wasn't any sign of his car in the open garage and street, she wondered if he'd already left. *I should have called first instead of coming unannounced*, she thought, hearing someone shout her name.

"Vanessa! You look great!" Maruschka called from an upstairs window. "Dad's out right now. Please come in, the front door's open. I'm in my bedroom making phone calls. I'll be with you shortly."

Taking her cue, Vanessa walked into the small kitchen, where she kicked off her shoes, poured herself a glass of tap water and then fell into a chair at the table. Rummaging through her bag, she looked for something to write on so she could leave a message saying how grateful she was to be let in but had to leave. *Perhaps there's a notepad and pen in the entrance?* Walking barefoot into the dark hall, Vanessa saw a yellow pad on the mantelpiece, stumbling on a ripped piece of paper beneath her feet on the carpet. Bending to pick it up, she read the name and number scribbled on it. *Hannah! So she's the reason Mark snubbed me . . . I've got to get the hell out of here before he returns!*

Forgetting to leave a message, Vanessa put the offending note on the mantelpiece. Tears of humiliation stung her eyes, and she was mortified that she'd thought he felt something for her. Stumbling out the front door and into her car, she was halfway home when she had a sudden change of heart. Turning the car round, heading towards Richmond, she was determined to find out if Mark and Hannah were seeing each other behind her back.

★

HELENE FERMONT

"You? W-why are you here?" Hannah stammered, turning red with fury seeing who was standing there on her doorstep.

"You came back to me! I knew you would eventually . . . looking just as pretty!" As she moved to slam the door shut, Mark asked, "Why are you being like this? I thought you'd be pleased to see me."

"Pleased? I want you to leave this instant!" she shouted, eyes cold.

"But you're back . . . Surely that means you still have feelings for me?" Mark was shaking all over.

"I live here with Ben! When will you get into your head I don't care about you?"

"You're lying! The two of you were over years ago. After what took place in his office . . ." Mark said, nearly suffocating with anger and resentment.

"You're more deluded than I imagined. Leave now or I'll call the police!" Hannah was praying Ben was on his way back from the patisserie where he'd gone to pick up food for the picnic they'd planned with friends in Richmond Park later.

"I'll not leave until you tell me why you're treating me like this." Mark hissed, putting a foot inside the door.

"Stop making a fool of yourself!" Hannah shouted, certain the neighbours could hear them.

"You're sexy when you get angry," Mark replied in a thick voice, taking in her sultry green eyes, red hair and almost transparent shirt. He was aching to touch her. "My daughter's back in my life! So is my son with Vanessa. I did what you asked: I sorted myself out." Stalling for time, Hannah feigned interest.

"That's wonderful. Look, why don't we put this unfortunate incident behind us? Just leave and that'll be an end to it."

496

"Not until you talk to me," Mark insisted. "Why are you so hostile towards me?"

"Because I couldn't care less about you!" *Dear God, please make him leave!* Mark's face darkened. Pushing her aside, he grabbed her arm roughly.

"You sure as hell didn't object to having me around back then."

"Please don't do something you'll regret . . ." But Mark had lost control, kissing her mouth; the mixture of stale beer and Polo mints on his breath almost making her wretch. Hannah slipped out of his grasp and ran into the kitchen.

"Come near me again and I'll scream so loudly, the neighbours will come to my rescue!" Sensing how frightened she was, Mark took a step back.

"I'd never hurt you, baby . . . I love you."

"No you don't! You only think you do, it's too late to go back." *What is it about me that makes men assume they've permission to abuse me? First Linus, now Mark . . .*

Watching her standing at the kitchen sink, trying to calm down, Mark felt ashamed of himself. "I was wrong to do what I just did . . . Seeing you again brings it all back."

"Ben's all I ever wanted."

Hearing her say his name made him furious again. Pulling her into his arms, Mark kissed her hard on the mouth.

"Stop it! You make me sick!" Hannah cried, feeling his lips on her face, ears and neck.

"I know you want me, baby . . .." he groaned, one hand sliding up her thigh, much too aroused to stop. Pushing him off her, nails scratching his face, Hannah glimpsed Ben coming towards them through the open door.

"What the *hell* do you think you're doing?" he yelled, dropping his shopping and racing towards them. "Get your grubby hands off her or else . . . Hannah, call the police – that creep's going nowhere except prison!"

"Don't . . . please! I'll lose everything, my mother will die of shame – the kids won't have anything more to do with me!"

Ben punched him, square in the jaw. "Come near her and this house again . . ." Mark fell back painfully over a chair and landed in a heap on the floor.

"Not the police!" Hannah cried. "I just want to put this behind me . . ." She sobbed in Ben's arms.

"You're not thinking straight. What if that piece of scum attacks someone else?"

"I won't! I'm so ashamed . . . Please let me go," Mark begged.

Yanking him up from the floor and dragging him to the front door, Ben shoved him out onto the ground, shouting, "Next time I'll press charges against you! Now get the hell away from us before I change my mind." He slammed the door shut, and returned to the kitchen, where he gently rocked Hannah in his arms until she stopped trembling.

"No one will ever lay a finger on you again, little one – I'll make sure of it!"

Limping back to his car, his face hurting so much he wanted to scream, Mark somehow managed to drive back to Stanmore, unaware Vanessa had witnessed what happened between him and Ben, having pulled up outside the house just in time to see the scene on the doorstep.

My father was right . . . I let my personal feelings cloud my judgement, she thought, heading grimly towards Primrose Hill.

Waking up in the early hours of the morning, face burning so much he had to put disinfectant onto it, Mark cried out in agony. He was horrified by his reflection in the bathroom mirror, the scratches and bruising even worse than he'd imagined. As he crawled back into bed, it finally hit him.

But I'm not in love with her . . . I haven't been for years! Hannah's right: I was trying to relive the past . . . It's Vanessa I'm in love with! If she finds out about this, she'll cut me out of her and Jake's lives! There's always been something between us . . . even when we loathed each other . . .

After a restless sleep, he dragged himself out of bed and splashed ice cold water onto his face. He didn't bother with breakfast and was relieved to find a note from Maruschka, saying she was spending the night at his mother's. Grabbing the car keys on the mantelpiece in the entrance, his eyes fell on another note.

> *Vanessa was here yesterday morning – I hope you got to*
> *see each other.*
> *Maruschka.*

Next to it lay the other piece of paper with Hannah's name and number of the estate agent informing him she moved back in. Slowly he put two and two together. Shit! Please God don't let her have seen it! I've got to make her listen to me . . . Rushing out the door and driving to his mother's house, Mark saw his family come out to greet him.

"What's happened to your face?" Annuschka gasped.

"Have you been in a fight?" Maruschka asked.

"We'll talk inside . . ." Ten minutes later, finishing his coffee, Mark asked his daughter if Vanessa saw the note with Hannah's number scribbled on it.

"I don't have a clue . . . She was gone when I went downstairs to join her. You're white as a sheet. What's up?"

"I'll tell you later . . ." Mark groaned.

"You're lucky if she wants anything to do with you," Annuschka hissed, angry he'd forced himself on Hannah.

"What if they reported you to the police?" Maruschka added.

"You're both right and don't I know it!" he mumbled, thinking, *I've got to get through to the woman I love!*

"Please let me come in, Vanessa and I need to talk." Mark tried getting past Bernie whose face looked decidedly grim.

"She's not interested in anything you have to say – leave now or I'll throw you out!"

"This isn't how it seems . . . Five minutes, it's all I ask."

"It's all you're getting . . ." Bernie replied, a contemptuous expression in his eyes, just as Vanessa appeared, barefoot, with no make-up on and wearing old clothes.

"You've a nerve showing your face. Haven't you put me through enough?"

"Please hear me out, Vanessa. You need to listen to what I have to tell you about this . . . this bloody mess!" He followed her into Jake's room, relieved to find the boy was at school. "I know you saw that note. I should have come clean to you about Hannah but I was confused."

"The way you acted the other night didn't make sense. You're usually keen on spending time with our son. Before you continue to embarrass yourself and me, I need to tell you something. I was there, Mark . . . I saw everything you did."

"You were outside? I think I can figure out the rest." He was mortified she'd witnessed how he'd behaved with Hannah.

"Please listen to me . . . I beg you!"

"What's the point? You're still in love with her – even now you found out she's with Ben!" Vanessa wept.

"You're wrong . . . I kept telling myself I loved her, but last night I realised I fell out of love with her a long time ago – we only shared a brief fling. You're the only woman I love!" He sighed and left the room, saying over his shoulder, "Tell Jake I'll be in touch. I'll never forgive myself for causing you pain." Halfway towards the front door, Mark heard a whisper.

"Did you mean what you just told me?"

"Which part? That I'm sorry I hurt you or that I'm in love with you? You're all I want, Vanessa. I was an idiot doing what I did. Please say something – anything!" They'd spent too long not admitting how they felt. "I always knew it deep down. The way I behaved with Hannah was unforgiveable! I guess I just had to prove to myself it was over."

"You really love me?" Vanessa's eyes were moist with tears.

"I do . . . Don't you know how much I fancy you? I never met anyone as desirable, funny and loveable." Walking up to her, Mark kissed her on the lips, the smell of lavender and vanilla so intoxicating, he wished they were the only people in the house.

"You smell divine . . ." he whispered into her hair.

"Really? It's because I've sorted out the laundry and baked Jake's favourite pie! I used to think you were a pain in the ass. No manners whatsoever and those clothes . . ."

"And I told myself I didn't fancy you – not even if you were the only woman on the planet!"

"If only we'd owned up to how we felt instead of chasing ghosts." They were still kissing when Bernie appeared.

"Is everything as it should be, Vanessa?"

"What do you think?" She smiled. Mark and I sorted everything out."

"Well, you'd better start behaving or you'll answer to me," Bernie threatened, secretly pleased they'd made up. That evening

Mark sat at the table in his living room and wrote a letter of apology to Hannah and Ben, wishing them all the best.

"You actually believed him?" Ronald shouted, "He doesn't want *you*, only what's in it for him!"

"So you keep telling me but I'm not listening," Vanessa replied, fully aware how much Mark's presence in her and Jake's lives perturbed him.

Spending the weekends at Mark's house discovering they were just as physically compatible as before, Vanessa had even taken to wearing a mac similar to the one she'd worn the night she first seduced him. They'd been together for two months, alternating between his place and hotels when Mark had asked, "What'll happen when Ronald's gone?"

"We'll be free to live as we wish."

"It could be a while yet. You and Jake are welcome to stay with me and Maruschka."

"Don't tempt me," Vanessa had replied, watching him unbutton her top.

Now she and her father were busy arguing about her refusal to let him spend time with his grandson, introducing him to the business, when Ronald staggered a little.

"Do you want me to call for your doctor?" she asked, certain he was about to collapse.

"Stop fussing! You're the reason I'm upset – turning my grandson against me."

It was past 2am when Bernie came knocking on her bedroom door, shouting, "Ronald's had a fit! I found him on the floor in the kitchen." Throwing a robe over her nightgown, Vanessa ran downstairs to the basement, looking at the still body gasping for breath.

"Call an ambulance!" she shouted, Jake standing beside her, wide-eyed.

"Is Grandpa dead, Mom?" he asked in a shaky voice.

I did this to him, she thought, crouching next to her father. "The ambulance is on its way." Turning to look at her son, she said reassuringly, "We'll soon find out what's wrong."

"This isn't your fault," Bernie's voice trembled as he helped her to her feet. "He brought it on himself. I'll call Mark."

"Not just yet. Let's get him to A&E first."

As Ronald was carried out on a stretcher, Jake cried, "What if he dies, Mom?"

"Shh . . . let's not expect the worst," she replied, putting her arms around him. They sat on either side of her father at the back of the ambulance, all still in their pyjamas. *I wanted this for so long. Now it's happened, I can't feel a thing.* Ten minutes later they were in a sterile room, where the nurses attached tubes to his arms and legs. There was an oxygen mask on his face.

"It's not looking good," said the young duty doctor. "Is there someone we can call for you?"

"There's only us." Vanessa shook her head, feeling empty inside. After watching Ronald lying there looking so ill and defenceless, she turned to look at her son.

"Grandpa's very sick. Why don't you pull up a chair and talk to him, honey?"

"Only if you're here with me!" Jake cried.

"I'm not leaving you."

They'd been sitting there for an hour when Mark entered the room.

"I'm here now. Bernie told me what happened."

"Grandpa's dying, Dad," Jake sobbed, holding onto his father's arm.

"Isn't there anything that can be done?" Mark asked.

"I doubt it," Vanessa mumbled. At that moment the doctor returned, his eyes serious. "It's as I suspected: Mr Westbrook suffered a massive stroke. There's nothing more we can do. I'm sorry to be the bearer of tragic news."

"How long do we have?" Mark's voice was tense.

"It's only a matter of hours, if that. I can ask one of the nurses to give Ms Westbrook a sedative if she needs to sleep."

"No! It's for the best we're alert when . . ." Vanessa was unable to finish the sentence for fear of upsetting her son.

"Talk to him . . . he can still hear you."

I'm the last person he wants to hear before he dies! she thought, listening to her father's laboured breathing. Suddenly his hand touched hers.

"Don't leave me!" Ronald rasped, looking petrified. She asked Mark to take her son outside into the corridor.

Bending to kiss his grandfather's forehead, Jake whispered, "Goodbye Grandpa. Thanks for everything you did for me," looking down on him one final time before leaving.

"Come closer – time's running out."

"I'm sorry," she replied in an wooden voice.

"You and Jake will be set up for life! You'll soon have everything you always wanted, Vanessa . . . No more interfering from me." That familiar anger bubbling up inside, Vanessa snapped.

"Not everyone's like you! Money's not everything."

"It came out the wrong way," Ronald tightened his grip on her hand. "I failed you, my own daughter!"

What the hell is he talking about? He's detested me since I was born, she thought, convinced he was hallucinating.

"I let you down, but it's too late for regrets. Jake's a credit to you." As he clawed at the oxygen mask, Ronald asked, "Can you forgive me . . . for being so . . . hard . . . on . . . you?" His voice faltered. Numb to her core, Vanessa nodded.

"You're forgiven." She watched his eyes close, a peaceful expression on his face.

"He's in a coma. It won't be long now," the doctor said, taking her father's pulse. He paused for a moment. "Mr Westbrook has passed away. My sincere condolences."

"I need some air! Please excuse me," Vanessa whispered, running out into the corridor and Mark's arms.

"It's over, Daddy's dead!" she said, feeling his reassuring arms around her.

"I'm here for you both. What did he say to you?" Sighing, Vanessa looked into his eyes.

"What I longed to hear all my life . . . only it's too late now." Ronald had long since killed whatever affection she once felt for him.

"That man died not knowing what it means to love! You and Jake are at long last free to live as you wish." By now Bernie had arrived. Offering his condolences, he suggested he should arrange the funeral, leaving the family time to grieve.

"You're always here for us . . . Bernie's right, Mom; Grandpa's gone. He can't bully you anymore."

My son's right! I'll not mourn the father I never had. He never said he loved me.

The funeral came and went in less than a week. It was a small affair, attended by some business associates, Bernie, Vanessa and Jake. Afterwards mother and son let themselves be fussed over by Mark, Annuschka and Maruschka.

Wondering if she was expected to honour the agreement she

and her father signed, Vanessa heard Mark ask if she'd agree to be his wife. Shaking her head, she replied, "We're good as we are."

"You're saying that because of my track record." Mark was hurt but understood now was not perhaps the right time.

"Of course not! If it ain't broke, why fix it?"

"Maybe later?"

"Perhaps . . . when things calm down." She was referring to her and Jake's inheritance.

"I admire you, Vanessa, only you would be capable of pulling something like this off!" Ronald's old friend and associate, Richard McKenzie, remarked. At eighty, tall and lean with deep-set grey eyes, he was nothing like her father, for he possessed something as rare as a big heart: something almost unheard of in the world of finance.

"You think I can do it?" she whispered.

"Without a doubt! Ronald treated you appallingly. Imagine the impact you'd have had if he'd let you . . . Now stop worrying about that blasted agreement – I'll see to it you and Jake are no longer beholden to him." Reminding her to keep him updated about her plan, Richard pulled her close, then watched her leave the luxurious offices in Park lane, beaming.

Getting back into old routines at work, Annabelle was appointed manager of the cosmetics and lingerie department at a brand new department store opening on Regent's Street, and was kept busy preparing for the early awaited launch. When the big day arrived, she left Clara with Rebecka and Michael, and prepared herself for duty, feeling slightly nervous.

She was nursing a glass of sparkling champagne in a corner of the large foyer when her American boss, Bill Paterson, strode up to her, looking dashing in a midnight-blue suit. In his late fifties, the millionaire mogul bore a strong resemblance to Paul Newman, with the same intense blue eyes, fair hair and athletic build.

"Who's the lucky guy? You look stunning in that satin gown . . . red suits you." With her blonde hair falling down her back, he thought Annabelle was the most beautiful woman he'd ever seen.

"Why, you kept your accent," she said, surprised he was taking such an interest in her. "British people aren't as outspoken as Americans . . . I'm flattered by the compliment." Sipping his champagne, Bill smiled, revealing an even set of white teeth.

"Will you let me take you out to dinner? It's not a proposition, only a request to get to know you better." Avoiding looking into his eyes, Annabelle shook her head.

"I'm not in the habit of dating someone I hardly know . . . We're practically strangers!" She instantly regretted saying too much.

"I'm sorry you feel that way. It wasn't my intention to insult you," Bill replied, not knowing what else to say to her.

"I'm sorry too. I've not been out on a date for a very long time. It wasn't so long ago I was divorced . . ." She flushed prettily in embarrassment.

"Join the club! I split up from my ex a while ago – a mutual friend told me she'd met someone a lot younger, referring to him as her 'toy boy'. Monica's a wonderful woman, I wish her every happiness." Looking deep into her eyes, Bill tried his luck once more. "So, what do you think? I promise to behave like a gentleman!" Sensing she was just as vulnerable as he was, he couldn't get her out of his mind. Having had an amicable divorce, recently Bill had been actively seeking someone with whom to share his life. "I want us to meet outside of this place. You're extremely popular among staff and clients. Everyone speaks very highly of you."

"I've a three-year-old daughter. Perhaps her father won't mind babysitting her," Annabelle whispered, blushing a second time.

"I bet she's every bit as beautiful as her mother!" Annabelle looked down at her hands.

"Clara has my smile. Apart from that, she's the spitting image of her father . . . I'm sorry. You're wasting your time on me, I'm not very good company at the moment."

"I disagree! There's nobody I'd rather spend time with. You may think this odd but I'm rather bad at socialising. You don't have to make an impression on me, Annabelle. Please say yes. We seem to have quite a lot of things in common."

"You're very kind . . ." she said in a small voice, reprimanding herself for revealing too much.

What did that guy do to her? I'd never have left a bombshell like her.

"This is my card, your details are on file in my office," Bill told her, adding, "Take care of yourself. I'll be in touch very soon."

They arranged to meet in a top London restaurant the following week and that was the start of their friendship. Several weeks later, Annabelle invited him to her and Clara's home, the latter exclaiming: "You're nearly as handsome as my Daddy!"

Bill's eyes lit up each time she and Annabelle showed their appreciation when receiving gifts of toys and expensive pieces of jewellery. They were having dinner at Mr Chow in Knightsbridge when halfway through the meal Bill asked if she wanted to see his house in Belgravia.

"I'm not sure. Would you mind awfully if we take it slowly?" Annabelle wasn't sure if she was ready to embark on a new relationship.

"You're scared I'll hurt you . . . That'll never happen! I'm in love with you, Annabelle," Bill answered, reaching over to kiss her lips.

Melanie told Ben the news when they met up for a drink at The Flask in Hampstead Village.

"Bill's the best thing that's ever happened to her, he single-handedly brought her out of her shell!"

Similarly, Clara told everyone Mummy had met a nice man called Bill, adding, "Rambles likes him too!"

"Was it something I said?" Bill asked, concerned, as he watched her pick at her food in Scalini, their favourite Italian restaurant in Knightsbridge.

"Sorry . . . I was thinking about what you told me the other night."

"I meant every word! I'm in love with you and want us to spend the rest of our lives together, angel."

"How can you be so sure? We've known each other for less than a year . . ." *I'm in love with him! Bill's not like the others; I'm the only woman for him.*

Pulling his chair closer, Bill smiled. "The moment I first met you, I knew you were 'the one'."

Bursting into tears, Annabelle put a finger on his lips.

"I'm only crying because I'm happy! My first husband cheated on me every chance he got . . . The second was still in love with his ex . . . Clara's the only good thing that came out of that marriage. Ben's not a bad person. He tried so hard to live up to my expectations. But you're the only man who loves me, not someone else! A friend once told me I needed to come to terms with the past, my father's suicide and ex-husbands. I've since concluded they're not my responsibility. You can't help who you fall in love with." Suddenly she couldn't stop talking and she poured her heart out, bathing in the love and warmth in his eyes.

"You've been through so much. Am I more than just a friend?" Bill asked quietly.

"Can't you tell? I'm in love with you, how could I not be?" Annabelle cried, kissing him through her tears.

Seeing the house in Belgravia for the first time, Annabelle admired the view from the roof terrace, the spacious rooms decorated in soft pastels, and the mixture of modern and antique furniture. Fascinated, she listened to Bill describing his idyllic childhood in Brighton. His eyes misted over when he described how he'd lost his beloved parents, Joy and Harry, in a car accident soon after his twenty-first birthday.

"I ought to get rid of my parents' home yet I can't bring myself to do it. You must think I'm crazy . . .."

"Not in the least. I'd probably feel the same."

"I kept my parents' old cleaner and gardener: Maria and Terry are married. It feels good knowing they're looking after it." Hesitating for a moment, Bill reached for her hand, asking if she wanted to see the rest of the house. Nodding, not trusting herself to speak, Annabelle followed behind upstairs to the master bedroom.

"I love you, angel . . . Please let me show you how much."

Starved of love and affection, aching for his touch, Annabelle bowed her head as, scooping her up into his arms, Bill gently laid her down on the enormous bed and proceeded to make love to her, making her feel like the most desirable and cherished woman that ever lived. Hours later, after showering together in the luxurious en suite bathroom, Bill suggested they have breakfast in bed. He returned from the kitchen bringing bagels with smoked salmon and chocolate croissants.

"I'd given up on finding someone like you . . . You and Clara mean the world to me." Still in awe of what had just happened between them, Annabelle took in her surroundings.

"Ours is a shoebox compared to this house."

"That's strictly not true . . . Yours is cosy and close to Regent's Park. I'm so much in love with you, angel."

It took every bit of strength asking him to drive her home, but she knew she must as Rebecka expected her to collect Clara prior to attending a little friend's birthday party later that morning.

"Only if you answer my question."

"I don't recall you asking me anything."

Going down on one knee, Bill looked into her eyes.

"Will you do me the great honour of becoming my wife?"

As his words sunk in, tears sprang to her eyes.

"Are you sacking me?" she teased.

"Certainly not! Good staff are hard to come by!" he joked, but his eyes were serious.

"You're expecting me to continue working for you when we're married?" she asked, playing along with his little game.

"No, I'm not! But if it's what you want, I'll not prevent you. I'm happy if you are, angel."

"My answer's yes!" she cried, her only thought: *Ben's not the love of my life anymore – Bill is.*

One week later, Annabelle was awaiting her daughter's return after the little girl had spent the day with her father. She opened the front door and Clara threw herself into her arms.

"I hope we're on time. I wasn't sure if you and Bill had made plans?" Ben asked politely, thinking she looked great in a black and white trouser suit.

"Bill's a very special man," she replied mysteriously.

"I'm pleased. You deserve the best."

"There's something I want to talk to you about. Let's go inside." He followed her into the living room, where they sat in silence for a moment, watching Clara play with her cat.

"Bill's asked me to marry him," Annabelle said. "I accepted. I never thought I'd say this: I'm happy for you, Ben ... truly." Delighted for her, Ben reached tentatively for her hand. He was surprised to see tears welling up in her eyes.

"What's wrong?"

"Nothing. I'm just so very happy. And sorry for the way I behaved ... Perhaps given time you and I can resume our friendship?"

"I'd like that as well. You said you've something to tell me?"

"I do. Seeing as Bill's part of our daughter's life, it's only fair Hannah gets the same opportunity." Ben began to interrupt, but she stopped him. "Please let me finish. I want to do this my way." Listening to her, Ben knew she forgave him.

"I'm not sure I understand what you mean ... yet I'm very grateful!" As he kissed her cheek to say goodbye, Annabelle felt nothing but affection for him, promising to soon be in touch.

"We'll keep this between ourselves for the time being," she commented, shutting the door behind him.

As they parked outside the pretty house in the quiet cul-de-sac, Clara asked, "Is this where Daddy and Hannah live, Mummy?" Her eyes shone with excitement.

"That's right." It felt strange walking up the path. The blue and yellow curtains in the window caught her eye.

"Does Daddy know we're here?" Clara persisted, looking adorable in a pink dress with teddy bears printed all over it.

"No he doesn't ... it's a surprise," Annabelle replied, butterflies at the pit of her stomach.

"Can I push the bell?"

Annabelle was about to respond, when they heard footsteps approaching on the inside. The door opened wide by a petite redhead with the biggest green eyes Clara had ever seen.

"My God . . . it's you!" Hannah's jaw dropped at the surreal sight of Ben's ex-wife and child come to visit. She couldn't help but wish she'd bothered with make-up and nice clothes instead of faded jeans and t-shirt.

"Perhaps we've come at an inconvenient time? I ought to have called first . . ."

"Of course not! Please come inside – Ben's out buying bread and cakes. He'll be back soon." Annabelle and Clara followed Hannah into the cosy kitchen, where she asked if they wanted something to eat or drink.

"Please don't go to any trouble," Annabelle said, feeling just as tense as the other woman.

Ben's daughter's here in our house! "Would you like a glass of milk and a chocolate cookie?" she asked the small girl.

"Yes please! I like the colour of your hair. You're almost as pretty as my Mummy!"

Hannah dared to glance at Ben's ex-wife. She was tall, blonde and eye-catching in black trousers and a white satin blouse. "Your daughter's gorgeous . . . you must be very proud of her."

"Very. I can't imagine life without her."

They were sipping their coffee when Ben walked in the door, shocked to see who was seated at the kitchen table.

"You kept your promise," he said, putting a brown bag on the floor next to the sink, automatically fetching a tissue to clean his daughter's face and hands.

"We've outstayed our welcome. Say thank you for the biscuits, honey." Annabelle started to put on her jacket.

"Please stay," cried Hannah. "We've plenty of food to go round. I made pasta with salmon, dill and *crème fraîche*."

"You'd like that, wouldn't you, pumpkin?" Ben asked, looking at Clara.

"Yummy, I love pasta!" she replied.

"That's settled then!" he laughed, helping Hannah get everything ready. After making small talk for a while with Annabelle and Clara, he went up to the woman he loved and whispered in her ear.

"It's a miracle . . . I love you, little one."

By the time they'd finished their meal and were eating strawberries with ice-cream for dessert, all of them were chatting and laughing as if they were old friends.

"Look at the time!" Annabelle exclaimed. "We've been here for hours! Thank you for a lovely meal."

"I want to stay!" Clara blurted stubbornly.

"What about Rambles?" Ben asked.

"That's my cat," Clara explained to Hannah. "Have you got any pets?"

"No I haven't but I'd like to meet yours . . ."

"Can I visit you and Hannah in Sweden, Daddy?"

Exchanging glances with the mother of his child, Ben replied, "Nothing's been decided yet . . .."

"We'll talk about it later, honey . . . We'd better leave, seeing as we have a long journey ahead of us."

"Can I see you again?" Clara asked Hannah.

"That's for your mother to decide."

"Of course you can! You'll be spending lots of time with Hannah and Daddy."

"I love you, Mummy!" Clara shouted, chubby arms around her mother's neck.

"I know how difficult this must have been for you," Ben said, following Annabelle and their daughter out to the car. "Thank you from the bottom of my heart." As he bent to kiss her cheek, Clara piped up.

"Can I give Hannah a hug, Mummy?"

"Go for it! Our girl's extremely affectionate, you'd better get used to it."

As Hannah felt Clara's small body next to hers, she smiled at the young girl's comment: "You smell nice!"

"Charlie's my mother's favourite fragrance."

"Is she pretty too?"

"She was very beautiful when she was alive," Hannah whispered, a sad smile playing on her lips.

"That's awful! I want my Mummy to live forever!"

"Then you must take very good care of her." It was her way of showing how grateful she was to Annabelle for letting her be part of her daughter's life.

A few months later, with Clara and Melanie as their only witnesses, Annabelle and Bill were married in a small chateau on the outskirts of Paris, celebrating their honeymoon on the French Riviera. Opting to divide their time between the house in Regent's Park, his Paris flat and Belgravia Mansion, they also spent the odd sunny weekend in his parental home in Brighton, and Clara would go to stay with Hannah and Ben in Richmond.

"I don't believe it!" Sanna exclaimed when she called one night in early spring. "You and Annabelle being civil to each other? Wow. So when are you and Ben walking down the aisle? The poor guy must be petrified to ask you again, seeing as you always turn him down . . . Perhaps it's your turn to ask him?"

Hannah and Ben were in the conservatory enjoying a late leisurely breakfast in early June when she put down her cutlery and turned to look at him. "There's something I want to ask you."

"What is it? You look serious," Ben asked, putting down his croissant.

I've got to get this right! "You know how much I love you, don't you?"

"The feeling's mutual, darling. What is it?"

"Will you marry me?"

Thinking he was dreaming, Ben pulled her into his arms.

"It should be me asking you! I had it all figured out, you beat me to it . . ."

"What's your answer?" she persisted, holding her breath.

"What do you think? Yes, yes, yes!" Ben shouted, deliriously happy she'd finally agreed to become his wife.

"We'll have a civil ceremony as my parents aren't alive," she said, voice trembling slightly. "Where will we hold the reception?" The words were no sooner out of her mouth when the same thought entered their minds.

"It makes perfect sense! We'll keep it to ourselves a while longer."

Selling his share of the law firm to Collin some time later, Ben asked Hannah what she wanted to do about the house in Richmond.

"It's yours to do with as you wish," he reminded her.

"I guess letting it is an option until we decide where to live . . ." she told him.

There was a mischievous expression in her eyes.

Epilogue

Mayfair, June 2014

THE LILY FORRESTER Foundation For Research Into Mental Disorders opened its doors to the public on a warm, balmy night; the brainchild of the woman smiling at the crowd from the stage. Vanessa stood, to the applause of those in awe of the charity aimed at transforming lives irrelevant of background, circumstances and gender.

Spotting the beaming faces of Jake, Bernie, Maruschka and Mark in the audience below, Vanessa raised her glass, addressing everyone invited to take part.

"Thank you for being here tonight! Losing my mother at an early age was the singularly most devastating experience of my entire life. In those days depression was an ugly word. If she was alive today, I firmly believe the outcome would have been very different . . .

"Growing up without a mother and grandmother to my son, I thank God every day we're healthy and happy. Please join me in a toast to The Lily Forrester Foundation, a bright future and new beginnings!"

The audience burst into applause for the hostess, who was wearing a specially designed Donna Karan gown and diamond necklace. Bursting with pride, Jake whispered in his mother's ear as she stepped down from the stage.

"You did it, Mom! Because of you, millions of people will get the care and treatment they deserve!"

Born into an emotionally deprived environment, Vanessa Westbrook had truly succeeded in turning her life around, something in its own right well worth celebrating.

Limhamn, August 2014

Celebrating after taking their vows at a local registry office earlier that day, Hannah and Ben gazed around them at the people gathered at the reception in the picturesque villa both referred to as home. It was the perfect venue for a late summer party.

"You look stunning in your mother's vintage Pucci dress, darling," Ben said, kissing his bride.

"You don't look so bad either! That blue suit goes beautifully with your silver grey hair."

Having agreed to take his surname, Hannah Isaacs touched her wedding band. Bittersweet tears welled up in her eyes as her brother began play their mother's favourite song, 'The Best Of Times' from *La Cage Aux Folles* on the piano in the living room. Guests helped themselves to champagne and the scrumptious buffet of smoked salmon, potato salad and strawberries with cream laid out in the dining room. Ben's daughter sat happily on her grandmother's lap, looking very pretty in a white silk dress, flowers in her hair.

"Isn't it great we get to spend Christmas with Clara at our house in Richmond? My parents booked an early morning flight because Annabelle and Bill want to take her with them to Brighton."

"We're fortunate to live part of the year in London, the rest here in Limhamn," Hannah replied, watching Melanie, Sanna and Rosie talk amongst themselves.

"Let's go outside," Ben suggested, the intoxicating scent of Zadie's roses filling the air.

Looking up at the blue sky above them, Hannah asked, "Do you suppose my parents, Granny and Ella are looking down at us?"

"Without a doubt. If there's such a thing as angels, they're the closest thing. I love you, little one, always have – always will."

Smiling at him, Hannah whispered softly, "Until we meet again," before following the man she loved back into the house and the next chapter of their lives.

ACKNOWLEDGEMENTS

I wish to express gratitude to the following people; My wonderful editor Bryony Sutherland, you're the best! Fabulous graphic designer Jennie Rawlings, your image perfectly captures the essence of the novel! Phenomenal all round publishing consultant Heather O'Connell, your outstanding input and knowledge are indispensable! Book marketing expert Palamedes PR, your professionalism and enthusiasm are much appreciated! At last but not least; To everyone who encouraged and supported me, especially my gorgeous cat Teddy, whose consistent love and loyalty never cease to amaze me.